SAVAGE TEXAS
A GOOD DAY TO DIE

SAVAGE TEXAS
A GOOD DAY TO DIE

William W. Johnstone
with J. A. Johnstone

PINNACLE BOOKS
Kensington Publishing Corp.
www.kensingtonbooks.com

PINNACLE BOOKS are published by

Kensington Publishing Corp.
119 West 40th Street
New York, NY 10018

PUBLISHER'S NOTE
Following the death of William W. Johnstone, the Johnstone family is working with a carefully selected writer to organize and complete Mr. Johnstone's outlines and many unfinished manuscripts to create additional novels in all of his series like The Last Gunfighter, Mountain Man, and Eagles, among others. This novel was inspired by Mr. Johnstone's superb storytelling.

All Kensington titles, imprints, and distributed lines are available at special quantity discounts for bulk purchases for sales promotions, premiums, fund-raising, educational, or institutional use. Special book excerpts or customized printings can also be created to fit specific needs. For details, write or phone the office of the Kensington special sales manager: Kensington Publishing Corp., 119 West 40th Street, New York, NY 10018, attn: Special Sales Department; phone 1-800-221-2647.

PINNACLE BOOKS and the Pinnacle logo are Reg. U.S. Pat. & TM Off.
The WWJ steer head logo is a trademark of Kensington Publishing Corp.

ISBN-13: 978-0-7860-2810-8
ISBN-10: 0-7860-2810-6

First printing: July 2012

10 9 8 7 6 5 4 3 2 1

Printed in the United States of America

ONE

On a night in late May 1866, Comanche Chief Red Hand took up the Fire Lance to proclaim the opening of the warm weather raiding season—a time of torture, plunder, and murder. For warlike Comanche braves, the best time of the year.

Six hundred and more Comanche men, women, and children were camped near a stream in a valley north of the Texas panhandle, on land between the Canadian and Arkansas rivers. The site, Arrowhead Rock, lay deep in the heart of the vast, untamed territory of Comancheria, home grounds of the tribal nation.

The gathering was made up mostly of two main subgroups, the Bison Eyes and the Dawn Hawks, along with a number of lesser clans, relations, and allies.

Red Hand, a Bison Eye, was a rising star who had led a number of successful raids in recent seasons past. Many braves, especially those of the younger generation, were eager to attach themselves to him.

Others had come to hear him out and make up their own minds about whether or not to follow his lead. Not a few had come to keep a wary eye on him and see what he was up to.

All brought their families with them, from the oldest squaws to the youngest babes in arms. They brought their tipis and personal belongings, horse herds, and even dogs.

The Comanche were a mobile folk, nomads who followed the buffalo herds across the Great Plains. They spent much of their lives on horseback and were superb riders. They were fierce fighters, arguably the most dangerous Indian tribe in the West. They gloried in the title of Lords of the Southern Plains.

Farther southwest—much farther—lay the lands of the Apache, relentless desert warriors of fearsome repute. During their seasonal wanderings Comanches raided Apaches as the opportunity presented itself, but the Apache did not strike north to raid Comancheria. This stark fact spoke volumes about the relative deadliness of the two.

The camp on the valley stream was unusual in its size, the tribesmen generally preferring to travel in much smaller groups. The temporary settlement had come into being in response to Red Hand's invitation, taken by his emissaries to the various interested parties. Invitation, not summons.

A high-spirited individual, the Comanche brave

was jealous of his freedom and rights. His allegiance was freely given and just as freely withdrawn. Warriors of great deeds were respected, but not slavishly submitted to. A leader gained followers by ability and success; incompetence and failure inevitably incited mass desertions.

It was a mark of Red Hand's prowess that so many had come to hear his words.

The campsite at Arrowhead Rock lay on a well-watered patch of grassy ground. Cone-shaped tipis massed along the stream banks. Smoke from many cooking fires hazed the area. The tipis had been given over to women and children; the men were elsewhere. Packs of half-wild, half-starved dogs chased each other around the campgrounds, snarling and yapping.

The horse herds were picketed nearby. Comanches reckoned their wealth in horses, as white men did in gold. The greater the thief, the more he was respected and envied by his fellows.

For such a conclave, an informal truce reigned, whereby the braves of various clans held in check their craving to steal each other's horses . . . mostly.

North of the camp, a long bowshot away, the land dipped into a shallow basin, a hollow serving as a kind of natural amphitheater. It was spacious enough to comfortably hold the two hundred and more warriors assembled there under a horned moon. No females were present at the basin.

To a man, they were in prime physical condition. There was no place in the Comanche nation for weaklings. Men were warriors, doing the hunting, raiding, fighting, and killing—sometimes dying. Women did all the other work, the drudgery of the tribe.

The braves were high-spirited, raucous. Much horseplay and boasting of big brags occurred. It had been a long winter; they looked forward to the wild free life of raiding south with eager anticipation. An air of keen interest hung over them as they waited impatiently for Red Hand to take the fore.

At the northern center rim of the basin stood a triangular-shaped rock about twenty feet high. Shaped like an arrowhead planted point-up in the ground, it gave the site its name. Among Comanche warrior society, the arrowhead was an emblem of power and danger, giving the stone an aura of magical potency.

A fire blazed near its base. Yellow-red tongues of flame leaped upward, wreathed with spirals of blue-gray smoke. Between the fire and the rock, a stout wooden stake eight feet tall had been driven into the ground.

The braves faced the rock, Bison Eyes grouped on the left, Dawn Hawks on the right. Both clans were strong, numerous, and well respected. Nearly evenly matched in numbers and fighting prowess, they were great rivals.

A stir went through the crowd. Something was happening.

A handful of shadowy figures stepped out from behind the rock, coming into view of those assembled in the hollow. They ranked themselves in a line behind the fire, forming up like a guard of honor in advance of their leader. Underlit by the flames' red glare, they could be seen and recognized.

Mighty warriors all, men of renown, they made up Red Hand's inner circle of trusted advisors and henchmen, his lieutenants.

Ten Scalps was a giant of a man, one of the strongest warriors in the Comanche nation. He'd taken ten scalps as a youth during his first raid. After that he stopped counting.

Sun Dog, his face wider than it was long, had dark eyes glinting like chips of black glass.

Little Bells, with twin strings of tiny silver bells plaited into his lion's mane of shoulder-length hair, stood tall.

Badger was short and squat, with tremendous upper body strength and oversized, pawlike hands.

Black Robe, clad in a garment he'd stripped from a Mexican priest he'd slain and scalped, was next. Part long coat, part cape, the tattered garment gave him a weird, batlike outline.

The cadre's appearance was greeted by the crowd with appreciative whoops, shrieks, and howls. The five stood motionless, faces impassive, arms folded across their chests. They held the pose for a long time, their stillness contrasting with the crowd's mounting excitement.

After a moment, a lone man emerged from behind the rock into the firelight. He wore a war bonnet and carried a lance.

The Bison Eyes clansmen vented loud, full-throated cries of welcome, for the newcomer was none other than their own great man, Red Hand. But Red Hand's entrance was almost as well received by the rival Dawn Hawks.

He was a man of power, a doer of great deeds. He had stature. He had stolen many horses, enslaved many captives, killed many foes. With skill and daring he had won much fame throughout the plains and deep into Mexico.

Circling around to the front of Arrowhead Rock, Red Hand scrambled up onto a ledge four feet above the ground. Facing the assembled, he showed himself to them. Roughly thirty years of age, he was in full, vigorous prime, broad-shouldered, deep-chested, and long-limbed. Thick coal-black hair, full and unbound, framed a long, sharp-featured face. His eyes were deepset, burning.

He was crowned with a splendid eagle-feather war bonnet whose train reached down his back. He wore a simple breechcloth and knee-length antelope skin boots. A hunting knife hung on his hip.

From fingertips to wrists, the backs of his hands were painted with greasy red coloring, markings that were stripes, wavvy lines, crescent moons, and arrows. His right hand clenched the lance, holding it upright with its base resting atop the rocky ledge. Ten feet long, it was tipped with a wickedly sharp, barbed spear blade.

This was no Comanche war spear. He had taken

it in Mexico the summer before from a mounted lancer, one of the legions of crack cavalry troops sent by France's Emperor Napoleon III to protect his ally Maximilian of Austria-Hungary.

Red Hand knew nothing of the crowned heads of Europe nor of Napoleon III's mad dream of a New World Empire that had prompted him to install a Hapsburg royal on the throne of Mexico. Red Hand knew killing, though, dodging the lancer's lunging spear thrust, dragging him down off his fine horse, and cutting his throat.

Word of this enviable weapon spread far and wide among the Comanches. More than a prize, the lance became a talisman of Red Hand's prestige. It evoked no small interest, with many braves pressing forward, craning for a better look.

Red Hand lifted the weapon, shaking it triumphantly in the air. It was met by a fresh round of appreciative whoops.

Notably lacking in enthusiasm, was Wahtonka, a Dawn Hawks chief standing in the front rank of his clan. He, too, was a great man, with many daring deeds of blood to his credit. But he was fifty years old, a generation older than Red Hand.

Of medium height, Wahtonka was lean and wiry; all bone, sinews, and tendons. His hair, parted in the middle of his scalp, was worn in two long, gray-flecked braids. His face was deeply lined, his mouth downturned, dour.

Red Hand's enthusiastic audience did nothing to

lighten his mood. Others were not so constrained in their appreciation of the upstart, Wahtonka noticed, including many of his own Dawn Hawks. Too many.

The young men were loud in their whooping and hollering, and a number of older, more established warriors also stamped and shouted for Red Hand.

Wahtonka cut a side glance at Laughing Bear standing beside him. Laughing Bear was of his generation, himself a mighty warrior, though with few deeds in recent years to his credit. He was Wahtonka's kinsman and most trusted ally.

Laughing Bear was heavyset, with sloping shoulders and a blocky torso, thick in the middle. His features were broad and lumpish. The gaze of his small round eyes was bleak. He looked as if he had not laughed in years. Red Hand's appearance this night had not struck forth in him any spirit of mirth. He shared Wahtonka's grave concerns about the growing Red Hand problem.

The hero of the hour basked for a moment in the gusty reception given him, before motioning for silence. The Comanches quieted down, though scattered shrieks and screams continued to rise from some of the more excitable types. The clamor subsided, though the crowd kept up a continual buzzing.

"Brothers! I went in search of a vision," Red Hand began, his voice big and booming. "I went in search of a vision—and I have found it!"

The warriors' cheers echoed across the nighted prairie.

Red Hand's face split in a wicked grin, showing strong white teeth. "In the old times life was good. The game was thick. Birds filled the skies. The buffalo were many, covering the ground as far as the eye could see." He had a far-off look in his eyes, as if gazing through the distance of space and time in search of such onetime abundance.

He frowned, his gaze hardening, dark passions clouding his features. "Then came the white men," he said, voice thick, almost choking on the words.

The mood of the braves turned. Whoops and screeches faded, replaced by sullen, ominous mutterings accompanied by much solemn nodding of heads in agreement. Red Hand was voicing their universal complaint against the hated invaders who were destroying a cherished way of life.

"First were the Mexicans, with their high-handed ways," he said, thrusting his lance toward the south, the direction from which the initial trespassers hailed.

"They came in suits of iron, calling themselves 'conquerers.'" Red Hand sneered at the conquistadors who had emerged from Mexico some three hundred and fifty years earlier. It might have been yesterday, so fresh and strong was his hate.

"They rode—horses!" Red Hand's eyes bulged as he assumed an expression of pop-eyed amazement, his clowning provoking shouts and laughter.

"We had never seen horses before. The horses were good!"

He paused, then punched the rest of it across. "We killed the men and took their horses! We burned the settlements and killed and killed until only cowards were left alive, and we sent them running back to Mexico!"

The braves spasmed with screaming delight, some shouting themselves hoarse.

Red Hand waited for a lull in the tumult, then continued. "From that day till now, they have never dared return to our hunting grounds. We could have wiped them off the face of the earth, chasing them into the Great Water, had we so desired. Aye, for we Comanche are a mighty folk, and a warlike one. But we were merciful. We took pity on the poor weak creatures and let them live, so they could keep on breeding fine horses for us to steal.

"One black day, out from where the sun rises, came the Texans."

Texans—the Comanches' generic term for Anglos, English-speaking whites.

"Texans! They, too, wanted to steal our land and enslave us. They had guns! The guns were good. So we killed the Texans and took their guns and killed more, whipping and burning until they wept like frightened children!

"Not all did we kill, for we Comanches are a merciful people. We let some live so we could take more guns and powder and bullets from them.

Their horses are good to steal, too! And their women!

"But the Comanche is too tender hearted for his own good," he said, shaking his head as if in sorrow. "For a time, all was well. But no more. The Texans forget the lesson we taught them in blood and fire. They come creeping back, pressing at our lands in ever-greater numbers. They will eat up the earth if they are not stopped.

"What to do, brothers, what to do? I prayed to the Great Spirit to send me an answer. And I dreamed a dream. The sky cracked open! The clouds parted, and an arm reached down between them—a mighty red arm, holding a burning spear. The Fire Lance!

"The hand darted the spear. It flew down to earth, striking the ground with a thunderclap. When the smoke cleared, I alone was left standing, for all around me the Texans lay fallen on the ground. Man, woman and child—dead! Dead all, from oldest to youngest, from greatest to most small. All dead. And this was not the least of wonders.

"Everywhere a white person had fallen, a buffalo rose up. Here, there, everywhere a buffalo! They filled the plains with a thundering herd, filling my heart with joy. So it was shown to me in a dream, as I tell it to you. But I tell you this. It was no dream, but a vision!"

Wild stirrings shot through the crowd, a storm of potential energy yearning to be released.

"A true vision!" Red Hand bellowed.

The braves chafed at the bit, straining to break loose, but Red Hand shouted down the rising tumult. "The Great Spirit has shown us the Way— kill the Texans! Take up the Fire Lance! Kill and burn until the last white has fled from these lands, never to be seen again! The buffalo will once more grow thick and fat! All will be well, as in the days of our fathers!"

Brandishing his lance, Red Hand shook it at the heavens. Pandemonium erupted, a near riot. The hollow basin became a howling bedlam as the wild crowd went wilder.

So great was the uproar that, in the tipis, the women and children marveled to hear it. Any outsider, red or white, hearing it crashing across the plains, would have taken fright.

Red Hand hopped down off the ledge that had served him as a platform and stepped back into the shadows, partly withdrawing from the scene while the disturbance played itself out. His henchmen followed.

Presently, order was restored, if not peace and quiet. The braves settled down, in their restless way.

Red Hand put his head together with his five-man cadre, giving orders.

Carrying out his command, Sun Dog and Little Bells moved around to the east side of Arrowhead Rock, where a lone tipi stood off by itself in the gloom beyond the firelight. Sun Dog lifted the front flap and went inside.

A moment later, a figure emerged headfirst through the opening as if violently flung outward, falling facedown in the dirt at Little Bells's feet.

Sun Dog reappeared. He and Little Bells bracketed a sorry figure, grabbing him by the arms and hauling him to his feet. The newcomer was a white man in cavalry blue. A Long Knife, one of the hated pony soldiers!

There was a collective intake of breath from the mob in the hollow, followed by ominous mutterings and growlings. As one, they pressed forward.

The captive wore a torn blue tunic and pants with a yellow strip down the sides. He was barefoot. His hands were tied in front of him by rawhide strips cutting deep into the flesh of his wrists. He sagged, legs folding at the knees. He would have fallen if Sun Dog and Little Bells hadn't been holding him up.

He was Butch Hardesty, a robber, rapist, and back-shooting murderer. He had a system. When the law got too hot on his trail, he would enlist in the army and disappear in the ranks, losing himself among blue-clad troopers and distant frontier posts. When the pursuit cooled off, he would steal a horse and rifle and go "over the hill," deserting to resume his outlaw career. He'd go about his business until the law started dogging him again, once more repeating the cycle.

In the last years of the War Between the States, he worked his way west across the country, finally winding up at lonesome Fort Pardee in north central Texas. He deserted again, and had the extreme bad luck to cross paths with some of Red Hand's scouts. He'd been doubly unfortunate in being taken alive.

He'd been beaten, starved, abused, and tortured near the extreme. But not all the way to destruction. Red Hand needed him alive. He had a use for him. Hardesty was taken north, to the conclave at Arrowhead Rock. Kept alive and on hand—for what?

Out of the tipi stepped a weird hybrid creature, man-shaped, with a monstrous shaggy horned head.

Coming into the light, the apparition was revealed to be an aged Comanche, pot-bellied and thin-shanked. He wore a brown woolly buffalo hide head-dress complete with horns. He was Medicine Hat, Red Hand's own shaman, herbalist, devil doctor, and sorcerer.

Half carrying and half dragging Hardesty, Sun Dog and Little Bells hustled him to the front of the rock. Medicine Hat shambled after them, mumbling to himself.

The cavalryman produced no small effect on the crowd. Like a magnifying lens focusing the sun's rays into a single burning beam, the trooper provided a focus for the braves' bloodlust and demonic energies.

Hardesty was brought to the stake and bound to it. Ropes made of braided buffalo hide strips lashed him to the pole with hands tied above his head. Too

weak to stand on his own two feet, the ropes held
him up.

When Comanches took an enemy alive, they
tortured him, expecting no less should they be
taken. Torture was an important element of the
warrior society. How a man stood up to it showed
what he was made of. It was entertaining, too—to
those not on the receiving end.

Hardesty bore the marks of starvation and abuse.
His face was mottled with purple-black bruises, features swollen, one blackened eye narrowed to a
glinting slit. His mouth hung open. His shirt was
ripped open down the middle, his bare torso
having been sliced and gouged. Cactus thorns had
been driven under his fingernails and toenails.
Twigs had been tied between fingers and toes and
set aflame. The soles of his feet had been skinned,
then roasted.

Firelight caused shadows to crawl and slide
across Hardesty's bound form. He seemed as much
dead as alive.

Black Robe now went to work on him with a
knife whose blade was heated red-hot. It brought
Hardesty around, his bellows of pain booming in
the basin.

Badger shot some arrows into Hardesty's arms
and legs, careful to ensure that no wound was
mortal.

Each new infliction was greeted with shouts by
the braves. It was great sport.

Hardesty was scum and he knew it, but he played

his string out to the end. His mouth worked, cursing his captors. "The joke's on you, ya ignorant savages. I ain't cavalry a'tall. I'm a deserter. I quit the army, you dumb sons of bitches, haw haw! How d'you like that? Ya heathen devils."

A few Comanches had a smattering of English, but were unable to make out his words. All liked his show of spirit, however.

"The gods are happiest when the sacrifice is strong," Red Hand said. "Make ready for the Fire Lance."

Medicine Hat muttered agreement with a toothless mouth, spittle wetting his pointed chin. Reaching into his bag of tricks, he pulled out a gourd. It was dried and hollowed out, with a long neck serving as a kind of spout. The end of the spout was sealed by a stopper. Pulling the plug, he closed on the captive.

Hardesty slumped against the ropes, head down, and chin resting on top of his chest. He looked up out of the tops of his eyes, his pain-wracked gaze registering little more than a mute flicker of animal awareness.

Red Hand moved forward, out of the shadows into the light. It could be seen that his face was freshly striped with black paint.

War paint! The sight of which sent an electric thrill surging through the throng.

Red Hand motioned Medicine Hat to proceed. The shaman's moccasined feet shuffled in the dust, doing a little ceremonial dance. Mouthing spells, prayers, and incantations, Medicine Hat neared Hardesty, then backed away, repeating the action several times.

He held the gourd over the captive's head and. began pouring the vessel's contents on Hardesty's head, shoulders, chest, and belly, dousing him with a dark, foul-smelling liquid. Compounded of rendered animal fats, grease, and mineral oils, the stuff was used as a fire starter to quicken the lighting of campfires. It gurgled as it spewed from the spout.

Groans escaped Hardesty as his upper body was coated with the stuff. Medicine Hat poured until the gourd was empty. He stepped away from Hardesty, who looked as if he'd been drenched with glistening brown oil.

Red Hand moved forward, the center of all eyes.

The shaman was a great one for brewing up various potions, powders, and salves. Earlier, he had applied a special ointment to the spear blade of Red Hat's lance. The main ingredient of the mixture was a thick, sticky pine tar resin blended with vegetable and herbal oils. It coated the blade, showing as a gummy residue that dulled the brilliance of the steel's metallic shine.

Red Hand's movements took on a deliberate, ritualistic quality. Holding the lance in both hands, he raised it horizontally over his head and shook it at the heavens. Lowering it, he dipped the blade into the heart of the fire. A few beats passed before the slow-burning ointment flared up, wrapping the blade in blue flames.

Red Hand lifted the lance, tilting it skyward for all to see. The blade was a wedge of blue fire, burning with an eerie, mystic glow—a ghost light, a weird effect both impressive and unnerving.

Quivering with emotion, Red Hand's clear, strong voice rang out. "Lo! The Fire Lance!"

He touched the burning spear to Hardesty's well-oiled chest. Blue fire sparked from the blade tip, leaping to the oily substance coating the captive's flesh. The fire-starting compound burst into bright hot flames, wrapping Hardesty in a skin of fire, turning him into a human torch.

He blazed with a hot yellow-red-orange light. The burning had a crackling sound, like flags being whipped by a high wind.

Hardesty writhed, screaming as he was burned alive. Fire cut through the ropes binding him to the stake. Before he could break free, he was speared by Red Hand, who skewered him in the middle.

Red Hand opened up Hardesty's belly, spilling his guts. He gave a final twist to the blade before withdrawing it. He faced the man of fire, lance leveled for another thrust if needed.

Hardesty collapsed, falling in a blazing heap. The fire spread to some nearby grass and brush, setting them alight.

At a sign from Red Hand, members of his five-man cadre rushed up with blankets, using them to beat out the fires. Streamers of blue-gray smoke rose up. The night was thick with the smell of burning flesh.

Red Hand thrust the blue-burning spear blade into a dirt mound. When it was surfaced, the mystic glow was extinguished, the blade glowing a dull red.

Chaos, near anarchy, reigned among the Comanches. The horde erupted in a frenzy, many breaking into spontaneous war dances.

Above all others was heard the voice of Red Hand. "Take up the Fire Lance! Kill the Texans!"

Much later, when all was quiet, Wahtonka and Laughing Bear stood off by themselves in a secluded place, putting their heads together. The horned moon was low in the west, the stars were paling, the eastern sky was lightening.

"What should we do?" Laughing Bear asked.

"What can we do? Go with Red Hand to make war on the whites." Wahtonka shrugged. "Any raid is better than none," he added, philosophically.

Laughing Bear grunted agreement. "Waugh! That is true."

"We shall see if the Great Spirit truly spoke to Red Hand, if his vision comes to pass," Wahtonka said. "If not—may his bones bleach in the sand!"

Two

The town of Hangtree, county seat of Hangtree County, Texas, was known to most folks, except for a few town boosters and straitlaced respectable types, as Hangtown. So it was to Johnny Cross, a native son of the region.

Located in north central Texas, Hangtree County lay west of Palo Pinto County and east of the Llano Estacado, known as the Staked Plains, whose vast emptiness was bare of towns or settlements for hundreds of square miles. Hangtown squatted on the lip of that unbounded immensity.

The old Cross ranch lay some miles west of town, nestled at the foot of the eastern range of the Broken Hills, called the Breaks. Beyond the Breaks lay the beginnings of the Staked Plains.

Johnny, the last living member of the Cross family, had come back to Hangtree after the war. He lived at the ranch with his old buddy Luke Pettigrew, two not-so-ex-Rebels trying to make a go of it in the hard times of the year following the fall of the Confederacy. They were partners in a mustang venture. Hundreds of mustangs ran wild and free in the Breaks and Johnny and Luke sold whatever they could catch.

Growing up in Hangtree, Johnny and Luke were boyhood pals. When war came in 1861, both were quick to fight for the South, like most of the men-folk in the Lone Star state. Luke joined up with Hood's Texans, a hard-fighting outfit that had made its mark in most of the big battles of the war. In the last year of the conflict, a Yankee cannonball had taken off his left leg below the knee. A wooden leg took its place.

Johnny Cross had followed a different path. For good or ill, his star had led him to throw in with Quantrill's Raiders, legendary in its own way, though not with the bright, untarnished glory of Hood's fighting force. Johnny spent the next four years serving with that dark command, living mostly on horseback, fighting his way through the bloody guerrilla warfare of the border states.

A dead shot when he first joined Quantrill, he soon became a formidable pistol fighter and long rider, a cool-nerved killing machine. His comrades in arms included the likes of Bloody Bill Anderson, the Younger brothers, and Frank and Jesse James.

The bushwhackers' war in Kansas and Missouri was a murky, dirty business where the lines blurred between soldier and civilian, valor and savagery, and it was easy to lose one's way.

When Richmond fell and Dixie folded in '65, Quantrill and his men received no amnesty. They were wanted outlaws with a price on their heads. On the dodge, plying the gunman's trade, Johnny Cross worked his way back to Hangtree County, where he wasn't wanted for anything—yet.

A dangerous place, the county was one of the most violent locales on the frontier. Trouble came frequently and fast, and Johnny was in his element. He and Luke crossed trails and teamed up. A mysterious stranger named Sam Heller—a damned Yankee but a first-class fighting man—roped them into bucking a murderous outlaw gang.*

When the gunsmoke cleared, Johnny and Luke had come out of it with whole skins and a nice chunk of reward money.

Johnny and Luke saddled up and pointed their horses east along the Hangtree Trail, heading into town to blow off some steam after working hard during the week. Hangtown was a couple hours ride from the ranch, but then, Texas was big. Every place in Texas was a fair piece away from everywhere else.

They rode out in the morning, when it was still cool. Texas in late June got hot early and stayed that way long after sundown. The Hangtree Trail

*See *Savage Texas,* the first volume in the series.

was a dirt road stretching east-west across the county. It had rained the night before, washing things clean and wetting down the dust. The sky was cloudless blue, the grass and trees bright green.

Luke Pettigrew was long and lean. War wounds left him hollow-eyed, sunken-cheeked and gaunt. He was starting to fill out, but there was still something of a half-starved wolf about him. Tufts of gray-brown hair stuck out on the sides of his head under his hat, and the sharp tips of canine teeth showed over the edge of his lips.

He was mounted on a big bay horse, a rifle fixed to the right-hand side of the saddle and a crutch on the left. He was good with a rifle, fair with a pistol. A sawed-off shotgun hung in a holster on his right hip, for when the fighting got up close and personal.

Johnny Cross was of medium height, athletic, and compactly knit. He had black hair and hazel eyes that sometimes looked brown, sometimes yellow, depending on the light and his moods. He was clean shaven, something of a rarity when most men wore beards or mustaches.

When he'd been with Quantrill, he lived rough in the field, going weeks, months without a shave, haircut, or bath and wearing the same clothes night and day until they began coming apart, shredding off his body. These days, he set a high value on bathing, shaving, and clean clothes. His nature was fastidious, catlike even.

He wore a flat-crowned black hat, a dark broad-cloth jacket, and a gray button-down shirt. His black denim pants hung over his army-issue boots. A pair of hip-holstered Colt .44s showed beneath his jacket. A lightweight pistol was tucked away in one of his jacket pockets, a carbine was tucked into his saddle scabbard, and a couple more pistols were stashed in his saddlebags.

Riding with Quantrill had taught him the value of having plenty of firepower where he could get to it fast. Returning to Hangtree had firmed up that belief.

Ahead lay a low ridge running north-south, cut at right angles by the Hangtree Trail. Hangtown lay just east of the rise.

North of the trail rose the Hanging Tree, a towering dead oak, silver-gray and lightning-blasted. It had broken limbs sticking out from its sides. At its foot, lay black, sticklike crosses, slanting wooden grave markers, and weedy mounds of Boot Hill, burial place of the poor, the lost, and the damned.

South of the trail, the rise was topped by a white-painted wooden church with a bell tower topped by an obelisk-shaped steeple. Nearby was the church-yard cemetery, neat and well kept.

Johnny and Luke crested the ridge. On the far side, the trail dipped and ran east into Hangtown. Once in town, the road became Trail Street, the main drag. It was paralleled on the north by Commerce Street, south by Mace Street.

At the east end of Trail Street stood the courthouse and the jail, Hangtown's only stone buildings, built in the 1850s. The courthouse fronted east, a two-story brown sandstone structure with a clock tower. The jail fronted north, its long walls running north-south, a one-story brick building with iron bars on the windows. South central of town a jumble of adobe houses and wooden huts grouped around an oval plaza. Mextown.

Southwest of town was a grassy open field with a stream running through it. A wagon train was camped there, with more than two dozen wagons arranged in a circle. Horses and oxen were pastured nearby. Smoke rose from cooking fires. People moved to and fro, youngsters weaving in and out around them.

Johnny and Luke rode down the ridge into town. It was a little past ten o'clock in the morning.

Saturdays were usually busy in Hangtown. Ranchers and their families from all over the county came in to trade, barter, or buy. The fine late June weather had brought them out in big numbers. Wagons lined boardwalk sidewalks fronting the stores on both sides of Trail Street. Groups of kids ran up and down the street, playing tag.

Many cowboys and ranch hands worked only a half day on Saturday; they would start coming in after twelve noon. The week's wages burned a hole in their pockets, itching to be spent on whiskey, women, and gambling.

Johnny and Luke put their horses up at Hobson's Livery stables and corral, which was south of the jail. Once the horses were squared away, Johnny said, "Let's get some chow."

"Hell, let's get a drink," Luke said.

"Chow first. It's early yet."

Luke gave in with poor grace and they went into Mabel's Café. They sat at a table, ordered breakfast, and soon were digging into a big meal of steak and eggs, biscuits, and coffee.

Fortified, they exited the restaurant a few minutes later. Johnny reached into an inside breast pocket of his jacket for one of several long, thin cigars he kept there. He bit the end off, spat it out, and lit up. Luke used a penknife to cut a chaw off a plug of tobacco, stuck it in the side of his mouth, and commenced to work on it.

They moved on, north to Trail Street. With his crutch wedged under his left arm, Luke swung along with the facility that comes with much practice. Men with missing limbs were a commonplace throughout the land in the war's aftermath.

Johnny padded along at a nice easy pace so as not to get Luke winded. Besides, he was in no hurry. Turning left at Trail Street, they went west along its south side, nodding to acquaintances, saying hello in passing. Johnny smoked his cigar, trailing blue-gray smoke. Luke squirted tobacco juice from time to time.

Johnny liked to watch the passing parade, especially the pretty girls, the town misses, and ranchers' daughters. They were bright eyed, with well-scrubbed shining faces.

Their wayward sisters, denizens of the saloons and the houses, were mostly still abed, not yet astir. Johnny liked them well enough, too—perhaps too well. But they belonged to a half world of gamblers, barkeeps, whores, hardcases, and thrill seekers—sinners all. They were nightbirds who flew when the sun went down.

At ten-thirty in the morning, respectable folk held sway, crowding the wooden plank sidewalks fronting the stores. Luke flattened against a wall to dodge a gang of kids chasing each other, shouting back and forth. He and Johnny made their way west, sidestepping knots of people.

"Lot of strangers in town," Luke said.

"Must come from that wagon train, Major Adams's outfit," Johnny said.

The strangers were a rough-hewn lot, decent-seeming enough, but bearing the look of having done a lot of hard traveling with a long way yet to go. Some were staring, others shy, but all had the aspect of wayfarers. Pilgrims.

"Where're they going, Johnny?"

"West to Anvil Flats and then across the plains to the Santa Fe Trail, I reckon."

"And then?"

Johnny shrugged. "Denver, or the mines in Arizona or Nevada. California, maybe. Who knows?"

"Damn fools." Luke jetted some tobacco juice into the street. "I mean, the ones taking their families with them."

"Can't leave 'em behind," Johnny said reasonably.

"Well, maybe not. But they got a hard road ahead. Lucky to make it without losing their hair."

"Major Adams knows his business, they say."

"They say."

"His wagons have gotten through so far."

"Not all of them. Injins and outlaws, desert and mountains did for more'n a few."

"That ain't the Major's fault. They knew their chances when they set out," Johnny countered. "Anyhow, what've they got to go back to? Most of them are Southrons. All they own is their wagons and what's in them."

"They're lucky Billy Yank left them that much," Luke said.

They crossed the street to the Cattleman Hotel with its raised front porch and verandah. A half dozen wooden steps accessed it, with another such stairway leading down at the opposite end. Johnny and Luke went around it, walking in the street fronting the structure.

"Ever get a hankering to go wandering again, Johnny? See what's over the next hill, break new trails?"

"Not lately. I've been a rolling stone for a long time. I'd like to stay put for a while. You?"

"Can't say as I've got itchy feet, seeing as I only got one foot left to get a itch on. Hangtown ain't nothing special to me, now that the rest of us Pettigrews is either dead and gone or moved on. But it'll do for now."

"Why'd you ask, then?"

"Seeing them pilgrims got me to wondering, that's all."

Across the street was the Alamo Bar, a high-toned watering hole. Farther west, on the next block, was Lockhart's Emporium, the biggest general store in the county.

A stout middle-aged matron with a couple kids clinging to her skirts stood outside the store. A lightweight, four-wheeled cart drawn by a single horse was drawn up alongside the boardwalk.

A store clerk laden with packages came out the front door. He was young and thin, with a book-keeper's green-shaded visor on his head. He wore a white bib apron over a long-sleeved striped shirt and pants. The bulky parcels wrapped in brown paper and tied with string were held in front of him against his chest, piled so high he couldn't see over them. He navigated by peeking around and to the side of them.

He was followed by a young woman. She held two bundles by the strings, one in each hand, arms at her sides. Masses of dark brown hair were pinned up at the top of her head. She had wide dark eyes, high cheekbones, and a well-formed, clean-lined face. In a yellow dress, she was slim, straight, and shapely.

She was worth looking at, and Johnny Cross did just that.

The storeclerk and the young woman set the packages down in the back of the cart and went back into the store.

"Good-looking gal," Johnny stated. "Seems familiar, somehow."

"That's Fay—Fay Lockhart, hoss," Luke said, laughing. "Don't you recognize her?"

"She's filled out nicely since the last time I saw her. I'd have bet she would have been long gone from Hangtown. She always talked about how much she hated it here and couldn't wait to leave."

"She's been gone, and now she's back. Like you."

"And you!"

"No staying away from Hangtown, is there? Calls you home. Fay got married and moved away, but here she is, back at the same ol' stand."

"Married to who?" Johnny pressed.

"Some stranger, name of Devereaux. Cavalry officer. Way I heard it, they met while she was visiting kinfolk in Houston. He was on leave. They courted in a whirl and got hitched. He went back to join his troops and got killed a month or two later. Fay came back here to live with her folks."

Johnny thought that over. "Believe I'll go say hello to the widow."

"That'd be right sociable of you."

"I'm a sociable fellow, Luke."

"With a pretty girl, you are."

Johnny didn't deny it. "Coming?"

Luke shook his head. "She's your friend."

"Yours, too."

"I knew her to say hello to, back in the day. That's 'cause I was a friend of yours. Elsewise we moved in different circles. Them high-and-mighty Lockharts don't have no truck for us Pettigrews."

"For the Crosses, neither," Johnny said.

"You and her got along pretty good, I do recall."

Johnny tried to wave it away. "Kid stuff."

"She ain't no kid now," Luke said.

"I noticed."

Luke indicated some empty rocking chairs on the front porch of the Cattleman Hotel. "I'll set there for a while, take a load off."

"Them stairs ain't gonna be a problem?"

"I can handle 'em."

"I'll be along directly, then."

"Take your time. Tell Fay I said hello, for what it's worth. If she even remembers me. Regrets about her dead husband and all—you know."

"Sure." Johnny tossed the stub of his cigar into the street, where it landed with a splash of tiny orange-red embers. Crossing the street, he climbed the three low, wooden steps to the boardwalk. He took off his hat, running a hand through straight, longish black hair, pushing it back off his forehead and behind his ears. He put the hat back on, tilting it to a not-too-rakish angle.

Unconsciously squaring his shoulders, he took a deep breath and went into Lockhart's Emporium for the first time in over five years.

It was a big rectangular space, with a short wall fronting the street. Rows of shelves filled with goods lined both long walls. Beyond the door lay an open center aisle flanked by trestle tables, bins, and barrels filled with merchandise—everything imaginable. From black broadcloth jackets and gingham dresses to bolts of cloth, needles, and thread. Hardware, including plows, tools, harnesses, traces and saddles. Cracker barrels and casks of nails, sacks of beans and flour, rows of canned goods. Luxuries and necessities, it was filled with a world of stuff.

Owner Russ Lockhart, Fay's father, was absent from the premises. No doubt he was at the big table in a private dining room at the Cattleman Hotel, where his brother-in-law, town boss Wade Hutto, held court every Saturday morning, attended by Hangtown's gentry of bankers, merchants, and big ranchers. The Saturday morning meets were one of the few things that could entice Russ Lockhart out from behind the store's cash register.

The store was busy, crowded with customers. Johnny didn't have to look hard to find Fay. She just naturally stood out from the rest as she showed a bonnet to a townswoman. Her aunt Nell, a sour-faced old biddy, was helping out.

A watchful young woman who kept a wary eye on the clientele, Fay glanced up to see who had entered. She saw a handsome, well-dressed young man about her own age, a not-so-usual sight that made her look twice.

"Would you take care of this lady, Aunt Nell? I'll only be a moment." Not waiting for an answer, Fay put the bonnet down, scooting out from behind the counter and down the center aisle.

Nell started to squawk, choking it off as Fay kept moving toward the newcomer, her eyes shining, smiling warmly. "Johnny! Johnny Cross!"

"Howdy, Fay. Long time no see."

She reached out with both arms, taking his hands, squeezing them warmly. He couldn't help noticing a thin gold band circling the base of her ring finger. Wedding band.

Unsure how to respond, he was a bit awkward.

Fay leaned forward, kissing him lightly on the cheek. His skin tingled at the contact. Some free-falling strands of her hair brushed his face, smelling sweet. Intoxicating.

She stepped back, still holding his hands, looking him over. "It's so good to see you!"

She released him, hands falling to her sides. "I heard you were back. I was wondering when we'd run into each other. Why didn't you come to see me sooner?"

"I've been busy getting settled back at the ranch, fixing the old place up," he said.

"You've been busy, all right. Everybody's talking about how you cleaned up that awful outlaw gang. You're a hero, Johnny!"

"Don't believe everything you hear, Fay. These things are like fish stories, they get all puffed up in the telling. I just pitched in and helped out a little where I could, that's all."

"Don't be so modest. It was a wonderful thing you did. Not a man or woman was safe with those killers on the loose."

"Nice of you to say so, anyhow. I was sorry to hear about your loss, Fay. Your husband, that is. Real sorry."

Fay's face clouded, emotion flickering across it. Her blue eyes were shadowed and sorrowful, her mouth turned down at the corners. "Thank you, Johnny. Lamar—Captain Devereaux—was a gallant officer and a gentleman."

"I'm sure."

"You would have liked him."

Johnny wasn't so sure about that, but he nodded as if he was.

Fay said, "Who hasn't lost someone in the war? Your brother, Cal . . ."

Johnny shook his head. "No, Cal didn't make it."

"That's what I heard. Now it's my turn to say I'm sorry."

"Thanks."

Behind the counter, Aunt Nell snapped, "Fay! I could use some help here!"

"In a minute, Aunt Nell. I'm talking with an old friend."

Nell thrust her head forward, peering at the young man. "Johnny Cross! Land's sakes! I didn't recognize you. It's the first time I ever saw you in clean clothes."

"Nell!" Fay said sharply.

Johnny touched the tip of his hat brim to the older woman. "And a good morning to you, ma'am."

"Is it? We'll see," Nell said, her tone and expression indicating otherwise.

"So you're going to be staying in Hangtree?" Fay asked.

"For a while," Johnny answered.

"Good. I'm glad." Faye smiled, putting the full force of her considerable personal appeal behind it.

Johnny felt it all the way down to his toes as he became distantly aware of some kind of commotion brewing outside. It was like the buzzing of a nearby fly that hadn't quite yet begun to pestify.

Somebody shouted out in the street. People in the store started moving up front to see what it was all about.

A man outside was yelling, going on about something at some length and sounding distinctly unhappy.

Muffled by distance, Johnny couldn't make out the words. But he didn't care for the man's tone. Something about it, some raw, ragging note of derision, made the back of his neck start to get hot.

Fay frowned, glancing toward the storefront windows.

"What's all that commotion?" Nell said, sharp voiced with irritation.

"Some drunk, probably," a stiff-faced rancher put in.

"Hmph! And before noon, too! I declare I don't know what this town is coming to!" Nell exclaimed.

"He don't sound like no happy drunk," Johnny noted. He was just getting reacquainted with lovely Fay when a shot sounded.

"Uh-oh." *That's Hangtown for you,* he thought.

A fellow can't even strike up a chat with a pretty girl on Saturday morning without gunplay breaking out.

Fay started toward the door. Nell thrust out a hand as if to arrest her progress. "Fay, don't—"

Others moved toward the storefront for a better look. Johnny, cat-quick, rushed up the center aisle, smoothly interposing himself between Fay and the open doorway. "You want to be careful when bullets are flying, Fay. Best wait here where it's safe. I'll go take a look."

She started to say something but he was already out the door. The disturbance was centered two streets east on Trail Street. Only the one shot had been fired. The shouting continued, however, with no letup. It was louder and more abusive than before.

Johnny started toward it, then glanced back to see what Fay was doing. She stood just inside the doorway looking out but not following.

Glancing right, Johnny saw Luke standing along the rail of the Cattleman's front porch, facing toward the ruckus. He breathed a silent prayer of thanks that Luke wasn't involved in the fracas. Trouble had a way of finding Luke, and vice versa.

Of course, Luke thought the same thing about Johnny. They were both right, but at least, they were both well out of the trouble this time.

The street ahead was emptying. Scrambling for the sidelines, some sheltered in doorways, alcoves, or behind abutments. Others, farther away, thinking themselves safe, stood out in the open, craning to see what the ruckus was all about.

Men came out of the hotel lobby and dining room in a rush to see what was happening. They stood flattened behind upright pillars, crouched behind rocking chairs, peeking around corners. Staring oval faces clustered in the front entrance, others pressed against the windows.

Luke stood leaning for support against a porch column. Johnny pressed forward, boot heels scuffing on the plank boardwalk, until he crossed the street and climbed up on the porch. "Hey, Luke."

"You're just in time for the show."

Two men faced off in the square where a side-street met Trail Street. They were at opposite ends of the square, one at the northeast corner, the other at the southwest, facing each other across the diagonal.

A man standing near Luke peeked out from behind a white column. "Bliss Stafford's gunning for Damon Bolt! Called him out!"

"He must be crazy." Another man stood on one knee, peering between the bars of the porch rail.

"Crazy drunk," said a third.

"I seen it all," said the first speaker. "Damon was going to the barbershop when young Stafford ran out of the hotel and drew on him."

"He must've been inside laying for him," the second man said.

Damon Bolt was the owner of the Golden Spur, a saloon and gambling hall frequented by a fast, hot-blooded sporting crowd. A riverboat gambler from New Orleans, he'd come west after the war, settling in Hangtown.

Johnny knew him casually. He liked the man, what he'd seen of him. Liked the way he handled himself. Bliss Stafford was unknown to him. It was the first time he'd heard the name.

Bliss Stafford stood with his back to the hotel. Hatless, he showed a mop of yellow-gold curls. His expensive clothes were rumpled and wrinkled, as though he'd slept in them. He crouched with a smoking gun in his right hand, swaying, as though reeling under a wind only he could sense.

Opposite him stood Damon Bolt. His right hand rested near the butt of a holstered gun worn low on the right hip. He was tall and thin, almost gaunt, with a high pale forehead and deepset dark eyes. The hair on his head and his mustache were raven black.

He wore a brown morning coat, red cravat, tan waistcoat, and brown pants. His neat, small feet were encased in shiny brown boots. He seemed calm and self-possessed, oblivious of being under a drawn gun.

Bliss Stafford circled around to one side, angling for a better line of fire on Damon. His movements showed his face in three-quarter profile to those on the hotel's front porch.

He seemed younger than Johnny, and more immature. Handsome in an overripe way, his looks were spoiled by a sullen, sneering mouth. His face was flushed, his eyes were red.

Johnny nudged Luke. "Who's this here Stafford?" he asked, low-voiced.

"Stafford family came in last year," Luke said, speaking out of the side of his mouth. "Ranchers— a hard-nosed bunch. Bought up some prime land on the South Fork. Ramrod Ranch, they call it. Got more gun hands than cowhands riding for the brand. Bliss is the youngest, the baby of the family. A mean drunk and not much better sober."

"He must be a damned fool, calling out Damon Bolt," Johnny whispered.

The man standing by the white column turned and gave them a sharp look. "Walk soft, strangers. Bliss has killed his man and more. All the Staffords have. A bad outfit to buck."

"I'll take my chances," Johnny said. "But thanks for the advice," he added, seeing from the other's demeanor that he meant only to pass along a friendly warning.

Bliss Stafford drew himself up. "I'm calling you out, gambler!"

"I have no quarrel with you, Stafford," Damon Bolt said.

"I got a quarrel with you. You should never have got between me and Francine."

Damon frowned. "This is hardly the time or place to bandy words about a lady, sir."

"Things were fine between us until you horned in!" Bliss shouted.

"You are mistaken, sir. Miss Hayes has made it clear your attentions to her are unwelcome."

"You're a liar!"

Damon shook his head, seeming more in sorrow than in anger, almost pitying the young man.

Bliss's face, already florid, reddened further as he went on. "You're a fine one with all your fancy talk, making out like you're a real Southern gentleman. You ain't fooling nobody. Everybody in town knows what you are—a four-flushing tinhorn and whoremonger!"

Damon gave off a chill. "Have a care, sir. Say what you will about me, but I don't care to hear the ladies in my employ being abused."

"You don't, eh? What are you going to do about it?"

"You're the one with the gun. What are you going to do?"

"I'm going to kill you."

A man stood at the head of a press of spectators thronging the front entrance of the hotel. He pushed forward, starting across the porch. He wore a broad-brimmed hat, good clothes, and shiny boots. He was fiftyish, trim, with a handsome head of silver hair, a neatly trimmed mustache, and the beginnings of a double chin.

He was Wade Hutto, a powerful man in the town and the county. He descended the front stairs into the street, circling round into the intersection. Moving at a measured pace, he approached the face-off from the side, showing himself to both men yet careful not to get between them.

Johnny nudged Luke with an elbow. "Looks like the bull of the woods is sticking his horns in."

"Must be something in it for him. Ol' Wade don't stick his neck out for nothing," Luke said.

In the street, Hutto harumphed. "What the devil are you two playing at?"

"Ask Stafford. He threw down on me," Damon said.

"You got a gun—use it," Bliss Stafford spat out.

"Put that gun away, Bliss," Hutto said.

"Like hell! This is no business of yours, Hutto. Back off before you get hurt," Bliss warned.

"Everything that happens in Hangtree is my business, you young jackaknapes," Hutto said, coloring.

"You might throw some weight with these tooth-less townmen, but nobody tells Bliss Stafford what to do."

"Vince might see it different."

Some color came into Bliss's face. "Yeah, well, Pa ain't here now."

"A good thing for you he's not, otherwise he'd knock some sense into you," Hutto said. "I've got a lot of respect for Vince, too much to let you go off half-cocked and get yourself into bad trouble, Bliss."

"I kicked over the traces a long time ago. Now I do what I please. And it pleases me to give this tin-horn what he's got coming to him."

Hutto turned to Damon. "Maybe I can get a

straight answer out of you, Bolt. What's this all about?"

Bliss Stafford spoke first. "It's about my girl, Francine. Damon's trying to keep me from her, keep us apart. That's why he's got to die."

Hutto looked grave, like a doctor giving a heedless patient bad news. "You're playing with fire, Bliss. Vince told you to forget about Francine Hayes."

"What does Pa know about it? He's old. I'm young! I got blood in my veins, hot blood, not ice water. Francine belongs to me. She's mine!" Bliss made a warning gesture with his free hand, dismissing Hutto. "I'm through talking. Slap leather, gambler!"

"Against a drawn gun?" Damon said lightly, the corners of his lips upturned in a mocking smile. "I think not."

Bliss Stafford thought that one over. From his deeply lined brow and fierce frown, it could be seen that thinking was hard work for him. Coming to a decision, he shoved his gun back in the holster. "There! Now we're even up. The odds good enough for you, now? There's nothing to stop you from reaching. Why don't you draw?"

"It's too nice a morning for killing," Damon said.

"Draw, damn you!"

Damon tsk-tsked in a tone of real or affected sadness. "You see how it is, Hutto? There's just no reasoning with the boy."

"Boy? Who you calling boy? You see a boy around

here, kill him. Because I surely mean to kill you," Bliss cried.

"Don't do it, Bolt," Hutto said.

"You're my witness, Hutto. You and everyone else here. I gave him every out," Damon said.

Bliss Stafford shook with rage. "Enough talk! I count to three and then I'm coming up shooting!"

"You're making a big mistake, Bliss," Damon said.

"One!"

"Still time to back off and save yourself."

"Two!"

"Shoot and be damned, then."

"Three!" Bliss drew his gun, clearing the holster.

A shot rang out.

Bliss jerked as a slug tore into his chest. The impact spun him around halfway, his leveled gun unfired.

Damon's gun was held hip-high, pointed at Bliss. A puff of gunsmoke hovered around the muzzle.

Bliss looked surprised. He crossed gazes with Hutto, whose face showed pity mingled with contempt, but no surprise. Bliss toppled, falling sideways into the dirt. A final trembling spasm marked the last of the life leaving him.

Hurrying west on Trail Street—too late!—came Sheriff Mack Barton and Deputy Clifton Smalls.

Damon stepped back. Turning, he covered the newcomers with his gun. The lawmen slowed to a halt.

Barton, in his mid-forties, had a face like the butt end of a smoked ham. A wide straight torso hung down from broad, sloping shoulders; his legs were short and bandy. He wore a dark hat, gray shirt, black string tie, and a thin black vest with a tin star pinned over the right breast.

A Colt .45 was holstered on the right hip of a well-worn gun belt. He'd stayed alive for a long time by not rushing into things blindly. He was not about to start.

Deputy Smalls was tall, thin, reedy. Storklike. His gun stayed holstered, too. He took his cue from his boss.

Wade Hutto hauled from his jacket pocket a handkerchief the size of a dinner napkin and mopped his face with it. He'd sweated plenty during the face-off. "Nice work, Sheriff. You managed to get here too late to stop it."

Few dared talk to Barton in that tone, including Hutto, except when he was rattled, as he was now.

"You got no call to speak to me like that, Wade," Barton said.

Hutto had put Barton in as sheriff. For most intents and purposes he was Hutto's man, but Barton had a stubborn maverick streak that showed itself when he was crowded—he was a real son of Texas. There was no sense in getting on his bad side anytime, but especially with a potential crisis brewing.

Hutto backed down. "You're right, of course, Sheriff. I spoke out of turn in the heat of the moment. Sorry."

"That's all right," Barton said gruffly.

"This is a hell of a mess!"

Damon eased his gun into the holster, hand loitering not too far from the gun butt.

"Might as well inspect the damage." Barton and Smalls edged around the body, Hutto joining them. Bliss Stafford lay twisted on the ground, upper body turned faceup. A dark red hole marked his left breast.

Barton glanced down at the body, making his quick, expert appraisal. "Dead."

"Deader'n hell," Smalls seconded, nodding.

Hutto turned to Damon. "You went and did it. You couldn't just wing him. Oh no. You had to kill him. Now it's Katie-bar-the-door! Oh, there'll be hell to pay when Vince hears of this. Why didn't you shoot the gun out of his hand, or just wound him?"

"Who do you think I am—Bill Hickock?" Damon retorted.

"You got him right through the heart. I call that pretty fair shooting!"

Damon shrugged.

Barton took off his hat, scratched his head. He heaved a great sigh. "What happened?"

"I was on my way to Lauter's Tonsorial Parlor for a shave and a haircut when Bliss came gunning for me. I wouldn't draw, but he fired on me anyhow," Damon said.

"What for did he have a mad on?—as if I didn't know," Barton said.

Damon was silent.

"Things finally came to a head over the Hayes gal," Hutto volunteered.

"Francine Hayes," Barton said.

"If that's her name, yes."

"Don't bull me, Wade. You know her name. We all do. Francine Hayes. Lord knows Bliss and Vince have been kicking up a ruckus about her lately. Little slip of a gal got Bliss all tied up in knots so he couldn't think straight," Barton said. "Not that he was ever much of one for using his head."

"Bliss wanted Miss Hayes to run off and elope with him," Damon said. "Impossible, of course, even if she was willing—which she wasn't. Vince would never have stood for it. He even sent his son Clay around to buy her off. Francine was willing about that, but Bliss was having none of it. He threatened to kill his own brother if he tried to interfere. Francine held out, for which Bliss blamed me. He thought if I was out of the way he'd have a clear field."

Damon looked around at the various witnesses and rubberneckers hemming in the scene. "You all saw it. Bliss would have it this way. He left me no choice. I had to defend myself."

"Mebbe, but that won't cut no ice with Vince," Barton said.

"I can stand it."

"You only think you can," Hutto said.

Damon looked at him. Hutto was first to break eye contact, looking away.

"A clearcut case of self-defense, Sheriff. Everybody saw it," Damon said.

"How many will swear to it at the inquest, though?"

Barton asked. The milling crowd shrank back, sheepish, none meeting the lawman's eyes. "Anybody?" Barton pressed.

"I will," Johnny Cross said, standing at the porch rail.

Barton stood with fists on hips, looking up at him. "Now why does that not surprise me?"

Johnny shrugged. He and the sheriff had a history, going back to Johnny's boyhood days when Barton was deputy.

"I reckon we still got the right of self-defense in this country. That Stafford fellow was on the prod, spoiling for a fight. Damon did what he had to do. I would've done the same, so would any man here. That's how I'll tell it in court," Johnny said.

"Me, too" Luke chimed in.

"Just a couple of public-spirited citizens, eh?'

"You know us, Sheriff. Always ready to help out the law," Johnny said.

Barton laughed out loud without humor at that one. "You only been back for a month or two so you might not be up to speed yet. What do you know about Vince Stafford and his Ramrod outfit?"

"Not a thing."

"A bad bunch to mess with."

"That supposed to make a difference to me?"

"Not you, you're too ornery." Barton turned to Luke. "You got no excuse, though. You've been back long enough to know the way of things."

"I ain't worried, Sheriff. I got you to protect me," Luke said, all innocent-faced.

"Yeah? Who's gonna protect me?"

"Deputy Smalls?" Johnny suggested.

"You boys don't give a good damn about nothing, do you? I like your nerve, if nothing else," Barton said. "It's your funeral. Don't say I didn't warn you."

"Duly noted," Johnny said cheerfully

Damon Bolt cleared his throat. "I'm free to go?"

"Free as air," Barton said. "If you're smart you'll keep going, a long way off from here."

"That's not my style, Sheriff."

"No, it wouldn't be. You'd rather stay and get killed."

"I'd rather stay," Damon conceded.

"We won't argue," the sheriff said.

"You know where to find me for the inquest."

"If you're still alive. Vince Stafford knows where to find you, too."

"I'll be waiting."

"He won't come alone."

"The undertaker can use the business. Things have been slow around here lately."

"Laugh while you can, Damon. It won't be so funny when the lid blows off this town."

"We'll see. We through here, Sheriff?"

"For now."

"I'll be on my way, then. I've got a date with the barber for a shave and a haircut," Damon said.

"Tell him to make the corpse presentable," Barton said sourly.

Damon nodded to Johnny and Luke. "Stop by the Spur later. I'll buy you a drink."

"It's a go," Johnny said. Luke nodded assent.

Damon went up the street to the barbershop and went inside.

"Decent fellow at that," Wade Hutto said, musing.

"Too bad he's got to die," Barton said.

Spectators gathered around the body of Bliss Stafford, gawking, buzzing. Deputy Smalls plucked at Barton's sleeve. "Somebody's got to tell Vince."

"You want to be the one to tell him his pup is dead?" Barton asked.

"No, thanks!"

"He'll find out soon enough," Wade Hutto said. "No doubt somebody's already on the way to the ranch to give him the word."

"Good news always travels fast," Barton said sarcastically.

"Careful, somebody might hear you," Hutto cautioned.

"At this point, who gives a damn?"

"I do," Hutto said. Gripping Barton's upper arm, he led him off to one side for a private chat.

"Somebody was bound to burn down Bliss Stafford sooner or later. He was a troublemaker and a damned nuisance," Barton said.

"Good riddance!" Hutto said heartily.

"Too bad it was the gambler. Some lone hand done it, some drifter, we could step back and wash our hands of it. But it ain't some nobody, it's Damon Bolt. He'll fight."

"He's got friends, too. Gun hawks. He'll make a mouthful for Vince at that. Hard to swallow."

"I hope he chokes on it," Barton said feelingly.

"Those Staffords have been getting too big for their britches. Trouble is, the town's in the way. Hangtown could get pretty badly torn up."

"No way to stop it. Blood will have blood. Vince won't rest till he's taken Damon's head."

"It's a damned shame, Mack. Say what you will about Bolt, he's a gentleman in his way. Vince makes a show of setting himself up as a rancher, but he's little better than an outlaw."

"He's a dog, a mangy cur. One with the taste of blood in his mouth," Barton said.

"Why not bring him to heel?" Johnny Cross asked.

Hutto and Barton started. Soft-footed Johnny had come up behind them without their knowing it.

"You shouldn't go around sneaking up on people. It's a bad habit," Barton said, with a show of reasonableness he was far from feeling.

"How much did you hear?" Hutto asked.

"Enough—and that's plenty. But I don't go telling tales out of school." Johnny got to the point. "Stafford's crowding you? Cut him down to size."

Hutto looked around to make sure nobody else was within earshot. Luke Pettigrew stood nearby, leaning on his crutch, grinning. But Luke was

Johnny's sideman and knew how to keep his mouth shut, too.

"The Ramrod outfit is a rough bunch," Hutto said.

"No shortage of gunmen in Hangtown," Johnny said.

"But they've got no quarrel with Stafford."

"Pay 'em. They'll fight readily enough. There's enough hardcases in the Dog Star Saloon alone for a decent-sized war, and you can buy most of 'em for a couple bottles of redeye."

Hutto sniffed. "What's Damon Bolt to me, that I should start a range war with the Ramrod to save his neck?"

"Stafford's spread is on the south fork of the Liberty River. You're the biggest landowner on South Fork," Johnny said. "How long before he makes a move on you?"

"He wouldn't dare!"

"Why not?"

Hutto had no ready answer to that one.

"Why let him pick the time and place? Hit him now before he hits you," Johnny said, speaking the siren song of the Tempter.

Hutto was not easily swayed. "Your concern for my welfare is touching. What's in it for you?"

"I like Damon. He'll fight. Round up enough guns to hit Stafford where he's not expecting it and you can muss him up pretty good. The way to stop 'em is to bust him up before he gets started."

"We'd be taking a long chance," Hutto said, torn, fretful.

"It's your town," Johnny said, "but it won't be for long if you let someody hoorah it whenever he likes."

"I need time to think things out."

"Think fast. Move faster."

"Just itching for a fight, ain't you?" Barton said.

"Uh-huh," Johnny said. "That's what I do."

THREE

Hangtown was thick with killers, robbers, rustlers, horse thieves, card cheats, drunks, wife beaters, whores, swindlers, pickpockets, and a host of petty crooks and mean-minded individuals. Yet in all this collection of flawed humanity, the consensus ranked Sam Heller pretty much at the bottom of the heap.

Sam Heller was a Yankee.

In Hangtree, Texas, June 1866, a Northerner was in a potentially hazardous position. The landscape teemed with well-armed, unreconstructed Rebels. The Civil War, as the government in Washington, D.C., insisted on labeling the late secessionist conflict, was officially at an end—everywhere but in Texas. A year and more after General Lee had surrendered at Appomatox, all the states of what had been the Confederacy were at peace (however uneasy) with the Union. All but Texas.

The last battle of the war was fought in the Lone Star State at Palmito Hill in May 1865, a month after Lee surrendered at Appomatox. A year later, the powers in Washington were holding that Texas was still in a state of active hostility. The Federal troops garrisoned in Fort Pardee in northwest Hangtree County were as much an occupation force to overawe the local inhabitants as they were a fighting force charged with suppressing hostile Comanches, Kiowas, and Lipan Apaches. The real pains of occupation had not yet even begun.

A Yankee stranger in Hangtown, Sam Heller was little better than an outcast, a pariah. A dead shot and relentless foeman who kept coming until an opponent was beaten or dead, Sam had won grudging respect from sullen and resentful neighbors. A respect borne largely of fear, but no less real for that. He was known as a man not to be trifled with, best left alone.

Sam was on good terms with Captain Ted Harrison, commanding officer at Fort Pardee. On several occasions, he had interceded with Army brass to mitigate some of the rigors of Hangtree's status as occupied territory. It had won him few friends.

On this fine Saturday morning in late June, he'd saddled his sure-footed steel-dust stallion at first light and rode out, following the long slanting slope into the highlands. Riding the hill country alone, he climbed to the summit of the Upland Plateau, topping the rim of the elevated landform covering much of north central Texas. Part of it cut diagonally southwest across Hangtree County, dividing it in two. North of the line was highlands, well-wooded hilly country. South lay vast, grassy plains.

Most of the population of the county lived on the flat, the ranch lands of Long Valley, watered by the North and South Forks of the Liberty River. The twin forks joined east of Hangtown, flowing southeast across the state.

The uplands were more sparsely settled. Some— not many—ranches and farms could be found there, most sited within ten miles or less of the plateau's south rim. It was wild country, well-wooded timber broken up by hills and ravines.

At midday, Sam trailed south, a fine, fresh-killed buck deer slung across the back of his horse. He'd had good hunting that morning.

In his full adult prime, Sam was a rugged, raw-boned Titan, six feet two inches tall, broad-shouldered, deep-chested, and long-limbed. He looked like a Viking on horseback, with a lion's mane of shaggy yellow hair and dark blue gunsight eyes. He wore a battered slouch hat, a green and brown checked shirt, brown denims, and boots.

An unusual sidearm hung in a custom-made holster at his right hip, a sawed-off Winchester Model 1866 rifle called a mule's-leg. Even cut down at the barrel and stock, it was still as long as his thighbone.

A pair of bandoliers loaded with spare cartridges was worn across his chest in an X. A Navy Colt .36 revolver was stuck in the top of his belt on his left side, worn butt out for a cross-belly draw. A Green River Bowie–type knife hung in a sheath at his left hip. Tied to the left-hand side of the saddle by rawhide thongs lashed to metal rings piercing the leather was a long, flat wooden box with a suitcase grip at one end. Its contents were a welcome equalizer to a man alone.

Set at the edge of the no-man's-land that was the Staked Plains, Hangtree County was a thoroughfare for outlaw gangs, renegades, hostile Indians, and even north-ranging Mexican bandidos.

Sam was an outlander, but he had business in that part of Texas. Important business—government business. And he meant to see the job through.

The hostility leveled at him by the townfolk was a bit wearing at times, and on such a day it was pure pleasure to ride off by himself into the hills and do some hunting. Deer, an animal more savory and less dangerous than Man.

When the hunt was crowned with success well, that was a goodness. Gutted and wrapped in a canvas sheet, the carcass of a fat buck was slung head down behind the back of the saddle and tied in place by some lengths of rope.

Dusty, the horse, didn't mind. He was used to Sam's ways and the scent of blood and death, animal or human, bothered him not at all. He was a warhorse.

Sam headed Dusty south toward the rim of the plateau, some miles distant. He had breakfasted at dawn before riding out. Since then, he'd refreshed himself on the trail solely with beef jerky and canteen water. His empty belly rumbled its displeasure.

Back in town, he'd sell the fresh kill to the butcher, after first having cut out some prime venison steaks. The cook at the Cattleman Hotel would grill those cuts of meat over a charcoal fire, serving them up the way Sam liked, charred at the edges and red and juicy on the inside. With fried potatoes and some cut up fresh tomatoes—*man!* Sam's mouth watered at the thought. He could all but taste it.

A game trail wound south through low hills shaped like sombrero crowns, overgrown with green woods. Sam followed the twisty path. Strong sunlight shone through leafy tree boughs. A bushytailed red squirrel darted along a branch, startling a bird into flight.

The hills shrank into mounds, low and squat, as he rode along the trail opening into a stretch of rolling fields. The sun was hotter without the shade to buffer it, but not too hot. Sam basked in its welcome warmth.

Reaching into his left breast pocket, he took out a corncob pipe and a leather tobacco pouch. Tamping the pipe bowl full of rough-cut, shredded tobacco, he struck a self-igniting lucifer on the side of his pant leg and lit up, puffing away. Smoke clouds wreathed his head as the mixture in the pipe glowed orange-red, and he enjoyed the sharp, tangy bite of the acrid smoke, venting clouds contentedly.

The ground sloped upward, rising toward a ridge running east-west. The trail entered the wooded incline, putting Sam once more in the shade. He crested the hill, pausing at the top.

Beyond lay a shallow valley, another ridge, and another. The series of ridges and valleys stretched some miles to the southern edge of the plateau.

Behind the nearest ridge a line of smoke rose into the sky, a thin black streak climbing into the heights. Sam drew slowly on his pipe, frowning. *Where there's smoke, there's fire. And where there's fire, there's usually people—which in these parts means caution.*

He hadn't ridden that way before, having topped the plateau early that morning, several miles farther east. Sighting his prey, he'd tracked the buck northwest into conical hills. Returning, he'd taken a different trail, one that went directly south, instead of retracing his original route along the southeast.

He'd chosen those hunting grounds to take him away from human habitation, to where the wild game was. In the upland, a small homestead could easily be nestled out of sight in a pocket draw or under the lee of a hill.

Sam's frown deepened. He'd forgotten to draw on his pipe and it had gone out. He exhaled softly across the lip into the bowl, blowing it clear of cool gray ashes. He stuck in his thumb, wedging the remains of the coarse-cut tobacco deep into the bowl, hardpacking it in place for later. A thrifty man, he was. Waste not, want not. He put the pipe back in his breast pocket, buttoning it shut.

The touch of his heels against Dusty's flanks started the animal forward, down the far side of the hill. He crossed a valley, uncomfortably aware of its openness. He started up the opposite slope, dotted with stands of timber, and zigzagged uphill, angling from one clump of trees to the next, using them for cover.

Nearing the crest, he reined Dusty to a halt and got down from the saddle. Taking the reins in one hand, his left—his right was his gun hand—he led the horse toward the summit. "You're an old woman, Sam Heller," he said to himself, "but . . ."

The ridgeline was rocky, with gaps in it. Approaching on foot, Sam neared the top without skylining, avoiding silhouetting himself against the blue backdrop where he could be seen by somebody on the other side of the ridge. Covering himself and the horse behind a rocky outcropping, he crouched and looked around.

The valley below was wide and deep. A dirt road ran along its middle, stretching east-west. A real road, not a game trail, making it Rimrock Road, the main thoroughfare running east-west across the south end of the plateau.

The line of smoke streaking the sky took its origin in the valley below. It pointed down, an elongated gray-black finger whose tip touched a wrecked, half-burned covered wagon. The bodies sprawled around it and the ground in the immediate area showed white, powdered white, as if touched by frost.

But it couldn't be frost, not in that heat.

The air was still, with barely the breath of a breeze to ruffle the thin feather of smoke rising from the smoldering wagon. Sam studied the scene, scanning it. Some minutes passed. The valley seemed empty, peopled only by the dead. More time passed, with no change in the surroundings.

"Well," Sam said to himself, sighing, "can't stay here all day." The ground looked safe, harboring no skulking bushwhackers, as far as he could tell.

How safe was it, though, with corpses strewn about?

He glanced at the deer slung across the horse's back. He should cut it loose, to lighten Dusty's burden if he had to run. But he had a powerful hankering for venison steaks. He was frontiersman enough to not throw away anything of value unless he damned well had to. He could always cut it loose later.

Sam mounted up. He undid the leather strap at the top of the long, custom-built holster and hauled out the mule's-leg. He rode through the gap, down the other side of the hill. No shots greeted him, no charging horsemen.

Dusty descended at a steady pace. Nearing the valley floor, Sam smelled wood smoke from the burned wagon. and other less pleasant odors, including burning flesh. Human flesh.

The big, bulky Conestoga wagon, the kind generally favored by emigrants wending their way westward to new lands, stood about a dozen paces to one side of the dirt road. Its passengers had suffered an interrupted journey. He closed in on it.

The horses were gone. They had been cut loose from the traces binding them to the wagon tongue, most likely stolen. Its canvas-topped covering had been consumed by fire. Scraps and shreds of the charred canvas littered the ground nearby. Part of the right-hand side of the wagon was scorched and burned, but the rest was intact.

The white powder dusting the ground around the wagon was flour. It had been poured out of a slashed-open sack. Much of it had been poured over the dead.

The wagon had been vandalized. Baggage was thrown out of the wagon, suitcases and trunks breaking open upon impact. Ransacked contents, pawed over, were strewn about the ground. Various items of household bric-a-brac were broken up—chairs, a table, a cabinet, and sacks of bean, grain, and seed.

A wagon train had arrived at Hangtown the night before, laying over in the campgrounds southwest of town. The victims must have been on their way to join them when they'd been attacked by marauders. The bodies strewn about appeared to be a family of seven—two oldsters, a gray-bearded man and an old woman; a middle-aged couple, probably man and wife; a beardless youth in his mid-teens; a twelve-year-old girl; and a boy of ten. Most of the bodies were naked, their nudity white and pale as grubs that swarm in the rotten wood of fallen trees.

Robbery and murder were frequent occurrences on the frontier, but this outrage was marked by an emphasis on torture and murder. It was ghoulish bloodletting, executed, no doubt, with lipsmacking relish.

The middle-aged man, squat and stocky, was tied upside down to the right rear wheel of the wagon, braided buffalo-hide ropes binding him in place. Underneath him was a slow-burning fire. His face and head were burned beyond recognition.

The gray-bearded oldster had been shot several times, none of them fatal. He'd been cut up pretty badly, his naked torso scored with multiple stab and slash wounds. His crotch was worked on with a hatchet, but that wasn't what killed him. He'd been scalped—alive—and then his skull was bashed in by stone-headed war clubs.

Nearby lay the corpse of a young girl, thin, scrawny, and long-limbed, about eleven or twelve years old. She'd been shot once through the side of the head. A mercy killing.

Sam guessed the old man had shot her before she could be taken alive by the raiders. Cheated of their fun, they'd taken their wrath out on him, killing him by slow degrees.

A teenage boy lay facedown in the grass, pierced with arrows.

The woman, middle-aged and thick bodied, lay on her back, faceup. She'd been raped, of course, not once but often. She'd been beaten, broken, mutilated, and scalped.

The old woman had had similar treatment. As an added refinement, a tree branch had been shoved between her legs and set on fire. Sam could only hope it had been done after she was dead.

"Devilments!" Sam muttered to himself. His voice sounded strange, a toad's croak, startling him. His mouth was bone dry.

Obscene butchery was nothing new to Sam Heller. He'd grown up in southwest Minnesota where the eastern branches of the Sioux roamed, raided, and killed, terrorizing settlers. In the Dakota badlands—what the Sioux considered their home grounds—he'd seen similar remains of pioneers, prospectors, and other white invaders.

No less enthusiastic aficionados of torture were the Apaches, whom he'd tangled with in Arizona and New Mexico territories. And he'd seen plenty of atrocities committed by and against soldiers and civilians of both sides during the Civil War.

This outrage figured to be the handiwork of Comanches.

Recent reports had reached Hangtown of Comanche raids on the plains west of the Breaks. Isolated incidents as yet, brutal and alarming, prompted the commanding officer at Fort Pardee to detail a cavalry troop to meet Major Adams's wagon train at

Anvil Flats and escort it safely to the Santa Fe Trail. There it would be met by another cavalry troop from a New Mexico fort. That rendezvous was scheduled for sometime that day.

Sam's scalp tingled, with good reason. He wore his yellow hair long, scout-style. It was a scout's way of taunting the savages, as if saying, *You can't take my hair.* For a moment, the boast rang a tad hollow. Still, he intended to keep his shoulder-length yellow hair intact for a while longer—a good while longer. Or die trying.

The prospect had been made less sure by the grisly evidence before his eyes of Comanche raiders.

Sam examined the sign. The marauders' tracks went east along Rimrock Road through the valley.

He cut the deer carcass loose and threw it in the brush.

Pointing Dusty's head south, he moved forward, climbing the north slope of the far ridge, up and out of the valley. Away.

FOUR

One second, they weren't there; the next, they were.

Seton Fisher was carrying water back to the ranch house from the stream. He had a full bucket in each hand, held by the handles. It was early afternoon, it was hot, and the buckets were heavy.

In his mid-forties, Fisher was strong armed and thick bodied. Sweat stung his eyes, blurring them. He paused, trying to blink them clear because he didn't want to interrupt toting the water back to the house by setting down a bucket to wipe his eyes clean.

Fisher's ranch was near the south rim of the Upland Plateau. It was a good location, but a hard go to eke out a living from the Texas hill country for himself and his family.

The site occupied a saddle between two ridges running east-west. The south ridge hid the edge of the plateau and the flat below, screening them from view. The north ridge lay on a flat below Sentry Hill, the most prominent landform in the area. Between them lay a valley of gently rolling grasslands—Seton Fisher's spread.

A small herd of cattle, widely scattered, grazed on the greenery. A south-flowing stream ran through the property. A flat-roofed house sat on a rise within walking distance of the water. Ringed by cottonwood trees, the rise gave welcome shade on hot summer days.

The ranch house faced south, a modest two-room dwelling with windows and a covered dogtrot passage connecting both rooms. Glass for the windows was an unaffordable luxury for the Fisher ranch. Most of the year, the windows were sealed with semitransparent oiled paper. During warm weather months, the window frames were left bare and uncovered to let in fresh air.

Outbuildings included an open-sided barn and a shed. Nearby were a haystack and a corral with several horses and a mule penned inside. The dooryard, an open space loosely bounded by the house and outbuildings, was nothing but brown dirt. Traffic by humans and domestic animals had trampled out the grass.

Fisher was squat and burly, with a barrel-shaped torso. His bushy eyebrows, the hair fringing his balding head, and a rufflike beard were all streaked with gray. He was a onetime cotton planter from the rich black-earth district around Dallas. His first wife being deceased, he'd taken a second wife, Ada, a war widow, and adopted her young daughter, Lydia.

War had killed King Cotton, closing down markets and causing Fisher, like so many others, to go bust. It had also killed his oldest son Emory, who'd fought and died for the Confederacy. His next-born, Eben, was in his midteens, but big for his age.

By 1864, Seton Fisher had feared the lad would be rounded up by the relentless recruiters of the Confederate army. He'd feared that he, too, was not immune from conscription since the army was taking pretty much any male able to stand on his own two feet who hadn't used those feet to make scarce while recruitment agents were scouring the district.

Seton Fisher had moved his family west, from Dallas to Forth Worth, then Weatherford and Mineral Wells, and still farther west until finally fetching to a halt in Hangtree County.

But there was no living to be made in Hangtown. Mindful of draft recruiters and their ceaseless quest for Confederate cannon fodder, Fisher had deemed it best to put more distance between his family and the haunts of men, claiming land on the flat west of the town.

The south rim of the plateau had looked right for his purposes. It was far enough from civilization to keep the authorities to a minimum, but not so far that he couldn't get to town within a half-day's ride to fetch supplies or flee to in case of an emergency.

Other ranches, farmhouses, and cabins lay scattered up on the south rim but their owners, like Seton Fisher, had a passion for seclusion and their own reasons for anonymity.

Brooding over the landscape lay the heights of Sentry Hill. A spring at its southern base was the source of Locust Lake, whose gray-green hue was the color of aged, weathered copper. The lake fed a number of streams running to the plateau's edge and down its southern face, coursing southeast across the flat.

Fisher settled his family on a tract of land between Sentry Hill and the south rim. The uplands were overrun by maverick cattle, runaway longhorns that had gone back to the brush. They thrived and thronged the hill country, multiplying there as they did on the flat and indeed throughout much of Texas during the war years. The increase would ultimately make a cattle kingdom of the Lone Star State—but not yet.

By hard work and great pains, the family had managed to gather and brand a small herd of longhorns, enough for their needs. Not until the family was well and truly settled did Seton Fisher discover the reason for the ready availability of good grazing land in Hangtree County.

The threat of imminent civil war in 1860 had caused the federal government to close a string of forts it maintained along the western frontier. Manned by cavalry, the forts had been strongholds designed to suppress raids by Comanches, Kiowas,

and Lipan Apaches. Washington needed the troops
for the coming war in the all-important theaters
east of the Mississippi.

When war broke out in 1861, the Texas branch
of the Confederacy was too hard pressed fighting
the Yanks along the Gulf Coast, in New Mexico, and
in East Texas along the Louisiana border, to spare
more than a handful of troops to take up the
Indian-fighting duties formerly handled by U.S.
cavalry and Texas Rangers.

In Hangtree County, settlers in the uplands
mostly picked up and moved out rather than stay
put and be massacred. However, with the settlers
largely gone, the Indians shunned their former
raiding grounds, knowing they were no longer fit
and ready sources of captives, scalps, and stolen
horses.

"Now you tell me!" was Fisher's reaction to these
disclosures, confided to him by residents of Hangtown during a memorable visit to barter cattle hides
and tallow for supplies.

It was too late for him to back out. He had filed
his claim, cleared the site of trees and brush, built
the house and outbuildings, and made the land his.
They had equity in it now—sweat equity. To give it
up was unthinkable.

Besides, the Comanche threat was overblown.
He thought the Hangtown locals were having fun
at the expense of the newcomer, the outsider,
telling tall tales to spook the greenhorn. That's
what he told himself and his wife. He pretty much

managed to convince himself and she knew better than to contradict him and get a beating for her troubles.

For a fact, few Comanches had been seen in those parts in recent years, said sightings having been reported in the Breaks and farther west. Seton Fisher was a stubborn man. So long as he and his family took reasonable precautions, they would be safe from Indians.

While the Fishers did not exactly flourish on the south rim, neither did they perish. Maverick cattle provided meat, hides, tallow, and, when ground up, powdered bones for fertilizer. There was wild game aplenty—deer, antelope, pheasant, quail, and such varmints as possum, raccoon, rabbit, and squirrel.

Seeds bought or bartered from the Hangtown feed store grew in vegetable patches near the ranch house yielding corn, tomatoes, cucumbers, melons and such. Ada and her daughter Lydia tended to the gardening, as well as the cooking, cleaning, mending, and washing.

Fisher and his sixteen-year-old son Eben did the heavy labor, clearing, hewing, building, herding and branding cattle, and the like. Built like a bull, Fisher was a hard, tireless worker.

Son Eben got his growth early. He was a big, hulking youth, a towering man-boy. He did his chores like he was told—as long as his Pa was there to oversee him every minute. Fisher despaired of Eben ever making his way all by his lonesome.

Eben was in the dooryard chopping wood when

his pa returned from the stream with two full buckets of water.

Although big and strong, Eben was clumsy and ill-coordinated. Coarse dark hair fell across his face into his eyes. Flailing away at sectioned log rounds with a double-headed ax, he seemed more likely to cut off some toes rather than split firewood. Working harder, as if to impress his pa with his industry, he made a noisy task of it, grunting with the effort of each stroke, splinters and wood chips flying this way and that, making a mess.

Hot, tired, and thirsty, Fisher wasn't fooled. His shoulders, arms, and neck ached from the effort of fetching water for the house cistern. His mouth and throat were dry, parched. He longed for some refreshment. But it was easier to keep moving and stumble along, rather than having to resume from a dead start. He'd dip a ladle into a bucket, taking a long drink of cool, fresh water once he reached the house and set down his heavy load.

He closed his eyes for an instant, squeezing them shut. Red and yellow suns and pinwheels blazed against the black backdrop inside his eyelids.

He opened his eyes. He saw intruders.

Indians!

Comanches.

Four braves on horseback emerged from behind a screen of trees on the west, on his left side. They'd come as if out of nowhere, materializing like phantoms.

Fisher shook his head, wondering if perhaps

that's all they were—hallucinations brought on by too much sun on his bare head.

They looked hard and cruel. Dangerous.

Reeling, he staggered back a step. A giant invisible hand squeezed his gut, the bottom of his stomach feeling as though it had fallen out. He stood frozen in the middle of the yard, buckets in hand, a stone's throw from the ranch house, Through an uncurtained window, he saw a flash of movement as Ada crossed in front of the window, moving around in the room. She hadn't seen the invaders.

Eben stood with his back to the Indians, chopping wood full tilt, sending the chips flying, blissfully unaware of the intruders.

The horses' hooves trod softly on the brown dirt of the yard. There was a faint musical whispering. Soft as the first pattering fall of raindrops, it was the jingling of tiny bells. An odd, jarring note, the musical chimings came from several strips of little silver bells no bigger than a berry. They were strung at regular intervals on rawhide thongs, braided into strands of shiny black shoulder-length hair framing the face of the Comanche riding slightly in advance of the other three.

Seton Fisher was unaware that he was in the presence of Little Bells, a member of the Bison Eyes clan and a valued henchman of War Chief Red Hand. He knew only that he and the rest of his family were in danger, deadly danger.

He wondered if he looked as sick as he felt. He had no weapon at hand. He owned a rifle, two pistols, and a shotgun, but they were all in the house. *Why weigh myself down with a gun while carrying out ordinary household chores?* he had thought earlier.

Too late, he knew why, and cursed himself for being a damned fool.

Little Bells's lithe, wiry limbs were knotted with ropy strands of muscle wrapped in veins. A red bandanna circled his forehead. Beneath it, his hair hung loose and free, a strand of silver bells on each side of his face. Deep-set eyes peered out from under an overhanging brow. His swarthy, copper-hued face was painted with vertical and horizontal black stripes. War paint.

He wore a salmon-colored shirt, a breechcloth, and deer-hide boots. He rode a brown horse with a high-backed Comanche style wooden saddle, holding the reins in one hand and a rifle in the other. The rifle was decorated by a pair of feathers tied below the muzzle by a rawhide thong.

The three braves with him were armed. Greasy Grass carried an army carbine. Thorn had a single-shot rifled musket. A bow was slung across Firecloud's back and a quiver of arrows hung over a shoulder. A six-gun was stuck into a braided rawhide belt holding up his breechclout.

They stopped between Fisher and the ranch house, their expressions remote, impassive.

Some men cling to hope no matter how grim the facts. *Why assume the worst?* Fisher asked himself silently. He'd handled stray Indians before. They were great ones for trying to get something for nothing from settlers. High-handed, high-stomached, full of themselves, they did not beg, they demanded. Feed them a meal, give them a few trinkets, baubles, and blankets to sate their savage vanity and childlike greed and they'd be on their way. That's how it had always been in the past, in other places.

But those Indians hadn't been Comanches, staring down Fisher on the lonely heights of the hill country.

Eben kept on huffing and puffing, making the chips fly as he continued to chop wood, oblivious to the danger at hand.

Damned young fool! He always was slow on the uptake, that boy.

Seton Fisher glared and called to him in a stage whisper, his voice a croak. "Hsst! Hsst! Eben. Eben!"

"What, Pa?" Eben said, not looking up from the woodpile.

"Over here, ya derned idjit!"

Eben straightened up, turning around with ax in hand. "Yow!"

"Easy, boy," Fisher said.

Eben's expression of shocked surprise might have been almost comical in its grotesque exaggeration if the situation had not been so direfully real. He cried, "Injuns! Oh Lordy!"

"Keep still, boy! We can't show weak," Fisher hissed.

"Gawd!"

"Quit your bawling and carrying on."

"What're we gonna do, Pa?"

Fisher trembled, agitating the pails of water he held. Water slopped over the top of a bucket, splattering on the ground. Fat droplets were soaked up by the brown dirt.

He set the buckets down on the ground, knees creaking. He straightened, never once taking his eyes off Little Bells.

Little Bells grimaced, baring his teeth. Seconds passed before Fisher realized the Indian was not making faces, but grinning. It was hard to tell the difference. The grin was accompanied by a dry chuckle, sounding like a barking cough.

Little Bells glanced at Thorn beside him on his left, the turning of his head setting off a jingling of the silvery bells. Thorn smiled.

Little Bells turned to the right, toward Greasy Grass. Grinning away, he nodded at the other, as if to encourage him. The lower half of Greasy Grass's face split in a knife-blade smile, sharp, toothy, and mirthless.

Little Bells beamed down at Fisher, who forced a half grin. He looked sick. Little Bells's smile widened, laugh lines crinkling around dark eyes. His chuckling ripened into laughter.

Exchanging glances with his sidemen, he motioned them to join in. Greasy Grass and Thorn laughed loudly. Firecloud remained aloof, stone faced.

Little Bells gestured to Fisher, as if encouraging him to join in the merriment. Seton forced a laugh, sounding like he had a bone stuck in his throat and was trying to clear it.

Apparently that really tickled Little Bells, who laughed out loud. Greasy Grass and Thorn laughed along with him. Firecloud's blank-faced silence remained unbroken.

Little Bells motioned for Seton Fisher to continue. Fisher made a show of laughing it up. *If that's what the savage wants, best play along,* he thought, and made a braying jackass of himself.

Suddenly, without warning Little Bells frowned, falling silent.

Taking their cue from him, Greasy Grass and Thorn stopped laughing, turning it off as abruptly as though it had never been at all. The Comanches smiled no more.

Fisher's face was ashen. Little Bells pointed his rifle at Seton.

"What . . . what's happening, Pa?" Eben choked. "I'm kilt."

Little Bells fired once, the bullet tearing through Fisher. He crumpled, falling backward.

Firecloud burst out laughing.

"Pa!" Eben remembered the ax in his hands. Hefting it high above his head, he rushed Little Bells, sobbing. "Crazy murderin' redskins!"

Little Bells swung the rifle toward Eben and fired. Eben swayed but kept lurching forward, his big feet kicking up clouds of brown dirt.

Another slug tore into him, knocking him down.

* * *

Inside the west wing of the ranch house, Lydia was mending a croker sack with needle and thread. At thirteen, she was slim, coltish, with long, straight, dirty-blond hair worn in a pair of braids framing a thin, fine-featured face. Dark brown eyes contrasted with fair hair and skin. She wore a lilac-colored, cotton floral-print dress and a pair of flat-heeled, lace-up ankle boots.

Her mother sat nearby, folding towels.

Lydia stopped working and looked up at her ma.

"Quit your daydreaming, gal."

"I'm out of thread, Ma."

"Get some more. You know where it is."

"Yes, Ma." Sighing, Lydia rose and left the room.

Her mother watched her leave, then stood and walked past the front window on her way to put away the towels. In her early thirties, Ada looked ten years older, the wreck of one who'd once been fancied by appreciative males as "a damned handsome woman." Hard times and privation had worn her down. Her gray-streaked brown hair was pinned up so as not to interfere with the daily round of household chores. A deeply lined, square-shaped face showed a strong chin and a lot of jaw.

Movement outside caught her eye as four Indians on horseback cut off Seton and Eben from the house. Immediately, she closed and barred the front door, and shuttered the front window. Stuffing her pockets with shells from a box nestled on a ledge nearby, she grabbed the shotgun from where it stood against the wall beside the front door. Her eyes, usually dull with fatigue, were hard and intent.

Lydia went through the dogtrot into the east room. The twin of its opposite number, it was a low-ceilinged cube, bright where sunlight shone through the south-facing window and dim where shadows massed.

A rear corner had been partitioned into a kind of alcove, which was used as a storeroom. The windowless enclosure was thick with stuffy brown gloom.

Lydia stepped inside, looking for the wicker basket containing her mother's sewing kit with its spare bobbins of thread. She rummaged through boxes of household goods and domestic implements in search of the kit, but couldn't find it.

Hunkering down, not wanting to soil her dress by kneeling on the hard-packed dirt floor, she searched the lower shelves. The sewing kit continued to elude her. Frowning, she started pulling out boxes and looking inside them.

She grew aware of a commotion outside. Like a garment snagged on a nail, her attention was caught up by the sound of laughter—a sound rarely heard on the hardscrabble, just-getting-by-if-that Fisher ranch.

Lydia's frown deepened. She disliked something in the laughter, a note of meanness. Or craziness. Or both.

The laughter stopped. Lydia rose to see what it was all about. After the gloom of the storage space, the sunlight shafting through the window was dazzling. She squinted against it, eyes narrowed.

A shot sounded from outside.

Ada Jenks Fisher came barreling out of the west room. Usually too worn out by hard work for speed, she moved fast, rushing along the dogtrot into the east room, carrying the shotgun. Brushing past Lydia, she slammed the front window shutters closed. Made of hardwood several inches thick, they had loopholes for shooting through. "Help me bar the window! Quick!"

A voice started screaming, ragged, high-pitched. *Eben?*

Another shot boomed, followed by an outcry.

A third shot.

Silence.

Laughter again, thinner than before.

"Ma, what?"

"Quick!"

Stung, Lydia took hold of a stout wooden bar lying on the floor below the window. With both hands, she lifted it and wrestled it into the pair of U-shaped metal staples bracketing the window frame. Ada's free hand helped push it solidly into place.

No sooner was the job done than Ada caught Lydia by the arm, clutching her thin wrist. Turning, she started back the way she came, pulling Lydia after her with a wrench that nearly yanked her off her feet.

"Ma! You're hurting me!"

"Hush up, you fool girl!"

They hustled through the dogtrot into the west room, shadowed in brown murk.

Outside, screaming broke out, raw and terrible. Counterpointing the screams came shrill exultant cries, sounding like a cross between a screech owl and a coyote.

Lydia put her hand to her mouth, gasping. "What is it, Ma?"

"Indians!"

The rear half of the west room was partitioned into two cramped, criblike rooms. Blankets strung on head-high, horizontal poles served as doors. Ada went into a room, pulling Lydia, dazed and numb, after her.

The room was hot, dim, and stuffy. Set high in the rear wall was a small, square window. The shutter was open, unfastened.

Ada put her mouth close to Lydia's ear, speaking low. "Comanches killed Fisher," she rasped, "and from the sound of things, they're doing the same to Eben."

"Comanches! What're we gonna do, Ma?"

"You're gonna run like you never ran in all your born days, missy."

Ada shoved Lydia toward the window. It opened on a long, grassy field bordered by woods on the east and west. The field stretched a hundred yards north to a dirt road that intersected it at right angles—Rimrock Road. Beyond the road lay a thicket of woods, with Sentry Hill peeking over the treetops.

"Climb out the window and run for the brush." Ada indicated a patch of woods on the east, right-hand side of the field. "Get under cover as soon as you can. Don't try to reach the road. It's too far away. Hide and don't come out no matter what you hear."

"What about you, Ma?"

"I'll follow you."

Lydia climbed on the narrow, wooden plank bed under the window and put a leg through the open space above it, scraping the back of her thigh against the windowsill. Holding the frame with both hands, she pulled her other leg after her.

She sat on the sill, bent forward from the waist. It was a tight fit.

Frightful noises came from the front of the house, rising and falling.

Lydia paused, hesitant. Ada put a hand on the girl's back and pushed her forward.

Lydia fell to the ground, feet and ankles tingling from the impact. She turned, looking back. "Come on, Ma," she urged.

"You go first, gal," Ada said.

"Ma—"

"I'll cover you. Don't argue. Git!"

Lydia started forward, angling toward the tree-line east of the house. She felt naked and exposed in the open. The sun shone brightly on green grass.

She was about ten trembling paces away from the house when a Comanche rode out of the west woods. He'd been posted there earlier to keep watch on the road.

He put heels to his horse's flanks, kicking it into motion, intending to run the girl down. It was better sport than he'd dared hope for.

Ada saw him coming. She shouldered the shotgun, planting both feet squarely on the dirt floor. When the brave drew abreast of the window she pulled the triggers, giving him both barrels. A booming blast of buckshot blew him off the horse.

Stung by a few pellets, the horse reared, shrieking. It raced toward the road.

Ada broke the shotgun, shucking expended cartridges out of the bores. Reaching into a front pocket of her apron, she took out two fresh shells and reloaded.

Lydia stood frozen in place.

Ada cried, "Run!"

"I ain't leaving you, Ma!"

Ada shook her head. "I'll hold off them red devils as long as I can. Go, before they get us both. I'm gonna give 'em what for. Don't let it be in vain."

"Ma, no!"

Ada smiled sadly. "You always minded your momma. Don't stop now. I love you, darlin'. God save you!"

"Mama, please."

"*Run!*"

Lydia stumbled a few steps forward, sobbing. She looked back, blinking away tears. Ada lifted a hand in farewell, and moved away from the window, lost from view.

Lydia staggered away from the house, weaving toward the trees. She caught sight of the dead Comanche sprawled on the ground, his upper body a wet, red ruin from the double-barreled shotgun blast. Recoiling, she lurched away from him, stiff-legged.

Ada nodded approvingly to herself as she saw Lydia closing on the treeline. She had thought about keeping Lydia with her and making a stand against the Comanches. The ranch house had guns, ammunition, and solid walls. But the roof was made of wood. The braves would set fire to it to burn them out. It was better to distract the Comanches, keep them focused on the front of the house while Lydia escaped through the rear.

The plan had almost gone awry thanks to the brave hidden in the west woods. Luckily he'd showed himself in time for Ada to down him, and there didn't seem to be anyone else posted there. She had to keep the others busy for as long as she could.

Lydia reached the safety of the trees, ducking into the greenery and disappearing inside the thicket.

Ada crossed to the shuttered window in the front

and peered through a loophole. She saw three braves, all on foot. To her left, near the corral, Firecloud was hitching the reins of a horse to a top rail of the corral fence. The reins of another were wrapped around his forearm to forestall the animal from getting loose. Two other horses had already been hitched to another section of fence.

In the middle ground, Thorn was finishing up the last of Eben, chopping him up alive with the ax. He'd set down his musket to do the job properly. The grisly task had splattered him with the red stuff from head to toe, but he didn't seem to mind. Eben gurgled, choking out a death rattle.

In line with the shuttered west front window, Greasy Grass hunkered down beside the body of Fisher, working on him with a scalping knife. Fisher's hair was thin on top, balding, but that didn't spare him the indignity of mutilation.

Largely free of body hair themselves, the Comanche were amused and intrigued by its presence among whites. Sometimes along with the scalp they took the sideburns or a beard, or all three. Occasionally they took the full face, skinning it off the corpse's skull, to make a mask of it, a cured and dried mask for their warrior society lodge. Such macabre curios made treasured heirlooms—keepsakes.

Frowning with intense concentration, Greasy Grass leaned into his handiwork, shifting and squirming to make a series of sharp, precise cuts to take Fisher's beard, along with much of the face that went with it.

Ada thrust the shotgun muzzle through the loophole, pointing it at him. Greasy Grasss had time enough to look up and no more.

Ada squeezed a trigger, the blast pulping his head. She was careful to use only one barrel. Swinging the shotgun to the left, she tried for Thorn, wielding the ax on what was left of Eben.

Thorn was too fast for her. In one movement he flung the ax at her and threw himself to the side, diving headfirst to the ground. Ada pulled the second trigger a split second too late, hitting only empty air.

The ax came hurtling at her end over end. *Thunk!* It struck blade-first, burying itself deep in the wooden shutter a handbreadth above the loophole.

Thorn came out of his dive in a roll, grabbed his musket, and fired. A round tore through the shutter, missing Ada by inches.

The shotgun was empty. She cleared it and grabbed two fresh shells out of her apron pocket but dropped one. It rolled in a half circle on the hardpacked dirt floor. She fumbled a shell into place, took another from her pocket and loaded it into the second barrel, ready for another go-round.

Lydia had not gone far. Once inside the thicket, she paused at the edge. Crouching on hands and knees, sheltering beside a tree trunk, she peered through a gap in the underbrush. She could see the rear of the house and, to the left of it, part of the barn and corral.

She was afraid to move, afraid to go and afraid to stay. She couldn't stop shivering. Her mouth was open, panting, but she couldn't catch her breath.

A shotgun boomed. Lydia cried out involuntarily, clapping hands over her mouth.

A second boom blasted.

A Comanche rounded the rear corner of the west room, coming into view.

Little Bells. Knife in hand, he sneaked up on the back window.

Lydia thought it was shuttered, but she was wrong. Ada had closed it but in her haste had fastened it improperly. It hung slightly ajar.

Little Bells put the knife between his teeth, freeing his hands to reach up and open the shutter. Taking hold of the windowsill, he boosted himself up, wriggling snakelike through the window into the house.

Fear for herself and fear for her mother warred within Lydia. *The Comanche is going to sneak up on Ma from behind and take her unawares.*

Lydia rose, parting the brush and stepping into the open field. She started toward the house. The empty black square of the open rear window was a sinister portent of ill omen. "Ma, look out! The back window!"

Her voice sounded impossibly thin and faint in

her ears, unable to carry its message of warning into the house so Ada could hear it.

Inside, Ada peered through the loophole of the west room's front window. The handle of the ax stuck in the shutter panel, blocking some of her narrow field of vision.

Thorn and Firecloud had taken cover. She saw no sign of them. The shotgun was charged with a double load of shot but no targets presented themselves.

A faint, high-pitched shrilling came to Ada's ears. She recognized it as Lydia's voice, though she was unable to make out the words. Her heart sank. She mumbled, "That fool girl, didn't she have enough sense to stay hidden in the brush and keep silent? Or has she been taken?"

Nearer, came a soft sound at the edges of her hearing. A sound innocent in itself, but infinitely dangerous in its current context, it was a faint jingling as of tiny chimes.

At the same instant, Ada became aware of a menacing presence hovering nearby, a sensation not unlike that which seizes a rabbit when the shadow of a hawk passes over it.

She sensed a rush of motion at her back and turned, swinging the shotgun around with her.

A heavy, solid mass crashed into her, all but knocking her off her feet. She was swept across the floor and slammed into a wall. Little Bells crept closer to her, strong and relentless.

Ada realized her mistakes. She'd seen four

horses but only three braves and hadn't fastened the rear window shutter properly. Two missteps in a contest where the slightest oversight could prove fatal

Little Bells's clawlike hands fastened on the shotgun barrel, trying to rip the weapon from her grasp, nearly breaking her finger in the trigger guard.

He swung the barrel upward, causing Ada to jerk one of its double triggers. The gun fired, spewing deafening noise, flame, and smoke, and blowing a hole through the roof.

Their faces were only inches apart as they struggled. A frontier woman by birth, Ada had come up in a hard school. She tried to knee her attacker, but he blocked it with his thigh.

Little Bells rocked her with a vicious backhand, knocking the back of her head against the wall so hard she saw stars. The blow caught her in the mouth, splitting her lips and sending blood droplets flying.

Ada fought to keep hold of the shotgun, but she could feel it slipping from her grip. He struck again, with a closed fist to her jaw. Blackness thrust inward around the edges of her awareness. There was a roaring in her ears. Her legs folded and she collapsed, sliding with her back against the wall and sitting down hard.

Little Bells tore the shotgun from her nerveless fingers and glared at her. His white eyeballs gleamed out from the raccoon's mask of black war paint banded around his eyes.

The shotgun was a prize. He would keep it. Holding it in one hand, he used his other hand to grab a fistful of her hair and dragged her across the room to the door. He shrieked his distinguishing war cry, alerting his fellows that he was in control of the situation.

Unbarring the door, he flung it open. He hauled Ada to her feet and threw her through the open doorway, out into the yard. She fell, sprawling in the dirt, dazed, semiconscious.

Happy and exultant, Thorn and Firecloud emerged from behind cover, showing themselves. Still clutching the scalping knife, the corpse of Greasy Grass lay stretched out beside Seton Fisher.

Little Bells had subdued the woman, and she was his by right of conquest. He shrugged. Interested not so much in womanflesh as horseflesh, he went to the corral to appraise the horses and take the best for himself, as was his right as leader. The others could do what they wanted with the woman. She was too old for him. He liked them young.

The killing had excited Firecloud. He stood over Ada as she tried to rise from her hands and knees. He kicked her in the belly, doubling her up. She fell on her side.

Thorn laughed, moving in to watch.

Firecloud shucked off his bow and quiver of arrows, laying them on the ground. He flung Ada on her back and straddled her on his knees. Slapping, punching and bloodying her further excited him.

Leering, he grabbed fistfuls of fabric at the front of her dress and tore it open. Shredding it, he bared the soft, abundant flesh of her upper body.

He lifted her skirts, bunching them up around her middle, and pulled down her drawers, ripping them off.

Firecloud threw himself on top of her. Under his breechcloth, he was hard. Rampant and ready, he took hold of himself and lunged into her, ripping, tearing, thrusting.

Lydia stood midway between the back of the house and the treeline. She couldn't see what was happening, but she could hear it—the fierce exultant shrieks and agonized outcries. She'd been unable to warn her mother and save her. She now risked the same fate.

The sound of hoofbeats broke her paralysis of will. A gut-twisting jolt of fear told her she was undone. Panicked, she turned to run for the brush.

A lone mounted man rode east on the road north of the ranch. A white man.

Changing direction, Lydia started toward him, terrified that he wouldn't see her and would ride on. The road seemed a long way off. She waved her arms over her head. "Wait, wait! Help, please! Help!"

From the corral, Little Bells heard the thin, wailing cries and things fell into place in his head. When he was in the house, he'd thought he'd heard a voice calling from somewhere outside. The woman had put up unexpected resistance, more fight than he'd bargained for, and in the excitement, he'd ignored the cries, forgetting them.

Hearing them again, he ignored them no more. Running to his horse, he unhitched it and climbed on its back. Drawing his rifle from the saddle scabbard, he turned the horse's head north and kicked the animal into a run. He rode between the east side of the house and the trees, breaking into the open field. A young female, a slip of a girl, ran toward the road, yellow braids streaming after her.

Lydia's long thin legs flashed, a blur of motion. War whoops sounded behind her. She glanced back only to have her worst fears confirmed. A brave on horseback was pursuing her, and he was closer to her than she was to the stranger.

She couldn't outrun a horse, but gave it a good try. Legs scissoring, she ran all out, scenery flashing by. She tripped over a half-buried root and fell forward, sprawling in the dirt and weeds.

Not fair! It isn't fair! Lydia got to her feet, swaying unsteadily. She looked over her shoulder and realized the Comanche was only a few horse lengths away and closing. As she stared at him, something changed in his face and he swung up his rifle.

Tensing, Lydia braced herself for the shattering impact of a bullet.

With Sentry Hill on his left, Sam Heller searched for a way off the south rim of the plateau. The uplands were crawling with Comanches and the sooner he was quits of it, the better the chances of keeping his hair. He'd been ducking scouting parties for several hours.

He worked his way east on Rimrock Road, looking for a safe route down the south slope. He'd passed several ranches along the way in the last hour, and the one yonder was the first one he'd seen not burned to the ground.

Nearing it, he heard shots.

The mule's-leg cleared the holster, filling his hand. Looking southward, he saw a long field leading to a ranch house.

A girl raced across the field toward the road, waving her arms to attract his attention, crying out to him. He couldn't make out the words but he didn't have to. Her fear and desperation were plain to see. Sam turned Dusty toward her, angling across the field as the girl stumbled and fell.

A Comanche swung into view, charging north.

"Yah!" Sam put the boot heels to Dusty's flanks, and gripped the reins between his teeth, freeing both hands to work the mule's-leg.

The Comanche had a rifle. Veering off from his pursuit of the girl, he changed course to meet Sam head-on.

Little Bells fired first, his rifle bullet zooming past Sam's ear like a fat bumblebee buzzing by. Sam fired second, but better, tagging the Comanche dead center.

The Indian shuddered.

A second round followed, ripping into him. A third knocked him backward off his horse, and Little Bells hit the ground hard.

Sam hauled on the reins with his left hand. Dusty slowed. Little Bells's riderless horse rushed past and kept on going.

Sam reined in short of the fallen Comanche. A glance showed the brave was as dead as they come.

Nearby, the girl stood swaying, shaken but unhit, gasping. "More of them—at the house. Ma! They've got her!

"How many?" Sam asked.

"Don't know."

"Go hide in the brush. I'll be back for you. If not—stay there till it's dark and then try to make it to the flat."

"Hurry, please! They're killing her!"

Sam rode toward the house, coming in on the west side, a shifty tactic that might edge the odds a hair more in his favor. He rounded the corner, entering the dirt yard.

Firecloud was on top of Ada, raping her in the dirt. Thorn stood nearby, armed with Greasy

Grass's carbine, preferring it to the single-shot musket he'd discarded.

Sam reined in hard, pulling Dusty up short. The horse reared, rising on his hind legs as Sam shot Thorn.

As the hooves of Dusty's forelegs touched ground, Sam shot Thorn again, watching as he fell in the dirt.

Firecloud raised himself up on elbows and knees. Quickly, Ada reached under him, clawing the six-gun out of the top of his belt. She shoved the muzzle into his belly and worked the trigger, emptying the gun into him. His gut came undone, spilling entrails.

Dying, Firecloud drew his knife and plunged it into Ada, burying it in her heart.

Thorn was still twitching. Sam swung down off his horse and shot him again. Thorn stopped twitching.

Ada and Firecloud were dead—leaving Sam and the girl alone in a country alive with Comanches on the warpath.

FIVE

Johnny Cross and Luke Pettigrew stopped in the Dog Star saloon, a dive on the south side of Hangtown. The saloon was a long, low, shotgun-style shed.

Outside, it was midday, inside, twilight time. Day or night, a smoky gray dusk compounded of gloom, smoke, and whiskey fumes reigned over the place.

A bar ran along one long wall. Tables and chairs were grouped along the opposite wall. The saloon featured raw whiskey at a low tap. A couple whores plied their trade in a back room.

Behind the bar, drinks were served up by Squint McCray, proprietor. Two men, shiftless, lazy loafers who were reasonably honest as long as he had his eye on them, worked for him. Some joked that he'd developed the squint from watching the help closely.

That was untrue. The squint was the result of a wound sustained in a knife fight, causing one of his eyelids to have a permanent droop. The undamaged eye glared fiercely, as if outraged at having to do the work of two good eyes.

McCray preferred to hire relatives. The men were his cousins; one of the whores was his niece. The other whore was unrelated to him, McCray having no other female kin in that line of work. When he caught kinfolk in one of their petty dishonesties, as he inevitably did, he made allowances for them. Being family, he let them off with a roughing up or at worst, a beating. He didn't have to bust them up bad, club them, cut them, or shoot them, as he might have felt duty-bound to chastise those with whom he shared no ties of blood.

As for the whore who was no kin of his, she was scrupulously honest. She turned over to McCray all the money she made from rolling drunks, meekly accepting whatever portion of the loot he doled out to her in recompense.

Such docility vexed him. It wasn't natural. As a result he kept an even closer watch on her. He found himself wishing he could catch her stealing so he could let her off with a beating and break the tension created by her seeming integrity.

Watchful as always, Johnny stood with Luke at the head of the bar where it made a little L-shaped jog near the entrance. Angled sideways with his back to the wall, he watched the patrons' comings, goings, and carryings-on.

He drank with his right hand—his gun hand—his left hanging down loose and easy near the butt of the gun holstered on his left hip. He was faster and more deadly accurate with a gun in his left hand than most men were with either hand.

Luke leaned against the bar with his back to the door, facing the rear of the building. He could see the full length of the saloon, all but the entrance, and Johnny had that covered. Between them, they had the whole place under view.

They weren't expecting trouble, but they weren't not expecting it, either. After all, this was Hangtown.

At the bar, you took your drinks standing up, since there were no stools. If you wanted to drink and sit down, you took a chair at one of the tables. Had Johnny and Luke been planning to stay a while, they would have taken a table, to give Luke a chance to rest his good leg.

Luke's feet, the one of flesh and blood and the wooden one, were firmly planted on the sawdust-covered floor. His crutch was beside him, propped against the edge of the bar.

The Dog Star drew a rough crowd, attracting more than its share of local hardcases. Few were out and out villains, but most were no better than they had to be. Small ranchers who weren't above using a running iron to put their brand on other men's cattle, cowboys too ornery or alcoholic or both to hold a job for long, horse thieves, gun hawks, drifters, tinhorns, skirt chasers, saddle tramps—a lively crew. The saloon was packed with them, thronging the bar and the tables.

Johnny caught Squint's eye, the good one, a round and fiercely glaring orb. He motioned for a refill. McCray nodded, reaching under the bar for a bottle of the higher-line brand of whiskey he kept for more demanding, better-paying customers.

He filled Johnny's cup, a wooden tumbler, and Luke's too, while he was at it. All the cups in the saloon were made of wood. It cut down on breakage, especially during brawls. Fridays and Saturdays were usually good for a half-dozen brawls each night.

"Have one on me, Squint," Johnny said.

"Don't mind if I do." McCray grinned, showing the few teeth he had, black and broken. Setting another cup on the bar top, he poured himself a drink. Raising it, he said, "Mud in your eye."

He didn't mind having fun with his name, so long as he was instigating it. Let somebody else make sport of it, though, and there could be trouble.

"Here's how," Johnny said.

"Health," said Luke, gesturing with his cup.

They drank up. McCray tossed his back like it was water, with as little seeming effect. Johnny drained his cup without flinching, but a deep red flush overspread his bronzed face. Luke did the same, eyes watering, an involuntary twitch firing a couple times at the corner of his mouth.

"Good for what ails you," McCray said cheerfully.

"Smooth," Johnny said, a mite breathless.

"Yeah," Luke coughed out.

"It's my special brand, for them what appreciates the quality," McCray said. "The secret's in the aging."

"A whole week, huh?" Luke said sarcastically.

"Eight days! It's that extra day that makes the difference."

"As long as you're in the neighborhood, might as well hit 'em again," Johnny said, "and don't skip yourself."

McCray refilled the three tumblers. "This one's on the house, boys."

"Thank you kindly, Squint," Johnny said.

"Right generous of you," Luke said.

They all three drank the round slower, a sip at a time.

"Ain't seen much of you boys lately," McCray remarked.

"We've been out at the ranch, mustanging," Johnny said.

"You picked a good day to come in, what with the shooting and all."

"You see it, Squint?" Luke asked.

"And leave the place to those no-account thieving kinfolk of mine? Not on your life, brother. Although it almost would've been worth it to see Bliss Stafford get a bellyful of lead."

"No bellyful. Shot through the heart," Luke said.

"You seen it, huh?" McCray leaned forward eagerly, elbows on the bar.

"Sure 'nuff. A sweet piece of gunplay it was, too."

"Worked out good for me."

"How's that, Squint?"

McCray looked around the saloon, his good eye glinting. "Nothing like a killing for bringing 'em in," he said, beaming. "Saturdays is always good, but we're doing a land office business. It's the shooting what done it. Folks like to talk it up over their cups, kick it around."

"What're they saying?" Johnny asked.

McCray looked around, then leaned in farther. There was little worry about being overheard amid the noise and tumult of the hard-drinking, rowdy crowd. But the Dog Star was the kind of place where patrons naturally put their heads together as if cooking up some scheme—crooked, more likely than not.

McCray was just being confidential and cautious. "You ain't gonna find too many tears being shed over Bliss Stafford. Too bad about Damon, though."

"What for? He ain't the one who got kilt," Luke said.

"Not yet. But he's not long for this earth." McCray shook his head, the corners of his mouth downturned. "Damned shame, though. Him being a genuine hero of the Confederacy and all."

"That right?" Johnny said.

"Ain't you heard? Damon was part of that outfit that whupped that Yankee General Banks and his army at the junction of the Teche and Atchefalaya rivers. Chased 'em clear out of the Red River country."

"That's hard country. Swampland when it rains,

near-desert when it don't, and not much good any time."

"Sounds like you been there," McCray said shrewdly.

"Just passing through," Johnny said. After the war, he'd knocked around for a while in the East Texas Louisiana borderland with Lone Star hellions Cullen Baker, Bill Longley, and such. Johnny was still wanted in those parts.

"Reckon the Staffords will come gunning for Damon?" he asked, changing the subject.

"Depend on it," McCray said flatly. "The old man's a mean one on the best of days, and this ain't gonna be one of them, not with his fair-haired boy dead with Damon's bullets in him."

"A fair duel," Johnny said.

"That won't make no never-mind to Vince Stafford, no sir. Them other sons of his are a handful, too. Fact is, they could all use killing. Hard to beat, though. Clay's pure hell with a gun and Quent's meaner than a rattlesnake. And they won't come alone. They'll bring the whole Ramrod bunch, and that's a passel of bad hombres."

Two men came in through the front door, one at a time, cutting the conversation short.

The first was about forty, round faced, with a neatly trimmed black beard. His eyes were bright, calculating. He looked like a prosperous rancher or businessman, well fed, well dressed. Those types were at a premium in Hangtown . . . in all of post-war Texas, for that matter.

A pair of big-caliber guns were worn holstered low on his hips, below a soft swelling roundness of belly. The bright shrewd eyes and low-slung guns didn't quite fit the image of man of affairs that he presented.

The second man was in his mid-twenties. His hat was set back on his head so the brim tilted up at a near-vertical angle. A brown hat with a round crown, broad flat brim, and a snakeskin hatband. He was thin, bony, sharp-featured, with slitted eyes, a knife-blade nose, and a thin-lipped mouth. A holstered gun was slung low on his right hip, his hand hovering near it.

The duo moved apart, so that neither stood with his back framed by the open doorway. They stood at the front of the saloon, facing the rear, eyeing the place as if looking for something, or more likely, someone.

Johnny recognized them. The older man was Wyck Joslyn, the younger was known only as Stingaree. Joslyn was a gun for hire, a professional with many kills under his belt. Johnny had heard that Joslyn had tried to sell his services to town boss Wade Hutto. But Hutto already had top gunhand Boone Lassiter on his payroll and wasn't hiring. He wasn't looking to make trouble, either, not with a Yankee cavalry troop garrisoned upcountry at Fort Pardee. Stingaree was a fast young gun looking to make a name for himself.

Joslyn and Stingaree were regulars at the Alamo Bar, the pricey establishment patronized by a high-living, free-spending crowd. A fellow could burn through a lot of money fast at the Alamo. Both being at somewhat loose ends, the two had fallen in together.

They were suspected of having pulled several stagecoach and highway robberies farther east in Palo Pinto and Tarrant counties, but nothing had been proven against them yet. They'd stayed out of trouble in Hangtown, giving Sheriff Mack Barton no cause to brace them.

Wyck Joslyn's restless gaze brushed Johnny's, making eye contact for a brief beat. Johnny nodded, tilting his head an inch or two in casual acknowledgment, not making a thing out of it one way or the other.

Joslyn's gaze moved on, looking beyond Johnny to others, seeking. Finding what he was looking for, he started forward, Stingaree falling into step beside him. Stingaree was a small man who carried himself like a big man, swaggering all cock-o'-the-walk.

They went down the center aisle and even in that rough crowd, men made way for them, moving aside.

Some men at the far end of the bar called out for more whiskey. "Like to stand around jawing with y'all, but we got some thirsty folks here," McCray said.

Johnny slapped a dollar coin down on the bar.

"Thanks, gents," McCray said, scooping it up and scuttling off to serve some more customers.

"Some barkeeps, you buy 'em a drink, they say, 'I'll have it later,' or 'I'll have a cigar, instead.' Not ol' Squint. You buy him a drink, he drinks it, by God! I like that," Luke said.

"Hell, he'll even buy you one on the house once in a while," Johnny said.

"I like that, too."

"Wyck Joslyn's a long way off his stomping grounds," Johnny said, a bit too casually.

Luke cut him a side glance. "The Dog Star's a far cry from his usual fancy digs. What do you figure he's doing here?

"Maybe we'll find out."

Joslyn and Stingaree reached the end of the long aisle. At the left rear corner an odd trio sat huddled around a table, hunched over their drinks like vultures over carrion.

Wild and woolly characters, they looked more like mountain men than cattlemen. All had long hair and stringy beards. Ragged scarecrow figures with harsh bony faces and hard eyes, they shared a family resemblance

Each of the three wore some part of a Confederate Army uniform. One sported a gray hat with a faded, frayed yellow-braided hatband. Another was wrapped by a long, tattered knee-length gray overcoat. The third wore baggy gray breeches tucked into the tops of black cavalry boots.

A long-barreled, single-shot smoothbore musket was leaning up in a nearby corner.

Johnny and Luke eyed the trio nonchalantly, as if they weren't looking at them.

"The Fromes Boys," Johnny said.

"You know 'em?" Luke said, surprised.

"I've seen 'em around. In Quinto, up in the Nations."

Quinto was a flyspeck town in the middle of a sun-baked plain in what would someday be the Oklahoma Territory, a refuge for deserters, drifters and outlaws.

"They're brothers from the Tennessee hill country, wanted all over the map. They're on the dodge, so they never stay in any one place for too long," Johnny said.

"Man! They's really unreconstructed," Luke said, shaking his head.

"They never was constructed in the first place," Johnny said dryly. "Zeb, Tetch and Jeeter. Zeb's the one with the Billy Goat chin whiskers. Tetch is the big one. Jeeter's the red-haired, sneaky looking one. The Fromes Boys. Three of the meanest faces you ever did see."

"They look mighty unsociable at that," said Luke.

"Zeb's so sour he'd cross the street to kick a sleeping dog," Johnny said. "I seen him do it once. I should've shot him then."

Despite the crowded conditions in the saloon, the other patrons had left a space around the brothers. The Fromeses sat off by themselves, hunched over their whiskey, glaring out at the world.

They looked none too welcoming, but Wyck Joslyn was undeterred. He went to their table, Stingaree lagging behind.

The brothers looked up as one. Three sets of hard eyes fastened on Joslyn, pinning him. Zeb, the oldest, was possessed of a particularly forbidding gaze. Dark irises were completely surrounded by white eyeball, giving an intent, spooky quality to his unblinking stare.

Few men could have stood under those gun-sight eyes without qualms, but Wyck Joslyn seemed unabashed.

Joslyn did some fast talking and not much of it. Just as well—the brothers weren't much for palavering. Whatever his pitch, he must have put it over.

The Fromeses exchanged glances, Tetch and Jeeter looking to Zeb for guidance.

Zeb nodded grudgingly. That went by his way of being an invitation. Joslyn pulled a chair from a nearby empty table, drew it up to the Fromes's table, and sat down. He motioned to Stingaree, telling him something, giving him instructions.

Stingaree went to the bar, shouldering aside several patrons. They were no pushovers, but when they saw he was associated with the evil-eyed Fromeses, they sidled off without protest.

Stingaree got a couple bottles and two cups from McCray, bringing them to the brothers' table. He dragged a chair away from the wall and sat down at the table.

Neither Joslyn nor Stingaree sat with his back to the front door. Both angled their chairs around to the sides so they were partially turned to the front and could keep an eye on it. The chairs extended out from the table like wings.

Joslyn uncorked the bottle and filled Zeb Fromes's cup, followed by Tetch's and then Jeeter's. Then he poured for Stingaree, and lastly, himself. All drank, with no particular evidence of good fellowship, cordiality, or even relish for whiskey. Joslyn did some more talking, not drinking much.

"Quite a coalition." Johnny stepped away from the bar. "Let's mosey. I could use some fresh air."

Luke nodded. Fixing the crutch under his left arm, he swung around facing the door. He and Johnny went out, into the street. No porch or boardwalk fronted the Dog Star saloon, just hard-packed dirt under their feet.

High overhead the noonday sun beat down, blanketing the surroundings in bright hot glare.

"Now, what do you suppose Wyck Joslyn's about with the Fromes Boys?" Johnny asked.

"Cooking up some mischief," Luke said.

"Sure, but what?"

"Whatever it is, it'll probably come to fruit before too long."

Johnny nodded. He lit a cigar and got it going. South of the Dog Star the buildings were few and far between. A wide expanse of bare dirt mixed with patches of short, tough grass was broken by a handful of straggly trees and bushes.

Beyond lay Mextown, where the Spanish-speaking people of the town lived. A cluster of whitewashed adobe huts and wooden shacks grouped around an oval plaza centered by a shallow, water-filled basin. The area was watered by irrigation troughs fed by a stream snaking across the plains south of town. Small yards and vegetable gardens were marked off by wooden pole fences. A burro hitched to a pole walked around in circles, turning a waterwheel. A youngster walked beside the animal, beating its hindquarters with a stick when it slowed.

West of Mextown lay a big open green space with a rivulet running through it. It was used as a camping ground by westbound wagon trains, Hangtown being the last settlement until New Mexico.

The site was occupied by Major Adams's outfit. About two dozen wagons were in motion. Most were Conestoga-style covered wagons but there were some freight wagons and even one or two high-sided caravan wagons. Hitched to the wagons were teams of horses, mules, or oxen.

Scores of men, women and children thronged the scene. Families for the most part, along with scouts and others of Major Adams's crew.

The wagon train was breaking camp and moving out. It was a slow, laborious process with lots of jockeying for position, balky animals, and clumsy wagon handling.

One by one, the wagons began forming into a long, single-file column. The movement kicked up a tremendous amount of dust, brown clouds rising skyward, shot through with shafts of sunlight. The line of the column angled northwest to pick up the Hangtree trail outside the town limits.

"There go the pilgrims," Johnny said.

Luke, chewing tobacco, let fly with a spurt of brown juice. "Them greenhorns can't even hardly form up in a single line without fouling up. It's like herding cats."

"Smart to move 'em out now. The Major knows what he's doing. Those folks could only get into trouble in Hangtown on a Saturday night—'specially this Saturday night."

"They'll wish they stayed put if they cross trails with any Comanches out on the Llano," said Luke.

"They're gonna link up with the cavalry out at Anvil Flats."

"Anything that keeps the bluebellies out of town is all right with me."

"Amen to that."

"Where to now, Johnny?"

"How about the Golden Spur?"

"I knew that was coming."

Johnny tried to look innocent. "Don't you want to see the famous Francine Hayes, who drives men wild?"

"The Staffords would like to see her too, I bet," Luke said. "All hell's gone break loose when that bunch hits town."

"It'll take some time for them to round up their men and ride in from South Fork," Johnny said.

"They've had time."

"We're just going for a looksee, Luke. We'll have a drink or two and be on our way before the storm breaks."

Luke laughed. "You probably even believe it."

"Sure I do, or I wouldn't have said it."

"Some folks, trouble follows them. But you, Johnny—you follow trouble."

"I start it. Hell, that's where the fun is."

Luke sighed. "When you put it that way, I cain't say no."

Johnny grinned. "Things have been getting too blamed quiet lately, anyhow."

Luke shook his head. "Not for long. I got me a feeling."

SIX

The Golden Spur and the courthouse were next-door neighbors. A side street ran between them. The rear of the courthouse faced the Golden Spur, as if turning its back on all the drinking, gambling, and whoring of the pleasure palace.

Occupying its own square lot, the Golden Spur was isolated from its neighbors. The two-story wooden frame building fronted south on Trail Street, a rectangle whose long sides ran north-south.

A portion of the façade extended above the roofline, forming a broad, flat flare on which the name GOLDEN SPUR was blazoned in big, bold red letters trimmed with gilt paint. Behind the flare, concealed by it, a man with a rifle sat perched on the flat rooftop. He was Monk, the saloon's bouncer. He was keeping watch for the Staffords and their Ramrod Ranch riders.

The usual gang of loafers and regulars found

sitting in the shade on the front porch was absent. They had gone elsewhere to avoid being in the line of fire when the Ramrod bunch came to town.

The entrance of the Golden Spur opened on a large, high-ceilinged space. A long bar stretched along the right-hand wall; on the left side were tables and chairs, most of which were set aside for gambling. It was set with card tables, a Wheel of Chance, and birdcage dice games.

Opposite the front door, toward the rear of the building, a wide central staircase rose to a second-floor mezzanine, with balcony wings extending along two long side walls. Under the mezzanine were rooms used as offices by the saloon's owners, Damon Bolt and his business partner, Mrs. Frye.

Ordinarily, by the noontide hour on a Saturday the Golden Spur would have been doing a brisk trade in gambling, women, and whiskey. Now, it was all but deserted. Abandoned but for its staffers, a number of whom were about to take their leave.

Seated alone at a card table was Damon. Facing the front door, he was playing solitaire, dealing out the cards to himself, arranging them in neat rows by suit and number.

The big room was quiet, hushed. The soft slap of each card could be heard as it was laid down faceup on the table. A pistol lay near his right hand. A bottle of bourbon and a glass stood by his left.

Morrissey, the barkeep, stood behind the bar, wiping the countertop with a damp cloth. It didn't need wiping, but he liked to keep busy. He looked like a barkeep should look, big, bluff, with hair parted down the middle, a black handlebar mustache, and wearing a striped shirt with sleeve garters.

On the other side of the bar stood Creed Teece, the house's resident hired gun. He was loading cartridges into a Henry's repeating rifle. A brown hat with the brim turned up at the sides sat on top of his head. He had a spade-shaped face, big ears that stuck out, long narrow eyes and a bushy mustache. He wore a six-gun on his right hip.

He looked like what he was, a working cowboy, one who worked at the Way of the Gun.

The stillness was shattered by the exodus of whores. Mrs. Frye had rounded them up in their rooms upstairs and herded them down to the ground floor. Some of the youngest, freshest whores in the territory—Cherokee, Nicole, Penny, Vangie, Daryah, and Kate—they had on their traveling clothes. They were covered up and looked "respectable" enough. Their bags were packed, carpetbags and suitcases, a hatbox or two.

Mrs. Frye had burnt-orange hair and wore a green satin dress. She was thirty, with a long horse face, pinpoint green eyes, thin sharp nose, and a full-lipped, generous mouth. She was bony, angular, with high pointy breasts, and lean hips. Her long legs, what could be seen of them under her ankle-length dress, were her best feature.

She stood at the bar, the whores gathered around her. A few showed grim, white-lipped faces. One or two had moist eyes and quivering chins. They would have taken it a lot harder if Mrs. Frye hadn't already paid them off for their work up to date. That was Damon's idea; he always paid his debts, for good or ill.

At Mrs. Frye's prompting, Morrissey poured out shots for all. She raised her glass. "Drink up, gals, time's a-wasting." Her voice had a harsh Midwest twang. "It ain't often the house is buying, so get it while you can."

At the table, Damon filled a shot glass. He rose, holding it up. "Your very good health, ladies. Until we meet again. May it be soon."

Mrs. Frye nodded. "The sooner we get back to business, the better." She raised her glass a little higher. "Luck!"

She tossed her drink back like a man, unflinching. The others drained their glasses fast or slow, according to their tolerance for strong drink.

Having emptied his glass, Damon threw it against the wall, where it shattered, causing some of the girls to jump. He sat down, picked up the deck of cards, and resumed playing his game of Solitaire where he had left off.

Mrs. Frye set her glass on the bar. "On your way, girls." Turning around, she called out, "Swamper!"

"Yes, ma'am!" The man came shuffling to the fore. He was a cheerful derelict, an old drunk who was kept around to do various scut work and chores in return for room and board. His lodgings consisted of a bedroll in the corner of the kitchen and his board was made up mainly of whiskey.

He had long, stringy gray hair, bloodshot eyes, and a face full of broken, spidery blue veins where it was not covered by a straggly beard. He wore a red-and-black flannel shirt, bib denim overalls and hobnailed boots. An oversized horse pistol was stuck into a hip pocket, gun butt jutting out.

"Take the girls over to Honey Bailey's," Mrs. Frye said. Honey was a brothel keeper, a friendly rival. Her "house" was a few streets north of the Spur. Mrs. Frye turned to the girls. "You girls can stay at Honey's until the trouble's blown over. Worse comes to worse, you'll all find work there. With what you've got to sell, none of you will have to worry about starving."

She turned back to Swamper. "Take them out the back way. Wait until Monk gives you the word."

"Yes, ma'am. C'mon, ladies."

The women picked up their bags. Swamper started toward the rear of the building, weaving slightly. The women followed.

"Good luck, Damon," one said.

"Thank you, my dear."

"Get on with you and don't bother the man," Mrs. Frye said, shooing the whores on their way.

Swamper led them through a passageway behind the staircase to the back door that opened onto Commerce Street. He opened the door and stuck his head outside. The street was quiet. Only a handful of people were scattered along its length, none showing evidence of any hostile intent.

Exiting, Swamper staggered a few paces away

from the back of the building. He tilted his head back, looking up at the roof. Cupping a hand to his mouth, he bawled, "Hey Monk, what d'you say?"

The bouncer, up on the roof keeping watch for Ramrod riders, shouted, "All clear!"

Mrs. Frye hurried the whores out of the building into the street. "There's only five of you—one's missing. Wait up, Swamper." Cursing under her breath, she went back to the main floor.

The sixth whore, Nicole, stood lingering by the staircase. She was plain faced, with a sensational figure. Her eyes were downcast, her expression sullen, a stubborn set to her chin.

"What're you waiting for, a special invitation? Git!" Mrs. Frye exclaimed.

Nicole stayed in place. "What about Francine?"

"Never you mind," Mrs. Frye snapped. "Other arrangements are being made for her."

"What arrangements?"

"That's none of your business. On your way!"

Nicole squared her shoulders. "I'm making it my business. Francine's my friend."

"Why, you little—" Ruling her female charges with a free hand, Mrs. Frye was quick to lash out if anyone got out of line. She raised a hand to slap Nicole's face.

"Mrs. Frye! Kindly desist, if you please," Damon called.

Mrs. Frye restrained herself with some difficulty. "I don't take sass from tarts!"

"Your disciplinary zeal is well known, but in this

case we might make an exception. Loyalty is such a rare virtue that I hate to discourage it."

Damon rose, crossing to the rear of the building. He went to his office, opened the door, and stuck his head inside. "Francine, if you'd be good enough to step out here for a moment."

Francine Hayes exited the office, stepping into view. White-blond hair framed a fine-featured, heart-shaped face. Dark blue eyes contrasted with her light hair and fair skin, making the orbs seem deeper and more alluring. She wore no face powder, lipstick or rouge; her clearcut features were vivid without cosmetics. A demure, blue-and-white checked gingham dress covered her from neck to ankles, though not concealing a high-breasted, slim-waisted physique.

"What is it, Damon?" she asked.

"Nicole's worried about you."

Francine went to Nicole, putting her hands on Nicole's upper arms. "You're sweet."

"Ain't you comin' with the rest of us?" Nicole asked.

"No, I'm staying here."

"Why?"

"I don't want to bring any trouble down on Miz Bailey or you girls. You won't be bothered if I'm not with you."

"Why should we be bothered?"

Francine smiled sadly. "Staffords are hard and unforgiving. They might take it out on anybody giving me shelter. I'll be safer here and the rest of you will be safer without me."

"I'll stay with you," Nicole declared.

"You'd just put yourself in danger. I don't want that."

Nicole's agitation grew. "You're the only friend I got. I ain't gonna run out on you."

"We'll take care of Francine," Damon said. "You'd just be one more distraction, Nicole."

"Please."

"The longer you wait, the more danger you're putting all of us in. Francine most of all," Mrs. Frye insisted.

"Please, Nicole, for my sake," Francine urged.

Nicole nodded and blinked rapidly, her chin quivering. Tears spilled down her cheeks. Francine hugged her and kissed her cheek, then she and Mrs. Frye escorted Nicole through the passageway and out the back door.

Nicole joined the others. Swamper led them across the street, north up a side street, around a corner, and out of sight.

Francine and Mrs. Frye returned to the main floor. Mrs. Frye studied the other. "You all right, Francine?"

"Yes, Mrs. Frye. I'll be in my room." Francine climbed the stairs to the second floor, crossing the balcony to a door, opening it and going inside.

Mrs. Frye cut a glance at Damon. He poured her

a drink. She drank it. He went to the table, sat down, and resumed his card game.

Johnny Cross and Luke Pettigrew entered the Golden Spur.

"We're closed, gents," Mrs. Frye said.

Luke gave her a big grin. "Aw, Miz Frye, after I done humped my way over here on my one good leg, you ain't gone send me away without one measly little old drink?"

"Save the blarney. You walked in, you can walk out," she said.

Damon cleared his throat. "I think we can make an exception, Mrs. Frye. Belly up, gentlemen, and have one on the Spur."

Luke beamed. "That's a go!"

"You're a gentleman, Damon," Johnny said.

"Am I? How nice it would be to think so," Damon said, returning to his card game.

Johnny and Luke made their way to the bar. "Howdy, Creed," Luke said.

"Creed." Johnny nodded to the other.

"Hey, y'all," Creed Teece mumbled.

"How's it goin'?" Johnny asked.

"Can't complain," Teece said. "You?"

"I'm getting along."

Morrissey poured drinks for Johnny and Luke. They downed them, setting empty glasses on the countertop. Johnny slapped a coin down. "How about letting me buy one?"

"Why not?" Teece said. Morrissey poured three shots.

"Pour one for yourself," Johnny said.

"Thankee," the barkeep said, filling a fourth glass. "How about you, Miz Frye?"

"I'll pass, cowboy. But I'll take the money."

"Now, Mrs. Frye," Damon chided.

"The way things are going today, we could use it. Well, all right, I can't say no."

"I heard that about you," Luke joked.

"No to a drink."

"I heard that, too."

She gave Luke a hard look. "Don't push your luck, hayseed."

"What'll you have, Damon?" Johnny asked.

"This'll do me fine, thanks," Damon said, reaching for the bottle on the table and refilling his glass.

"Mud in your eye," Johnny toasted.

They drank.

"Enjoy yourself while you can," Mrs. Frye said, "the climate here's liable to turn distinctly unhealthy anytime now."

"That so?" Luke said.

"Too much lead in the air."

"Maybe sooner than you think." Johnny's tone was sharp, pointed.

Wyck Joslyn and Stingaree came in through the front door.

Luke whistled through his teeth. "They dogging us, Johnny?"

"Dogging somebody, maybe," Johnny said low voiced. "Keep a close hand by that scattergun."

"I always do."

Creed Teece glanced at the newcomers, his gaze hooded. "Something I should know about?"

"Stay loose and ready," Johnny said.

"Those two clowns?"

"They've been making some new friends lately."

Damon kept turning up the cards and placing them down, slowly and deliberately. Mrs. Frye went into the office, closing the door behind her.

Wyck Joslyn walked softly, carefully putting one foot before the other as he advanced toward the end of the bar nearest the entrance. Stingaree swaggered alongside him, all loose jointed. They stopped more or less on a line with where Damon was sitting.

The saloon owner went on playing cards, seemingly oblivious.

Wyck Joslyn looked around, scanning the scene. His gaze took in Johnny and Luke and he nodded to them. "Looks like you boys had the same idea as us."

Johnny said, "Oh? What's that?"

"To have a drink here, what else?" Joslyn rapped his knuckles on the bar. "Whiskey, barkeep."

"Make it two," Stingaree said.

Morrissey picked up two glasses and a bottle, carrying them to the end of the bar. He set down the glasses and poured. Wyck Joslyn laid a few coins on the counter. He turned and raised a glass in his left hand. "Nice shooting today, Damon."

Damon glanced up. A soft slap sounded as he laid down another card. "I'm still here."

"Couldn't have done better myself."

"No?"

"Hell, Wyck's just being modest," Stingaree said, scoffing. "He could do better."

"Could be," Damon said, shrugging. Turning over the cards.

Wyck Joslyn's face split in a broad grin. "My young friend here tends to get overly excited. Something about a gunfight does that to him. Don't mind him."

"I don't," Damon said.

Slap. He laid a card down. Black ten on red jack.

"You've got my admiration," Joslyn went on. "It takes plenty of guts to go against Vince Stafford."

"You a friend of his?" Creed Teece asked, hard-nosed and unfriendly.

Wyck Joslyn made a throwaway gesture. "I don't even know the man. I know of him, though. Hard not to. He throws a long shadow, him and that Ramrod outfit of his."

He spoke not to Teece but to Damon. "Stafford's not likely to take too kindly to you putting his boy in the graveyard."

"So? Where do you come in?" Damon said.

Slap. Another card hit the table. Red five on black six.

"Stafford's got a lot of guns riding for his brand.

Maybe you could use a couple good guns on your side, to kind of even up the odds," Wyck Joslyn said.

Slap. Black eight on red nine.

"You selling?" Damon asked.

"You buying?" Joslyn countered.

Slap.

"Our guns are for hire, Stingaree and me, but we don't come cheap." Joslyn indicated Johnny and Luke. "Maybe you've already hired on those two."

Johnny laughed. "Leave us out of it. We came in for a drink."

"I'm a lover, not a fighter," Luke said solemnly.

"So much the better. That leaves us a clear field of play," Joslyn said.

"Any gun can play," said Johnny.

Wyck Joslyn looked around. "Nice place. You must make a lot of money, Damon."

"Barely breaking even, with all the overhead." Damon turned up a card. Red queen. He laid it on a black king.

"Bosh. You're poor-mouthing. I appreciate horse trading but time's running out," Joslyn said.

"Oh?"

"Stafford's liable to ride in anytime."

"You don't say."

Noise sounded at the back of the building, like somebody bumping into a chair.

Slap.

Damon placed a black ace on a red deuce.

Ace of Spades.

Death card.

Three men came rushing out of the rear passageway, out from behind the staircase. Zeb, Tetch, & Jeeter. The Fromes Boys.

Johnny Cross had been looking for the Fromeses from the moment Joslyn and Stingaree entered. The duo had been thick as thieves with the brothers when he'd last seen them in the Dog Star Saloon. He knew they were up to something. Once Joslyn and Stingaree showed themselves at the Golden Spur, Johnny was waiting for the other shoe to drop.

The sounds in the back of the building, faint but telling, had given him his cue. In a flash it all came clear to him. Wyck Joslyn was stalling for time, waiting for the brothers to make their play so he and Stingaree could make use of the diversion.

Johnny stepped away from the bar, filling his hands with the twin .44s holstered at his sides. He faced the rear as the brothers came in shooting wildly, throwing lead to screen them while they got in place for the kill.

Zeb leveled his musket hip-high, shouted, "Gambler!" and swung the musket toward Damon. A bullet struck him, knocking him sideways with a crashing thud of flesh being impacted by hot lead. Johnny had struck first, ventilating him.

By reflex, Zeb jerked the trigger, firing a wild round that missed Damon, and dancing sideways to stay on his feet, Johnny fired again, the second slug spinning Zeb around, causing him to drop the musket and topple to the floor.

On either side of him, Tetch and Jeeter, six-guns in hand, blasted away, pumping out bullets, slinging lead. Johnny slung some back at them.

At the first sign of trouble, Damon snatched up the gun on the card table, firing even as Wyck Joslyn and Stingaree slapped leather, hauling out their guns.

Stingaree was fast, his gun clearing leather first. But Joslyn was in his way, blocking the shot, trying to make his own.

Damon and Joslyn fired at the same time. Joslyn missed, his bullet whizzing past the gambler's head. Damon scored, dropping a .45 round in Joslyn's middle.

Wyck Joslyn's face contorted in agony. He seemed to implode, shrinking into himself, falling back against Stingaree.

Gun in hand, Stingaree fought to get clear, angling to open up a line of fire. The top of his head exploded, spewing blood, brains, bone. He'd been felled by the gun in Creed Teece's hand.

A bullet from Tetch Fromes's gun punched a hole into the side of the wooden bar near Johnny Cross. Johnny returned fire, tagging Tetch, knocking him down.

A line of fire stabbed from the gun of Jeeter Fromes, missing Johnny and drilling the mirror behind the bar. The looking glass starred, frosting with a spiderweb of cracks radiating out from the bullet hole.

Johnny shot Jeeter Fromes twice, first dropping

him to his knees as he tried to bring his gun up. Then Johnny shot him between the eyes.

Tetch was up on one knee, holding his gun in both hands, swinging it toward Johnny.

A thunderclap boomed as Luke opened up with his sawed-off shotgun. He leaned against the bar, propping an elbow on the counter to hold himself up while he cut loose with a blast.

Tetch came apart in mid-center, a raw, red mess spilling loopy gray strands of intestines where his belly had been before being pulped by buckshot.

The gunfire fell silent. A cloud of gray-white gun smoke hung in the air in the middle of the big room. Bodies littered the floor.

Behind the bar, Morrissey straightened up, shotgun in hand. When the shooting started, he'd ducked down and grabbed for the weapon he kept handy in case of trouble. But by the time he brought it up and clear of the bar, he was too late. That's how fast the action had gone down.

The victors looked around, guns in hand. No more challengers presented themselves.

The bullet-pierced mirror came undone all at once, splintering into what seemed like a thousand glittering crystal shards, clattering down on the wooden plank floorboards behind the bar.

Zeb Fromes was still alive. He lay on his side, twitching, legs working like those of a dog who dreams of running. Johnny reached out with his pistol to deliver the coup de grâce, sending a bullet crashing through the mountaineer's brain.

After a pause, the office door at the rear of the building opened, an orange-haired head cautiously peeking around the corner of a doorframe. Mrs. Frye looked out, surveying the carnage. "God!"

"You can come out now," Damon said, his voice steady.

Mrs. Frye emerged, stepping onto the main floor. "God," she repeated, then, "What happened?"

"I'm a mite bewildered myself." Damon turned to Johnny Cross. "Perhaps you can shed some light on the subject, sir?"

"Glad to," Johnny said. "Luke and me were over to the Dog Star earlier, when we saw Wyck Joslyn and Stingaree getting together with the Fromes Boys."

Indicating the brothers' three corpses sprawled around the foot of the staircase, Damon said, "I take it those are the gentlemen in question."

Johnny nodded. "No-account trash—cutthroats, back shooters. Only reason for Wyck Joslyn to be roping in the likes of them was to be cooking up some badness. When he and Stingaree came in here, it all fell into place. You was the target, Damon. Joslyn must've figured Stafford would pay big money for your scalp.

"I had a hunch the Fromeses wouldn't be too far off. Wyck was stringing you along, stalling for time while the brothers got in place. When they came charging in, I was ready for 'em. Luke, too."

"That's right," Luke agreed.

At the left rear corner of the second floor, a

vertical wooden ladder bolted to the wall rose to a square-shaped hatch in the ceiling. A head and pair of shoulders came thrusting out of the hatch. Monk looked down at the main room below. "You okay, boss?" he shouted.

"Yes!"

"Anybody hurt?"

"Nobody important."

"What happened?"

"Somebody made a bad bet."

Monk climbed down the ladder, a rifle in one hand. He was balding, bullet-headed, bearded, with powerful shoulders and arms, and bowed, bandy legs. He crossed to the edge of the balcony and leaned over the balustrade, surveying the carnage below.

"Whoo-whee! Who's them deaders—Staffords?"

"Outriders trying to cut in," Damon said.

Mrs. Frye stood with hands on hips, head tilted, looking up at Monk. "Where were you when they sneaked in through the back?" she asked, indicating the bodies of the Fromeses.

"Up on the roof," Monk said.

"A fine lookout you are!"

"Staffords got to come in from the south. I was watching for *them*. I can't look everywhere, Miz Frye, it's a big roof!"

"Get back up there and keep your eyes open this time."

"Yes, ma'am." Monk went to the ladder, scrambling up through the trapdoor hatch and out of sight.

Francine came out of her room and stood at the balcony rail. "Everyone all right?"

"The ones on our side are," Mrs. Frye said. "Come down and join the party."

"No, thanks." Francine put a hand to her mouth. "I think I'm going to be sick." Turning, she hurried back into her room, slamming the door shut.

Damon faced Johnny. "Gutsy play that, turning your back on Joslyn and his partner to shoot it out with the brothers."

"I'm a betting man myself. I figured you and Creed could handle Wyck and Stingaree," Johnny said.

"Quite a gamble."

Johnny shook his head, smiling. "A sure thing."

"Your faith in us is heartening, if possibly misplaced. In any case, I thank you, sir. I thank you both," Damon said, addressing Johnny and Luke. "And now I suggest you clear out while you can, before Stafford arrives."

"What! And miss all the fun?" Johnny joked, but he meant it, too.

"Fun, he calls it," Mrs. Frye said. "If you think tying into two dozen red-hot killers is fun."

"Happens, I do," said Johnny. "It wouldn't be the first time, neither."

"Why buck the Ramrod? Vince Stafford's got no grudge against you," Damon said.

"It's early yet," Johnny said.

"Wait till he gets to know us better," Luke chimed in.

Mrs. Frye's eyes narrowed as she looked over the duo. "I don't get it. What's in it for you? I mean, why make this your fight?"

"Damned if I know," Johnny answered. "Maybe because the Spur is the one place in town with square-deal, straight-up card games and dice. No crooked tables or watered-down whiskey. Maybe I liked the way you handled yourself, Damon, when young Stafford braced you. Or maybe I was overdue to kill Zeb Fromes for kicking an ol' hound dog who never did him any harm. I got distracted that day and Zeb got away from me.

"Could be I'm just a natural-born Rebel with a liking for lost causes and kicking up trouble and siding with y'all promises to deliver plenty of both. Who knows? Like I said, I ain't entirely sure why myself."

Mrs. Frye gave Luke the once-over, appraising him with cold-eyed calculation. "And you, where do you fit in in all this?"

"Me? Oh, I'm with him." Luke indicated Johnny. His attitude said that explained it all. For him it did.

A slight smile played around Damon's lips. "Betting on the Golden Spur now could be considered a long shot."

"Them's the kind that pays off best," Johnny said.

Damon reached into one of his pants' front

pockets, pulling out a fat roll of high-denomination greenbacks. "The house always makes good."

"Whoa," Johnny said, holding his hands up, palms-out. "Put your money away, I ain't sniffing around for a payday."

"The workman is worthy of his hire, they say."

"When I sell my gun, that's business. When I side with a man, that's different. Money's got nothing to do with it."

Damon stuffed the roll back in his pocket. "My apologies, sir. I misread the situation. No insult meant or implied."

"None taken," Johnny said.

"A couple of go-to-hell Texas gun hawks, in it for the fun of it?" Mrs. Frye said. "The funny thing is with you two, I almost believe it."

"'Course, you want to buy us a drink or ten to show your appreciation, we wouldn't take that as no insult, not even a little bit," Luke said.

"You got yourself a deal, stud," Mrs. Frye said.

"Let's all step over to the bar and get better acquainted," Damon said. Nobody found fault with his suggestion. They went to the bar, where Morrissey was already setting them up, laying out glasses on the countertop.

"Drink up," Damon invited, "as much as you want. It's on the house."

All drank, several rounds.

"I believe we got the best of that bargain. Ol' Luke can sure put it away," Johnny said.

"I got me a hollow leg," Luke said, nodding. He rapped his knuckles against his wooden limb. "For real."

"Never mind," Mrs. Frye said airily, "Damon'll win it all back in cards, and more."

Presently Damon, Mrs. Frye, and Creed Teece were all called away on various errands relating to the reception they were preparing for Vince Stafford and company. Morrissey was at the other end of the bar, removing bottles from the back shelf below the mirror and stowing them under the wooden counter for safekeeping.

Johnny and Luke were by themselves for the moment. They spoke low voiced, for their own hearing alone.

"I don't get it," Luke said. "Why not take Damon's money, if he's giving it out?"

"The friendship of a man like Damon Bolt's worth more than money. That's a friend worth having, if we mean to stick in Hangtown," Johnny said.

"If he don't get killed. Or we don't."

"That's where the gamble comes in. I'll take a chance on him, and I sure ain't gonna bet against us. Trust me, once the ball starts rolling, there'll be plenty of money to pick up from action on the side."

"You're calling it, hoss," Luke said, shrugging. "Too much thinking makes my head hurt."

"I think that's the whiskey," Johnny pointed out.

Luke studied his glass, peering into it, surprised

to find it empty. "Thanks for reminding me. Believe I'll have another." Reaching for a nearby bottle, he refilled his glass. "You?"

"Why not?" Johnny said. "This killing is thirsty work."

SEVEN

Ten minutes after the shooting, Wade Hutto and Sheriff Mack Barton entered the Golden Spur. They came alone, just the two of them, to show their lack of hostile intent. Deputy Smalls and a half dozen hangers-on from Hutto's party waited outside. The sheriff of Hangtown had no hangers-on, except maybe Deputy Smalls.

Barton had the glum, stolid air of a man doing a disagreeable duty. "Now what?"

"They came in looking for trouble," Damon Bolt said, pointing to the five corpses littering the floor. "They found it."

"You're in an all-fired hurry to get yourself killed," Hutto snapped.

"Yet they are dead, while I am still alive," Damon said, smiling thinly.

Johnny and Luke were at the bar. Creed Teece was there, too, standing slightly apart from them.

Their faces were turned toward the newcomers. Morrissey was behind the bar, keeping out of Swamper's way while the latter cleaned up pieces of broken mirror.

Swamper wore grimy work gloves. He was picking up the bigger pieces of broken glass and making a racket as he tossed them into an empty bucket. He'd clean up the smaller pieces later with a broom and dustpan.

Barton circled the three bodies stretched out in front of the staircase, each outlined by handfuls of sawdust Swamper had spread on the floor around them, to soak up the blood. The sheriff cheered up at sight of the corpses. "The Fromes Boys! It was only a matter of time before they got shot or hung. Saves the town the price of three hangman's ropes. That's a break." The lines at the corners of his eyes crinkled upwards.

"Any reward on 'em?" Johnny asked.

"Not in Hangtree," Barton said, his good humor increasing at the thought that the county need pay out no funds to be rid of three such potential troublemakers. He went to the far end of the bar to look at the two corpses there.

"Who killed Joslyn?" he asked.

"I did," Damon said.

"And Stingaree?"

"Mine," said Creed Teece.

Barton nodded. He didn't take any notes. It

wasn't an investigation. He was just curious. He rejoined Hutto, who stood to the side, facing Damon.

"That's how it begins. Vince isn't even in town and already there's killing," Hutto said.

"It wipes five undesirables off the books, at no cost to the taxpayers," Barton said.

"There is that."

Mrs. Frye came out from behind the closed door of the office, where she'd been fortifying herself with a glass of whiskey and a laudanum chaser. A medicinal tincture of opium, laudanum was widely available with no prescription needed, despite its addictive properties. The drug contracted the pupils of her eyes to pinpoints. "How about getting those bodies out of here?"

"Who, me?" Barton said, taken aback.

"You're the sheriff. They're lawbreakers. That falls under your jurisdiction."

Barton snorted, shaking his head. "I'm a lawman, not an undertaker."

"In this town, there's not much difference." Mrs. Frye turned to Hutto. "What do I pay taxes for? Believe you me, I pay plenty! If the town won't take them away, I'll have them thrown out in the street."

"We'll take care of it," Hutto said, making placating gestures. As the man whose slate of hand-picked candidates included the mayor and most of the town council, Hutto was ever mindful that it was an election year. The Golden Spur swung a nice handful of votes, or would, depending on how many of its staff and associates were still alive come Election Day.

"We're gonna need a place to put the bodies," Barton said. "These, and more to come."

"Plenty more," Hutto agreed grimly.

"You own half the property in town and hold the paper on the other half. Any ideas?"

Hutto rubbed his chin thoughtfully. "We've got young Stafford in a storeroom at the courthouse, but that's a special case."

"Oh yes," Barton said, his tone flat, neutral. "Special."

"Can't turn the courthouse into a mortuary."

"How about the carriage house behind the Cattleman?"

"Not there," Hutto said, shocked. "It's the best hotel in town!"

"There's a storage shed behind the lumberyard," Barton suggested.

"That'll do it." Hutto motioned to his hangers-on standing outside looking through the front windows. A couple of them entered.

"Run over to the lumberyard and tell Tuttle we're temporarily commandeering his storage shed. Tell him I'll square it with him so he's not out of pocket for any inconvenience," Hutto said.

"Okay, Wade." The fellows started for the door.

"Wait a minute," Hutto called after them.

They paused and turned back.

"Get a cart or wagon to haul the bodies out. Have Hobson at the livery stable fix you up," Hutto said.

"Right!" the hangers-on chorused, and out they went.

Mrs. Frye turned some of her dissatisfaction on Barton. "What's the law going to be doing when Stafford makes his move?"

"I'm working on it," Barton said evasively.

"I bet."

"Try the Dog Star," Johnny Cross said. He and Luke sat at a table between the bar and the front door. "I hear the Ramrod brand ain't too popular around there."

"Where do you fit in this, Cross?" Hutto questioned.

"Just helping out."

"Careful you don't help yourself into Boot Hill!"

"I'll be careful, Mr. Hutto. Very careful," Johnny said with mock solemnity.

"Bah!" Hutto was one of those fellows who can say *Bah!* without looking ridiculous. He turned to Damon. "You could help by clearing out of town. And take that Francine Hayes with you."

Damon glanced with seeming mildness at the other. Hutto looked away, not making eye contact.

"You touch me on a point of pride, sir," Damon said. "Miss Hayes is entirely blameless in this matter. She's the offended party here. It's no fault of hers that a boor like the late Bliss Stafford tried to force unwanted attentions on her. I'm sure you agree that I did what I had to do, and that no Southern gentleman could do less."

Hutto backed off. "I'm not arguing the point. Legally you were in the right. Isn't that so, Sheriff?"

"A clearcut case of self-defense," Barton said.

"But Vince Stafford won't see it like that," Hutto pressed. "He'll make it a blood feud, him and Clay and Quent. They'll have twenty guns and more backing them up. You're a gambler, you know better than to buck those odds. Get out of town."

"That would make things easier for you," Mrs. Frye said.

"You're damned right it would!" Hutto said fervently.

"If you were me, would you run?" Damon asked.

"I'm not you and right now I'm damned glad of it!"

"And you, Sheriff? Would you run?"

"It's not the same." Barton fidgeted, uncomfortable with the question.

"Why not?"

"I wear a badge. A lawman who runs is finished, washed up."

"It's the same with me."

"You're dead if you stick," Hutto warned.

"I'll take that bet," Damon said.

Mrs. Frye thrust her face forward. "All your fine talk about the law! What about Damon? The law's supposed to protect him, too. Where's Hangtown going to be if you let Stafford ride roughshod over it?"

Hutto was silent.

Barton looked troubled, angry. "I'll do what I think is best for every man, woman, and child in Hangtree. What happens to them if I get killed trying to keep Vince from doing what he's hell-bent for leather on doing, namely evening up on Damon for killing Bliss? Who stands between him and them then? I'll do what I can to head him off, but don't expect miracles."

Damon said, "Not a gambling man, Sheriff?"

"Not when the whole town is part of the ante. Sorry."

"That's all right. I'll pull my own chestnuts out of the fire."

An awkward silence followed, broken by Hutto clearing his throat. "We're through here." He looked at the sheriff. "Coming, Barton?"

"Yeah."

Hutto started for the front door. Barton followed, taking a few steps, then pausing. "I'll do what I can, but I ain't making no promises."

"Can't ask for more than that," Damon said.

"For what it's worth—good luck," said Barton. He and Hutto went out.

Eight

Sam Heller cleaned up in the aftermath of the Comanche raid on the Fisher ranch. Climbing down off Dusty, he hitched the horse to the corral fence, away from where the Comanche horses were hitched. He holstered the mule's-leg and took hold of his Navy Colt .36, holding it in his right hand.

He crossed to the front entrance of the house, eyeing the braves sprawled in the yard for any signs of life. He'd put a bullet in any who so much as twitched. None did.

The house had to be cleared, to make sure no one was lurking inside, foe or, less likely, friend. Sam went through the open doorway, into the west room. He walked softly, gun ready. The smell of gunpowder hung heavy; gray-white gunsmoke drifted in midair.

Sam looked around, his hearing pitched to the highest level for a whisper of sound betraying the presence of anyone within. It was tricky work—a panicked settler could kill him just as dead as a Comanche could.

There was no one in his immediate view. Gun leveled, Sam used his free hand to part the blankets hanging from a metal rod screening off the rear of the room and stepped inside.

The partitioned-off space was empty. The rear window gaped open. Sam went to it, looking outside.

The girl was crossing the field toward the house. She moved slowly, stiff-legged, like she was walking in her sleep. She stared straight ahead, unaware of him at the window.

Two dead Indians lay in the grass, the one Sam had killed and one slain by a shotgun blast. Their horses were nowhere to be seen. *Not so good,* Sam thought. He didn't want any horses running loose to attract attention to the ranch. Comanche attention.

He turned, going through the dogtrot into the east room. It was empty, too.

Going outside, Sam started making the rounds of the fallen braves in the dooryard, making sure they were dead. Double sure. He'd checked before going into the house, but the possible threat of a lurker within had prevented him from a too-scrupulous inspection.

He wasn't taking a chance on any of them having enough life left in them to be a threat. It was an old trick of downed foes, white or red, to sham, playing possum, waiting for an opportunity to jump an unwary enemy. Sam had pressed his luck to the full already and didn't want to crowd it further.

No worry about the brave with the scalping knife. Much of his head had been blown apart by a load of 12-gauge buckshot. The settler he'd been working on with the knife was no less dead.

Nasty stuff, but Sam wasn't squeamish. Which was just as well, when he got a good look at the overgrown man-boy who'd been chopped up with the ax.

Sam was less certain about the brave who'd been raping the woman, approaching him with care. The brave was stretched out facedown on top of his victim. Her upturned face was showing. She looked dead as could be, open eyes glazed and unblinking.

Sam approached from the side, gun pointed at the back of the Indian's head, ready to shoot. Getting the toe of his boot under the brave's chest, he half kicked, half lifted the body off the woman. The brave was heavy; Sam grunted with the effort of moving him.

The body rolled off the woman, flopping onto its back. The bullets the woman had pumped into him with his own gun had inflicted a mortal wound, but not soon enough. He'd lived long enough to knife her. The blade was buried to the hilt in the woman's left breast.

Sam closed her eyes. He pulled her dress down where it was bunched up around her waist, covering her up. Sighing heavily, he straightened up. He stuck the Navy Colt into his waistband on his left hip, unholstered the mule's-leg and reloaded it with cartridges from one of his bandoliers.

The girl stood at the southwest corner of the house, her flat-eyed gaze taking in the whole scene. She stood very straight, hands clenched into fists at her sides. Her face was deathly pale. Sam went to her, trying to get between her and the bodies to block her view.

He hoped she wasn't going to scream. He was in a tight enough spot without her going into hysterics. They both were. Not that he would have blamed her for throwing a fit.

Sam studied her face. Her eyes were wide, dry. A nerve twitched in the corner of her mouth.

No way to sugarcoat it, best say it the way it was. "Your people are all dead. I'm sorry." He kept his voice low, so as not to startle her. But his mouth and throat were dry and his words came out harsh and croaking.

She started forward, but he stood in her way, stopping her. "There's nothing you can do for 'em. I checked."

She nodded, holding herself so taut Sam wouldn't have been surprised to hear her corded neck muscles twanging with the movement. He watched her intently. She didn't scream, didn't faint.

"Are you hurt?" he asked.

She shook her head.

"I've got to leave you for a minute, to check on those two braves behind the house, make sure they're dead. Will you be all right?"

She nodded yes.

"If you hear any shots, that'll be me, so don't let it scare you. I'll be right back. Then we're gonna get out of here." Sam stepped around her, starting forward, then paused. "Your folks are safe from hurt now. Best not to look if you can. You don't want to see them."

She was silent, staring at the bodies. Sam went around to the back of the house, drawing the mule's-leg. He fired a shot into the heads of both braves, loaded two fresh cartridges into the receiver to replace the ones he'd expended, and returned to the front of the house. The girl was nowhere in sight. Sam's flash of alarm was stilled by the sound of movement coming from inside.

She came out through the doorway carrying a stack of folded blankets. Setting them down beside the body of her mother, she took a blanket off the top of the pile, unfolded it, and spread it over the corpse.

Sam was reassured somewhat. The youngster was taking it better than he had thought she might, having just survived the slaughter of her family. Plenty of adults, even hardened frontier types, would have gone to pieces from the experience. But she might shatter anytime at the drop of a hat.

Sam knew they had to keep moving. Picking up a blanket, he covered the man-boy—most of him. A few body parts were scattered out of reach of the blanket. He helped the girl lay a blanket over her father.

She turned, starting toward the house.

"Where you going?"

"Getting a gun," Lydia said.

Sam had been unsure if she had been shocked into speechlessness. That she could talk was heartening. He needed all the encouragement he could get. Things looked mighty grim for them. He'd been lucky to evade several bands of braves earlier after first encountering the slain emigrants and their half-burned wagon. Alone, it would have beeen touch and go whether or not he could slip the net of Comanches he'd seen covering the area. With a youngster in tow, the odds against him went up dramatically.

"Make it fast. We've got to move," he called after her.

Lydia went inside, making no reply. A minute or two later she returned, carrying a rifle and a box of cartridges. It was a Henry's, a repeater—a good gun. She took some cartridges out of the box and started loading it, She handled it like she knew what she was doing.

Sam said, "We're in a heap of trouble, miss. The upland is thick with Comanches. Looks like the whole blamed tribe is on the warpath. More could come along any minute. We've got to get down to the flat, fast. Later when it's safe we can come back and give your folks a Christian burial. But now we got to run. Savvy?"

"I savvy," Lydia said.

"Good. Let's mount up and ride."

"I'll take Brownie."

"Brownie? Who's that?"

"My horse. I'm not leaving him behind."

Brownie, a strong, solid-looking gelding with good lines, was in the corral. The Comanches' horses were saddled up, but there was no telling what their dispositions were like. Sam didn't want to chance the girl being unable to control a strange mount. Best let her ride the animal she was used to and that was used to her.

Lydia went into the barn with him and pointed out a saddle. Sam carried it out while she toted a blanket. Brownie was anxious, unnerved by the blood, shooting, and violent death. Sam sympathized. He knew how the horse felt.

Lydia stood inside the end of the corral farthest away from where the Comanches' horses were tied up. Brownie came to her when she called him. She stroked the horse's muzzle and patted its neck, speaking softly to him, gentling him down. She put a bridle on him, then led him out through the corral door Sam had opened.

Sam unhitched the Comanche horses from the fence one by one and led them into the corral, then closed the door, penning them with the other horses. He didn't want them wandering off, attracting Indian scouting parties to the ranch.

Lydia spread the blanket over Brownie's back; Sam saddled him. She adjusted the saddle girth and the height of the stirrups, her movements deft and sure, her pale, slim-fingered hands steady.

Taking two handfuls of cartridges from the box,

Lydia stuffed them into a pair of deep pockets at the front of her dress. She put the box in a saddle bag. There was no scabbard, but a set of leather ties allowed her to secure the rifle to the side of the saddle.

"My name's Sam, Sam Heller. What's yours?"

Lydia's eyes narrowed. "Why?"

"So I can call you something besides Miss."

"You talk funny. You're a Yankee," she said accusingly.

"That's right."

"Hmmph. Miss will do just fine, thank you very much."

"The war's over, in case you hadn't heard."

"That's a sneaking Yankee lie. God bless the Confederacy and Robert E. Lee!"

Sam showed a quirked half smile. "Comanches don't make no difference between Yankees and Rebels, you know."

"Well, I do." Lydia Fisher had been raised to believe that Yankees were the Devil. The stranger had no tail, and if he had horns they were hidden under his hat, but she trusted him no more than she had to. Trouble was, she had to, at least until she was off the plateau and safe among decent, civilized Southern folk.Sighing, Sam mounted up on Dusty.

She swung herself up on Brownie's back. The horse's eyes bulged, nostrils flaring. He pawed the ground, sidling. Leaning forward, Lydia patted

Brownie's muscular neck, murmuring comforting sounds into his pointed ears.

"Sure you can handle him?" Sam asked.

"Don't worry about me, Mister Yank. Brownie'll be okay once we get away from here."

"What's the fastest way off the plateau? Can we get down from there?" Sam pointed directly south where a ridgeline screened the edge of the plateau from sight.

Lydia shook her head. "Can't go that way, it's too steep. No way down. The nearest trail's Hopper Glen, a half mile or so down the road."

"Can we go through the woods? Any trails?"

She shook her head. "The brush is too thick. Got to take the road."

"Great," Sam said sourly. He and Lydia rode between the house and the woods, north across the field. Sam rode ahead, to scout Rimrock Road bordering the edge of the property. It was empty in both directions, as far as the eye could see.

Lydia came alongside him. They turned right on the road, going east. She did not look back at the ranch, not once, not even a glance.

"You look like you know how to handle that rifle," Sam said.

"I do. Here in the hills, it's shoot straight the first time, or you don't eat," Lydia said.

"Lord knows you got plenty of reason to want to even up. But don't shoot straight off if you see a Comanche. Make sure he sees us first."

"What d'you expect me to do? Throw flowers at him?"

"Just don't give away our position if you don't have to."

After a fifth of a mile, the belt of woods on the south gave way to fields dotted with dirt mounds and stands of timber. "Best stay off the road if we can. The Comanches are out in force," Sam advised.

They turned right, angling southeast for several hundred yards. A game trail wound east through low, rounded hills. They followed it.

"We're coming on the Oakley ranch," Lydia said after a while.

Sam couldn't see it. "Where?"

"Not far. There's a brook, then a rise. It's on the other side."

A low, tree-covered ridge ran north-south, a stream winding along its western foot. Smoke showed over the treetops, a hazy gray curtain. Sam reined to a halt, Lydia pulling up beside him. Sam shucked the mule's-leg out of its holster, holding the reins in his free hand.

Lydia looked stricken. "The Oakleys?"

"Comanches got there first," Sam said, shaking his head.

"Maybe it's not too late to help."

"Hear any shooting?"

"No."

"It's too late, girl. Comanches have already been and done. Any Oakleys left alive, they'd be shooting and the Comanches would be shooting back. It's over."

"You don't know that for a fact."

"I ain't risking my hair to find out," Sam said. "You?"

"No," Lydia said, swallowing hard.

"Let's get clear." *If we can,* he thought. He pointed his horse north, Lydia following. They rode along the base of the ridge until they struck Rimrock Road, running east through a gap in the ridge.

Sam scouted the road. It looked clear. Quickly, he and Lydia crossed over to a long, grassy slope and trailed north along the foot of the ridge. He holstered the mule's-leg as they rode on.

The ridge flattened out as the long grassy slope crested. Beyond, in the middle distance rose Sentry Hill, its base hidden by thick woods.

Sam and Lydia made a right-hand turn, going east once again. Below, a line of trees screened the Oakley ranch from view, but they could see the inverted pyramid of smoke rising amid the mass of leafy green boughs. Black at the base, it lightened to gray as it fanned out into the sky.

The fugitive duo crossed an open space, coming to a thicket of woods. Riding south along the tree-line, they searched for an opening. A gap showed, revealing a game trail winding east through the brush. Sam and Lydia entered the narrow passage, forcing them to ride single file. Sam took the point, Lydia following. Shady groves alternated with sunny glades.

The trail bent southeast, the ground sloping downward. Once again, they crossed Rimrock Road. Beyond, the trail angled south. It widened, and they rode side by side.

The slope leveled off, the trail continuing south. The woods thinned out, showing bright, open sky. Ahead on the left, a massive shape loomed.

"Stickerbush Knob. We're almost at Hopper Glen," Lydia said in a hushed voice. "The glen'll take us down to the flat."

Stickerbush Knob was a sugarloaf-shaped mound, slant-sided and round-topped, with a rocky dome rising out of its south end. Its sides were covered with scraggly brush, dwarf trees, and weedy undergrowth. They rode south along its west side.

Sam halted a short distance from the knob's south end. Lydia reined in, too, sour faced. "What for you stopping?" she demanded.

"Ever heard of 'look before you leap'? I don't want to go down the glen to find Comanches there," Sam said.

They spoke in whispers.

"I'm gonna climb the mound and take a look-see." Sam dismounted and hitched Dusty's reins to the branch of a bush. "Sit tight. I'll be back directly."

"What if redskins get you?" Lydia asked.

"Then I won't be back."

"What'll I do?"

"Run."

"How'll I know if they got you?"

"If you hear shooting and war whoops, ride out. Leave Dusty behind in case I make it."

"I'll wait." Lydia looked doubtful. She loosened her rifle, holding it across the saddle, her eyes wide and watchful.

Sam didn't blame her, he felt doubtful himself. But it was dangerous country and he'd feel better if he got the lay of the land. Trust the Comanches to set scouts watching the south slope to look for escapees. If he could spot them in advance, he and Lydia would have a better chance of evading them. He padded to the foot of the mound, glad he had on hunting moccasins instead of boots. Stepping carefully, he avoided treading on fallen twigs.

He didn't think the girl would steal his horse and abandon him. She didn't seem the type, but he'd figured folks wrong before, especially females, young ones, too. Besides, nobody could ride Dusty but Sam, as more than one horse thief had found out to their dismay. A sharp whistle from him and Dusty would come running.

At first glance, the thorn bushes massed at the base of the mound seemed impenetrable, but a closer look revealed gaps in the wall of brush. Slipping through an opening, Sam started up a fan of loose dirt and stone. He kept a sharp eye out for snakes; rattlers especially liked the kind of loose rock piles heaped up at the bottom of the mound. His feet turned sideways, Sam climbed to the top of the fan on the edges of his soles for better traction and to minimize disturbances of the dirt. His passage was noiseless.

Above the fan, the dirt was hardpacked and covered with short, thick, colorless grass, eliminating the need to climb sideways. Spurs and slabs of bare rock jutted out at odd angles, serving as stepping-stones as he scaled the slope. Stems of gnarly bushes served as handholds.

He broke clear of the tops of the trees hemming the mound, out of the shade and into sunlight. The midday sun was high and hot, causing him to break into fresh sweat. His shadow, a small blob of blackness, pooled at his feet.

Above and to his right, a rock ledge thrust out from the side of the hill. Circling around toward it, he clambered up onto the shelf. It was about four feet wide. He was a hundred feet above the ground. Through spaces in the tree boughs he could see the girl and the horses.

He climbed up the ledge up for another forty feet before it gave on to a wide, platformlike outcropping that decked the mound's south end like a natural terrace. A rocky, razor-backed ridge ran north-south along most of the summit, cutting it in half and screening the opposite side. A tilted, round-topped slab stood thirty feet high, blocking most of the terrace, making it impossible for Sam to get around to the other side.

V-shaped gaps in the ridge looked promising. The notch in the nearest gap was wide enough for him to pass through. The gray-brown rock had plenty of handholds and footholds as Sam climbed up eight feet to the bottom of the V, four feet wide and lined with hardpacked dirt.

He looked for snakes—looked hard—but didn't see any, before easing into the notch. He started through to the other side.

Somebody cleared his throat . . . and it wasn't Sam. He froze.

The man hawked something up and spat. The Navy Colt filled Sam's hand as if it had leaped into it.

Silence.

Sam inched forward, wary of any betraying noise. Crouching, legs bent at the knees, he moved ahead with infinite care.

He stuck his head out past the edge of the rock just enough to look beyond it. A dirt-covered ledge lay eight feet below the bottom of the notch on its east side. The ledge was six feet wide, a narrow game trail running along its length.

To the left, about ten feet away, a spur thrust out from the side of the ridge, narrowing the ledge by half.

To the right, the ledge continued for another thirty feet, widening out into a rounded outcropping twenty feet wide. A Comanche squatted near the edge, holding a rifle across the tops of his thighs. He scanned the vista below, his back to Sam.

Sam could have finished him off with the gun but he didn't want to shoot, not knowing if there were other Comanches in the area. The throat clearing had sounded closer than he was, but placing locations was tricky when you had only sound to go on. He stuck his gun back in his waistband, wedging it in tightly.

The side of the notch was steep but not so much so that he couldn't climb it. Testing each handhold and foothold before trusting his weight to it, he went up the south side of the notch like a lizard climbing a rock wall.

The top of the ridge was four feet across at its widest, narrower in other places. It stretched unbroken to the round-topped slab at the end of the mound.

Sam drew the Green River knife at his left hip. It came free of the sheath with nary a whisper. Fashioned after the famous Bowie knife, the weapon had a foot-long blade with narrow blood grooves running horizontally below its upper edge, a wickedly sharp point, and a razor-keen cutting edge. The maker's mark GREEN RIVER was engraved on the shining steel just above the crossbar guard.

Wrapping his hand around the hilt, Sam started forward. Bent low, almost double, he soft-footed along the ridgetop. Stealthy though he was, he didn't trust his ability to sneak up on the Comanche by crossing the ledge. Comanches were spooky folk, ever-alert, wary. Sam reckoned he had a better chance of closing on his foe undetected by approaching from an unexpected direction, coming from above.

He reached the end of the ridge, the round-topped slab barring further progress, and estimated his prospects. He was ten feet above the ledge; the Comanche was some fifteen feet away from the base of the ridge—too far to risk a long dive. The Indian was so close to the edge that Sam was likely to go over the side with him.

He'd have to get closer. He didn't like that part of it, but then he didn't like running into a Comanche scout, either.

Easing over the steep side of the ridge, Sam lowered himself to the boulder jutting out five feet below him, dislodging a few tiny pebbles in the process.

The Comanche stiffened.

Sam hopped down to the ledge, lunging toward the brave. The Comanche stood and spun around, swinging his rifle toward the intruder. Closing with him, Sam slapped his left hand on top of the rifle barrel, holding it in place for an instant.

Wiry and strong, the brave broke free, but that split-second delay made all the difference, allowing Sam to thrust his knife deep in the other's vitals.

Burying the blade below the breastbone, Sam thrust up and deeper, seeking the other's heart.

They struggled, hand-to-hand, face-to-face. The knife point found its mark deep in the Comanche's left breast.

Sam saw the light go out in the other's eyes. Blood, so dark it looked black, filled the brave's gaping mouth, spilling down the sides. The rifle slipped from his hands, clattering on stone, but did not go off.

Sam gave the blade a final, wicked twist before withdrawing it. The Comanche collapsed. Sam panted for breath as if he'd run a race. He wiped the blade clean on the brave's shirt.

Looking around, he saw that the rocky platform overlooked the south end of the plateau and the flat below, making it a natural observation post. Going to the edge, he scanned the landscape.

The south slope of the plateau was less than a half mile away. It was cut by a gully that reached down to the flat. Trees lined both sides of the cut; through them he glimpsed a down-rushing stream.

The round-topped slab blocked the hill's south end, barring him from the west side. Turning, he started back toward the notch, planning to return the way he had come. Without warning a Comanche rounded the spur thrusting out into the ledge.

He and Sam saw each other at the same time. Nine feet of space stood between them. The brave wore a red headband over two black braids and held a rifle at his side. Surprise, wrath, and indignation flickered across his face. He must be the throat clearer.

Sam still had the knife in hand.

It was tricky, throwing it by the hilt rather than by the blade—a complicating factor. A knife of that size needed some fourteen feet to make a complete turn in midair when thrown. Throwing it by the hilt, the knife should make a half turn in seven feet, bringing the point in line with its target.

A master knife thrower, Sam calculated at lightning speed, took a step forward to compensate for the extra feet between him and his goal, and threw the knife.

The brave raised his rifle.

The knife took him dead center in the middle of his torso, striking home with a *thunk*. The blow exerted a paralyzing effect, keeping him from crying out. He staggered, venting a noise between a grunt and a snort.

His rage knew no bounds, but he was already too dead to do anything about it. He sat down hard in the middle of the ledge, then flopped on his back, lying faceup.

Sam drew his Colt. Any more Comanches and he would come up shooting, no matter what. Stepping around the spur, he saw that the rest of the ledge was empty, untenanted.

He went to the edge and looked down. Two horses were hitched to a tree in a nook at the foot of the east side of the mound, presumably the horses of the Comanche sentinels.

Looking up, Sam turned his gaze to the north. Sentry Hill loomed in the middle ground, dominating the scene. There were no real mountains as such in that part of Texas but it was a high hill, hundreds of feet tall.

At the foot of its south face, two rocky spurs reached out like outstretched arms, forming a horseshoe shape with the ends pointed southward. The horseshoe enclosed Locust Lake. Near the base of the hill a spring rose, feeding a broad, shallow green lake.

Haze overhung the lake and the woods bordering it. Not a haze of fog or moisture but of smoke— woodsmoke, coming from dozens of campfires burning at various sites around the area. The fires of a Comanche camp, a small army of several hundred braves. Poised on the high ground, they were in position to swoop down in force on Hangtree County.

The sight shook Sam Heller. He rubbed his eyes and looked again to make sure he wasn't seeing things. The unnerving image persisted.

Rounding the rock spur, he recovered his knife, wiped it clean, and sheathed it. He wedged his gun in place, climbed up to the notch, and squirmed through. He wasted no time descending the west side of the mound.

The girl had stuck. She was still in place, mounted on horseback with rifle in hand.

Sam unhitched Dusty and swung up into the saddle.

"Did something happen? What did you see?" Lydia asked.

"Too much," Sam said. "Let's ride!"

NINE

Sam and Lydia entered Hopper Glen. It began as a gully, narrow and high-sided, walls spreading out as the cut descended the south slope of the plateau. A stream ran through it, part of the overflow from the lake at Sentry Hill. It was heavily wooded.

The trees gave and they took away, providing cover for the duo while potentially concealing any lurking Comanches. A thin trail ran along the west bank of the stream.

Sam and Lydia rode down it single file, Sam in the lead.

He fought the urge to race down the cut and streak across the plains to Hangtown. That was the surest way to get killed. The terrain was treacherous for man and mount alike. Tangled thickets, snaky vines, and low-hanging branches could knock a too hasty rider senseless. Gopher holes and rocky spurs could trip up a horse and break its leg or send it plummeting down a steep drop.

A canopy of treetops roofed the glen, filling it with cool shadows. The smell of foliage and moist earth was thick. Knee-high green rushes lined the stream banks. A silver thread of falling water widened into a series of shallow pools.

Hopper Glen took its name from the hordes of grasshoppers infesting it. The grassy ground was thick with active insects the color of new leaves. A number of them lay crushed along the trail, trod under by the hooves of horses that had passed that way earlier. How much earlier, Sam couldn't tell.

A splashing sound stung him into reaching for his sidearm, until he realized it was only a false alarm, caused by a bullfrog jumping into a pond. Sam's hand drifted away from the mule's-leg. Not too far away, though.

Sam halted at a pile of horse droppings on the trail, Lydia reining in behind him. Getting down from the horse, he hunkered down beside the spoor, prodding and poking it with a twig.

He rose, standing beside Dusty, resting a hand on top of the saddle horn. Lydia looked questioningly at him. "Comanches have been down this way, about five or six of them," he said, low voiced.

"Maybe it's white folks," Lydia said.

Sam shook his head. "Couple of the ponies were unshod, Indian-style. The spoor's partly dried, so they passed this way a couple hours ago."

"What do we do?"

"Same thing we've been doing. Keep going with our eyes open."

Lydia nodded. Sam mounted and they started forward. Down and down they rode, descending two-thirds of the long, rolling hill. The glen, having in the course of its descent widened into a ravine, culminated in a gorge at the bottom third of the slope. The west side of the gorge was bordered by a rocky promontory about seventy-five feet high. Commanding a broad view of the flat below for many a mile, the summit would make a fine observation post.

The trail forked in two directions. One branch followed a saddle-shaped ridge to the cliff top; the other dipped down into the gorge along the east face of the cliff.

The cliff trail showed crushed grasshoppers, trampled weeds, and hoof prints on patches of bare ground. Sam glimpsed motion through a gap in the bushes on the summit. "We just found the scouting party," he whispered.

Lydia gazed steadily at him, level-eyed.

"Can't get past 'em without going through 'em," Sam said.

Rocks and brush hid the Comanches on the summit from view. He couldn't see them, they couldn't see him. If he'd had a clear sightline on them he could have picked them off from a distance. The mule's-leg was no long gun, lacking the accuracy even of a carbine, but he had a remedy for that in the flat wooden box tied to the side of the saddle. Too bad he couldn't put it to use. He'd have to do it the hard way.

He and Lydia backed their horses behind a bend in the trail hiding them from anyone on the cliff top. They dismounted, Sam leading Dusty into a small glade to one side of the trail. Lydia followed, leading Brownie. He handed Dusty's reins to her.

"If I don't make it, get off the trail and hide till dark. Then go down to the flat and break for Hangtown," Sam said.

Lydia nodded, wide-eyed and deathly pale.

"But I'll make it." Sam smiled.

She eyed him, unblinking.

Sam loosed the mule's-leg, holding it at his side. He went to the edge of the bend, peering around it. He couldn't see anyone on the cliff top looking in his direction.

He started along the cliff trail, moving in a half crouch, hugging the brush alongside the dirt path. He padded down the saddle ridge, chest tight and a heavy weight in his stomach. Walking softly, he darted from one side of the trail to the other from time to time, taking advantage of the cover provided by a tree trunk or rock.

The dirt path dipped, then rose to the cliff top, running between a line of trees, eight to ten feet tall, with snaky trunks and busy boughs massed at the near side of the summit. Through spaces in the brush, Sam saw horses milling about.

He sneaked up to the trees.

Five horses, saddled and ready to ride, were tied to a hitching line in a shallow natural basin. No watchman guarded them.

On the far side of the bowl rose a man-high arc of massive boulders, tilted slabs, and jagged spurs. A gap between them opened on the rest of the cliff top, framing an oblong of blue sky. From behind came the sound of voices rising and falling, an alien tongue harsh and guttural, thick with consonants.

The absence of a guard on the horses was a break. The Comanches must be almighty sure of their mastery of the plateau, Sam thought. He wondered how long it would be before the two dead lookouts at Stickerbush Knob were discovered, sending another scouting party or two down the glen—if they weren't already on their way. Time was running out.

He edged along the tree line, staying downwind of the horses. Comanche horses tended to shy away from strangers. About half the horses in the string were unshod mounts with the distinctive wooden saddles of the tribe. They were all hitched to a lead rope, but had been left unhobbled for a fast getaway.

Easing out from behind the trees, Sam drew his knife and cut the lead rope. The horses sidled, dancing and restless. He slashed the nearest horse on its haunch, a quick shallow cut. It was a cruel trick he'd learned from Apaches, but effective. The animal shrieked, rearing, then bolting.

The other horses panicked. Sam went among them, slapping their rumps with his hat to get them moving. They needed little encouragement, following the horse already in flight.

Sam dodged, flattening his back against a rock slab on the east side of the gap between the boulders. The stampeding horses ran along the summit up the cliff trail. He breathed a silent prayer of thanks that he'd left the girl holding their horses in a glade safely off the trail. Pounding hoofbeats counterpointed his own hammering heartbeat. He couldn't tell where one left off and the other began.

The wait for the the Comanches was not a long one. Loss of horses meant disaster for them, combining the threat of imminent danger with a potential loss of prestige on possibly the most important raid of their lives. With it came the sting of the biter bit. Horse thieves supreme, they did not look kindly on the theft of their own mounts. No one is more outraged than a thief who gets robbed.

The braves came running, charging out of the narrow gap one by one. Legs flashing, arms pumping, moccasined feet thudding softly, they climbed between the boulders and into the open.

They fanned out, racing to intercept the fleeing horses. One brave turned to shout something to another and caught sight of Sam. He was the first to die, as Sam cut loose with the mule's-leg.

Holding the trigger down, working the lever, Sam milled out bullets, cutting down two more braves. The mule's-leg spat chopped the first three before they could do more than realize his presence and the inevitability of their own deaths. Sizzling rounds lanced living flesh, copper-hued bodies spinning and wheeling in sudden violent death.

A fourth brave was off to one side from the others. Sam leveled the mule's-leg at him as the brave raised a tomahawk, arm bent for throwing. The brave lurched as three rounds tore into him, then toppled, weapon unthrown.

A fifth Comanche came rushing out from between the boulders, blindly firing a rifle. Perhaps he'd been a bit slower to react than the others, or perhaps he'd been farthest from the gap when the stampede started.

Drawing abreast of Sam, he glimpsed him out of the corner of his eye. He stopped short, whirling, bringing his rifle around as he lunged toward the foe.

Sam fired first. The mule's-leg was shorter, its cut-down barrel having less distance to traverse. The blast caught the charging brave in the belly at point-blank range, blowing a hole out the back of his spine. The muzzle flare from the mule's-leg scorched his shirt, setting it on fire.

Dying, the brave bowled into Sam, knocking him off balance. Sam slipped on a loose stone, losing his footing. He fell backward, fetching the back of his head against a half-buried rock with a sharp crack that made him see stars. The brave fell on top of him, pinning his lower body. Fighting a wave of blackness that threatened to engulf his senses, Sam held onto his weapon like a drowning man clutching a lifeline.

Bullets tore through the empty air above him,

ripping a line of holes into the face of the boulder. Stinging stone chips sprayed him with streaks of pain that cut through the darkness crashing down on him.

He rolled onto his side, trying to kick away the corpse weighing down on his legs. The blackness retreated. Through a streaming curtain of colored lights, Sam saw that one of the first three braves he'd cut down was not killed but only wounded. The Comanche was on his feet, staggering forward, shooting. He'd been hit in the left side, which glistened wetly with dark red blood.

Raising himself on an elbow, Sam returned fire, cutting the brave's legs out from under him. Still game, the brave dropped to his knees, shooting. A round buzzed past Sam's head, flattening into a lead smear on a boulder behind him.

Sam kept firing. The brave lurched, swaying on his knees before pitching forward to sprawl face-first in the dirt. Sam put another slug into him to make sure, planting it dead center in the crown of his head and blowing it apart.

Breathing gustily, Sam dragged his legs clear of the dead weight of the body pinning them down. The back of his head was an aching soreness, each pulsing heartbeat felt as if it would split his skull.

He sat up, back braced against the boulder for support. He looked around for his hat, but didn't see it.

That dark slouch hat meant a lot to him. A treasured gift, it had been given to him back in the war by General Ulysses S. Grant, after Sam had earlier expressed his admiration for the hard-fighting commander's battered but virtually indestructible campaign hat. Grant had gotten him one like it. It was new then; hard campaigning in wars national and local had made it comfortable as an old shoe, familiar as a second skin.

Abruptly, Sam realized he was still wearing the headgear, scrunched down around his ears on top of his head. He must've hit his head harder than he thought. Taking the hat off, he reached around to the back of his skull, fingertips gingerly probing.

His head felt oversized, enlarged. He expected his hand to come away bloody but when he held it out in front of himself he was surprised to see that it was dry. Not only the bone but the skin covering it was unbroken. He murmured to himself, "Lucky!"

The hat had cushioned his skull, blunting the impact when he banged it against the rock. Sam put a fist inside the lopsided crown, pushing out most of the worst of the dents. He fitted the hat back on his head, breath hissing through clenched teeth at the pain.

Getting his legs under him, he rose shakily to his feet. Dizziness made him sick to his stomach. He kept the gorge down and the sickness passed.

Five Comanches lay sprawled around him. Two he was dead sure of: the brave he'd shot at point-blank range and the one he'd shot through the top of the head. The others looked dead, but he delivered the coup de grâce of a bullet in the head to each of them.

The mule's-leg had spat out a lot of lead, but with a capacity of seventeen rounds, he could afford it. He reloaded, fingers initially thick and fumbling as he pulled the first cartridges from their loops on the bandolier and fed them into the receiver. The dizziness receded as he executed the practiced routine, recovering much of his usual dexterity toward the end.

He made sure his Navy Colt and Green River knife were in place. He wanted nothing so much as to stagger back to his horse and ride out, but knew he'd be a fool not to take advantage of the prime vantage point. Steadying himself, he went through the gap toward the far end of the cliff top.

Beyond the boulders lay a patch of stony ground shaped like an egg with the narrow end pointed toward the edge. Measuring about twenty feet at its longest axis, the outcropping was covered by thick, tough grass and bare, brown clay. It looked like the hide of an animal afflicted with the mange. Shards of a shattered brown whiskey jug lay strewn about, explaining the Comanches' lack of proper precautions. Sam told himself that he'd've gotten them all anyway even if they hadn't been drunk. He almost believed it.

He prowled around, still too unsure of his footing to go too close to the edge. The cliff top thrust out into nothingness like the bow of a ship coursing through sky-blue seas, giving a panoramic view of the countryside below.

The south slope of the plateau was a rampart stretching for miles to east and west. In some places, it showed long, gently rising hills which could easily be climbed by even the least sure-footed horses and their riders; in others, fault lines created jagged ravines, steep gullies, and precipices that only a mountain goat could climb. Some sections were thickly forested, with woods spilling out into the flat; others were bare of all but a few sparsely scattered bushes and clumps of dwarf trees. The slope was marbled with thin blue veins that were brooks, streams, rivulets and runs, branching out across the plains.

More important, Sam Heller saw no Comanches in view, not on the slope or the near ground of the flat. In the middle distance, there were various widespread dots of motion that could have been roaming cattle or mounted men—they were too far away to make out.

Turning, gazing inland across the tops of the boulders walling off the summit, Sam saw thin lines of sparsely scattered smoke rising from among the thick-belted trees of the plateau. He knew them for the grave markers of burned ranch houses, farms, and wagons, but they would have been meaningless to any unknowing passersby on the plains, if any there were.

Sam went back the way he came, passing through the boulder gap. He picked up each Comanche's rifle and broke it in the middle against a rock, wrecking it so it could never be used again. Two were repeating rifles, so new they still had the grease on them.

"I'd give a plenty to know who's supplying repeaters to the Comanches," he said to himself.

He walked the cliff trail back to the fork. The stampeded horses had long since fled, a thin brown smudge of dust in the sky the only sign of their passing. With all the Comanches gathered at Locust Lake, the horses would not escape discovery for long. The braves were expert trackers, so—best get a move on.

Sam neared the glade at the side of the trail. Lydia stepped into view, holding a rifle at her side and the horses' reins in her other hand. Blue eyes glittered in the taut white mask of a face framed by a pair of yellow braids.

Had he expected some great effusion of emotion at his safe return, some reaction, even, Sam would have been disappointed. But he wasn't one for such expectations.

"Took your time, didn't you?" Lydia said.

Was she joking? If she was, it would be a good sign, but Sam couldn't tell. Her expression was dead serious. He showed a halfway grin. "Any trouble?"

She shook her head. "I heard the shooting. How many did you kill?"

"Five," he said, not bragging, just a simple statement of fact.

She nodded. Sam took Dusty's reins from her and mounted up. Lydia climbed on Brownie.

"Let's ride," Sam said.

"You're the one holding things up. I've been waiting on you," Lydia said.

"Yes, ma'am," Sam said sarcastically, taking the point. They followed the trail's east fork to the bottom of the glen on the flat.

TEN

The stream widened out below Hopper Glen, running east through a belt of woods at the foot of the plateau's south slope. Sam was glad to have the cover of the trees hiding him and the girl from any hostiles roaming flat or heights.

When they were a mile or so away from the glen he judged it was safe to water the horses. Dusty and Brownie stood at stream's edge, heads down, drinking thirstily. Swarms of gnats hovered over some of the shallow pools and side pockets.

Sam's sore head throbbed. He longed for a smoke but the betraying scent of burned tobacco would carry a long way in the outdoors. A drink of whiskey would have been even better, if he hadn' taken the head-knocking. As it was, he was afraid drink would make it worse, so he abstained from tapping the bottle in his saddlebag.

Hauling back on the reins, he caused Dusty to l his snout out of the stream. "Don't let the anim;

drink too much. It's bad for 'em. Slows 'em down and that's bad for us."

Lydia urged her horse away from the water.

"We'll trail east through the woods as long as they hold out, then break out across the flat to Old Mission Road," Sam said.

"Hangtown's a long way off," Lydia said doubtfully.

"We're not going to Hangtown. We're going to a ranch I know. It's a lot closer."

Scorn replaced doubt on the girl's face. "With all them Comanches out on the warpath? What ranch could hold out against them?"

"This one can. It's held out against Comanches or a hundred years. It's built like a fort—Rancho Grande."

"I know of it," she said, unimpressed. "A big read, owned by Mexes. They got no use for glos, Mister Yank, in case you ain't heard."

"I know a few folks there."

"Friends of yours?" She sneered.

"Yes and no."

ydia laughed without humor. "If that ain't a ee for you! Talking out of both sides of your h and not a straight answer out of either."

s complicated. I've got a few amigos there, me others who'd cheerfully cut my throat," id. "But even enemies put aside their differhen Comanches are on the loose. They'll be n extra gun."

"Two guns," Lydia said quickly. "I can shoot, too. And I got me some evening-up to do."

Sam nodded, urging his horse forward. The girl followed. "Yankees and Mexes! This state is sure going to the dogs," she muttered.

"Let's hope it doesn't go to the Comanches."

Lydia was silent after that. They rode on. The woods were thick with wildlife. Birds flew overhead, and small critters such as hares, chipmunks, and red and gray squirrels scurried through the under-brush. Deer tracks showed on muddy stream banks. Sam regretted the prime deer carcass he'd had to cut loose on the heights.

A mile went by, then two. The woods followed the base of the slope. When the slant began to curve north, away from where Sam wanted to go, they paused at the edge of the treeline, scanning the broad, empty plains. Sam took a piece of jerky from his saddlebag, cut off a slice and offered it to Lydia.

"I ain't hungry," she said.

"It'll help you keep up your strength. You might need it," Sam said.

"Can't eat. Ain't got the stomach for it."

"You want some later, just sing out."

She shook her head.

Sam shrugged. "Looks clear. Might as well head out."

They rode out from under the trees, into the open. Sam bit off a chunk of jerky, wedging it in the back corner of his teeth. Sipping some water from his canteen, he held it in his mouth to soften up the jerky, tough as a boot sole.

The sun was high and hot. The flat stretched out toward the horizon, a vast, sprawling tableland under the Big Sky, almost dizzying in its size and scope. Rolling plains were broken by rises, hollows, and stands of timber. The grass was a rich bright green, slightly yellowing at the tips and edges.

Good grazing land for cattle and, not so very long ago, for buffalo. But the buffalo herds were thinning out, their numbers shrinking every season.

The prime source of sustenance for the Comanches, buffalo supplied them with meat, hides, sinews for bowstrings, bones for tools and implements, and hooves for glue. They followed the herds, hunting them when they weren't busy hunting two-legged prey.

A rock wall running north-south far in the western distance were the Broken Hills, that jumble of peaks, cliffs, and promontories known as The Breaks. A scant handful of bold and/or solitude-minded settlers lived along its eastern edge, dangerous country to roost in. Sam wondered how many would be left alive once the Comanche raid had run its course.

He steered a course to the southeast. The hollow feeling in the pit of his belly deepened as the covering thicket of the woods fell behind. From time to time he turned in the saddle, looking back to scan the scene for hostiles.

The horses moved along at a brisk gait. Sam set

a not too fast pace, leaving the horses plenty of reserve in case they had to run. He also didn't want to raise a telltale cloud of dust that would finger them to enemy eyes.

The girl wasn't much for talking, which suited him fine. Not that he blamed her. On the other hand, he didn't want her thinking overmuch on what she'd experienced. Still, how could she not?

Sam's eyes were active in a stony face as he surveyed the landscape. Several miles passed. The land rose and fell like long rolling swells on the open sea—but it was a sea of grass. The duo crossed two streams, or maybe the same stream twice, winding and doubling back on itself. It was hard to judge such things, in the lonesome Titan immensity. Sam devoutly wished it would stay lonesome.

He and Lydia rode side by side. Breaking the silence at last, she said, "What you doing in these parts, anyhow? Ain't Yankeeland good enough for you?"

"I like to roam," Sam said.

"Reckon you wish you'd kept on moving instead of lighting in Hangtree," she said, something like a smirk showing on her mouth for an instant.

"You might have something there," Sam said evenly.

"What for you come up on the hills?"

"A day's hunting."

"Now you're being hunted," Lydia said with a flash of bright, innocent malice. "How do you like that?"

"How do you like it?" he countered.

The girl fell silent, her face set in a sullen cast.

Presently they struck a trail, not even a dirt road but a trail, running east-west. "We're getting close. This trail runs parallel to Old Mission Road, which lies six, seven miles farther south," Sam said.

They crossed the trail at a tangent, continuing on their southeasterly course. A long shallow incline topped out on a grassy table dotted with stands of timber and patches of brush. Bunches of longhorned cattle wandered in the distance.

A patch of dust, no bigger than a man's thumb held at arm's length, smudged the blue sky of the southwest quadrant. Sam squinted at it. Its source, whatever it was, was as yet unseen. An involuntary grunt escaped him.

Lydia saw what he was looking at. "Them?" she asked, her tone dull, fatalistic.

"Don't know. Could be a herd of longhorns, or some ranch hands out riding."

"There ain't no ranches here," the girl pointed out.

"There's that," Sam admitted.

"So?"

"Let's see what they do. To run now would kick up more dust and mebbe tip 'em off if they ain't already seen us."

"They say them Comanches don't miss much."

"They do say that."

Keeping on their course, Sam fought the urge to put his boot heels into Dusty's flanks and break into a run. The patch of dust changed direction, moving parallel to their course.

"They're following us," Lydia said.

"Looks like," said Sam.

They continued across a long stretch of open ground, their progress seeming agonizingly slow. There was no cover to be had in the near or middle ground, just open flatland.

The source of the nearing dust cloud revealed itself as a blur of moving black dots, marching antlike across a green table. That seeming slowness was only an illusion caused by vastness, for the space between the duo and the unknowns was steadily narrowing.

"Riders," Sam said, "about a dozen."

"Run for it?" Lydia asked.

"You a good rider?"

"I ain't gonna fall off Brownie, if that's what you're asking, Mister Yank."

"Put some speed on but don't go all out just yet, save something for later. Ride!"

The chase was on. That it was a chase, there could be no doubt. The duo's horses broke into a run. Dusty was faster than Brownie but Sam held him back, letting the girl ride several lengths ahead of him. He wanted to know where she was at all times.

As for the pursuers, he only had to look back over his shoulder to see where they were. The pack moved up fast, kicking up dust. The not-so-distant brown plume grew into a pillar rising into the sky.

Whoops and shrieks sounded, thin and far-off, but no less ominous for that.

Comanches! Too near to be outdistanced in the long run, and no sheltering ravines or thickets of wood in which to lose them. Hunters not easily shaken once they had the scent of blood in their nostrils. They were still a fair piece off, but the gap was steadily decreasing.

Sam had a plan, desperate though it might be, but he was looking for more advantageous terrain to set it in motion.

Up ahead, he saw a slight break in the unreeling emptiness of the flat—a rock outcropping, a handful of boulders, and a couple of scraggly trees.

Sam pointed it out to Lydia, shouting, "Make for the rocks!"

"What'll we do there?"

"Fight!"

That seemed to satisfy the girl. She rode all out for the rocks, leaning far forward on the coursing horse, almost doubled over Brownie's muscular, dark-maned neck. A good little rider at that, Sam noted approvingly.

The landscape was a breathless blur as they closed on the rocks. Hoofbeats pounded, digging dirt. Some man-sized boulders stood heaped around a gnarly mesquite tree and a scruff of brush.

Sam and Lydia pulled up to a halt in the lee of the boulders. Their bases were planted deep in the turf. Behind the rocks was a bowl-shaped depression, little more than a foot deep and about ten feet wide.

They dismounted. Lydia said, "What good's this? Injins'll just ride around it."

"It's a place to make a stand, better than you might think." Pulling his blade, Sam cut the rawhide thongs securing the long, flat wooden box to the metal rings in the side of the saddle. Gripping the case by its suitcase handle, he carefully set it down against a rock.

Taking hold of the bridle, he pulled his horse's head down and to the side, urging, "Down boy, down! You know the drill!"

Dusty did know it. He was a veteran warhorse, survivor of many past battles. Legs bending, the animal knelt down in the bowl and lay on his side, flanks quivering as he panted for breath. It was a trick that had served him well in many a hot firefight. Sam wanted to minimize the chances of Dusty being hit by a stray slug; he set a lot of store by the animal.

Brownie didn't know the trick and wasn't minded to follow suit, going by Lydia's inability to make him obey.

Sam said, "Tie your horse to the tree! Tie him good so he can't break loose!"

Lydia hesitated.

"Comanches won't shoot him. They want him alive."

"But your horse laid down."

"Dusty's been in the war and knows what to do.

Brownie don't and this ain't the time to try and learn him!"

The charging Comanches were several hundred yards away. Every inch of that fast-narrowing gap meant the difference between life and death. Lydia hitched Brownie to the tree and ran over to Sam with her rifle in hand.

"Take cover behind the rocks and keep your head down, girl."

"The hell you say, Mister Yank. I aim to kill me some of them red devils!"

Sam chuckled, amused despite himself. "I believe you will at that, missy. Keep your nerve and we might just get out of this alive."

"I reckon I can stand anything an ol' heathen Northerner can, and more!"

Sam was done talking. He went down on one knee, laying the wooden box flat on the ground. He unfastened twin brass snaps at the join, opening the case.

"What for you fiddling with that?" Lydia asked.

"I've got a . . . secret weapon, you might say." Sam lifted the lid of the wooden box, exposing its contents. Within the hollows of a black crushed-velvet encasing lay several pieces of hardware: an elongated rifle barrel, a wooden stock, and a telescopic gunsight.

Crouching behind a chest-high rock, Lydia took up a shooting position, placing the Henry rifle across the boulder's flat top and snugging the butt of the stock into a hollow of her thin shoulder.

"Them Injins is getting awful close," she said, her thin voice quivering.

"Don't shoot yet. It's a waste of ammunition. Wait'll they get closer," Sam said.

"Mister, they're getting too danged close!" Lydia raised her voice to be heard over the drumbeat of galloping hooves, the whoop and shriek of fast-closing raiders.

Her face was stiff, the pupils of her eyes blue-rimmed black dots, large and swimming. She kept glancing from the charging Comanches to Sam, to see what he was doing.

Sam loosed the mule's-leg from its holster. The hardware in the case was custom-designed for the cut-down Winchester. Practiced hands moving with expert sureness, Sam freed the elongated rifle barrel from its casing. Its butt end was expertly tooled, machined with spiraling grooves that ensured a perfect fit when joined to the muzzle of the Winchester's sawed-off barrel. Sam screwed the long barrel into place, a final twist bringing its front sight post up with a click to the deadline-center vertical.

Taking the smoothly polished wooden butt stock from its holder, he fitted its forward end over the butt end of the short-handled mule's-leg. The stock's open central slot fit snugly over the rear of the weapon.

A pair of screws with flat, thumbnail-shaped ends was set in place in holes drilled in opposite ends at the head of the stock. Strong, dextrous fingers worked them, turning them in place in corresponding holes in the Winchester's chopped handle.

The mule's-leg, cut-down for quick access when in the saddle or in the close quarters of a saloon or back alley, was transformed into a long rifle, with the precision and accuracy of the same.

The wood case held a telescopic sight, too, but there was neither time nor need for attaching it; the Comanches were too close.

Sam muttered under his breath. "Their blood is up. They're hot for the kill, the dirty so and so's."

"Hey, mister," Lydia said, "don't let them take me alive!"

"Don't be in such an all-fired hurry to die," Sam said.

Lydia, desperate, was insistent. "I ain't no kid. I know what happens to girls they catch! Promise you won't let that happen to me."

"It won't."

"Swear it!"

"I swear." Sam shouldered the long rifle. Bringing it into play, he went to work.

Black Robes. That's what the Comanches called the Catholic priests who had first come with the conquistadors.

In their misguided zeal the priests sought to convert the Indian tribes of the southwest. Comanches were bemused by these strange ones who clothed themselves in long black robes with high, stiff white collars, wearing crosses on chains around their necks. It was clear, though, that they were the Mexicans' shamans and spiritual leaders, like the medicine men of their own tribes.

The Black Robes had odd ways of doing things, even for whites—queer prohibitions and obligations—all designed to set them apart from more worldly individuals and bring them into contact with the god-devils of the Invisible World. Some had strong medicine indeed, chanting prayers of their faith while undergoing hideous tortures of cutting, burning, mutilation, and other bedevilments devised by Comanches to test the mettle of captive priests. The ironclad conquistadors came and went but the Mexicans and their Black Robes remained.

During the summer of 1865, Red Hand had led his followers on a raid south across the Rio Grande deep into Mexico. One of his trusted henchman, a cruel and wily warrior of proven ability, killed the priest of a pueblo village during a skirmish. The pueblo was a clump of adobe houses inhabited by white-clad peasants with wicker-and-straw sandals. It yielded slim pickings, with few decent horses or weapons to plunder or captives to enslave and torment.

The village had a church, a high-walled structure which the raiders gutted and burned. The Black Robe priest died well, hard but well. Red Hand's henchman stripped the corpse of its black robe, donning it.

The Comanche wore the clerical garb like a long-sleeved coat or cape, splitting and cutting it to maximize his freedom of movement. The garment gave him power, not the power of a shaman such as Medicine Hat, but still, an aura of otherworldly menace enhancing his death-dealing capabilities in the material world.

It set the henchman apart from his fellows, who in the time-honored way of the tribe began calling him "Black Robe." His old name, the name by which he had previously been known to one and all, was dropped, forgotten as if it never was. Henceforth he was—Black Robe.

Now, a year later, Black Robe's priestly vestment was somewhat the worse for wear. Weathered and bloodstained, it was ripe with the smoke of countless campfires, the burning of villages, and the blood of many foes. It was tattered and frayed, with torn seams showing at the shoulders and across the back. It was decorated with strips of buckskin fringe along the arms and brightened with beads and scraps of colored ribbons.

Black Robe's mission, given him by Red Hand himself, was to lead a band of scouts down on the flatland, making sure that no White Eyes from the plateau escaped the slaughter to warn their fellows in the ranches and town.

Black Robe's party was one of several advance parties operating deep in enemy territory, land the Comanches regarded as theirs by right. These bands would begin the encirclement and isolation of the town of the Hanging Tree.

The tribesmen well knew the Hanging Tree and hated it. More than a few of their number had been caught in times past by the hated Texans and hung on a rope by the neck from the lightning-blasted tree at the edge of town. It was a bad thing, an evil act, for Comanche tradition decreed that any warrior slain by hanging was unable to enter the Happy Hunting Ground, his spirit condemned to wander the winds forever in bodiless, endless limbo.

It was good that Red Hand had united the bravest of the brave under the Fire Lance to take and sack the town, killing the Texans, save for such captives to be taken as slaves or given up to the torture.

Black Robe's band had been busy, raiding small ranches in the Breaks, burning them out and killing their occupants. Moving east, they slew a number of hapless travelers crossing the flat. A good day in all, but the next day would be better. The next day was the Day of the Great Raid.

For now, Black Robe and his men still had work to do, scouring the plains for such whites as they could find and take. Chance favored them with the sight of two more victims riding out in the open.

The gods were kind, for one of the fugitives was female. She would afford Black Robe and the others some trifling amusement throughout the night before being put to death before dawn light of the Day of the Great Raid, assuming she lived through the ordeal of rape and horror.

As for the man, he would be killed, probably outright, though if he could be taken alive, great sport would be had putting him to the torture.

Black Robe led his band in pursuit. As always, the prey sought to escape, though their fate was a foregone conclusion. Two against twelve, miles from the nearest ranch with no cover and nowhere to run, they were doomed.

Black Robe was surprised when the fugitives broke off the chase to stand and fight. "A great joke, eh, my brothers!" he crowed.

How the other braves laughed! Perhaps one or two of them would be wounded or even killed during the chase, adding the spice of danger to the chase. So much the better! Each brave was confident his own personal power would protect him from harm and ensure that ill luck would befall one of the others.

A Comanche band in full charge was an impressive sight, fearsome to those unfortunate enough to be the object of their wrath. Closing on the rocks and skinny tree where the fugitives would stage their pathetically futile defense, Black Robe was chagrined to find his pony unexpectedly faltering.

The animal favored one leg, causing it to lose speed. From the feel of the mount under him, Black Robe guessed the cause was nothing more serious than a pebble caught under a hoof of one of the forelegs. Had the distance been greater or the foe more formidable, he would have halted to dislodge the obstruction, but his galloping band was fast nearing the two in the rocks and there was no time to waste.

He resolved to ride the horse full out. If the hardship crippled or lamed it, he would replace it with one of the Texans' horses. Still, it was irritating to lose his place at the head of the charge while his fellows overtook him on uninjured mounts. As leader he must ever be at the fore, outdoing others in deeds of valor and horsemanship.

Furious, he kicked the horse's flanks with his heels, cursing the animal, urging it to greater speed. His efforts were for naught. Worse, the animal's pace slowed even further.

In battle, in the heat of the chase, rank and precedence counted for nothing; each warrior must show himself to best effect, seeking always to surpass all others. No brave slowed to wait for Black Robe to catch up. In truth, each was secretly delighted by the ill luck suddenly afflicting their vaunted leader.

It had all the makings of a great jest, one that would be told and retold around the campfire with relish—just the kind of reversal of fortune a Comanche delighted in, so long as it happened to the other fellow and not himself. What a joke if Black Robe was last in line to take enjoyment of the leavings of the girl, after all the other braves had had her first! Ah, the sly jokes and smirks at his impotent fury at being bested!

Though perhaps not too openly, for Black Robe was a fierce fighter with a wicked temper, a well-respected killer. Still, he who comes first to the spoils is first served.

Advancing in a loose, wide arc, the riders fanned out on both sides and rode rings around the two whites in the rocks. The man would be downed quickly no doubt, but not the female; she must be taken alive and intact. A slip of a girl with a pair of yellow braids bracketing a wide-eyed, ghostly face.

Shouting and catcalling to each other to be heard over the clamor of the charge, the braves marveled. "Look, she has a rifle!"

"Waugh! That is good! She has spirit!"

Like Black Robe, about a third of the band were similarly armed with repeating rifles. Others had cavalry carbines or single-shot rifled muskets. Several relied on the bow and arrow and their skill at letting loose shaft after shaft in quick succession.

The Comanches opened fire, rifles cracking. Arrows whizzed, arcing through the air, and falling well short of the mark, but getting the range.

Sam had readied to take out Black Robe first. Kill the leader and break the spirit of the band. But when he fell behind, Sam swung his rifle toward the Indian at the head of the charge. Lining him up in his sights, he squeezed the trigger. Tagged dead center, the lead brave fell off his horse.

Sam swung the rifle slightly to one side, sighting on the next in line. The trigger was pulled, the rifle barked, and another man went down. The riderless horse raced away.

Sam picked off a third Comanche. He was knocking them down like targets in a shooting gallery, the deed done as passionlessly as if he were clearing a row of tin ducks. Shot followed shot in quick succession from his long rifle. Each shot hit its mark, killing a man.

Once or twice when Sam targeted a foe, the wounded warrior remained upright, still on horseback. With barely a pause Sam shot again and that man fell and died.

The braves focused their ire and weapons on the source of the furious firepower. Bullets smashed into the rock shielding Sam like hail peppering a flat roof. A round clipped the edge of his hat brim, nicking a half-moon shaped hole out of it.

Arrows shattered on the slabs of the rock pile, spraying Lydia's face with stinging splinters, but missing her eyes. That stung her into action. Drawing a bead on a Comanche, she fired—and missed.

Taking aim again, she discovered her target's horse was empty, the brave having been felled by Sam, who had already moved on to the next foe.

It was done without thinking—point, squeeze the trigger, kill a man, find the next target.

A rider on the right flank of the arc of charging braves swung farther to the right, his purpose to swing around the rocks and get behind the defenders. He was on Lydia's left.

Adjusting her aim to lead him, Lydia fired. Hit,

the brave spasmed, the rifle slipping from his hands. He clutched his horse's flowing mane with both hands, holding on tight. Losing his grip, he slipped off the side of the horse, spilling into the dust.

Of the twelve braves who'd begun the charge, only six remained on horseback by the time they'd halved the distance between them and the rocks. The charge was breaking up, falling apart.

The surviving braves were stunned by the vicious counterstrike. It was like riding full tilt into a wall of hot lead. Comanches were no strangers to the repeating rifle, more than a few of them were similarly armed. But none had ever come face-to-face with a repeater wielded by such a dead shot as Sam Heller.

Even their best marksmen were at a disadvantage. They were on horseback, charging across uneven ground. Sam, dismounted, worked from a stable firing platform.

He had some cover. The Comanches had none. They were being decimated by a sharpshooter with the world's latest and most lethal application of mechanized mass death available to a lone individual.

The braves were no fools. They were in the game to kill, not to die, but it was all happening too fast for them to break off the charge. No sooner did they realize the damage done than it was too late to turn back. They had a mountain lion by the tail. Or rather, he had them.

That was the edge Sam Heller had been counting on. With his repeating rifle he could pick off most, if not all, of the attackers before they closed with him.

The last of the Comanche band was very close indeed. Outriders on the flanks turned their horses's heads, peeling off from the charge. Or trying to. Sam wasn't going to let them circle around the rocks and get behind him. He picked off a brave at his extreme left. A beat later, he felled an outrider wheeling to the right.

Black Robe's rage at being undone by his lamed horse was supplanted by stunned amazement as the ranks of his band thinned visibly with each passing second. What had first seemed great sport was becoming a blistering fight for survival, one his side was losing.

He took heart in the surety that all was not lost. His gods had not deserted him. What he had taken for a cruel jest of fate laming his mount had become the instrument of his salvation. Had he been at the head of the charge, he would have been the first to fall to the White Eyes with the Devil Gun. But luck was still with Black Robe, affording him an opportunity to turn disaster into victory.

Holding on to the horse's neck with one bent arm, hooking the back of an ankle around his saddle's high wooden cantle, he hung down on his horse's right-hand side. This put the animal's body between him and the foeman's Devil Gun, covering him as he swung right to get behind the rocks on Sam's left. Half lurching, half loping, the horse was still game, still coming on.

Black Robe clutched his rifle in one hand, the barrel protruding beneath the horse's snout as he lined it up for a shot at Sam.

Sam was busy burning down a last lone brave who'd almost reached the rocks on a head-long charge. He drilled him through the heart.

Lydia saw Black Robe coming, but he was too well screened behind the far side of the horse to present much of a target to her. He glimpsed the girl with the yellow braids as she rose and turned, pointing a rifle in his direction. A flare rimmed the muzzle of her weapon as she fired.

Thinking fast, Lydia shot not at the brave but at his horse. The horse stumbled, forelegs folding, tumbling headfirst. Black Robe was thrown, cartwheeling to the hard ground.

He rolled to a stop, battered and dazed, semiconscious. He was empty handed, having lost the rifle in the fall. Somehow he rose, standing shakily on two feet.

Sam shot him. Black Robe's awareness was blotted out by the darkness of complete and illimitable death.

Sam Heller looked around. Dead bodies lay all about; riderless horses scattered in every direction. Like himself, the girl was unhit, unhurt. She put a hand against a rock to steady herself. "Hey, mister!"

Sam looked at her.

"My name is Lydia—Lydia Fisher."

Sam realized that up till now he hadn't known her name. "Glad to know you, Miss Fisher."

"Lydia," she said, sticking out a hand.

He shook it. "Call me Sam."

ELEVEN

It was quiet in the Golden Spur, as if the earlier outburst of violence had never been. The dead bodies had long since been carted away. Sawdust thrown down by Swamper had soaked up the blood. He swept it up, mopping the stains with a bucket of hot water, lye soap, and a scrub brush. Their washed-out shadows darkened the floorboards.

"That's enough," Mrs. Frye said. "There'll be more later—or sooner."

Swamper tossed the scrub brush into the bucket and put everything away, then crashed on his mattress in a corner of the kitchen to sleep off some of the booze he'd guzzled in the aftermath of the shootings.

A long case clock stood between two windows on the west wall of the main hall. In height and shape it was not unlike a coffin standing on end. Black and gold it was, made of ebony wood with gilt trimmings. An ivory-colored clock dial was decorated with images of the sun, moon, and stars; sun and moon were depicted with the human faces of Old Sol and the Man in the Moon.

The hands on the clock pointed to a little after seven in the evening. The interior of the case was filled with clockwork gears and a pendulum, each *ticktock* sounding as sharp and clear as a gun hammer being thumbed back into place.

Damon Bolt sat in place at the table facing the front door, playing his game of solitaire. Whether it was the same game as before or a new one made no difference to him. He continued to play with an undiminished air of concentration and a steady hand, despite the fact that the level of whiskey in his bottle had declined noticeably in the last hour or so.

Mrs. Frye had retreated to the office behind the staircase. The door had been left open to hear if anything was going on outside the room. She sat behind a desk, going over the accounts. Her steel-tipped ink pen made rustling, scratchy sounds on the ledger pages as she brought the entries up to date.

Out front, Morrissey stood behind the bar, absently polishing up glasses with a thin towel. A double-barreled shotgun lay on its side on the countertop, near at hand. The front pockets of his white bib apron bulged with shotgun shells.

Behind him, the wall showed the ghostly outline where the mirror had hung before a stray slug had shot it to pieces. The horizontal oblong was discolored compared to the rest of the cream-colored wall.

Across from the barkeep, Creed Teece sat on a long-legged stool at the bar, eating a late lunch. "Damned if I'm goin' off my feed on account of a dustup that ain't even happened yet," he said with his mouth full. The thick, juicy steak that Morrissey had cooked covered his plate, the slabbed beef looking about as big as a doormat.

Teece went at it hard with knife and fork, his face almost parallel to the plate as he wolfed down his food. Strong white teeth tore at red-dripping meat, the juices running down his chin. The knotted clumps of muscle at the corners of his square jaw worked hard to chew the steak. From time to time he washed it down with great gulps from a tumbler full of whiskey, which the barkeep was quick to refill when it showed signs of running out.

Monk the bouncer was still up on the roof of the building, keeping watch.

Johnny Cross and Luke Pettigrew sat at a table off to the side of the bar, with a clear view of the main floor and front entrance. They drank beer out of solid, long-handled glass mugs. They'd switched from whiskey to beer earlier to keep from getting too big a skinful too early in the day.

"We got enough hands here to work up a decent poker game," Luke said, looking around.

"The cards'd only get in the way of your drinking," Johnny said.

"You ain't exactly been on the water wagon yourself." Luke drained his glass, setting the empty mug down on the table and smacking his lips. He wiped his mouth on his sleeve. Pushing his chair back, he reached down under the table, straightening the wooden leg that had been bent at a right angle and extending it in a straight line out to the side. His fingers worked on the hinge screws of the artificial limb, locking it into place.

He gripped the back of his chair with one hand and the edge of the table with another. Johnny took hold of the table to steady it. Luke hefted himself up out of the chair, on to his feet. Bending forward, he picked up the crutch which lay across a third chair at the table.

Luke snugged the crutch's padded crossbar under his left arm and planted its tip firmly on the floorboards. "Got to see a man about a horse."

Johnny nodded absently, watching tiny bubbles rise in his beer. Luke made his way limping to the bar. "Where's the donnicker?"

"Through that door and down the hall, first door on your right," Morrissey said, gesturing at a swinging door set in a near corner of the rear wall.

"Much obliged," Luke said, making his way to the convenience.

Johnny sipped some beer. Holding the mug up, he gazed at the wash of foamy suds sliding down the inside of the glass. From behind came soft footfalls, the rustle of a long skirt and petticoats. Glancing over his shoulder, he saw Francine Hayes coming out of a back room.

She went to the bar and spoke softly to Morrissey. Reaching under the bar, he set an unopened bottle of whiskey on the countertop. He put two glasses down beside it. Francine picked up the bottle and glasses and started toward Johnny.

Johnny eyed her admiringly without getting over-heated about it. She was a good-looking gal, a real beauty. Champagne-colored hair, blueberry eyes, a ripe red mouth that turned up at the corners. A dress of some shiny, satiny material hugged her slim, well-formed body. It was a pleasure just to watch her move.

Francine stood at the table, smiling. "Buy you a drink, cowboy?"

"That's a switch. Usually it's the fellow who buys a gal a drink," Johnny said.

"It's an unusual day."

"And it ain't hardly even got rolling yet."

"Compliments of the house," she said, brandish-ing the bottle.

Johnny rose, indicating an empty chair. "Please."

"Thank you." Francine set the bottle and glasses down on the table.

Johnny held the back of the chair, pushing it toward the table after she sat down. He tasted her perfume in his nostrils, light and elusive, yet making his senses tingle.

"You're a gentleman, sir."

"Shoot, all us Texas boys is gentlemen."

She cut him a sceptical side glance, a wry twist to her lips. "Not all."

"Maybe not," he allowed as he sat down, turning his chair to face her.

Indicating the bottle, Francine said. "If you would be so kind . . ."

"Glad to." He broke the seal and uncorked the bottle, loosing the rich, dark scent of prime Kentucky bourbon. It smelled almost as heady as her perfume. Almost, but not quite. He filled a shot glass, setting it down before her. "No water for a chaser?"

"Why, do you need one?" she countered.

"I was thinking of you."

"I take it straight. Especially today."

"Can't say as I blame you." Johhny filled the other glass, raising it.

Francine raised her glass. "Here's luck."

"Mud in your eye," Johnny said.

They drank. She tossed hers back in a gulp, drinking it down, shuddering a little. Color came into her cheeks, some of the tautness leaving her face.

"Good." Johnny smacked his lips.

"Have another," Francine invited.

"Why not?" He refilled their glasses.

She sipped hers. Johnny slowed down, too.

She studied his face, thoughtful. "I know you."

His eyebrows rose. "I'd remember if we ever met before. I never get that drunk."

"I mean, I know who you are. You've been in

here before. You and your friend were pointed out to me."

He'd forgotten about Luke. Where was he? Looking up, he saw his buddy standing at the bar, chatting with Morrissey. Catching Johnny's eye, Luke winked at him behind Francine where she couldn't see him. Johnny grinned to himself. Luke had nice timing. He knew when not to show up. Now that was a friend.

"You're John Cross, the gunfighter," Francine said.

Johnny smiled, shaking his head. "I'm Johnny Cross, the mustanger. I catch and sell wild horses for a living."

"Why be coy? I've seen what you can do with a gun."

"I can take care of myself."

"You're very good."

"You're pretty good yourself, Miss Hayes."

"It's Francine . . . John."

"Call me Johnny, Francine."

"All right, Johnny. How is it we never met before?"

"Luke and I are kind of busy out at the ranch. We don't get into town much. You're new here."

She nodded. "I've only been at the Spur for a few weeks. Long enough to get into trouble, though."

"No shortage of that in Hangtown. Is it too late for you to clear out?"

"Is that polite? Trying to get rid of me when you hardly know me. Usually it takes longer than that for someone to tire of me," Francine said, pouting.

"What am I saying? I must be drunk."

"And here I thought you were a gentleman."

"You must be drunk."

"Not yet."

"I meant that the party is liable to get rough when the Ramrod crowd rides in," Johnny explained.

"I've got nowhere to go. Why are you sticking?"

Johnny shrugged. "Maybe I don't like to see a pretty gal get pushed around."

"I was hoping that was the reason," Francine said huskily, gifting him with a full-force smile he could feel clear down to his toes.

"Or maybe I'm just an ornery critter that likes to fight," he added.

"That I believe!" she said, laughing. "You like me, Johnny?"

"Sure, what's not to like?"

"I know you do. I can tell. I like you, too. But watch out."

"Why?"

"I'm dangerous."

"All women are dangerous."

Francine's smile faded, the corners of her mouth turning down as she got serious. "I mean it. Look at Bliss Stafford. He got killed because of me."

"Don't talk dumb," Johnny said, frowning, his yellow cat eyes glinting. "I saw it. Stafford got hisself killed because he was a damned fool, a troublemaker who thought he was fast with a gun. He picked a fight with someone who was faster. That's all."

"You knew him?" Francine asked.

"Hell, no."

"You described him pretty well."

"I know the type. There's some like him in every saloon from here to the Mississippi. Too many. Seems I happen to meet more than my share, and they all want to fight me."

Francine showed a quirked smile. "Bliss. Bliss! Was ever anyone so misnamed? All he ever brought was heartache and trouble. He was a swine who thought he was God's gift to women. The harder I tried to discourage him, the more he wanted me. He kept after me, wouldn't let me be."

"No need to explain. What's done is done."

"I want you to understand." Francine put her hand on his, squeezing it. "I like you, Johnny. I like you a lot."

She let go of his hand. "His brother Clay came to see me a couple times. I suppose you heard about that?" Francine asked, studying his face.

"No." he said, though in truth he had heard a few comments along those lines earlier.

"Clay Stafford offered me money to leave his kid brother alone and go away. As if that would have done any good! I'd have gone away for free if I hadn't known Bliss would follow me wherever I went. I begged Clay to ride herd on Bliss and keep him out of my life. He couldn't stop him. Not even Vince Stafford himself could hold Bliss in line. At least here I knew that Damon would protect me."

"Bliss ain't gonna bother you no more, Francine."

"No. But his father and brothers will come for my scalp."

"They ain't gonna bother you. Not while I'm around . . . and I'll be around." Johnny's youthful face was set in hard lines, his eyes bright and cold. None could doubt that he meant business and when he was in that mood few would dare to balk him.

"Thanks, Johnny. You're sweet." Francine blinked back tears. Leaning forward, she rested her slim, long-fingered hands on his shoulders and kissed him on the cheek. Her long, white-blond hair brushed his face.

"I better go before I make a fool of myself by crying my head off." She rose from her chair and crossed to the staircase. Climbing to the second floor, she walked along the mezzanine and into her room, closing the door behind her.

Luke returned to the table. "What happened, hoss? Looked like you and that little gal was getting along nicely, then up she jumps and runs away."

"Who knows why women do what they do?" Johnny wondered. "At least she left the bourbon," he said, reaching for the bottle.

Mrs. Frye came out of the office to check on some item of business with Damon. Standing at his side, she laid an open ledger on the table before him, pointing out an entry about which she had some questions. While they were talking, a man came in through the front entrance.

He was Ace High Olcutt, a card dealer employed by the Golden Spur. He was thin faced, with wavy black hair slicked back and a pencil-thin mustache. He walked fast, a sheepish expression on his face.

"I thought we'd seen the last of you, Ace High," Mrs. Frye said, a cynical twist to her mouth.

"I got a week's wages owing," Olcutt said, avoiding her eyes, and Damon's.

"What's the hurry? Going somewhere?" She needled him, already knowing the answer.

"I'm clearing out," the dealer said.

Damon looked up, his expression calm and mild. He smiled gently. "Quitting us, Ace High?"

Olcutt squirmed, uncomfortable and awkward. "I'm a gambler, not a gunman."

Damon nodded. "The Golden Spur always pays in full, you know that. If you would be so good, Mrs. Frye?"

"I'll take care of it, Damon. Come in the office and we'll settle up, Ace High." Mrs. Frye turned, heading to the rear of the building.

"Thanks." Olcutt followed her into the office.

"Looks like Ace High is running out on us," Morrissey observed.

"He's a yellowbelly." Creed Teece spoke without rancor, as if commenting on a change in the weather.

"I thought he had more sand than that."

"Now you know better."

The business transacted quickly. Olcutt soon emerged from the office. He went upstairs to his room. A few minutes later he came out, carpetbag in hand, descending the staircase. He started toward the front.

"Paid in full?" Damon asked.

Olcutt halted. "Yes."

"That's fine."

Olcutt squirmed, shifting his weight from one foot to the other. "Well . . . I'll be on my way."

"Sorry to see you go," Damon said.

"You know how it is, boss. No hard feelings?"

"No hard feelings."

Mrs. Frye stood by the Wheel of Chance, an oversized numbered gaming wheel mounted vertically on a table stand. Her arm was bent at the elbow, one hand resting on the Wheel's rim. "You're a gambling man, Ace High. Care to make a sporting proposition? Stake your wages on a turn of the wheel? Red or black, double or nothing?"

Ace High looked like he was thinking about it for a few seconds before shaking his head. "No thanks, I'll pass."

"Too rich for your blood, eh? Looks like the house holds its edge after all," Mrs. Frye said.

Damon had already returned to his game of solitaire.

"Well—so long," Olcutt said lamely.

"Good luck," Damon said indifferently, his attention elsewhere.

Olcutt scuttled away toward the front entrance. Mrs. Frye gave the wheel a turn, setting it motion.

It made a loud clickety-clacking noise as it spun, causing Olcutt to flinch.

"Hah!" Mrs. Frye's mocking laughter was a harsh crow's caw.

Olcutt went out, not looking back.

Mrs. Frye crossed to Damon. "Can you beat that. Damon? After all you've done for him, pulling him out of the gutter and giving him a good job, and then the louse walks out on you!"

"I took a chance on him. Can't win them all."

"Burns me up anyway." She stood beside him, resting a hand on his shoulder, watching silently as his restless hands worked the cards.

"What about you, Mrs. Frye? Can't I persuade you to find a safer place, at least for now?"

"Nobody runs me out of the Golden Spur, Damon. Nobody! I worked too hard for my half of it. So let's have no more nonsense."

"As you will. I never argue with a lady."

"I'm no lady."

"I beg to differ."

"That's arguing."

Damon took her hand, raising it to his lips and kissing the back of it.

Outside was the sound of riders pulling up in front of the place. Not many, no more than a few. And not the Ramrod bunch. Monk on the roof would have given the alert. Still, everyone in the Golden

Spur looked up to see what it was about, things being what they were.

A delay of a half minute or so occurred while the newcomers tied up their horses at the hitching post. Boot heels clattered as they climbed the stairs, crossing the front porch to the entrance.

Inside, Mrs. Frye gripped the back of Damon's chair, her knuckles whitening.

The batwing doors swung open, admitting two men. One was tall and lean, with a long horse face, bright eyes, and buck teeth. Flint Ryan.

The other was square built, muscular, with long black hair and a thin mustache that came down on the sides of his mouth. He was Anglo with Mexican blood, maybe some Indian blood, too. He was Charley Bronco.

Tension eased in the Spur. The newcomers were friends.

"Sorry, gents, this is a private party," Mrs. Frye said.

"We know. We brung some party favors." Bronco patted twin-holstered guns.

"We rode in as soon as we heard the news. Afraid we'd be late for the fun," Flint said, "but it looks like we got here in time."

Damon rose, looking thoughtful, troubled. "I appreciate the sentiment, gentlemen, but I can't allow you to put yourselves in harm's way."

"Save your breath, Damon. You can't fancy-talk us out of this go-round. Hell, you're our favorite gambling man. Losing to you in a poker game is the next best thing to winning," Flint said.

"We got a right to be here. You can't turn us down, not with all the money we've lost at the tables," Charley Bronco said.

Damon shrugged in a gesture of hopelessness. Turning to Mrs. Frye, he said, "What can you do with men like this?"

"I know what I do, but you don't have the anatomy for it. Best say 'welcome aboard' and give them a drink," Mrs. Frye said.

Damon did exactly that. Handshaking and backslapping all around was followed by a round at the bar.

Flint exclaimed, "Free drinks, Bronco!"

"No wonder the man was trying to get rid of us," Bronco answered.

Morrissey poured, filling glasses for all including Damon and Mrs. Frye, and one for himself.

"We was down in Waco when you boys had that dustup with the Harbin gang. Sorry we missed it," Flint said to Johnny and Luke.

"This one has all the makings of a pretty good shooting match," Johnny volunteered.

"I'm looking forward to it."

Damon raised his glass, the others following. "A toast, gentlemen . . . and lady"—he nodded to Mrs. Fry—"confusion to the enemy!"

"That—and plenty of hot lead!" Luke chimed in.

They drank. His glass empty, Damon threw it in the

corner, shattering it. An instant later, Mrs. Frye did the same, followed by Morrissey and Creed Teece.

"What for did you do that?" Bronco asked.

"For luck," Mrs. Frye said.

"Busting the glasses?"

"Glasses we've got plenty of, cowboy."

Bronco and Flint exchanged glances. "Must be one of them fancy New Orleans ways," Bronco said, shrugging.

An outburst of breaking glass ensued as the rest of them hurled empty glasses against the wall.

A dawning light of comprehension showed in Bronco's eyes. "Now I know why he thunk that up. No glasses, we can't cadge no more free drinks."

"I told you—glasses we've got plenty of," Mrs. Frye said. "Set 'em up, barkeep! Hell, give 'em each their own bottle if they want it!"

"Now that's what I call being sociable!" Luke exclaimed.

"He'd storm Hell if you gave him a beer chaser," Johnny joked.

Upstairs, Monk stuck his head upside down through the trapdoor hatch, shouting, "They's coming! They's coming! The Staffords are riding into town!"

TWELVE

The Staffords and their Ramrod Ranch riders had come to Hangtown. They rode in from the south, going north on River Road between the town and Swift Creek. They rode in a column, twenty-one men in all.

The point man rode alone. Vince Stafford. Patriarch and boss, he was proud, profane, upright, and unbowed. White-haired, gray-bearded, and thick-bodied, he was mean faced and scowling, and not necessarily because of his son Bliss's death. It was how he looked most of the time. He wore a gun belt on his right hip and had a repeating rifle tucked into a saddle scabbard.

Behind him, riding side by side yet as far apart as possible, were the two surviving Stafford sons, adults both, Clay and Quentin.

Quentin—Quent—the firstborn, was hulking and brutish. As firstborn he should have been in line to be Vince's inheritor. But Nature and the patriarch had long since determined the line of succession should skip the eldest and fall on second-born Clay. That, and Clay's own cunning, ruthlessness, and quick gun.

Quent resented the situation, but not enough to do something about it. The last time he dared to try, Clay pistol-whipped him into a whimpering heap. Known as "the Ramrod's ramrod," Clay was the one Vince called on to see that the dirty work got done and done right.

Bliss had been the youngest, the "baby of the family." He was Vince Stafford's first dead son, a dubious distinction his father meant to capitalize on during the foray into Hangtown.

Behind the Staffords, the Ramrod riders came on in threes, their precedence in the column determined by the pecking order of their gun skills.

In the first nonfamily rank were Dan Oxblood, Ted Claiborne, and Kev Huddy.

Oxblood was the only outsider, a gun for hire who'd been brought on for this venture. Thick, glossy brick-red hair was combed straight back from his forehead. He had green eyes, wore a black hat and garments, and a left-handed gun. He rode a handsome white stallion.

Claiborne and Huddy were Ramrod regulars, though they were kept on the payroll for their skill as gun hands, not ranch hands. Claiborne, thirty, was heavyset, deliberate, slow-talking and easy-walking—quick with a gun. Huddy, in his early twenties, was skinny with a sharp nose, thick lips, and long, lank dirty-blond hair.

In the next rank came Kaw, Dimaree, and Marblay. Good guns all, dependable and nervy. They lay somewhere on the cusp between working cowboys and gunmen. They could break a horse, ride herd, rope and brand a dogie with the best of them, their gun handling skills better than most.

The same could be said of Duncan, Lord, and Carney, next in line. Top hands and good men in a fight.

The rest of the bunch were ranch hands first, but any cowboy worth his feed must count a six-gun as one of his working tools and be able to use it quickly and accurately. They were all of that, and had less compunction than most when called on by the boss to kill a man.

Most of the Ramrod outfit had come along. Only a handful remained at the ranch to keep an eye on herd and property.

The group rode steadily at a measured pace. There was something formal and ominous, sinister even, about their deliberate gait. It had a funereal pace. They passed the grounds where the wagon train had been encamped, then Mextown.

Vince Stafford slowed still more, reining in at Hangtree Trail running east-west at right angles to River Road. Once in town, the trail became Trail Street, keeping that name until exiting on the west side between the church and Boot Hill, then resuming once more as Hangtree Trail.

Aware, attentive to his father's actions, Clay Stafford raised an arm, signaling the others behind him to halt. The riders slowed to a stop, bunching up.

Vince said, "Dress 'em up, Clay. The Staffords are coming to town. Let's show 'em something!"

Clay rose in the saddle, turning toward the rear. Cupping hand to mouth, he shouted, "Look sharp, men! Dress up those lines! Keep a length between each rank. Move!"

A lot of shuffling, backing and moving around agitated the column in response to Clay's command.

"Me too, Clay?" Dan Oxblood drawled, his tone light, but on the right side of insolence—barely.

"For a specialist like you, the rules don't apply. But I'd think the great Dan Oxblood would just naturally want to show some pride of place," Clay said, showing his habitual sneer.

"Show that in everything I do," Oxblood said genially.

"For what you're being paid, you should."

Kev Huddy snickered. Ted Claiborne looked faintly disapproving. Oxblood brought his horse in line with the other two in his rank.

Vince Stafford said, "Tell the boys, Clay."

"You know what the boss said! Nobody makes a play until he gives the word!" Clay shouted.

"I'll shoot the first man who slaps leather without

my say-so," Vince rumbled, loud enough to be heard at the end of the column.

Turning his horse's head to the left, Vince made a left-hand turn onto Hangtree Trail, going west. He was about twenty yards outside the town proper. Rank by rank, the column followed. The patriarch set the pace at a slow walk,

Shouts from somewhere in town testified that the Staffords' arrival had not gone unnoticed. People began clearing off the street fast.

Ahead lay the jail and courthouse. The building housed a trial room on the first floor; on the second floor were the various offices of mayor, notary, and town council. The administrative center of the county seat, it archived county records, trial documents, land titles, certificates of birth, death, marriage and the like. Open Saturdays for a half-day's business, it was now closed. Across from its front lay a small plaza, a square of grass and some shade trees with a couple benches beneath.

A slanted wooden awning protruded from the north face of the top of the jail. Leaning against the middle support post was Deputy Smalls. Seeing riders at the edge of town, he turned and went into the jail.

Shoulder-high plank board partitions walled off the building into two halves, a gap in the middle of the wall allowing access to both sections. The front half held the sheriff's office; the rear held four narrow cells, two each on either side of the center aisle. Three cells were empty. The fourth was occupied by a drunk who lay on his side on a wooden pallet facing the wall, snoring and occasionally crying out in a fitful sleep.

Up front, on the east side of the space, stood a dark, wooden desk with a swivel chair behind it, the sheriff's desk. It faced the front door. In the two corners on that side were cabinets with drawers for holding records. Most of the drawers were empty; Mack Barton wasn't big on doing paperwork, and his deputy was barely literate. Sometimes Smalls kept a bag lunch in one of the drawers.

Between the cabinets was a wall-mounted, glass-fronted gun locker lined with rifles and shotguns. Much of the rest of the wall was papered with an assortment of Wanted posters, some current, others years out of date. Standing well out in front of the desk was a brass cuspidor. The sheriff didn't chaw, he smoked, but plenty of upright, taxpaying citizens did chaw and it was there to accommodate them. A square-topped wooden table with two chairs edged the front wall.

Behind the desk sat the sheriff, smoking a cigar and reading a six-month-old copy of the *Police Gazette*.

He looked up as Smalls rushed in, leaving the door open.

"They're here," Smalls said, excited but trying not to show it. Barton didn't like it when his deputy got excited. He thought it was unprofessional.

Barton didn't need to ask who. He just said, "How many?"

"About twenty."

"Where?"

"Coming in from River Road. Coming slow, but coming."

Putting down his magazine and wedging the cigar in the corner of his mouth, Barton gripped the edge of his desk with big, meaty hands that had beaten many a malefactor and detainee senseless. With a great grunt he hauled himself upright, standing on two legs.

"Lord! How I hate to get up out of my chair!" he said feelingly. His eyes glinted, a danger sign to those who disturbed the peace—his peace.

Smalls crossed to an opposite corner, reaching for a shotgun he'd left standing there earlier.

"The cells are empty except for that one drunk. Let him go and send him on his way," Barton said.

"Without paying no fine?" Smalls said, goggling.

"He's got no money to pay. You ought to know, you turned out his pockets."

Smalls didn't deny it; Barton had been watching at the time. "Let him serve on the work gang."

"To hell with it. I got bigger fish to fry. The county can fill out its quota with somebody else."

"Mr. Hutto ain't gonna like that."

"Who's gonna tell him? You?"

Smalls contrived to look shocked and indignant at the same time. "You know me better than that, Mack! I know how to keep my mouth shut."

"All right, I didn't ask for a testimonial. Shake a leg and shoo the rumpot out of the cell."

"I checked on him a little while ago. He's dead drunk!"

"Drag him out back and leave him in the alley," Barton said. Before the other could comply, the sheriff thought better of it. "No. It don't look good to have a drunk sleeping it off behind the jail. Let him be where he is, it's his lookout. Hell, whatever happens he'll probably sleep through the whole thing."

"Okay, Mack."

"Let's get to it, then." They went out, Barton locking the front door behind him. "If we both get killed, the poor guy 'll probably starve to death in there." The thought tickled him and he chuckled.

He looked east on Trail Street and saw the Ramrod riders coming in. "Head over to the Cattleman and spread the word. You know what to do."

"Let me go with you, Mack," Smalls urged. "I'll cover your back."

"No sense both of us getting killed," Barton said The deputy's face fell. "Think it'll be that bad?"

"Naw. If I did, I'd send you and I'd go to the Cattleman."

Smalls looked at him uncomprehendingly.

"That's a joke, jackass," Barton snapped.

"Oh."

"I don't want to provoke Stafford any more than I have to—which is what the sight of you and that shotgun would do."

"Shoot, there ain't no getting on his good side, no matter what you do."

Barton was plesantly surprised by this glimmer of wit. "You're catching on, Deputy. There may be hope for you yet."

"I'd like to go along, though."

"Forget it. You just make sure Hutto does what he's supposed to."

Smalls looked doubtful. "Mr. Hutto ain't much on listening to other folks."

"He will when you tell him he won't have much of a town left if he don't play things like we planned. You tell him I said that. Get going, Deputy."

"Watch yourself, Mack."

"You picked a fine time to get sentimental!"

"Hell, you're the only one who ever trusted me—or hired me—to do a job . . . that wasn't kin."

"Do it, then. And remember, Smalls, I aim to be sheriff here for a long time. Now, git!"

"Yes, sir!" Smalls hurried west on Trail Street.

Barton stepped out from under the shade of the awning, into the sunlit street. He turned, facing east. Glancing down at his chest, he noticed that the tin star pinned over his left breast was filmed by dust. He swiped it with the sleeve of his right forearm, shining it up.

Taking a last puff on his cigar, he tossed it away and started down the middle of the street toward Vince Stafford.

Barton stood just past the courthouse with hands hanging easy and open at his sides. His expression, usually dour and harbitten, was more so. His narrow eyes shone like mica chips glinting in a rock face.

The column of riders came on, spearheaded by Vince mounted on a big brown horse, a charger, a Morgan type quarter horse.

The sheriff's gaze followed the line of riders behind the elder Stafford. Waspish Clay and dumb, mean Quent rode right behind their pa. Quent was big, oversized. Clay with the quick gun was the dangerous one, fast and smart. Too bad he couldn't talk some sense into Vince but then, nobody could.

Barton looked at Dan Oxblood behind the brothers. Gunfighter, outlaw, he'd somehow wrangled himself a full pardon from Yankee Captain Harrison at Fort Pardee for services rendered in taking down the Harbin gang. He was a fast draw, maybe the fastest one riding into town. Dangerous, he could like you and still kill. He'd regret it, but he'd do what had to be done—or not. The redhead was a creature of whims, unpredictable. No telling which way he'd jump.

Ted Claiborne and Kev Huddy were well-respected triggermen. Barton had never seen either of them at work, but he'd cleaned up after Claiborne in a shoot-out outside the Alamo Bar that left one foe dead and two others wounded.

The sheriff knew some of the others, too. They were a bad bunch to mess with.

Vince Stafford halted little more than a man's length away from Barton. The others followed their paymaster's lead, pulling up and reining in. Vince glared down at the sheriff. "You bucking me, lawman?"

Barton shook his head. "Thought you'd like to see the boy first."

"My boy Bliss . . ." Something like pain flickered across the part of Vince's face not hidden by a bushy, snow-white beard—hard bright eyes nesting in wrinkled pouches, flat squashed nose, and wide belligerent mouth. A spasm of intense emotion, powerfully held in cheek, was quickly stifled.

Barton indicated the courthouse with a tilt of his head. "He's in there."

"Show me," Vince demanded.

"Sheriff's trying to stall you, Pa," Quent said, pronouncing it "shurf." "You ain't gonna fall for that one, are you? The gambler—"

"He'll keep," Vince said curtly.

"He'll run, if he ain't long gone already."

"Damon won't run." Clay sighed, weary of Quent's stupidity, yet mocking it, too.

"What makes you so sure?" Quent asked.

"I've got eyes in my head and a brain behind them. I know people."

"Shut up, boys," Vince said. He turned to Barton. "The gambler?"

"At the Golden Spur. He ain't running, though I wish to hell he would."

"You a friend of his?"

"No, I want him out of town where he'll be somebody else's problem."

"Sensible enough, I suppose. Don't worry about it. He's my problem and I'll fix it," Vince said. "Take me to the boy."

Barton walked toward the courthouse front. Vince turned his horse and followed. Clay cut his horse out of the line, starting after them. Barton paused at the foot of the courthouse steps as Vince reined in, stepping down heavily from the saddle, joints creaking. He tied up his horse at the hitching rail.

Clay halted his horse, Vince squinting fiercely up at him. "Where you going, boy?"

"He was my brother," Clay answered.

"Oh? Where was you when Bliss got killed?"

"The same place as you, Pa. At the ranch."

"You should've been with him to keep him out of trouble."

"Nobody could keep Bliss out of trouble, Pa. You know that."

"You should've been there anyhow."

"I could run the ranch for you or I could nursemaid the kid, but not both. Each is a full-time job."

"So you chose not to be your brother's keeper. Well, what's done is done."

"Pa—"

"Stay here. Keep an eye on our men and on your dumbass brother."

"Minding Quent's a full-time job, too."

"Son, you are purely minded to argue with me and this is the wrong day for it," Vince said, his voice thick with rising fury held down with difficulty.

"Okay, Pa. Like you said." Clay turned his horse to rejoin the others.

Vince called after him. "Remember, they move on my say-so, not before."

"Sure, Pa."

Vince and Barton went up the stone steps of the courthouse to the double doors under the archway. Politely, Barton held a door open, but Vince brushed past him, opening the other door and stepping inside.

It was cooler out of the sunlight in the entrance hall. The building's lone occupant, a wraithlike figure at the far end of the hall, stopped pushing a broom and leaned on it, watching the two men approach, their footfalls echoing in the hushed space. A pace or two in the lead, Barton led the way to the closed door of a storeroom behind the staircase on the left of the hall.

The sweeper bobbed his head respectfully, mumbling some unintelligible greeting to the newcomers as they walked past. He was old, reedy, bone-thin, a living, rheumy-eyed mummy.

Yet Barton knew the sweeper was no older than Vince, possibly a few years younger. Stafford was a monster of vitality, an unnaturally energetic oldster by virtue of his domineering will.

The storeroom door was unlocked. Barton

opened it, and he and Vince went inside. A slanted ceiling followed the contours of the stairway under which it lay. A window was set in the west wall, butter-yellow sunlight shining through it. It had been left wide open to air the room out.

The walls were lined with bookcases whose shelves sagged with old ledgers and record books—county archives. There were stacks of tables and chairs, mostly broken; some stepladders, buckets of paint, and stained, rolled drop cloths.

A long table occupied the center of the floor. A manlike shape lay on top of it, lengthwise, covered with a sheet. The head lay at the end of the table nearest the window. A pair of booted feet protruded beyond the bottom of the sheet, toes-up.

Not a sound escaped Vince Stafford save for slow, heavy breathing.

Barton went out of the room to give him some privacy, not that Stafford had requested any. He closed the door behind him and walked to the open window at the end of the hall. Glad of the fresh air, he filled his lungs with it and looked out. He was sweating.

In the storeroom, Vince stood at the table's head, reaching for the sheet. His clawlike hand was steady as he turned the sheet down, uncovering the figure to its shoulders.

Bliss Stafford lay faceup, a rolled towel under the back of his head propping it up. He was dead only a few hours but already something stiff and waxy had crept into his face. His eyes were closed. The blood had been wiped clean from where it had spilled down the corners of his mouth, chin, and neck, but his shirt collar and front were stained with it.

Vince studied him. A long, unruly forelock curled down over his son's forehead, the tip of it hanging down into his eye. Vince brushed it back out of the way, smoothing it in place with the rest of the hairs on Bliss's head. A beat later, it came undone, once more falling over an eye.

The corners of Vince's lips quirked upward in what might have been the ghost of a smile, one as quickly laid as raised. His face resumed its stony stolidity, mouth clamped down in a tight line.

Looking out the window, a flash of motion caught the sheriff's eye just as he heard the doorknob on the storeroom door turn. Down near the Cattleman Hotel, several figures dashed from one side of the street to the other, seemingly to no purpose. He cursed under his breath.

He turned as Stafford stepped out in the hall. Vince's eyes were dry, his face cold. "I'll take care of things. Have him moved."

Barton nodded.

"I'm done here," Stafford said, starting toward the front of the building.

Barton followed, passing the sweeper. "Leave the front door unlocked, Jess. Some of Mr. Stafford's men'll be along directly for the body. Stay here till they come, then lock up and go home."

"Yessir, Sherrif Mack."

Vince and Barton went out. Small birds fluttered in the boughs of a shade tree on the small plaza's square plot of grass. The Ramrod bunch hadn't moved.

Clay was guarded, watchful. Quent stared off into space, mouth hanging half open, his thoughts, such as they were, far away.

Vince went to his horse, resting both hands on the saddle horn before hoisting himself up into place. The horse sagged noticeably under his weight. He walked the animal to the head of the column of riders.

Barton moved along the column slowly, the mass of mounted men looming up like a wall on one side of him. His face was leaden, his tread light. The next few moments would be critical.

"Clay, send a couple of the boys to fetch Joe Delagoa. He'll get the body ready for burial," Vince said.

Clay turned his horse, looking down the line toward the men who were more ranch hands than gun hands. "Farrell, Ritchie! Go fetch Joe Delagoa."

The two exchanged blank glances. "Who's he?" Farrell asked.

"The old Portugee carpenter, down to the lumberyard. Have him bring a wagon for Bliss. And, uh, be polite," Clay added as an afterthought.

"Gotcha, Clay," Farrell said. He and Ritchie peeled off, riding south down a side street.

Vince motioned Clay to him. They put their heads together. Vince was doing the talking, giving Clay some instructions. He spoke too low for Barton to make out the words.

Sitting up high on his white horse, Oxblood was rolling a cigarette. He opened the drawstring mouth of a tobacco pouch.

Barton ambled over to him. "When did you start riding for the Ramrod, Red?" The sheriff's tone was matter of fact, conversational.

"Since this afternoon, Sheriff," Oxblood said, a white-toothed grin splitting his wide, ruddy face.

"Selling your gun again, eh?"

"Just renting it."

"Can't stay away from the life, can you? You did a good job for the folks around here a little while back when you turned against Harbin and helped clean up the gang. You got pardoned so you could make a fresh start."

"That I did. But I like to keep my hand in, from time to time."

Pushing back his hat, Barton used his sleeve to mop a sweat-damp forehead. "This don't hardly seem like your kind of job, if you don't mind my saying."

"You'd speak up whether I minded or not. That's what I like about you, Mack," Oxblood said.

"I thought you liked Damon."

"I do. Everybody does . . . present company ex-cepted." Oxblood cut a side glance to indicate the

Staffords. "I ain't going against Damon. I'm here to balance the wheel in case Creed Teece steps into the play."

"That's what Damon pays him for."

"So now Vince is paying me."

"Teece is fast."

Holding a cigarette paper creased down the middle in one hand, Oxblood poured a small mound of tobacco into it from the pouch. Holding the drawstring between his teeth, he pulled the pouch closed, dropping it into his breast pocket. "Always wondered which of us is faster. What do you think, Mack?"

"I wouldn't know," the sheriff said.

"Maybe soon we'll all find out. If Teece steps in, I step in. Else, I'll just sit tight and watch the fireworks. I'd advise you to do the same."

"I ain't taking sides."

"If you ain't with Vince, you're agin' him. That's how he sees it."

"I'm for Hangtown."

"But is Hangtown for you? Good luck." Oxblood smoothed out the tobacco in the paper and started rolling it up, evening it out with his fingertips. He raised it to his mouth to lick the ends of the paper to stick it in down in place.

"Seeing as how you're giving out advice, Red, I'll do the same. A couple friends of yours are siding with Damon," Barton said.

"Who?"

"Johnny Cross and his one-legged pard."

Oxblood's face remained unchanged, but the

hand-rolled cigarette crumbled, coming apart in his hands. "Dang! What for are they horning in?"

Barton shrugged meaty shoulders. "Who knows why that Cross kid does anything? You tell me."

"He's a wild one. Hellacious. As for the gimp, he goes where Johnny goes, simple as that."

"They're siding Damon. So're a couple other fellows. Flint Ryan and Charley Bronco."

"Bronco I know, not t'other one."

Barton flashed a tight, nasty grin. "Maybe more fireworks than you expected, huh?"

"Anyone ever tell you you look real mean when you smile, Sheriff?"

"Yeah."

"I don't go up against friends," Oxblood said with an air of nonchalance. "As for the others, the only one I'm being paid to tackle is Teece. Him I don't like him, not even a little bit."

"Just letting you know the lay of the land," Barton said.

"And I appreciate it." Oxblood nodded.

Vince finished talking to Clay and glanced at Oxblood, annoyed. Ever alert to Vince's moods, Clay said, "What're you doing, Red? Telling the sheriff your life story?"

"Just jawing," Oxblood answered. "Man's a friend of mine."

"You ain't being paid for talking, gunfighter," Clay pointed out.

"I do it for free, seeing as how I'm naturally a sociable type fellow."

"We're through talking," Vince Stafford hissed.

"Fine," Oxblood said.

Barton circled around to the front of the column, casual-like, standing in the middle of the street facing them.

"That's the second time you've gotten between me and the town," Vince said, scowling.

"That's what they pay me for," Barton stated. "I want to make sure we're straight on a few things, Vince."

Clay rubbed his chin with the back of his hand. Quent lost the dreamy-eyed look, becoming aware of his surroundings for the first time in a while. His small round eyes widened, then narrowed. Behind the Staffords, a couple horses pawed the dirt with front hooves.

Sensing resistance, Vince Stafford didn't like it. "Straighten this out for me. Where were you when Bliss got kilt?"

"It was all over when I got there," Barton said.

"My boy was shot down like a dog in the streets of your town."

"He wasn't no boy. He was a man carrying a gun, and he knew how to use it."

"The gambler who shot Bliss, he in jail?"

"No."

"Why not?"

"Bliss was pushing it. Damon wanted to walk

away, but Bliss drew first. You can't jail a man for defending himself. That's the law."

"I don't rightly care for your kind of law. I follow a higher law. 'Blood shall have blood,' like the Good Book says. An eye for an eye." Vince spat.

"You didn't bring your whole outfit to town to take Bliss back home. What do you figure on doing?" the sheriff asked.

Vince reached down to one side of the saddle.

Barton almost slapped leather and drew until he realized the man was reaching for a looped circle of hempen rope. The coiled lariat was fixed to a saddle ring.

"I'm gonna hang the man who kilt my boy," Vince cried, brandishing the rope, shaking its looped length in the air. "But don't get yourself in an uproar, Sheriff. I'm gonna do everything right and proper, the good old-fashioned Hangtown way. I'm gonna slip the noose around the gambler's neck by myself and stretch him from a limb of the ol' Hanging Tree." Vince's voice quivered with malice, reveling in it.

Spewing little flecks of spittle, he went on. "That ain't all I'm gonna do. I'm gonna fix the whore what led my boy astray, too—cut her face up good and proper so that after this day no man's ever gonna be able to look at her again without puking!"

Clay started. "That's crazy talk, Pa! The girl had nothing to do with it!"

Vince turned on him. "How do you know? Was you there? Hell, no! So just keep your trap shut."

"I know Bliss, the way he was around women. Everybody knows! He saw a pretty girl he just had to have her, come hell or high water. If it wasn't this one, it would have been another," Clay quipped.

"But it was this one," Vince pressed. "What's her name? Francine? Sure, that's it. Francine. He talked about her enough, back at the ranch. Francine! She's the gambler's whore and because of her Bliss is dead and she's got to pay! They both do, and they will."

Clay's face reddened, teeth bared in a half snarl. "I didn't come out here to fight women, I came to get my brother's killer and—"

"You came because I told you! And you'll do like I tell you! And that's the end of it," Vince hollered, "unless you feel like bucking me, boy. Do you?"

After a pause, Clay made a visible effort to control himself. "You're the boss, Pa."

"Damned right, and don't you forget it."

Quent snickered. "Never learn, do you, Clay? There's no going agin' Pa once he's got his mind set—"

"Shut up, Quent. I take it from Pa, but I don't have to take it from you."

"Both of you shut up." Still holding the coiled lariat, Vince rested one hand on top of the saddle horn, put the other hand on it and leaned forward, glaring down at Barton, impassive and unmoved. "Now what do think of that, lawman?"

"I think Clay's talking sense and you ought to listen to him," Barton said. "Bracing Damon is one thing, but hurting a woman, cutting her, that's another. That's awful raw, even for Hangtown. Folks in these parts don't cotton to a man putting a bad hurt on a woman."

"Respectable women, not whores."

"Whores, too. There ain't so many of them around here that we can afford to lose one, especially not a pretty one."

That got a couple chuckles from the men, mostly the top guns who didn't give a damn and the riders too far in the back for Vince to know it was them laughing.

Vince got more irritated. "I showed my hand. Now it's time for you to lay your cards faceup on the table, Sheriff. What's your call? You plan on bucking me?"

"I didn't get this badge for being dumb," Barton began.

Some of the tension left Clay's face. Dan Oxblood smiled knowingly. Some of the men nodded their heads.

"I'm hired to protect Hangtree. I ain't so much of a fool as to risk the town getting tore up and innocent folks hurt and maybe killed to save Damon Bolt's neck. 'Sides, Damon's pretty good at taking care of himself . . . and he's got some friends with him."

"That's our lookout," Clay said.

"The gambler and the whore, I want 'em both," Vince said. "And I'll have 'em."

Clay frowned. "Damn it, Pa, he's going along! You don't got to rub his face in it."

"He's got to go along all the way."

"There's a condition," Barton drawled.

"I don't hold with conditions," Vince said.

"You want to fight a private war with the Golden Spur, that's your business. I may not like it, but I have to take it. But it's strictly between your crowd and his. Keep it private and the rest of the folks safely out of it."

"Nobody'll get hurt unless they get between me and what I'm after. If they do, God help 'em because I surely won't." Vince looked skyward, as if calling on the Lord to witness the truth of his words.

"Don't let things get out of hand, Vince."

"Suppose they do? Who's gonna stop me, you?"

"That's right." Barton nodded.

After a pause Oxblood laughed without mirth, breaking the deathly silence. "Whew! You do speak right up, don't you, Mack?"

The Ramrod riders flashed dark looks and muttered harsh words.

"Easy, men," Clay cautioned.

Vince gawked in disbelief. "I must've heard wrong."

"You heard right," Barton advised. "Listen up,

Stafford, and that goes for the rest of you, in case any of y'all are hard of hearing."

Quent swelled up, stung. "That's Mister Stafford to you—"

"Shut the hell up. Now get this. No man buffaloes Hangtree, no matter how big he thinks he is or how many guns he's got riding for him. It's been tried before and it never took and it ain't gonna take now."

"Big talk for one man," Vince said, sneering.

"I ain't alone." Barton turned, angling his body so he faced Vince and West Trail Street, careful not to turn his back on the Staffords. The rest of the bunch wouldn't make a play unless and until one of the family got the ball rolling first, he figured.

Raising his left arm slowly and deliberately, so as to not spook anybody into shooting, Barton waved a hand in the air. Armed men poured into the street from the front and side doors of the Cattleman Hotel and the Alamo Bar across from it.

"Don't nobody get trigger-happy, gents. You don't want to spoil your fun," Barton said.

Figures armed with rifles, shotguns, and handguns massed in the center of the street, filling it. A crowd of thirty or forty men stood facing the Ramrod riders. The hard-core center of them were Dog Star toughs, paired with hard-bitten ranchers and cold-faced townmen. Together, they made up the Hangtown militia.

"What's this? What do you think you're pulling?" Vince Stafford blustered.

"Hangtree got through the war without being sacked and burned by Yankees, deserters, or outlaws, and we aim to keep it that way. Them folks over there ain't minded to stand by and let the town go to Hades just because you or anyone else wants to run roughshod over it," Barton said.

"Seems to me you made a slight mistake in your calculations, Sheriff," Clay said, keeping his voice level. "Them fighting shopkeepers and store clerks and whatnot of yours—real bad hombres, I'm sure—they're down there. But you're here, all alone with us."

"I'll take my chances," Barton said, unimpressed.

"You're taking them, by God!" Vince cried.

Barton had been unsure whether the likes of Wade Hutto and Squint McCray could marshal their respective factions and get them in the street when the time came. That was the chancy part. Now that the confrontation had come to a head he felt cool, ready. "Them bad hombres you're making small of have homes and businesses to protect against looting and burning. Most of them were in the war and they can take care of themselves if they have to. See that they don't have to.

"Go fight your fight with Damon. That's your business. It's the Ramrod against the Spur and that's where it better stay. If it gets out of bounds, slops over where it can foul our nests—we'll make it our business. Savvy?"

Quent's open hand hovered over the butt of his holstered gun. "Almighty sure of yourself, ain't you?"

Barton eyed him, fixing him with a cold stare. "Just as sure as I am that you ain't gonna pull that gun, you overgrowed sack of horse droppings."

"Why, you dirty—"

"Don't try him, Quent," Clay said quickly.

"Back off, boy!" Vince yelled.

Quent held the pose for a beat, then slowly lowered his hand to his side, well clear of the gun.

"What I thought," Barton said, sneering.

"Don't crowd your luck," Vince cautioned. "Don't crowd us."

"You'll have your hands full with Damon and his pals. You're too smart to go against him and the town both," Barton said. "And don't forget about the Yanks at Fort Pardee. Give them an excuse to hunt you down and they'll clean up on the whole bunch of you and confiscate your herd and ranch for their troubles."

A voice from one of the militia men in the street called, "You okay, Sheriff?"

"Yeah!" Barton replied, not taking his eyes off the Ramrod riders. "I'm gonna walk out of here now and tell the folks you know the facts of life and will abide by them."

"I ain't forgetting this," Vince said feelingly.

"I can stand it," Barton retorted.

"Git and be damned. Keep out of my fight and you won't have any of ours."

"Done." The sheriff gave them all one last hard look. "Wonder how many of you will be alive by this time tomorrow?"

Barton turned and started walking, moving at a steady pace. It was so quiet he could hear the grit of street dirt scuffling against his leather boot soles. He fought to keep his shoulders and back muscles loose and untensed, but it was hard. He was half expecting bullets to come tearing into him any second.

He kept on walking, eyes front, not looking back. Drawing abreast of the Golden Spur, he cut a side-glance at it.

Johnny Cross stood framed in the doorway, arms folded on top of one of the hinged batwing doors. He rested his chin on his arms, yellow cat eyes unblinking, smiling lazily at the sheriff as he walked past.

Nearing the militiamen, a wall of vague oval faces began resolving into recognizable faces: town boss Wade Hutto, his top gun Boone Lassitter, Hutto's brother-in-law Russ Lockhart, Deputy Smalls, Squint McCray and a couple of his cousins, Karl from the gunstore, others.

Hutto moved forward to meet him. "How'd it go, Sheriff?"

"Vince listened to reason," Barton said, glad to note his voice held steady, without a quaver.

"That's great! Good work, Mack," Hutto enthused.

"The Ramrod bunch'll toe the line, but we still need to keep our guns loaded and ready to smash them down at the first sign of trouble—which could be soon—anytime."

"Whew! I don't mind telling you, that was a real nail-biter."

"You should've seen it from my end."

Trouble came sooner than Barton expected. It came without warning out of the west, in a mass of rushing horses, gunfire and war whoops—all accompanied by the ringing of church bells.

THIRTEEN

It was mid-afternoon when Sam Heller and Lydia Fisher reached Rancho Grande. One of the biggest spreads in the county, in all north central Texas for that matter, the ranch was bordered on the north by Old Mission Road and the south by the upper fork of the Liberty River.

Before getting too deep into Grande land, Sam and Lydia were intercepted by a band of vaqueros who patrolled the lush grasslands to deter trespassers, rustlers, and marauders. Ranch master Don Eduardo Castillo had no love for intruders on his private domain, especially Anglos, all of whom he lumped under the label "Texans" and whom he resented for what he felt was their steady encroachment on his land.

The outriders closed in. Mexican-Americans, they were hard men with grim, unfriendly faces under broad-brimmed sombreros and weapons—guns and rifles—held at the ready.

"I heard the Grande riders shoot white folks on sight," Lydia said.

"Not true," Sam answered. "Just pesky yellow-haired gals with braids," he added dryly.

Lydia looked unsure as to whether or not he was joking.

Sam was no stranger to the ranch, thanks to previous involvements with the Castillo clan. He was recognized by the jefe, boss of the vaquero band. Sam spoke a few sentences to him in rough, broken Spanish, a language he was learning but still a long way from mastering. He got his message across, though, especially the dreaded word *Comanche.*

Of no less dread import was the name *Mano Rojo*—Red Hand.

The jefe's face stiffened, his dark-eyed gaze hardening. Some of the vaqueros muttered curses. All checked their weapons and peered into the distance in search of war parties.

Mexicans and Comanches had been mortal enemies for more than three hundred years, since the first armor-shelled conquistadors ventured north from Mexico City across the Rio Grande. The rancho had battled for survival against the Comanches for over a century.

The jefe issued a series of rapid-fire comands to his men, who leaped into action. One wheeled his mount, spurring it southward at top speed toward the rancho, hidden from view by some low ridges. He raced all out to give warning.

Two more vaqueros peeled off from the group,

pointing their horses in opposite directions, one going east, the other going west, galloping away to spread the alert to other working parties tending the herds on the grazing lands.

The jefe and those remaining escorted Sam and Lydia to the ranch. Twenty minutes of hard riding brought them in sight of the main settlement.

Here was the core, the inner citadel of Rancho Grande. A sizeable tract of land was enclosed by thick adobe walls ten feet tall. The walls were pocked and cratered by rounds fired in numerous battles, some old, others of more recent vintage.

The main gate faced south. A set of stout, iron-bound dark wooden double doors stood open, allowing a view within. Square-faced columns topped by an adobe arch bracketed the entrance. A bronze bell hung from a black iron chain in the center of the archway. A dirt road stretched across the flat fronting the portal.

Sam, Lydia, and their vaquero escort rode in under the arch, through the gate, and into a wide courtyard. Stung by the advance rider's warning, the ranchero was abuzz with activity, swift and purposeful.

Within high, curved adobe walls, parapets accessed by stairways served as shooting platforms. Sentries on the walls scanned the horizon for sign of hostiles; none had yet appeared. Two-man teams toted crates of rifle ammunition, each man gripping a rope handle attached to a short end of the case. Laboring under the heavy load, they lugged the crates up the stairs onto the ramparts, broke open the lids with rifle butts, and began handing out boxes of cartridges. Riders rushed in and out of the main gate, going here and there on various vital errands.

The dirt-floored outer courtyard gave way to the stone-paved inner courtyard of a plaza. At its center was a wide, shallow adobe water basin and fountain, fed by a well. Bordering the plaza were outbuildings: stables, a tool and equipment shed, and storehouses filled with supplies of corn and sides of dried, smoked meat.

Beyond the fountain rose the main building, a three-story structure. An imposing edifice that fronted south, its slanted roof was shingled with orange ceramic tiles. Across the whitewashed adobe and stucco front black ironwork grilles hung on the windows. Ornate rails and balustrades covered the second floor balcony. Lush, extensive gardens and arcades lay on the west side of the building.

The jefe escorted Sam and Lydia into the inner courtyard. Nodding to Sam and raising a hand in curt salutation, the grim-faced chief turned, riding across the space and out the gate.

Sam and Lydia dismounted, holding their horses' reins. They were met by Hector Vasquez, the segundo, the foreman of the ranch.

He was topped by an outrageously oversized, broad-brimmed sombrero. Its tall crown narrowed to a curved peak, looking like an inverted horn of plenty. Spilling from under it was plenty of hombre, a bearish, barrel-chested, big-bellied man. A pear-shaped face was framed by masses of shaggy, salt-and-pepper hair. Dark black eyes looked out from a bronzed visage whose cheekbones and cheeks were pitted by remnants of long-ago small-pox scars.

He wore a black bolero jacket with silver trim and frogging, a white embroidered shirt whose front was strained by a massive swelling belly, black bell-bottom pants, and silver-spurred leather boots. Worn low under his big gut was a pair of six-guns in soft leather buscadero holsters.

"He looks like a bandit," Lydia whispered.

"He was, once," Sam said. "Don't worry, he's perfectly respectable now. Probably hasn't killed anybody this week."

Lydia looked at him out of the corners of her eyes.

"I'm joking."

Actually, there was no knowing if Vasquez had killed anybody lately or not. He'd obey cheerfully and with a will if ordered to do so by his patron, ranch master Don Eduardo.

Shiny sunburst rowels as big as silver dollars sparkled at the ends of his spurs as Vasquez made his way to them, raising a hand in greeting. "Trouble always follows you, gringo. What misery do you bring now?"

"Nothing a man like you can't handle, large one," Sam said.

"True. But I like to know who I'm shooting at."

"Comanches, mucho Comanches."

"So you say. Senor Diego says maybe you got scared by a few *los bravos Indios,* that's all."

Sam looked around at the bustling courtyard. Brawny, heavyset women in white blouses and colorful skirts filled ollas—water jugs—at the basin and carried them inside the hacienda. Gangly boys in baggy white shirts and pants and woven sandals, bent double under the weight of massive bundles of firewood and stowed them away in the outbuildings. Riders came and went, stable hands saddling and unsaddling horses.

Indicating the urgent movement going on around them, Sam said, "They seem to be taking it seriously enough. And you?"

"I think maybe there is going to be a fight," Vasquez said, grinning toothily. A fight was okay with him.

"Good thinking," Sam said.

"And . . . the señorita?" the segundo said, eyeing Lydia. "Who is she?"

"The last of her family. Comanches hit their ranch in the hills today," Sam said.

"Aiiee! *Pobrecito,* poor little one. A great misfortune for one so young."

"Old enough to kill a jefe of los Indios."

Vasquez gave the girl a second look, longer and more appraising. "So? Well, I expect no less from a friend of yours, young or old."

Sam handled the introduction. "Hector, meet

Lydia Fisher. Lydia, this is Senor Vasquez, ramrod of Rancho Grande."

Bending forward from the waist, Vasquez executed a courtly bow. "Welcome to our home, señorita. I am sorry for your loss."

"Thanks . . . *gracias,* Senor Vasquez." Lydia stuck her hand out for a handshake. It all but disappeared inside Vasquez's massive bear paw of a hand as he clasped hers lightly, shaking it.

Going to Dusty, Sam took his flat wooden gun case down from the side of the saddle. "I'll take this. And this." He reached for a rolled-up dark garment tied in place like a bedroll behind the back of the saddle and tucked it under his arm.

"Will you see that our horses are taken care of? They've had a long, hot ride," Sam said.

"It shall be done." Vasquez whistled, catching the eyes of a couple stable boys, who came on the run.

Lydia took her rifle from the saddle and held it under one arm.

"You will not need that here, señorita," Vasquez said.

"I ain't letting go of it till the last Comanche is killed or quits," Lydia said, her face set in stubborn lines.

"As you will," Vasquez said, nodding approvingly. "A fit companion for you, gringo."

The stable boys led the horses away. "Will Brownie be okay?" Lydia asked anxiously. "He's all I got now, him and the rifle."

"He'll be fine. I wouldn't leave Dusty if I thought differently," Sam said.

"Please come with me to the hacienda, if you will," Vasquez invited. He started toward the big house, Sam and Lydia following.

Sam eyed the fountain longingly. Hot, tired, and thirsty, he wanted nothing so much as to empty a jug of cool, clear water over his head. He resisted the temptation.

Rounding the basin, the trio followed a long, straight, flagged path leading to the entrance of the hacienda. The towering structure loomed over them as they neared it. Lydia followed close on Sam's heels. Vasquez knocked on the front door. It was opened by a servant woman.

"I'll leave you here, gringo. *Hasta la vista,*" Vasquez said.

"See you," Sam said. He and Lydia stepped inside. The high front hall with tiled floors was cool. Closing the door, the servant turned and went deeper into the house, gesturing for Sam and Lydia to follow, murmuring, "*Por favor.*"

They went down a long hall with white-painted stuccoed walls showing dark brown wooden rafter beams and beam-ends. The walls were hung with spiky, ornate crucifixes and somber portrait paintings in elaborate gilded frames. The portraits were so dark with age their subjects could barely be made out. An unlit iron chandelier hung on a chain from the ceiling.

Lydia said in a hushed voice, "It's like a palace."

"In its way, it is," Sam agreed.

The servant paused at the entrance of the great hall. "Señor Diego will see you now, señor. There are some refreshments prepared for the señorita. If she would be so good as to accompany me?"

Lydia grabbed Sam's arm. "I want to stay with you."

"It's all right. I won't be long," Sam said.

Lydia, unhappy and suspicious, allowed him to persuade her to go with the servant woman. She led Lydia down a side passage toward the rear of the house.

"Try not to shoot anybody," Sam called after her, only half joking.

A manservant appeared at the threshold of the hall's rounded archway, motioning for Sam to enter. Sam followed him into the grand hall, a spacious, chamber two stories high. Stone pillars were set at regular intervals along whitewashed walls. Brightly colored woven tapestries and woolen blankets were hung as decorations. The long west wall was pierced by a row of tall, slender windows with peaked tops.

In the grand hall were Diego Castillo and Lorena Castillo Delgado.

Diego was the sole surviving scion of the Castillo bloodline. Age thirty, tall, slim, and elegant, he looked every inch the grandee, imperious and arrogant. He wore custom-tailored clothes with expensive decorative lace at the throat and cuffs, and imported boots of hand-tooled Cordovan leather.

His father, Don Eduardo Castillo, was the patron, the master of Rancho Grande. Thus Diego must remain "Señor Diego," able to assume the honorific "Don Diego" only upon the death of his father. Don Eduardo enjoyed excellent health; a fact Sam guessed gave little pleasure to his impatient, ambitious son.

Lorena Castillo, born Lorena Delgado, was the childless widow of Don Eduardo's firstborn son. Originally from Mexico she lived at the ranch. She was dark with bold good looks and a sensational physique.

Masses of black hair fell past her shoulders, framing a wide, sculpted bronze face with wide brown eyes, and a full-lipped red slash of a mouth. She was garbed in a bolero jacket, starched white blouse, and tan riding breeches tucked into knee-high brown leather boots. She was smoking a small, thin black cigarillo and held a pumpkin glass of brandy.

She was a willful, passionate woman. Sam wanted to trust her. He trusted few women and fewer men. Diego he trusted not at all.

The manservant ushered in the newcomer, Diego dismissing him with a few words. Nodding acknowledgment of Sam's presence, Diego smiled thinly. "Ah, Señor Heller. Once again you grace us with your company."

He spoke excellent English. His and Lorena's

English was a lot better than Sam's smattering of Spanish.

"The pleasure is all mine, señor," said Sam.

"A sublime thrill, Lorena, no?" Diego murmured.

"No." Lorena shrugged, taking a sip of brandy, content for now to let Diego do the talking.

"You must forgive my father Don Eduardo for not being here to greet you in person. A slight indisposition has confined him to his bedchamber, alas," Diego said.

"Nothing serious, I hope," Sam said.

"Not at all, thank you. I am sure he will make a full recovery presently."

Presently? Most likely as soon as I leave, thought Sam, remembering the Don hated Anglos.

In the assumption that all Anglos were eager to rob him of his vast holdings, Don Eduardo was far from mistaken. His ownership, well documented by deeds, titles and Spanish land grants, was upheld by a small army of well-armed, hard-riding pistoleros. It was a signal mark of favor that an Anglo such as Sam Heller was even allowed under the Castillo roof.

Sam had rendered the family several important services in the past and might again in future, so the patriarch allowed him into the hacienda, while shunning direct contact with him, letting such encounters be carried out by his son and daughter-in-law.

"Señora Castillo," Sam said, "I regret we're not meeting under happier circumstances."

"Always a happiness to host a friend of Rancho Grande," Lorena said diffidently. "We saw your arrival through the window. The young one who was with you, who is she?"

"A friend, Lydia Fisher. A brave girl." Sam briefly outlined the circumstances that had thrown them together on the plateau and afterward. Diego smiled politely throughout his narrative. Lorena alternated puffs on her slim dark cigarillo with sips of brandy.

"A most remarkable account," Diego said when Sam had finished. "Yes, remarkable indeed."

"And every word of it is true," Sam said.

"Oh, I don't doubt that you crossed paths with some Comanche bravos. Since the end of the great war between your North and South, the savages have become emboldened, once more venturing on their old raiding trails. We have heard of packs of them striking out on the Llano. Some band or two may even be in the county, but surely not in the numbers you claim."

"Looks like the Rancho's getting ready to fight— and a good thing, too," Sam commented.

"That is none of my doing, I assure you. My father Don Eduardo has a long memory. The days of his adventurous youth, when the Comanche often tried their strength against the ranchero, is still fresh in his mind. He takes the path of greater caution. It was his order that the ranch be made ready in case of attack." Diego made a show of smiling tolerantly, as if amused and indulgent of the oldster's foibles. "In all honesty, I confess I do not share his alarm and in his place I would have done differently."

"I thought you might feel that way. Seeing is believing." Sam set the gun case flat on a drum-shaped side table to free his hands and unrolled the dark garment he'd brought with him, holding an end in both hands and letting it fall free in front of him. It smelled of sweat, smoke, and blood. "Take a look."

Diego's finely formed nostrils quivered in delicate disgust, expressing repugnance. Fascinated, Lorena moved closer for a better look. "What is it?"

"It belonged to the Comanche known as Black Robe. I took it off his dead body not long ago. He took it off a priest he killed. The story of how he got it is well known throughout the West. I reckon word of it might even have reached inside Rancho Grande," Sam said dryly.

The macabre trophy, with its elaborate bead-work, fringe, and other trimmings, was a master-piece of barbaric splendor. His pose of supercilious hauteur temporarily forgotten, Diego stared at it despite himself. Lorena eyed it with awe and unease.

"If you don't believe me, ask Vasquez or any of the vaqueros—I'm sure they know the story. They'll tell you that Black Robe is the lieutenant of Red Hand, the fiercest Comanche war chief in the territory. Red Hand, Mano Rojo. I'm sure you've heard of him."

Wide-eyed, lips parted, Lorena nodded in agreement. Diego had a worried look; a little twitch fired off in the corner of his mouth. "I suppose it is better for us to be prepared," he reluctantly conceded. "Though I find it hard to credit that even Mano Rojo would be so foolish as to try his strength against ours."

Gaining confidence as he spoke, he continued. "Let them come! They will break against the stone of our walls and the fire of our guns!"

"I'm sure," Sam said. "And now that I've said my piece, I'll be on my way."

"You're leaving? Where will you go?" Diego asked, surprised.

"I've done my bit here. I'm going to town. Hangtree's got to be warned that Red Hand and his Comanches are coming."

"Better to stay, safe behind the walls of the ranchero," Lorena said.

"Gracias, but if I don't spread the word, who will?" Sam said.

Lorena shrugged. "You are loco, gringo."

"Mebbe," Sam said, grinning. "I've kept one step ahead of the braves all day. With any luck, I'll stay that way. I'd like to ask a favor, though."

"With the service you have rendered us, we are hardly in a position to refuse," Diego said with ill grace.

"My horse Dusty is plumb worn out. I'd like to borrow a pair of horses, fast ones."

"Why two?" Diego asked.

"If I get chased, a fresh horse might give me that extra burst of speed to get clear."

"It shall be done as you wish."

"The girl, Lydia . . . I can't take her with me. I'd be much obliged if you'd let her stay here until the danger is over."

"*Claro*, Señor Heller. Of course," Lorena said quickly. "I will look after her until you return."

"Can't ask more than that. Thanks. I've got to warn you, though, she's a handful."

Lorena's thin smile showed her confidence in managing the girl.

Diego fidgeted, restless. "I must confer with the segundo to make sure our defenses are in order. Lorena will see to the horses and anything else you might need, Señor Heller. Your service to Rancho Grande is most appreciated and will not be forgotten. Now if you will excuse me, I will take my leave."

"Many thanks, señor," said Sam.

Diego hurried across the room, into the corridor, and out of sight.

"I'll keep this to convince any other Doubting Thomases," Sam said, rolling up Black Robe's cape. He picked up his gun case off the drum table, holding it by the suitcase-style handle. "I ain't had much to eat today. It would be a kindness if the cook could fix me up a cut of beef between two slices of bread."

"I think we can do better than that," Lorena said.

"That's all I want. I want to travel light, not be weighed down."

"Come with me."

They went out into the corridor. "I got to tell the girl I'm going. From what I've seen of her, she won't much care for staying behind," Sam said.

"She would like losing that yellow hair of hers to a Comanche scalp hunter even less." Lorena led Sam to the kitchen, where she gave orders to the cook. "I'll go tell one of the boys to get the horses ready." She turned and left the kitchen.

Lydia sat at a wooden table in a side room of the kitchen, picking idly at her plate. It was loaded with food, but she hadn't taken more than a few bites. A big glass of milk seemed equally untouched. Sam didn't blame her, he hated milk. Lydia's rifle stood propped upright in the corner.

She looked troubled by Sam's leave-taking. "I don't want to stay here, let me go with you."

Sam shook his head. "You've risked your neck enough for one day."

"I don't want to be alone with strangers—"

"Lorena—Señora Castillo—will look after you."

"She's a stranger. Anyhow, I don't need looking after."

"I believe it. In that case, you look after her."

"Men!" she said scornfully, wise for her age.

"Now don't go getting any ideas," Sam cautioned.
"You like her, don't you?"

"She's a friendly acquaintance, that's all."

"Is that what you call it?"

"I like lots of folks. I like you," he pointed out.

"Sure, but not in the same way," Lydia said.

The conversation was interrupted by the arrival of the cook, a stout moonfaced woman. She handed Sam a brown paper bag with a couple sandwiches inside. He thanked her and she went back to her chores.

"Got to be moving on, Lydia. I'll be back for you when the Comanche is whupped," Sam said.

Lydia sat with elbows on the table, tight little fists pressed against the side of her head, pouting.

"Ain't you gonna say good-bye?" Sam asked lightly. "No? Well, that's all right. We sure had ourselves some ride, coming off the plateau and across the flat. You done real good. Your folks would be proud of you. I'm proud of you. Proud to know you.

"See you soon," he said, starting toward the corridor.

"Mister Yank!" she called after him. He turned, looking back.

"Take care of yourself," Lydia said.

"I'll do that," Sam said, smiling. "And, Lydia— don't be too hard on the señora. For a great grand lady, she's ain't so bad."

He went into the corridor. Lorena came into

view at the far end of the passageway. He went to her. Rounding a corner, they entered a narrow hallway connecting two corridors. It was empty, with no doors or windows.

Lorena turned, leaning into him, pressing herself against him. His hands were full, but he wrapped his arms around her, crushing her to him.

They had an understanding. Soon after they'd first met, they both knew that eventually they'd get together in a physical way. Lorena's position as honored widow of the beloved dead elder son and the tight supervision under which Don Eduardo kept all females under his roof had thus far prevented Sam and Lorena from consummating their relationship. The wanting heat of desire kept Sam on the boil on the few occasions they were thrown together, but he was careful to hide his true feelings from prying eyes, keeping strong passions hidden behind an easygoing manner.

Crushing her red-lipped mouth with his, Sam kissed her hard. She kissed him back, putting her whole body into it. Her mouth was warm, moist, and spicy-sweet. He tasted it, tongue probing, demanding.

Sam's senses reeled. Reluctantly he disengaged, easing out of the embrace.

Lorena stepped back, her eyes shining. Moist lips parted, they quirked upward at the corners in a secret smile. "Now you know what you are fighting for," she murmured. "Stay alive, hombre."

"That's a promise," he said, somewhat out of breath.

"Otherwise you will leave two women unhappy."

"Two? How so?" he asked, puzzled.

"Me and your little friend."

"Lydia? Don't be silly," Sam scoffed. "She's only a kid!"

"They grow up fast at that age. I did."

"She's done enough growing up for one day. Look after her, will you? This is a big place and I'd hate to see her get lost. Especially if the Comanches come."

"Stay with us. We can use your gun."

Sam shook his head. "I've got to warn Hangtown."

"Why?" Lorena asked.

"Why? So they can protect themselves."

"They're Rebels, you're a Yankee. They hate you, you told me so. Is this not true?"

"Some of 'em ain't so bad. Besides, I've had my fill of seeing innocent folks massacred today."

"Strange hombre!" Lorena marveled, shaking her head in mixed exasperation and wonderment.

Enterering the opposite corridor, she looked cool and composed. Sam's forehead was beaded with sweat. He wiped it on his sleeve before entering the corridor.

They turned left, the corridor taking them to a side door. Lorena opened it and they stepped outside, into the sunlight. The door opened on the east side of the hacienda.

A vaquero waited patiently nearby, sitting his

horse. A lead rope hitched around his saddle horn trailed behind him to a string of three horses, all saddled and ready to go.

Sam knew him: Latigo, a pistolero with plenty of sand.

"Latigo will go with you," Lorena said.

"Thanks, but I don't need him. He travels fastest who travels alone," Sam said.

"Still, I will feel better if there is another along to watch your back. One gun more or less won't make any difference to the fortune of the Grande, but it could make a very great difference to you. Latigo is one of mine, loyal first to the Delgados, not the Castillos."

Sam nodded. "I've seen him at work. A good man."

"But bad enough to stay alive," Lorena said, "like you, amigo."

"And you!"

Sam crossed to Latigo. The pistolero, in his mid-twenties, was of medium height, with a runner's build. Beneath a sombrero, thick black hair was parted in the middle, the ends reaching down to his jawline. He sported a blue bandana headband. He had almond-shaped eyes and a thin mustache.

He lifted a hand in greeting, holding it palm-up for a beat before letting it fall to his side. "We meet again."

"Sure you want to go along?" Sam asked.

"Why not? It's a nice day for a ride," Latigo said.

"In that case, I'll stay here and you go."

"I don't like riding that much, gringo." Latigo's gaze dropped to the sawed-off Winchester in its special long holster hanging down Sam's right thigh. "I see you still have that trick gun, the Kick of the Burro."

"Mule's-leg, podner."

"What I said."

Sam went up and down the string of three horses, checking them out. The second in line, a piebald brown-and-white cow pony, was dressed with Sam's own saddle.

"They're all good but the pinto is the best. I had them put your saddle on it," Latigo said.

"I'll take your word for it. Thanks," Sam said, pleased. He liked the pinto's lines and appreciated being able to ride his own saddle, broken in to his specifications. It wasn't the same, riding with another man's leather underneath him.

He put the brown paper lunch bag into a saddlebag, then secured the rolled-up black robe behind the cantle. A length of rawhide thong helped rig the gun case on the saddle's left-hand side. Unfastening the lead rope, Sam cut the pinto out of the string.

Latigo took the rope, trailing the two reserve horses behind him. Sam stepped into the saddle, mounting up on the pinto.

"*Muchos gracias, señora,*" he said, nodding to Lorena, touching thumb and forefinger to his hat brim. A tip of the hat, polite and respectful.

"Vaya con Dios," she said, lifting a hand in seeming casual salutation and letting it fall. Entirely correct and proper, yet no more than that, for the great lady of the rancho.

Sam and Latigo walked their horses across the patio into the courtyard. In its center, a knot of vaqueros wrestled with Rancho Grande's ultimate weapon. The Long Tom, an old Spanish cannon about fourteen feet in length, was mounted on a carrier with four solid wooden wheels. It looked like it belonged on the gun deck of a Spanish galleon or pirate ship. It was very old, but effective. Its punishing firepower had broken more than a few Comanche onslaughts across the long years.

The handlers struggled to move the Long Tom into place, positioning it so that it anchored the defense of the courtyard and its field of fire encompassed the main gate in case of a breach.

Diego Castillo was up on a parapet, repositioning the riflemen along the wall. He was oblivious of Sam . . . or pretended to be. That suited Sam fine.

The front gate was in the process of being secured. One massive door was closed, the other stood open. Sam and Latigo exited single file, Sam first, Latigo following with the string of two horses behind.

Once they were clear of the portal and out in the open, Sam waited for Latigo so they could ride abreast. Behind them, eager hands wrestled with the slab door, pulling it closed with a dull, booming thud that reminded Sam unpleasantly of the closing of a coffin lid.

Latigo was looking at him. Perhaps they shared similar thoughts.

"That sounded like the crack of doom," Sam noted.

Latigo shrugged his shoulders. "*Quien sabe,* gringo? Who knows?"

FOURTEEN

Sam and Latigo heard the death throes of the doomed stagecoach before they saw it. It was early evening; long shadows were falling.

From beyond the next ridge came the drum of thundering hoofbeats. A coach jounced on overworked springs, the undercarriage rattling and banging, its iron-rimmed wooden wheels rumbling along a dirt road. Counterpointing the stagecoach's frantic flight came the clamor of raucous pursuit, more hoofbeats, shots, shrieks, war whoops and yowls, bloodcurdling in their feral intensity.

The ridge ran east-west. Sam and Latigo rode almost to the top, pausing just below the crest of the rise, showing only enough of their heads to let them see what was happening below without being seen.

On the far side of the ridge stretched the rutted dirt road of the Hangtree Trail. Sam and Latigo were west of Hangtown, east of the Breaks, and far enough away from both so that neither could be seen.

The stagecoach hurtled east, chased by a band of Comanches. It was flanked on both sides by a couple lead riders, the rest of the braves closely bringing up the rear. Prey and predators streaked by at a breakneck pace.

The braves harried the coach like wolves trying to bring down a lumbering bear closing in for the kill. Shots cracked, arrows whizzed. That the moment of truth was near could be seen from the fact the stagecoach was without a driver.

Two men would normally have occupied the seat up front, the driver and the shotgun messenger. But there was only one, and he was dead. He lay on his side sprawled across the driver's seat, inert save for the motion imparted by the plunging, bucking, roiling vehicle. Arrows jutted out of him.

The shotgun guard was nowhere to be seen. He must have fallen off somewhere farther back on the road, out of sight. Other arrows protruded from the coach's roof, sides, and back. That it was not yet a corpse wagon was told by intermittent shots and shrieks coming from inside it.

The course lay straight across the flat. Six terrified horses, yoked in tandem to the wagon pole, raced straight ahead, freed of all restraint now that no man's hand held the reins. The end would be soon. Comanche riders flanking the coach team whipped their mounts with leather quirts, urging them to greater speed to overtake the lead horses.

Once that was done the braves could grab the animals' headstalls, turning them and bringing them to a halt. Two were almost there, leaning dangerously far out of their saddles, hands reaching.

Their fellows were bunched up in a pack coming alongside and behind the vehicle. Copper-red, half naked, sinewy Comanches armed with rifles, lances, and bows and arrows failed to completely obscure the forms of passengers inside the coach.

A bowman riding abreast of the coach box reached over his shoulder to draw an arrow from the quiver hanging across his back. Fitting it to the bowstring of his curved composite bow fashioned from buffalo bones, he drew the string taut, angling for a shot.

A man in the coach shot at him with a six-gun, missing, but causing the bowman to slow down and fall back.

Jamming his hat down tight on his head to keep from losing it—the hat that is, not the head—Sam kicked his heels into the pinto's flanks, urging it forward. It lunged over the crest of the ridge and down the other side, tearing a slanting line across the gentle downhill slope and pounding across the flat.

Left to his own devices, Latigo would have abandoned the coach and its passengers to their fate. Not out of callousness or indifference, but out of prudence. He'd come up in a hard school and learned early not to take unnecesary risks. The coach folk were strangers, no kin or friends to him.

But Latigo had been charged to ride with Sam Heller and, having been so charged by Señora Lorena, was faithful to his duty. The gringo was loco, a madman. But ah, what magnificent madness!

With more than a few sighs and head shakes, Latigo took off after Sam, taking his mount and the two horses strung behind him over the top of the hill and down the other side.

On the pinto, Sam tore across the flat after the stagecoach and its pursuers. His horse was fresh, the coach was near. Behind, Latigo was coming up fast, leaning far forward in the saddle.

Comanches are not easily taken unawares, but the band of marauders was intent on its prey. The pinto closed the gap between itself and the rearmost of the braves. Sam drew the mule's-leg with his right hand, gripping the reins between his teeth.

Levering the cut-down Winchester, he opened with a fast-crackling volley of lead.

Three braves in the back of the pack were swept off their mounts and thrown to the ground, never to rise again.

The others now knew Sam was on their tail.

The stagecoach was slowing; so were the Comanches. A rider at the head of the team on the left-hand side held the headstall of the lead horse nearest him, trying to turn the animal.

The stagecoach rumbled to a halt. Sam rode up

along the left-hand side of the coach, closing on three braves clustered together.

The nearest, a bowman with arrow nocked and pointed at a passenger half leaning out of a window and shooting, turned and loosed the arrow at Sam. Narrowly missing his head, it whizzed past so close he could feel the air disturbed by its passage. Sam triggered a burst of rounds, drilling the archer and a rifle-wielding brave riding alongside him.

Latigo unsheathed a repeating carbine from its saddle scabbard and drove down on the stage-coach's right-hand side, firing at three Comanches grouped there.

Five braves, the trio faced by Latigo and the two on Sam's side, wheeled their mounts around, turning them to meet the threat. A brave with an eight-foot-lance rushed Sam, thrusting the spear-blade at him. Sam shot him in the torso, felling him.

A brave threw a tomahawk at Latigo and missed. A passenger stuck his arm out of the coach, gun in hand. He blazed away at the tomahawk thrower at point-blank range, burning him down.

The brave holding the lead horse in check released its headstall to bring his rifle in line with Sam. Sam fired first, knocking him to the ground. He urged the pinto forward.

The brave he'd felled was still alive, groping in the dirt for his weapon and catching it up. The pinto trampled him. Sam held the animal in place, its iron-shod hooves dancing atop the Comanche, hammering him into the dirt.

Sam moved on, rounding the front of the team and coming up behind the duo on the other side shooting it out with Latigo. Sam shot one in the back while Latigo downed the other.

Taking no chances with possible hair-triggered survivors, Sam shouted, "Don't shoot, We're friends!"

"Amen to that, brother!" a man's voice returned from inside the coach.

Sam and Latigo reined in, eyeing downed braves pouring red lifeblood onto the hardpacked dirt road, the ground soaking it up like a sponge. Swinging down from the saddle, Sam hitched the pinto's reins to an iron staple bolted to the side of the coach. Latigo similarly secured his horse, then checked the lead rope and two horses on the string. They checked out okay. He and Sam dropped finishing slugs into the skulls of the downed who looked like they were still breathing.

Inside the coach, a woman cried out, "Lord be praised!"

The stagecoach doors were flung open and two men climbed out.

Carbine in hand, Latigo climbed up on the front of the stagecoach. He set the hand brake, locking it into place, and checked the driver for signs of life. "Dead," he said, looking up.

Sam's clothes were damp with sweat and he was breathing hard. He started reloading, plucking cartridges from a bandolier and feeding them into the mule's-leg. He faced west, eyes scanning west and north. The immediate landscape was partly obscured by dust clouds kicked up by the chase. He tried to peer through them, frowning. It looked clear of more Comanches, for now.

One of the coach duo was a big, sandy-haired fellow with a handlebar mustache. He wore a baggy, rumpled brown suit with a tan vest and held a .32 pocket gun. The other, of medium height, was slight, birdlike and thin faced. He wore a derby hat, a natty green-and-black checked suit, and long, slim boots. His right arm at his side held a big-bore, heavy-caliber handgun pointed at the ground.

"I don't mind telling you, you and your friend saved our bacon, sir. Thought we were goners, sure," he said to Sam. He mopped his face with a damp handkerchief. "Whew!"

"Sam Heller's the name. My friend is Latigo."

"I'm Hal Brewster, salesman out of St. Louis," the second man introduced himself.

"Donny Donahue, same line and town," the sandy-haired man said. Drummers they were, traveling salesmen.

A woman inside the coach stuck her head outside. She was haggard, white lipped, and trembling. "One of my girls is hurt, hurt bad. Can you help her?"

"I'll take a look, ma'am." Holstering the mule's-leg, Sam stepped up into the coach's interior.

Two dead bodies lay heaped on the floor like sacks of dirty laundry, a man with the shaft of a broken arrow sticking out of his eye socket, and a woman with half her face shot away.

Occupying the rear seat was another woman and two girls. "I'm Mrs. Anderson, Mary Anderson." She and a girl about twelve years old were huddled around the wounded youngster. At the same time they were trying to keep their legs and feet as clear as they could of the corpses on the floor.

"I was taking my nieces Sally and June to meet their daddy in Dallas. June was hit," Mrs. Anderson said. "I don't know what to do!"

Sally was about the same age as Lydia Fisher. Long brown hair parted in the middle framed a deathly white oval face. Her eyes stood out like they were on stalks. She was shivering, and held herself so taut that she looked to Sam like she'd twang like a plucked bowstring if touched.

June, ten, was short and chubby with brown hair cut in bangs and a round face. She half sat, half lay in corner of the seat. The back of her head was cradled and propped up by a rolled-up fringed shawl. An arrow was stuck in the girl's chest high on the right side. Sam winced when he got a good look at it.

June's eyes were closed, her lids drawn taut, orbs bulging like walnuts behind them. Her lips were parted, a line of wetness clung in the corner of her mouth.

Mary Anderson peered over behind Sam's back, breathing hard. "She's not moving! Is she . . . ?"

Sam held the side of his head low over the girl, listening. Her breathing was faint, slow and laboring. "Still alive," he said, straightening up.

"Thank God!" Mary Anderson cried. June whimpered, tears spilling from half-closed eyes.

"Fainted, looks like," Sam surmised.

A twisted hand gripped his forearm, squeezing it. Mary Anderson was a bony, wiry, old-maid type, but at the moment her clutch was so strong Sam's flesh went numb under it. "How . . . how bad is it?" she asked.

"Not good, but it could be worse. There's no wheezing in her breath or bubbles in the blood around the wound, so it probably missed the lung. I ain't no doctor, mind," he added quickly.

"Can you pull the arrow out?"

"I don't know. Maybe not—too dangerous. Might do more harm than good. Better off leaving it be till we get to a doctor."

"What doctor? Where?" Hysteria rose in Mary Anderson's voice, threatening to break loose.

"We're not too far from town, six to eight miles. The sooner we get there, the better—for everybody."

"Isn't there anything that can be done now?"

"See that she don't move around much or jar that arrow against anything." Leaning toward the open doorway, Sam eased away from Mary Anderson as best he could with her death grip clutching on his arm. "Ma'am, please . . . I got to see about getting us moving."

She let go of him. Sam stepped down outside the coach. It was hot in the open under the declining sun, but not as close and stifling as it had seemed inside the coach. Sam flexed his fingers and shook out the arm, trying to get some feeling back into it.

Donahue was taking a long pull from a pint bottle of whiskey he had stowed somewhere on his person. His head was tilted back, throat muscles working. When he lowered it, his eyes watered and his face was red.

"Ah! Good for what ails you," he said, gasping. He proffered the bottle to his companion. "Brewster?"

"Thanks, Donny, I could use it!" Brewster had been reloading his six-gun. Putting the cylinder back in place, he stuffed the big gun in a hip pocket of his pants and took the bottle. Raising it to his lips, he thought twice and lowered it undrunk, holding it out to Sam. "Mister . . . ?"

"Thanks. I can use it," Sam said. The whiskey was strong, raw, and fiery, giving him a jolt—what he needed. A shadow fell across him. Latigo leaned over the passenger's side of the driver's seat, looking thirsty.

"Drink up, by God!" Donahue said.

Sam handed the bottle to Latigo, who drank deep. When Latigo handed it back to Sam, there was only mouthful or so left in the bottle—but then, there hadn't been all that much remaining when Sam passed it to him. Sam returned the bottle to Donahue, who finished it off and tossed it over his shoulder to the side of the road.

"Not to worry, there's plenty more where that came from. Got 'em in my bag. It's the only way to

get through this godforsaken country," Donahue said.

"Donny and me have been selling the territory
for our firms. We both got on the stagecoach in
Santa Fe. That's Apache country, but there's been
no sign of hostile Indians till now," Brewster said.

"These ain't Apaches. They're Comanches,"
Sam said.

"They're sure as hell hostile, whatever they are,"
Donahue said. "They came out of nowhere, hoot-
ing and a-hollering like banshees, running us
down."

"They're on the warpath. I saw a couple hundred
of 'em up in the north hills not more than a few
hours ago. This is the second bunch of 'em I've
seen on the flat."

Donahue started, white-skinned pallor showing
on his face under the red whiskey flush. "Good
God! Let's get out of here!"

"I aim to do just that as soon as we get squared
away," Sam said. "In the meantime, you gents could
help by gathering up any repeating rifles you see.
They could come in handy."

"Let's get to it, Donny," Brewster said.

"Watch out for live ones—Comanches, that is.
They look dead, but you never know when one's
playing possum. They're full of tricks," Sam said.

"I hear you, brother," Donahue acknowledged.
Reaching into the stagecoach, he grabbed his traveling bag. It rattled when he moved it. Opening the
top and reaching inside, he pulled out a pint bottle

of whiskey, uncorked it and chugged a quarter of its contents. It put the red back in his face. He offered it to Brewster.

"Maybe later," Brewster said.

"You?" Donahue asked, holding it out to Sam.

"Hell, yes. Thanks." Sam took a good, solid belt. It burned going down his throat, blossoming into a ball of liquid heat in his belly, rising to the top of his head.

Latigo's hand reached down from the top of the stagecoach. Sam put the bottle in it. Latigo drank up. The bottle was empty.

"Another dead soldier." Donahue took a fresh pint bottle from his bag, dropping it in a side jacket pocket. Putting the bag back in the coach, he joined Brewster who was already scavenging the bodies of the dead Comanches for rifles. A third of their number had been armed with repeaters, but some had been downed a good distance from where the stagecoach was halted. A couple rifles were strewn nearby.

Latigo heaved the driver off the side of the stagecoach. The body fell heavily, thudding to the ground, the impact startling a high thin cry of fright from twelve-year-old Sally in the coach.

Sam and Latigo gathered up their own horses, hitching them all to a string secured to the back of the vehicle. They moved quickly but surely, glancing up frequently to look north and west. Sam removed his gun case and saddlebags from his saddle, setting them down on the ground beside the stagecoach's open door.

Brewster and Donahue each managed to find a working rifle; Brewster also scavenging a bandolier half full of cartridges.

"Every bit helps," Sam said. "Give me a hand with these bodies."

He and Donahue stepped inside the coach and Latigo and Brewster followed. Sam and Donahue took hold of the dead man.

"Name's Perlmutter, Arkansas bound. Never did catch the lady's name, Lord help her," Donahue said.

"Mrs. Hamer," Brewster said. "I got to talking to her at a way station. Her husband died in California and she was going back east to live with her sister."

Mary Anderson started as Perlmutter's body was hauled across the coach floor. "What're you doing?!"

"Need to travel as light as we can, ma'am," Sam said.

"Can't you carry them in the back? Take them to town for a decent burial?"

"Folks'll come back for 'em later, when it's safe. It ain't safe now," Sam said. He and Donahue carried the body out of the coach and laid it down at the side of the road. Latigo and Brewster did the same with the body of the woman.

Sam stepped back into the coach. Setting himself, he leaned over June. She was still unconscious. She didn't look any worse, but she didn't look any better, either. Sam's left hand gripped the shaft of the arrow six inches above where it entered the girl's chest.

"What're you doing? You said it was too dangerous to take the arrow out," Mary Anderson said in a frantic rush of words.

"I been studying on the matter, ma'am, thinking it over. I reckon it'll be safer for the girl if I break off as much of the arrow as I can, before we set off. There'll be less danger of it bumping into something and doing her worse hurt, if we hit some rough ground." *Or get chased by more Comanches,* Sam thought, keeping it to himself. No sense scaring the poor woman even more.

Come to think of it, he was scared, too. Not for himself, but for June. He was taking a risk intervening. It would be easier to wash his hands of any responsibility and let things be. Easier for him, but not for the girl. Her chances were better if he acted now.

"Please, be careful!"

"I'll be very careful, ma'am. I wouldn't do it if it wasn't needful." Sam's right hand closed on the arrow a few inches inches above the top of his left fist where he gripped the shaft. His strong hands, the wrists as thick around as ax handles, were rock steady. A bead of sweat rolled down his nose.

He applied increasing pressure to the shaft, breaking it in two. It snapped with a sharp cracking sound. An involuntary outcry escaped Mary Anderson's lips.

June remained inert, seemingly undisturbed. Her breathing continued shallow but regular.

Sam eyed the wound where the arrow entered flesh. No fresh blood oozed up at the point of entry. "No harm done. It should help on the ride."

"Thank y-you," the woman murmured.

As Sam got out of the coach it occurred to him that it might have been wiser to carry out the first aid before drinking Donahue's whiskey. Then again, if he hadn't drunk it, he might not have ventured the effort at all. Conscious of the broken arrow in his hand, he threw it away. He took off his bandanna, using it to mop the sweat from his face, then retied it loosely around his neck.

Latigo sat up front in the driver's seat, clutching the reins.

"Ever drive one of these before?" Sam asked.

"I drive plenty wagons for Don Eduardo," Latigo answered, somewhat insulted.

That was good enough for Sam. Hefting his gun case, he climbed up onto the guard's side of the driver's seat. The drummers, Donahue and Brewster, got into the coach, sitting on the forward seat bench, each at a window, each armed with a repeating rifle taken from slain Comanches.

"Everybody ready?" Sam called.

"Let 'er rip!" Donahue replied.

"The lady have good hold of the girl?"

"She's all set."

"Ma'am?" Sam asked.

"Yes, I'm ready," Mary Anderson said, a tremor in her voice.

Sam nodded to Latigo.

Latigo released the hand brake, taking up the long reins. "Yah! *Vamonos!*" he shouted.

The team of horses started forward, straining against the harnesses. Wheels rolled and the stage-coach advanced. The horses fell into step, picking up the pace, carrying the stagecoach forward with them.

The road was hard and rutted. The vehicle's springs had taken a beating and didn't have much bounce left in them. Sam was conscious of every bump and jostle as the stagecoach increased its speed. It was going to be rough on June.

Setting the gun case on the tops of his thighs, Sam lifted the lid. He lifted the mule's-leg and started fixing the extended barrel in place. He could have put the long gun together on the back of a galloping horse and had, many times. Assembly swiftly completed, he put the gun case in the front boot, behind the footboard under the seat. Latigo's carbine was already stowed there.

The road ran more or less directly east over the plains, good green land with gentle rises and hollows, speckled with trees and rock piles. Latigo drove the team at a brisk pace, but not all out. The horses had used up a lot of energy fleeing their pursuers earlier, and he wanted to leave them with some reserves in case they had to bolt hell-bent-for-leather.

Sam's eyes scanned the north, on his left-hand side. Often he glanced back over his shoulder, west. The string of four horses trailing the rear of the stagecoach trotted along nicely.

The day was waning; the sun hung low in the west, an orange ball floating a few degrees above the skyline of the Breaks.

Sam faced front. The tallest object in Hangtown, the white church steeple, would be the first to show above the east horizon. He longed to see it. Several miles rolled past. On the north, a row of stepped ridges ran east-west, the nearest an eighth of a mile away.

A line suddenly formed along the crest—a long line made of mounted men ranked side by side. One second they weren't there; the next, they were.

Donahue stuck his head out of the stagecoach's paneless window, shouting, "Injins!"

Latigo was already urging the team forward, shouting, throwing a snap into the reins to get more speed out of them. The driver's long whip would have been of service, but it had gotten lost somewhere back on the road. Sam fired a shot close above the horses' heads to hasten them along.

A black wave of riders came rolling down the slope, whooping and hollering. No scouting party, this; it was a significant group, numbering perhaps forty braves in all.

Red Hand was not waiting for night to make his move. He was striking close to town by day. Sam wondered if the war chief had brought his whole force down from the hills and, if so, how close they were to Hangtown.

The stagecoach's race for life would be a close-run thing. It had a good lead and was off to a fast start, but riders on horseback were faster than horse-drawn coaches. And when the riders were peerless horsemen like the Comanches, the odds became narrower still.

The stagecoach careened along the road, wheels blurring, the landscape unrolling at high speed. Comanches angled across the flat, closing on the road. Some opened fire, bullets whipping through the air.

The nearest riders were those who'd been on the east flank of the line atop the hillcrest. The most distant, those who'd been on the west flank, crossed the road and plunged south, gradually curving southeast.

They were forming a crescent whose ends pointed east; their goal was to envelop the stagecoach on both sides, closing in on it with the tips of the horns and goring it preparatory to making the kill. Relentless, they were howling pack of hellhounds closing in on their quarry.

Gripping the side rail bordering the stagecoach roof, Sam climbed up on its flat top, rifle in hand. If any of the passengers' baggage had been mounted there, it had been shed sometime during the earlier pursuit, for the roof was clear and unencumbered.

Sam lay prone, facing west. He hooked the sides of his booted feet under the side rails to brace himself in place. The first Comanche bullets were a few missiles buzzing by through empty air. They were still too far away for bows and arrows to do any damage.

Sam opened up on the horsemen, firing from the prone position. He pointed the gun at a brave in the lead and shot him. A second shot felled the next.

The number of enemy shots increased, some tearing into the rear of the vehicle. It was the cue for Donahue and Brewster to stick their rifles out the windows and open fire.

The stagecoach plunged down a dip in the road, across a valley, and up the other side. Sam silently cursed each degree of slowness added by the slope. Sighting on a feather-bonneted brave on a tawny horse, he squeezed the trigger.

The brave lurched when hit, dropping his rifle. After a pause, he slumped sideways, falling off his horse.

Topping the rise, the stagecoach's front and rear wheels left the ground for an instant. Sam felt it in the pit of his stomach. The wheels touched down, the coach's upper works slamming against the undercarriage with a bone-jarring crash.

Latigo shouted, "Gringo! The town!"

Sam turned his head, looking east. Sunlight shone on the slim white obelisk of the church steeple, turning it to gold.

Three Comanches crested the rise behind the stagecoach. Sam shot the one in the middle. Knots of braves began swooping over the ridgetop. So many bullets were flying, it was as though the Comanches were pegging hornets' nests at the stagecoach, peppering it with hot lead stingers.

Riders at the tips of the curving horn drew abreast of the stagecoach. Sam downed several on his right-hand side. Point. Squeeze. Shoot. Kill a man.

Repeat. Point. Squeeze. Shoot. Kill!

Donahue and Brewster kept banging away with their rifles. Donahue engaged in a running gunfight with a Comanche closing in on him, finally potting him.

Ahead, the skyline of Hangtown rose into view: the white-steepled church and the Hanging Tree, a sketchy impression of jagged rooflines beyond.

The Comanches kept coming, seemingly ready to follow the stagecoach into town.

A sudden, savage attack on unwary townfolk might exact many casualties. Surely they could hear the shooting—unless they thought it was just a bunch of high-spirited cowboys shooting off their guns and whooping it up, giving the town a big hoorah before riding in—a not uncommon occurrence in Hangtown, especially on Saturday, when the ranch hands came in to blow off steam.

Sam turned, wriggling forward across the roof and dropping down into the front seat. He hunched down to keep his head from being shot off. Latigo, too, was leaning far forward, his chest a hand span or two above his knees as he worked the long reins.

Shouldering the rifle, Sam pointed it at the church belfry, the open-walled space below the bottom of the spire where the church bell hung. Its tolling was used to summon the faithful to Sunday services, but also to sound the alarm in case of fire or other emergency.

Sam squeezed off a shot, missing due to a sudden bounce of the stagecoach. Cursing under his breath, he tried again.

He was rewarded by the sound of a sharp ringing tone as a round struck the bell. Now he had the range. Sam fired again and again, each shot ringing the bell, shivering out a shrill alarm. A damned shame to use bullets to shoot a church bell instead of Comanches, but it had to be done.

Roosting up in the rafters inside the spire was a number of bats, startled into flight. Bursting into light of day, they were ragged dark shapes like scraps of black paper taking wing skyward.

The stagecoach burst through a gap, rattling past Hanging Tree on the north, towering over Boot Hill and the church and the well-kept cemetery on the south. The horses raced along a short open stretch leading to the west edge of town, where Hangtree Trail became Trail Street.

Usually at that hour on the shank of a Saturday afternoon, the streets were pretty well cleared. Generally, visiting families would have departed for their outlying ranches and night-crawling fun seekers would not yet have started making their rounds.

But Trail Street was crowded, a body of men massed in its middle, blocking it. And they were armed.

The stagecoach plunged toward them.

FIFTEEN

Pandemonium was loosed in Hangtown by the ringing church bell and the stagecoach's advent.

First, a distant clamor in the west nagged at the attention of the militiamen and Ramrod riders facing off at opposite ends of Trail Street. A crackle of noise like exploding firecrackers was immediately followed by the strident ringing of the church bell as it was struck by a series of shots.

"It's a double cross! I'll learn 'em, the dirty bastards!" Quentin pulled his gun, pointing it at Sheriff Mack Barton, standing at the other end of the street with his back to the courthouse.

Clay threw out a hand. "Don't!"

Oxblood sidled his horse into Quentin's, spoiling the latter's aim. The shot went wild, thudding into the side of a building.

Barton wasn't the sort to mull things over. He turned, slapping leather, leveling his gun on the

Stafford crowd. "No-account back shooters!" he said, looking for someone to plug.

Before the situation could explode into all-out gunfire between the two sides, the stagecoach made its entrance, barreling east on Trail Street—an irresistible force, with its six-horse team on the gallop, trailing four horses on a lead rope.

For the militiamen grouped in the street between the Cattleman Hotel and the Alamo Bar, it was run or be trampled. Rather than go under hooves and wheels, they scrambled for the sidelines. The sudden scattering kept the tense standoff from exploding into a battle royale.

Quentin turned on Oxblood, demanding, "What did ya do that for? You made me miss!"

Clay thrust a pointing finger west, shouting, "Indians!"

The bunch of Comanches who'd been in the lead, close behind the stagecoach, rushed through the gap between the church and Boot Hill and into town, shrieking and shooting. Confronted by armed townfolk gawking on the sides of the street, they opened up on them with bullets and arrows.

The initial rush caught many citizens flat-footed; the slow and the luckless were first to die.

Among the Ramrod crowd, horses milled, their riders confused and unsure. Guns were drawn. Somebody shouted, "What do we do, boss?"

"Get clear and shoot!" roared Vince Stafford.

"Shoot who?"

"Injins, ya blamed idjit!" Vince was good as his

word, pointing his six-gun at an oncoming brave
and banging away at him.

More Comanches came tearing over the west
ridge, some charging down the trail, others peeling
off to the sides to ride through Boot Hill and
around the church.

Barton checked, holding fire on the Staffords.
Comanches were pouring into town. Running half
crouched to the corner of the Cattleman Hotel, he
got around it and turned his gun on the braves.

The stagecoach tore wildly down the street.
Some militiamen were seriously brushed back by
the coursing horses and the sides of the coach,
knocking them ass-over-teakettle and sending them
sprawling. Luckily no one was run over or seriously
injured.

Caught up in the heat of the chase, the leaders of
the advance band of Comanches boldly attacked
with lightning swiftness. Riding into Hangtown, they
saw human targets, Texans, a plenitude of them.
Rifle muzzles swung into line, spitting flame and hot
lead. Archers quickly fitted arrows to bowstrings,
drawing them taut and loosing their shafts. Bullets
and arrows struck home, taking their toll.

A brave with a war lance turned his horse down a
side street, chasing a fleeing man. Leaning sideways
halfway out of the saddle, he speared the fugitive
in the back, releasing the lance at the last second.

The victim staggered a few steps forward of his
own momentum before falling facedown, the lance
sticking straight up out of his back. Tightly wheel-

ing his pony around, the brave headed back up the street, leaning over to pluck the lance from the dead body.

Deputy Smalls stepped out from an alcove holding a shotgun. He cut loose, blasting the spearman and spilling him into the street. Stung by buckshot, the pony screamed and raced away.

Clay Stafford shouted, "Move aside, boys! Take cover!" The Ramrod riders spurred their horses mostly to the north side of the street, getting behind the courthouse front, out of the way of the fast-closing stagecoach. The Stafford crowd held more than its share of quick-triggered gunmen; they already had guns in hand.

Sam Heller knew there was no point in running too far past the east limits of town, out in the open where Comanches could easily overtake and surround the stagecoach. Better to stay in town where there was plenty of firepower on the street to buck the invaders.

Glimpsing the group of mounted men by the courthouse, unaware of their identity or the crisis that had gripped Hangtown in the aftermath of Damon Bolt's killing Bliss Stafford, Sam saw the group as a godsend, there being strength in numbers.

Several of the foremost raiders were close behind the stagecoach and would not be denied their prize, not even in the heart of the White Eyes's stronghold.

Indicating the courthouse, Sam said, "Go left at street's end! Swing wide and head back into town!"

The stagecoach slowed, Latigo pulling back on the reins in order to make the turn without over-turning. The courthouse and jail zipped past as the stagecoach tore between them.

Working the lever of the hand brake, the brake pads shrieked against the iron-rimmed wheels. Latigo turned the team to the left, curving around the plaza fronting the courthouse. Team and stagecoach slewed in a wide, dizzying arc, throwing up a screen of dust.

For a heart-stopping instant the wheels on the coach's right-hand side left the ground, female screams shrilling from inside.

Sam one-handedly clutched a top rail on the stagecoach roof to keep from being thrown. The wheels touched down, joining the pair on the opposite side to churn up a thick plume of brown dust.

The lead rope at the rear of the coach parted, loosing the four horses trailing after. They went straight, running out of town and racing east.

Comanches chasing the stagecoach ran straight into a barrage launched by Ramrod riders. Crashing rounds of gunfire burst forth. The braves fired back, but they were outnumbered two-to-one by the gun hawks. Only half the braves survived that initial onslaught. Their charge took them beyond the town limits into the open.

The cloud of dust kicked up by the stagecoach on its high-speed turn worked to its advantage, cloaking it in airborne murk. Latigo turned the stagecoach onto Commerce Street.

A Comanche trio returned to the fray, emerging from the dust cloud in dogged pursuit. Firing back at them, Sam picked them off one, two, three.

The stagecoach had shed most of its speed while making the turn. Sam motioned for Latigo to turn into a side street on their left-hand side. "In there!"

Working the reins and the hand brake, Latigo wheeled the slowing stagecoach onto the street between the courthouse and the Golden Spur, providing a safe haven from the battle that continued to rage through the town. The vehicle jostled to a halt.

Recovering from the shock of the surprise attack, the townfolk had begun to regroup and return fire. The number of militiamen already grouped en masse in the street quickly mounted an effective counterstrike against the raiders. Also well armed and geared for trouble were those of the Ramrod, who fought back hard and fast.

In the grid of streets and cross streets comprising the heart of town, more braves spilled into the dirt, their ponies bolting free. The tide was turning.

Quick to adapt, the Comanches retreated from the costly fusillade on Trail Street. Their fight was not yet done, however. Breaking up into small groups of twos and threes, they spread out through the rest of town in search of less well-protected citizens.

A sodden drunk staggered out of an alley beside the Dog Star Saloon, where he had passed out sometime earlier. Confusing the pounding of his aching head with the racketing of gunfire and hoofbeats, he stood swaying just outside the alley mouth.

Seeing him, a Comanche bowman shot an arrow into his chest. The drunk reeled, staring bleary-eyed at the feathered shaft protruding from his torso. He remained on his feet.

A bowstring twanged for a second time, launching another arrow into the befuddled man. He dropped and died, bewildered by the cruel fate that had overtaken him.

A woman in a boardinghouse on a cross street north of the Alamo Bar went to the window to investigate the source of the racket. Standing at an open second-floor window, she was shot by a Comanche rifleman. She fell to the floor, sinking out of sight below the windowsill, and died.

Gunfire continued to pop elsewhere as the main clash on Trail Street subsided. From wounded townfolk came cries and screams, groans and mutterings, and calls for help. Wounded Comanches stayed grimly silent, due not only to their stoic nature but also the certainty they would live longer by not calling attention to themselves in the midst of their enemies.

A hard-core group of militiamen formed around Sheriff Barton and Boone Lassiter, Hutto's top gun. Among them were Hutto himself, Russ Lockhart, Deputy Smalls, and a steadily growing number of others.

"The red devils! Why, they haven't so much as shown their faces in Hangtree since before the war,"

Lockhart said, sounding as much offended as shocked.

"Well, they're here now," Barton said, reloading his six-gun.

"Looks like we got 'em on the run," somebody said.

"Keep your gun ready and your eyes open. You can't count on nothing where Comanches are concerned," Barton instructed. "Be like them to fake breaking off the attack, only to regroup and hit us again one more time."

"It could have been worse," Wade Hutto said. "If we hadn't gathered to buck the Ramrod, they would have fallen on this town like wolves on a sheepfold!"

"Wonder how Stafford's bunch made out?" said a clerk from the feed store, wearing a white bib apron over his clothes and toting a Henrys repeating rifle.

"If Vince caught a bullet it would solve a lot of problems." The rancher sounded hopeful. He had a small spread on the South Fork of the Liberty River, not far—meaning too close—from the Ramrod Ranch.

"You won't be rid of Vince so easily," Lassiter said, grinning. "He's too blamed ornery to be that obliging."

"We don't want to lose Vince just yet. We'll need every manjack we've got if the Comanches return," Barton said.

"They wouldn't dare!" Lockhart said.

"Why not?"

Nobody had an answer to that one.

Sporadic outbursts of gunfire and distant screams from outlying parts of town continued to be heard.

"Hell, they ain't quit yet." Deputy Smalls looked distinctly unwell—pale, pasty faced, and beaded with cold sweat.

"You're showing a little green around the gills, Deputy," Lassiter said, chuckling.

"I got excited and swallowed my chaw of tobaccy by mistake. I'm feeling mighty low down in the belly," Smalls complained.

Barton peered east on Trail Street. "Vince made it. He's still with us."

"Someone'll have to speak to him to arrange a truce until the Comanche threat is done," Hutto said.

"'Someone,' huh? Who could that be? As if I didn't know!" Barton exclaimed.

"You're doing a fine job, Mack. You're the only one can handle Stafford. He respects you."

"Respects me enough to put a bullet in my back!"

"That wasn't Vince. Looked like Quent shot at you," somebody said.

"Oh he did, did he?"

"Let's get squared away first," Hutto said quickly.

"I'll square Quent away," Barton fumed.

"We'll have to comb the town street by street to make sure the Comanches are all gone," Hutto said, trying to change the subject.

"Street by street? Hell, house by house," Boone

Lassiter said. "It'd be just like those devils for a few of them to find a hiding place to set for a few hours and let things calm down before cutting up again."

On the side street, Sam finished reloading his Winchester and climbed down from his perch. Latigo reached into the box under the seat, hauling out the carbine, which had remained unfired since he first took the reins of the stagecoach.

Sam put his face in a window of the coach. "How you folks doing in there?"

"Brewster's dead," Donahue said dully.

"Hell!" Sam looked in, seeing Brewster's body slumped in a heap on the floor.

"Sally and I are all right, but Junie started bleeding again, bad." Mary Anderson's dark eyes stared out of a strained white face. The front of June's dress was soaked with dark, fresh blood. "We've got to get her to a doctor."

"We will, Miz Anderson."

A Comanche rode west on Trail Street, flashing past the gap between the courthouse and the Golden Spur. Latigo fired, and the brave spilled into the street, lying motionless. The horse kept going, running out of sight.

Sam eyed the broken lead line tied to the rear of the stagecoach. "Looks like Don Eduardo is out four horses."

"He will love you all the more," Latigo said dryly.

"Blame the Comanches, not me!"

"He has love enough in his heart for both."

A door in the east wall of the Golden Spur creaked open. Sam and Latigo spun, pointing their rifles at it.

"Don't shoot, it's only me." Standing in the doorway, Johnny Cross raised his hands and smiled.

Sam and Latigo lowered their weapons.

"Trust a Yank to be in the middle of all that shooting and whatnot," Johnny said, shaking his head in mock sadness. "The bad penny always turns up somehow."

Sam looked him over. "I was thinking the same about you."

Sixteen

The girl, June, was dead. Sometime during the chase into town, the rough ride caused the arrowhead to cut something vital and she'd bled to death. A stricken Mary Anderson and her sobbing twelve-year-old niece were taken in tow by some of the women of the church committee and escorted to a place of safety. At least, as safe as any in Hangtown.

But how safe could that be, Sam wondered, with Red Hand's Comanches on the warpath within striking distance? He hoped he wouldn't find out . . . but he knew better.

Donahue picked up his traveling bag and took his sample cases out of the stagecoach's rear boot. Desirous of getting stinking drunk, he went into the nearest saloon, which happened to be the Golden Spur. Quickly apprised that he had found no safe harbor due to the Stafford threat, he went down the street to the Alamo Bar.

It was closed. Donahue disappeared into the Cattleman Hotel.

Sam and Latigo sat at the front of the stagecoach. "Could be a reward from the stagecoach line for bringing in their property," Sam mentioned. "If there is, we'll split it. If not, we'll sell the coach and horses and split the cash."

That sounded good to Latigo, who moved the team out and to Hobson's Livery Stable south of the jail.

Hobson had survived the raid intact and unharmed, as had his son and principal helper, a red-haired, freckle-faced kid. Hobson, a brawny titan who doubled as town blacksmith, wore a pair of holstered six-guns. He made arrangements to board the stagecoach team and the string of six horses. He asked no prying questions as Sam paid in hard cash, including something extra for the trouble of securing the coach.

He told Hobson what he'd seen on the plateau: burned-out ranches, slaughtered settlers, and the temporary camp of several hundred Comanches in Lago Gulch.

Hobson took the bad news with about as much excitement as if they were talking about the weather. He didn't crack too much.

Sam broke down the rifle, unfastening long barrel and stock and fitting them in the gun case. In the close confines of town, with its crowded saloons and narrow alleys, the cut-down mule's-leg was more convenient, faster to get into action.

He stuffed Black Robe's talismanic garment into one of his saddlebag pouches, draped the saddlebags over his left shoulder, and hefted his gun case. Latigo took his own saddlebags and carbine, and they took leave of Hobson.

A hundred yards south of the stables, on the far side of a weedy dirt field, lay Mextown. A handful of bodies, some of settlement folk and others of Comanches, lay strewn about on the ground. White-clad residents milled around, armed with muskets, shotguns, machetes, axes, and such potentially lethal implements as scythes, sickles, and flat-bladed hoes.

"Let's find the sheriff," Sam said.

Latigo made a sour face. He had no great fondness for gringos, less for lawmen. But Señora Lorena had told him to stick close to Sam, so he duly fell into step alongside him.

They walked north to Trail Street. The jail was closed up tight, nobody home except for an inmate in one of the cells, who gripped the bars of a window with both hands and stuck his face between them, bawling for somebody to come let him out. He was unhurt and scared half sober.

There wasn't anything Sam could do for him so he and Latigo moved on.

The sheriff wasn't hard to find. He was standing on the front porch of the Cattleman Hotel, surrounded by a cluster of the town's leading citizens, at least in their own estimation. A larger group of townfolk, mostly men but some women and children, were grouped in the street around the front of the hotel, facing Barton and the notables.

Now that the Comanches had been driven off, more people were emerging from behind bolted doors and shuttered windows to venture outside. Sam grinned wryly to himself. He was the bearer of ill tidings that, when they learned of it, would send most of them back running for cover.

Wanting to keep a low profile, Sam decided against bulling through the crowd and bracing the sheriff in public. Motioning to Latigo, he led him around behind the building to the back of the hotel. A waist-high white packet fence enclosed the backyard. They went through the gate and along a plank board pathway to the kitchen door. It was unlocked, opening into the kitchen. They walked through the kitchen and pushed open double swinging doors that accessed the main dining room, a large space filled with tables and chairs, but no diners. A half dozen white-aproned members of the kitchen staff, cooks, assistants and waiters, stood gathered under an archway, facing the front entrance.

Sam and Latigo came up behind them unnoticed. Sam put a hand on the shoulder of a waiter. The fellow started violently, giving a jolt to the other staff members alongside him.

"Easy," Sam said, "if I was a Comanche, I'd've had your scalp already."

"You're not supposed to be in here," the waiter said, frowning.

"Just passing through." Sam and Latigo went under the archway, across a central hall and into a lobby filled with overstuffed furniture and potted plants the size of small trees. Leafy green fronds screened the sunlight pouring in from the front bay windows, softening it.

On the other side of the hallway, standing near the front entrance where he could observe Barton and company organizing the townfolk, was Lloyd Garvey, the desk clerk, a prematurely aged young man with permanently hunched rounded shoulders. It took something on the order of an Indian attack to flush Garvey out from behind the front desk, where he customarily held court, dispensing room keys and keeping the rest of the staff on their toes.

"W-why, Mr. Heller," he said, catching sight of Sam, "what are you doing here?"

Sam didn't much cotton to his own cooking and ate dinner at the Cattleman several nights a week. The desk clerk was in a position to know plenty about the hotel's occupants and visitors, their comings and goings, and Sam's peculiar trade thrived on such bits of timely intelligence. He kept Garvey plied with gratuities to keep him nice and pliable.

Sam opened his hand, a gold coin nestling in his palm. He held it so only Garvey could see it, and that briefly. because Garvey made it disappear with smooth, well-oiled skill that comes of much practice. "How may I be of service?" he asked brightly.

"I want a word with the sheriff."

Garvey's face fell. "I can't interrupt him, I'm only the desk clerk."

"Tell Barton that if he wants to have a town to be sheriff of, he'd better listen to what I've got to say."

Garvey goggled, his eyes bulging, his Adam's apple bobbing.

"Give it to him just like I said it. If he gets sore, he'll be mad at me, not you, so you'll be in the clear. Make sure you tell him so only he can hear it. We don't want to go starting a panic."

"Well—okay," Garvey said, after much hemming and hawing. Swallowing hard, he took a deep breath and started forward on his errand.

Approaching Barton from the side, Garvey tugged at his sleeve. Startled at being interrupted by such a lackey, the sheriff could only assume the desk clerk had something worth hearing. "'Scuse me, folks." Barton leaned toward Garvey, turning an ear to him.

Speaking behind his hand, Garvey passed along Sam's words. Barton looked over his shoulder into the hotel. Sam gave him the high sign, motioning for Barton to come to him. The sheriff was a quick study. He blanked his expression, assuming a poker face before turning to face the buzzing crowd once more.

"Take over for a minute, Wade," he said out of the side of his mouth.

"Huh? What? Wait a minute," Hutto sputtered.

Barton entered the hotel, closing on Sam. Outside, Hutto had hold of Garvey's lapel and was no doubt inquiring into the latest odd turn of events. A quick study himself, Hutto recovered and commenced speechifying to the citizens, plying them with soothing generalities.

"You!" Barton said, face-to-face with Sam. "You brought the Comanches into town."

"Not hardly," Sam corrected.

Barton pointed a finger at Latigo. "And you too, huh? You're a long way from Rancho Grande."

"I wish I was there," Latigo said.

"That makes two of us. I wish you was there, too."

"We brought the stagecoach in. The Comanches wanted it, but we wouldn't give it to 'em," Sam said.

"You got some tall talking to do, mister," Barton declared.

He knew Sam Heller as a bounty hunter, a Yankee gunman who had drifted into town in the aftermath of the War Between the States and then just set, not moving on. A most mysterious fellow, he had somehow engineered the destruction of the Harbin gang, which was no mean feat. The stranger had some pull with the bluebelly commander of Fort Pardee, too, but that was no surprise. Those damned Yankees all stuck together. Barton had as little use for Sam as he had for any Northerner—none—yet he knew to let sleeping dogs lie. The sheriff was in no hurry to brace him to run him out of town. Even a Yankee bounty killer had his uses in a time and place where so many violent men flourished.

An excited Hutto made his way into the hotel, rushing up to Barton. "What's going on?"

"Let's step off to the side, in private," Sam said.

"Why?"

"This has got to be handled carefully." Sam turned, crossing to an alcove in the lobby, the others trailing after him. It was a nice secure space with nowhere for eavesdroppers to hide. "This'll do."

With the dead strewn about the streets and the cries of the wounded still ringing in their ears, Hutto and Barton needed little in the way of convincing when Sam told them that Red Hand and his Comanche warriors were gathered to hit Hangtown in force—and soon. Black Robe's famed garment, well known by ill repute in that part of the West, removed any lingering doubts.

"Red Hand's a bad one. Wahtonka knows when to pull in his horns, but Red Hand's looking to make a name for himself," Barton said, more dour than ever.

"What do we do?" Hutto asked, worried.

"Fight him."

"What about the troops from Fort Pardee?" Hutto asked. He and Barton looked to Sam, a Yankee with shadowy connections with Captain Harrison, the fort's Union Army commander.

Sam shook his head. "They're in force west of the Breaks, waiting to rendezvous with Major Adams's wagon train to escort it across the Staked Plains."

"Maybe Red Hand will attack them," Hutto said, hopeful, momentarily brightening.

"Why would he go against the cavalry when he doesn't have to?" Sam asked.

Hutto's face fell.

"Hangtown's a richer prize than any wagon train," Sam added.

Barton ground a fist into his palm. "Red Hand played the bluebellies—played us all. Those attacks on the plains were a decoy to lure the army away."

"The rendezvous point is less than a half day's ride away," Hutto said. "If we sent a rider out there to bring back the cavalry—"

Barton laughed mirthlessly. "Good luck finding somebody fool enough to take that ride, with Comanches on the loose. Staying here and blowing his brains out would be quicker and less painful."

"He'd have a better chance if he went out after dark. He could reach the troops and have them back well before sunup. Comanches don't attack at night, everybody knows that."

"They're not gonna let anybody ride through their lines, either."

"Still, it's a chance."

"Nobody's stopping you from asking for volunteers, Wade."

Hutto's gaze fell on Sam, measuring him.

"No, thanks," Sam said quickly.

"Would a hundred dollars in gold change your mind?"

"No."

"Two hundred?"

"I already ran the gauntlet today. Once is enough."

Hutto eyed Latigo. "How about you?"

"No comprende, señor."

"Don't bull us, Latigo," Barton said. "I know you speak good English."

Latigo grinned.

"You'd have to work a long time for Don Eduardo to make a hundred in gold," Hutto pressed.

"You told him two hundred," Latigo said, indicating Sam.

"All right, damn it, two hundred!"

"What good is money when you're dead, señor?"

"Bah! If you don't want it, somebody else will," Hutto said, with ill grace.

"Try some of the Dog Star crowd," Barton said. "Those galoots are wild and woolly enough to take a chance. Get 'em when they're good and drunk—which is most of the time."

Sam disagreed. "Best plan on fighting without the army. That's the way to bet it."

"Oh, brilliant! Got any more bright ideas, Heller?" Hutto asked, sarcastically.

"Yup. Get Stafford and Damon to call a cease-fire," Sam stated. Johnny Cross had told him about the standoff.

Hutto made a face. "Is that all?"

"No, but it's a start."

Barton mulled it over. "Damon might go for it. He's a gentleman. Vince's an ornery cuss, though, and right now he's got blood in his eye."

"If he's got no sense, his men might. They won't fancy losing their hair to some brave's scalping knife," Sam said.

"We could use the firepower. Those Ramrod guns already came in mighty handy," Barton admitted.

"It can't hurt to ask," Hutto agreed.

"That's what you think," Barton said sardonically. "Who's gonna put it up to him, you?"

"Ahem! Well, uh—that is—er, you're the sheriff, Mack."

"Somebody better put it to Stafford, and quick," Sam said, "before he gets it in his head to lock horns with Damon. Hangtown can't afford to lose any more men."

"You volunteering?"

"Now Sheriff, you know none of these Rebs'd listen to a damn Yankee like me."

"Hell, I don't know why *I'm* listening to you."

"Because you want to stay alive. And as long as you're listening, I've got few more ideas."

SEVENTEEN

Hangtown made ready for war, teeming with activity like a disturbed anthill. In addition to the two watchmen posted in the church bell tower, two more were stationed in the courthouse clock tower at the other side of town. That ensured against a Comanche sneak from east as well as west.

Two watchers in each observation post was protection against a lone sentry falling asleep, a very real threat in a town where whiskey flowed freely with no lack of passionate devotees.

Hutto found two volunteers willing to risk riding out to Anvil Flats in the Breaks to fetch the U.S. cavalry troop escorting Major Adams's wagon train. The two, Hapgood and Coleman, were each willing to make the attempt for one hundred dollars in gold—more money than either had ever seen in one place at one time.

Hapgood was a short, feisty bantamweight, tougher than leather, who'd survived some of the worst hell of the war. Coleman was a small rancher whose place had been foreclosed on by the bank when he couldn't make the payments.

Hutto wasn't such a fool as to put out any money in advance, and risk the recipient galloping away for all he was worth. The volunteers would be paid upon return with the troops. As soon as it got dark the messengers would go out separately, by different routes, to maximize the chances of at least one of them getting through.

The courthouse, the strongest and most secure structure in Hangtown, served as headquarters. Families from all parts of town streamed to it, women and children massing in the large, high-ceilinged courtroom.

Hangtown was too large to be defended as a whole. The heart of the defense was Four Corners, where the courthouse, the jail, the feed store, and the Golden Spur all met. Townfolk were leery of leaving treasured possessions unguarded in abandoned homes and shops, but were allowed to bring only water, food, weapons, and similar necessities into the courthouse.

The gathering included the folk of Mextown.

Wade Hutto had resisted when Sam Heller first broached the idea to him earlier in the Cattleman Hotel. "You can't mix white folks and Mexes in the same place," Hutto had protested. Aware of Latigo's cool-eyed glance falling on him, he quickly followed up by saying, "That is, the Mexican element want to stick to their own kind, just as we do."

"You speak true, señor," Latigo said coolly. "We no more want to be with you than you want to be with us."

"If we don't hang together, we'll all surely hang separately," Sam said.

"I've heard that before. Who said that?" asked Russ Lockhart, Hutto's high-strung, volatile brother-in-law.

"Abe Lincoln."

"Lincoln? Don't you dare mention that name around here!"

"Ben Franklin," Hutto said tiredly.

"Eh? What's that?"

"Benjamin Franklin said it, Russ. 'If we do not hang together we will surely all hang separately.'"

"Franklin, eh? I suppose that's all right then." Lockhart sniffed.

"You are all wrong," Latigo said gravely. "It was said by Benito Juarez."

"You're crazy!" Lockhart said.

"We've got to pull together if we want to win. If we learned anything from the last war, that's it," Sam reminded them.

"You'd do well not to bring up the war!" Lockhart sputtered.

Sam ignored him. "We need as much firepower in one place as we can get. Vince Stafford and Damon Bolt have postponed killing each other and agreed to a truce. The folk of Hangtown, Anglo and Mex, will have to forgo the pleasure of their prejudices till the Comanche is whupped—and believe me, that's a long way off from being a sure thing."

"You lowdown Yankee leveler, you," Lockhart said, shaking a small, bony fist under Sam's nose.

"Your differences will seem mighty small once those braves start coming at you, and keep coming," said Sam.

In the end there was nothing for Wade Hutto to do but concede the point. The indignity of mixing with one's "inferiors" paled against the possibility of roasting over a slow Comanche fire.

"Cheer up," Sam said. "If we get out of this alive, your boy Mayor Holloman will probably pick up a lot of votes in Mextown next election."

"Votes? We don't let Mexes vote," Hutto said.

"The commanding officer at Fort Pardee'll have something to say about that. There'll be some changes made come Election Day. Hope we're here to see it."

"You devil," Russ Lockhart said feelingly. "Is there no end to your base Northern scheming?"

Making no further comment, Sam joined his fellow delegation members—Latigo, Joe Delagoa and Wiley Crabbe—charged with persuading the folk of Mextown to combine rather than be conquered separately. Sam was a gringo, but it was hoped that as a generally shunned and despised outsider among the Anglo ruling class, his words might carry some weight. Coffin maker and stone carver Joe Delagoa, of Portuguese descent, made his home in Mextown. Wiley Crabbe, another cousin of the Dog Star's Squint McCray, had a common-law Mexican wife and a couple kids by her, giving him a dash of credibility with the Hispanic community. More impressive were his credentials as a skilled horseman and dead shot, attributes well respected by all ethnic groups throughout the West.

One of Don Eduardo's simpatico pistoleros, Latigo had the most pull, though the folk of Mextown were of decidedly two minds concerning the master of Rancho Grande. The grandee was haughty, remote, and had never lifted a finger to help them; on the other hand he was one of their own kind and held his own against the Anglos, which counted for something.

To Mextown rode the four, to confer with the alcalde, the headman, and the village elders. The raid earlier by the Comanches had left a number of folk killed and injured, adding urgency to the message of combine or die. No less persuasive was Black Robe's cassock, which Sam brought to buttress his case. The weird, fearsome talisman was a tangible warning sign shrieking Danger! Red Hand is coming!

Headman and elders immediately agreed and set about organizing the exodus from Mextown, adding their numbers to the scores of men, women, and children already assembled at the courthouse.

Clangor boomed as long, high-backed courtroom benches were taken apart to serve as barricades. Glass was knocked out of windows, a preemptive measure to protect against injuries from razor-sharp glass shards during a battle. Backs, seats, and struts from the disassembled benches were nailed in place as bulwarks at the bottom halves of the paneless windows.

The aftermath of the War Between the States was a time of scarcity throughout Texas and the rest of the South, but Hangtown had guns and ammunition aplenty. A sizeable arsenal was amassed, apart from the rifles, shotguns, and pistols with which the locals already went about armed.

Foodstuffs and supplies of fresh drinking water were stockpiled against a long siege. They were kept in a storeroom under lock and key, under the watchful eyes of guards posted by Barton.

Buckets of water were distributed throughout the building as prevention against fire. Buckets of sand were also in place to soak up slippery blood that might coat the floor.

The fact of it being Saturday worked to the advantage of the defenders. Many ranchers had come to town with their families. A fair number were still in Hangtown when the Comanches first struck. The vast majority of them survived. Their families were intact and in town.

A handful of families had split up earlier, with some members remaining in town while others dispersed back home to their ranches. After the attack, those in town were half crazed with fear and worry over the possible fate of loved ones at the ranch. They were in a tight spot—make a mad dash to the outlying ranches to rally their families and race back to town, risking death or capture by Red Hand's braves or stay put in town, separated from the rest of their family.

Hutto and the sheriff could not spare any men to assist in rounding up the outliers, not when the Comanches' main force might hit town at any time. Volunteers to escort such a suicide mission were few . . . actually none.

No one had the right to order men separated from their families to stay in the safety of town (such as it was) while those they loved were unknowingly threatened with the horrors of rape, torture, and death. The only option suggested was that these desperate men band together as a single force and go from ranch to ranch, collecting all their families before risking the return trip.

In the end that was done. Eight grim-faced men rode out together, vanishing over the horizon en route to the vast ranch lands along the forks of the Liberty River, wondering what they would find and if they would return.

A super-corral was hastily thrown up around the area of Hobson's livery stable to save as many horses from the Comanches as possible. The layout of the area lent itself to a more formidable stronghold than Hobson's rail fence. The rear of the jail and feed store, the front of the stable, and the side of the carpenter shop/lumberyard served as bulwarks of the enclosure. Four streets formed a grid. The street mouths were barricaded, sealed by wagons turned on their sides, hogshead barrels, and stacked hay bales. Anchored with weights, the wagons were backed by lines of hay bales to serve as shooting platforms, allowing defenders to take cover behind the upended wagons and shoot across their tops.

The longest open space was enclosed with two freight wagons turned on their sides. Gaps in the barricade were shored up with piles of tables, chairs, cords of firewood, and whatever else came to hand. The lumberyard supplied planks, beams and odd-sized pieces of scrap wood. Several openings were left at opposite ends of the enclosure, allowing quick and easy access while the barrier was being built. When the time came, they would be sealed with hay bales and hogsheads.

The flat roofs of the jail, feed store, and carpenter shop would serve as platforms for riflemen, as would the loft of the stable barn. Quantities of hay, oats, and water for horses were massed inside the enclosure, serving a double purpose of reinforcing makeshift walls.

Scores of horses were gathered for the penning. The Big Corral, as it was called, thronged with horses, stallions, mares, geldings, yearlings, colts, scrappy ponies, and massive quarter horses. A wealth of prime horseflesh—an irresistible target for Red Hand and his warrior braves.

A reserve stock was set aside to serve as a mounted

force against the Comanches, and to carry out errands and make the rounds around town.

The Staffords and the Ramrod bunch were centered in the feed store. Store-owner Dickerson had grudgingly consented to house the Ramrod riders in the building. Vince Stafford had come out in favor of it and Dickerson didn't want to go against him. Few did. A big building, it stood alone, sharing its lot with no adjacent structures, and almost directly opposite the Golden Spur and Damon Bolt, the special object (though not the only one) of Vince Stafford's ire. It was the prime reason Vince had proposed the arrangement; he could keep the gambling house under observation while waiting out the Comanche onslaught.

Stafford was a big customer of the store. Having the Ramrod riders lodged in the store might well protect it from being sacked and burned. On the other hand, they were rowdies and Dickerson feared losses from pilferage and vandalism. Still, he personally opted to stay in the courthouse along with his family, pinning his hopes on the sheriff's office being next door to the store where he could keep an eye on it. Besides, if they started tearing up the place, he could do nothing to stop them.

Ramrod men carried fifty- and one hundred-pound sacks of oats, grain, barley, and the like from the store, stacking them out in front of the building to form defensive breastworks. The Staffords were inside the store, well under cover, not showing themselves as potential targets of a well-aimed shot from the gambling house.

"What about the ranch, Pa? They's only a handful of the boys there," Quent asked.

"They got to take their chances like the rest of us. Here's where the battle will be fought and won. Red Hand will go for the big prize. Take Hangtown and he can pick off the ranches later. With any luck we'll break the Comanches here before they get to raiding the South Fork," Vince said.

"Hutto's sticking," Clay said. "You don't see him making any damn fool run for his ranch. Not with those scalp hunters out there."

Quent was restless, not one to sit still for too long, if at all. He paced back and forth. "What about them Mexes in the Spur?" he fumed.

Several dozen Mexican-Americans males, youths and adults, were housed in the gambling house.

"What of them?" Clay said. "They're here to fight Red Hand. When the fighting's over they'll go back to Mextown. They won't mix in our feud. They don't give a damn about white folks killing each other."

"I don't like it," Quent said.

"Don't get yourself in an uproar. When Red Hand's whipped, we take the gambler," said Clay.

"And his whore," Vince said quickly.

Clay groaned. "You still harping on that? For God's sake, Pa, let it go. It's crazy talk."

"Nothing crazy about doing what's right," Vince said. "It'll get done, too."

"I ain't killing no woman. I got to live in these parts. Nobody's hanging a woman-killer tag around my neck."

"I ain't gone kill her, if that's what making you go all yellow, Clay. I'm just going to make her wish she was dead, like my boy—your brother Bliss—or did you forget about him already?"

"I didn't forget, Pa."

"See that you don't."

"You sweet on that gal, Clay?" Quent said, snickering.

"I wouldn't have had nothing to do with her, if Pa hadn't sent me to buy her off," Clay said, coloring. "She'd've took the money, too, if it'd done any good. But Bliss would've gone chasing after her, no matter where she went. He just had to have her all to himself."

"And now he's dead, and they's gone be a reckoning," Vince Stafford said in a tone of finality.

Clay fell silent, exasperated.

Dusky shadows thickened in the feed store.

The Dog Star Saloon regulars, a hard-core nucleus of fifteen or so, clustered in and around the jail. Most of them had had more than a passing acquaintance with the hoosegow in the past, but this time things were different.

Using tables, chairs, barrels, and hay bales, they

built a barricade in front of the stone blockhouse, with wings extending along the sides for a man's length or so, forming a U-shape. Narrow openings at the sides allowed free passage. Finished, the men loitered around, loafing, smoking, talking, drinking, matching coins, and checking their weapons.

The sun had set, purple dusk deepening into night. Barton stood outside the barricade, smoking a cigar. He looked around. It was risky, putting the Ramrod bunch so close to the Golden Spur, but it kept both parties well away from the women and children forted up in the courthouse.

Closer to home, he eyed the Dog Star troops, shaking his head in mock disbelief. "What a crew! Looks like a posse should be chasing you fellows."

"Funny, huh? Us boys making our stand here at the jail, that is," Squint McCray said.

"Why not? For most of you, it's your home away from home. I ought to charge rent for all the time you rannigans have slept off a drunk back in the cells," Barton said.

"Rent? What do you think them fines were?"

Barton let it pass. "Where else are you and your crowd gonna light? Not in the courthouse with the respectable folk. They won't have you. Not in the Spur, Damon wouldn't chance all you booze hounds getting so close to his fine, high-priced liquor."

"Hard words, Sheriff, hard words."

"But true. And you sure don't want to bed down with Vince and friends."

McCray said a dirty word, then spat. "Shoot, I wouldn't piss on him if he was on fire."

"Maybe Red Hand'll do just that, and set him on fire for you not to piss on him," Barton quipped.

"I can hope. Anyhow, the jailhouse's the place to be. Good solid walls," reasoned McCray.

"You ought to know, you been behind 'em enough." Barton puffed on his cigar, the smoke clouds wreathing his head.

"Say, Sheriff, you wouldn't happen to have an extra seegar to spare, would you?" McCray wheedled.

Barton started to tell him where to go, then thought better of it for some unknown reason. He took a cigar out of his breast pocket. "Here."

"Why, thankee!" McCray said, surprised.

"Don't tell where you got it or all your pals'll be trying to bum a smoke from me," Barton warned.

"I'm a closed book," McCray said solemnly. He bit off the end of the cigar, spitting it out. He lit up, puffing away. "You're a gentleman, Sheriff."

"Just remember to vote for me come Election Day."

"I always do. Several times."

"Make sure you keep on doing it," Barton said. *If we're still around.*

EIGHTEEN

Dark was the night, and long.

Mrs. Frye knocked softly on the Spur's back office door. "Damon?" she said, low voiced. No answer. She turned the handle. The door was closed, but not locked. She entered, easing the door shut behind her.

A globe lamp provided the sole illumination. A window in the rear wall had plank boards nailed over it, covering it almost to the top. Above the planks, a narrow horizontal band of blackness showed through the glass. A couch stood against a side wall.

Damon Bolt sat behind a desk, arms folded on the desktop cushioning his head, which was turned to the side. His eyes were closed, his skin flushed. A snaky blue vein stood out on his high forehead, and sweat misted his face. Slow breathing came heavily. His jacket was draped across the back of his chair. A pair of pistols lay on the desktop, along with a whiskey bottle and an empty glass.

Mrs. Frye padded noiselessly behind the desk. She put a hand on his shoulder, gently shaking it. "Damon . . . Damon."

His slow, heavy breathing stopped and his eyelids slitted open. He lifted his head. "I'm not sleeping, Mrs. Frye. What time is it?"

"Eleven-thirty. Why don't you sack out on the couch? You'll be more comfortable."

"I'm fine."

She knew better than to argue. Crossing to the couch, she picked up a folded knit comforter that lay at one end, unfolded it, and draped it over the gambler's shoulders.

His head once again lay on pillowing arms. "Thank you."

"I'm going up to bed," she said.

"Tell Monk to wake me an hour before dawn."

"I will." Mrs. Frye lowered the flame on the lamp, dimming the light. A cone of bronze-colored light covered the desk and immediate area; beyond it swam yellow-brown shadows. She went to the door and paused. "Good night."

"'Night," he said.

She went out, closing the door.

Damon's eyes opened, peering blearily at the whiskey glass. Reaching for it, his hand closed around it, pulling it to him. Less than a mouthful of liquid lined the bottom of the glass. He raised his head and drank it.

Setting down the glass, he took hold of the bottle, tilting it to pour. The glass was three-quarters full when the bottle ran dry. Damon drank most of it, shuddering. He set the glass down, rested his head on his arms, and closed his eyes.

Mrs. Frye crossed the floor of the main room. Wall-mounted oil lamps broke up the big, barnlike space into zones of light and shadow. To economize, every other lamp in line had been extinguished, and those that burned had been trimmed low to not waste lamp oil. Besides, best not to have the place all lit up for fear of tempting Stafford's men into taking potshots at shadowy figures within. There was enough light to see by, and that was plenty. And, if she lived through Red Hand, she'd need every cent she could scrape up to rebuild.

The Golden Spur had been fortified. Boards were nailed over each window head-high, with plenty of loopholes and firing ports let into them, but the glass panes were still intact. Mrs. Frye was resigned to the likelihood of their destruction, but she refused to hurry the process. Window glass was expensive everywhere and hard to get that far west, especially the oversized front windowpanes. Maybe the Comanches wouldn't come; time enough to shoot out the glass if they did.

Strangers—Mexican-Americans from Mextown—were grouped at various places along the walls. There were dozens of them, ages ranging from graybeards to beardless youths. Their women, children, and oldsters were in the safety of the stonewalled courthouse.

Few if any of the men had ever before set foot inside the Golden Spur. It catered to those who could pay the freight. Some of the better-paid higher-ups at Rancho Grande were occasional customers, but rarely did the denizen of Mextown have enough gold in his pockets for a night at the Spur.

They'll have something to tell their grandkids about how they spent the night in the gilded palace of sin, Mrs. Frye thought. *If they live.*

It was the Yankee, Heller, whose idea it was for the Mexicans to fort up at the place. Mrs. Frye had been against it at the start, until Johnny Cross pointed out that the Ramrod bunch would be less likely to start trouble with all those extra armed men on the premises.

"That's one way to hedge a bet," Damon had remarked.

Never one to let her prejudices get in the way of her keen eye for the main chance, Mrs. Frye had agreed to admit the newcomers. She even allowed them kitchen privileges, to cook up a mess of beans and tortillas for their crowd. Any whiskey or beer they wanted, they had to pay for, though. There were few takers as the drinkers among them passed around bottles of tequila and mescal they had brought themselves.

Some of the men smoked and talked quietly, others slept or tried to. They sat on the floor, backs to the wall, their wide-brimmed straw hats pulled down over their eyes. Others lay stretched out on the floorboards, folded serapes cushioning their heads.

More than a few were armed with pistols. A goodly number of shotguns, from lightweight fowling pieces to trumpet-mouthed blunderbusses were close at hand. Some had rifles, mostly single-shot long guns and more than a few had unrifled muskets. Very few had repeating rifles. Everybody had blade weapons, machetes, belt knives, Spanish daggers, or stilettoes. Sharp-edged farm implements such as axes, scythes, hand sickles, and such were in evidence as well.

Mrs. Frye devoutly wished the fight with the Comanches would not come to such close quarters, but . . . it might.

Morrissey stood behind the bar, beefy forearms resting on the countertop. Monk the bouncer stood opposite him, tossing back drinks as though trying to make up for those hours spent earlier on the roof keeping watch under the the hot sun. Wiley Crabbe was there, too, soaking up free drinks.

Morrissey doled them out sparingly. A Dog Star boozehound like Wiley could soak up a lot of hooch if not kept on a tight rein.

Flint Ryan and Luke Pettigrew sat at a nearby table, yarning back and forth between sips of whiskey. Charley Bronco sat with his back to the wall, his chair tilted back with two legs raised into the air. With his hat covering his eyes and hands folded in his lap, he was sleeping, or maybe just resting his eyes.

Creed Teece was in his room, asleep. Passing by his door earlier, Mrs. Frye had heard him snoring away. Trust that bloodless cuss to be able to sleep even though a Comanche attack was imminent. He didn't have a nerve in his body. She envied him that ability. Maybe that's why he was so good at the gunman's trade.

Johnny Cross was nowhere to be seen, but Mrs. Frye knew where he was. She'd seen him going upstairs with Francine.

"Good night, men," she said, waving a hand in parting to the group around the bar. They bid her good night. *How many will be alive this time tomorrow night? Will I?*

To hell with it. She went upstairs, the revolver in a slitted side pocket of her skirt banging against her leg as she climbed the steps. She crossed the mezzanine to her room on the west side of the second floor. A night owl who slept by day, she needed a room free from morning's intrusive sunlight.

She glanced down the hall at Francine's closed door, her mercenary soul irked by the thought of one of her girls giving it away for free. Still, special times called for special circumstances.

Johnny Cross had already earned his keep during the shootout with Wyck Joslyn, Stingaree, and the Fromes Boys. Doubtless he'd prove his worth many more times before sundown tomorrow. He was proving it with Francine, if the muffled squeals and gasping outcries coming from behind her door were any indication.

"Ah, youth," Mrs. Frye murmured, a cynical half smile on her face. She opened her room door, letting in the hallway light so she could see what she was doing as she struck a match and lit the oil lamp atop her bedside night table.

She went back to the door, closing it, turning the key and locking it, leaving the key in the keyhole. Her room was clean and austere, with few decorations or creature comforts beyond a soft-mattressed bed.

Reaching into her skirt pocket, she took out her gun and set it on the bed. A short-barreled .44 revolver, the big-caliber six-gun had man-stopping power in every round. A lot of gun, but she knew how to use it . . . and had.

Sitting on the side of the bed, she untied the knotted laces of her ankle boots and took off the footwear. She removed her blouse and skirt, hanging them up. Underneath she wore a thin white cotton shift that covered her from shoulders to ankles. She peeled off dark knee-length stockings, rolled them up, and set them aside. Her body was good, supple, with high firm breasts, flat belly, lean hips and long rounded thighs tapering to slim ankles and small, narrow feet. It was a comfort to know that if the Spur burned down to the ground she still had something to sell to make a living.

She went to a chest of drawers standing against

one of the side walls. Opening the top drawer, she reached to the rear of it, taking a cigar box out from under some folded lingerie and setting it down atop the cabinet.

Her image glimmered and shifted in the oval mirror mounted on an H-shaped frame on top of the dresser. She was long-faced, more than a little horse-faced, but compensating for that were bright bold eyes, high cheekbones, and a ripe red slash of a mouth. A network of thin-lined wrinkles showed at the corners of her eyes, and a pair of vertical grooves ran from nostrils to chin, bracketing her mouth.

She unpinned her hair, freeing it so that it fell loose to her slim, smooth shoulders. Her mouth curved upward in an inward, secret smile. She looked as though she might have been getting ready for a visit from a lover. In a sense, she was.

Crossing to the bed, she set the cigar box down on the night table. It was warm in the room. She went to a window in the rear wall, parting the curtains and raising the window six inches, letting in the cool night air. Below lay only a bare wall. Not even the most agile Comanche could scale the wall to the window.

West of the window, Hangtown was dark, not a light burning. It occurred to her that she made a good target, outlined against the window's yellow rectangle. Closing the curtains, she went to the bed and sat down. Moving the .44 to the night table, out of the way, she opened the cigar box lid.

Inside was a small spirit alcohol lamp, a pair of golden needles not unlike knitting needles, an equally slim pipe tipped at one end by a thimble-sized bowl, and a plum-sized block of some gummy, blackish-brown substance wrapped in wax paper—Chandu, the Black Smoke.

Opium.

She took out the items, laying them out on the night table, her hands shaking slightly. Striking a match, she lit the spirit lamp's rope wick. It burned with a low blue flame.

Unwrapping the lump of opium, she used a golden needle to extract a pea-sized chunk of the stuff, spearing it on the tip. Using the flame of the spirit lamp, she set it alight, then blew it out. Thin lines of rich, aromatic smoke rose from it, the scent sending a wave of dizziness through her.

She placed the piece in the pipe bowl, hands trembling as she raised it to her lips. She took a puff, filling her lungs, holding it. She felt light-headed. She smoked some more, feeling as if she were in a train that had started moving, leaving the station. The Black Smoke was starting to come on. A cloud of purple-gray fog descended on her mind and senses, muffling them, taking her away.

She'd picked up the habit years ago, in her early days of whoredom. It was the one lover who never failed to satisfy. And it was always there for her—as long as she could pay for it. Run out of money and it would run out, too, like any faithless lover of mere flesh and blood.

Her eyes glazed, heavy-lidded; her mouth soft-
ened. The light from the globe lamp was too bright,
hurting her eyes. She turned the light down low,
muting it into soft sweet shadows where shapes
lurked, half-seen faces, images, and dreams.

Cares and fears fell away from her, sloughed off
like a snake shedding its skin. Let the world go to
hell, eternity beckoned in the seductive coils of spiraling strands of Black Smoke.

Several rooms down the hall and behind a door,
Johnny Cross sought a different brand of release,
grappling in sweet sweaty love-play with Francine
Hayes. Francine, with her angel face and figure of
passion, glowed naked in all the glory of her smooth,
flawless ivory skin.

She writhed under Johnny, wanton and knowing, her buttocks tightly clenched and quivering as
she lifted her hips off the mattress to meet his surging downstrokes. She was good, a hell of a ride, and
he'd had some of the best in his young, full life. He
gave as good as he got . . . or better.

Bedsprings creaked and squealed, the posts of
the brass-railed headstead hammering rhythmically
against the wall, chipping the paint and cracking the
plaster. Francine's face contorted in an ageless mask
of intense concentration. Her open mouth panting,
she moaned.

Her legs were lifted and bent at the knees, hugging
Johnny's sweat-slick flanks as he rode her on home to
glory. Pelvis working, gyrating, and meeting his
thrusts, she went over the edge, taking him with her.

At the climax, her mouth was close to his ear, her voice a breathless whisper that spoke louder than a shriek. "Save me, Johnny, save me. Don't let them kill me. Oh God, oh God. Save me!"

Frantic, but choice. That's Francine, Johnny thought. *Hell, I'd have saved her anyhow, but this sure seals the deal.*

NINETEEN

"Do you know the Truce of God, amigo?" Latigo asked.

"No," Sam said, "can't say as I do."

At midnight on the cloudy night, the moon was playing peek-a-boo with the clouds. Bright silver moonlight alternated with ghostly silver-black gloom. A farmer's old saw Sam had oft heard repeated during boyhood days in southwest Minnesota maintained that for the best crop yields, some planting was done by moonlight. He and Latigo were doing some planting of their own on the far west edge of Hangtown, sowing seeds of destruction to reap a crop of pure hell.

It was an idea he'd had, to lay out a special welcome mat for Red Hand. Surprise package, so to speak. He'd pitched it earlier to Hutto and Barton and through them to the Cattleman Crowd. The town powers had bought his idea.

Sam and Latigo were laying the groundwork to

make it happen. They were not the only agents of
the plan. Others were at work in other parts of
Hangtown, carrying out similar preparations.

Moonlight or shadow, which is best, Sam wondered.
Moonlight meant he could see better, but he could
also be seen. Shadow hid him, but also hid others
who were lurking.

Comanches, it was said, didn't attack at night.
Not true. They preferred not to attack at night, but
they weren't ones to pass up an opportunity no
matter what the hour, day or night.

Sam and Latigo labored on the flat below the
church and Boot Hill. With them were two horses,
and a mule laden down with sacks full of hardware:
bundled sticks of dynamite, wooden stakes, digging
implements, and strips of cloth.

We've got our necks stuck out a country mile,
thought Sam.

Two men in the church tower were keeping watch
for Comanches, but Sam preferred to trust his own
perceptions. Not that he trusted them so well.

A breeze was blowing from the west, making the
night air cool and fresh. Latigo held the horses'
reins and the mule's lead rope. Sam was down on
one knee beside a shallow hole on the ground. A
wooden stake had been hammered partway into
the hardpacked clay. A narrow band of cloth twelve
inches long was knotted around the top of the
stake. In the moonlight the cloth was gray; its true
color was red.

Sam placed a bundle of dynamite in the hole,

laying it on its side, lengthwise. Rising, he took up a spade, sticking the blade into a pile of dirt that had been excavated from the hole. Carefully—very carefully, for all the sticks of dynamite were fitted with blasting caps—he sprinkled the dirt over the bundled explosives.

The dirt mound disappeared quickly as he refilled the shallow hole. Using a leafy branch he'd broken off a bush, he evened off the dirt on top of the hole to disguise the marks of digging. Only the stake with the strip of cloth tied to it marked the spot where the dynamite had been buried.

Five more such banded stakes were studded at regular intervals across the broad apron of ground fronting the rise to the church.

Sam put the spade and the leafy branch in one of the burlap sacks slung across the mule's back. He rubbed his palms together, wiping the dust from them. "That'll do it for here," he said, low-voiced.

He and Latigo mounted up, Latigo holding the mule's lead rope. They started forward. The mule balked, staying in place. Latigo tugged on the rope several times, but the mule wouldn't budge. Leaning over in the saddle so his mouth was close to the mule's long ears, Latigo spoke softly to him in Spanish. The mule began moving in the desired direction.

"What'd you say to him?" Sam asked.

"I tell him I leave him for the Comanche," Latigo said. "Nothing they like better than roast mule meat."

They followed the dirt road up the rise, through

the gap between the two knolls and down the other side, riding toward Hangtown. "A couple more here should do it." Sam halted.

He and Latigo climbed down and dug two holes on the down slope, one a man's length below the crest, the other at the base. As before, bundles of dynamite went in the holes and were covered with dirt. Banded stakes marked out each hole. They talked as they worked, their voices hushed.

"Do you know the Truce of God, amigo?" Latigo asked again.

"No, can't say I do. What is it?"

"In Mexico, in the swamps around Vera Cruz on the coast, they say that when there is a great flood all the animals in the jungle flee to higher ground. Trapped all together, the creatures do not follow their natural way. *El Tigre*, the jaguar, falls not on the sheep to kill and eat it. The snake preys not on the rabbit, nor the fox on the chicken. All are at peace with each other until the waters go down. This is the Truce of God."

"Tell me, Latigo, have you ever seen this Truce of God?"

"In flood—no, for I have lived most of my life here on the plains of *Tejas*, where the floods are not so much. But with my own eyes I have seen something like it, during prairie fires. When animals flee the fire, none attacks the other."

"Because they all fear being eaten by the flames."

"So it is with the folk of Hangtown, no? Fear of

the Comanche is stronger than their hate for each other."

"It's a truce, mebbe, but not of God. The Lord and Hangtown are pretty far apart," Sam said.

"*Quien sabe, amigo.* Who knows?"

"Well, that's the way to bet it."

Sam brushed over the filled-in holes with the leafy branch, smoothing out the dirt. He and Latigo got on their horses and Sam rode up the side of the hill to the church, careful to stay off the road for fear that an iron-shod hoof could set off one of the tricky, touchy blasting caps.

He tilted his head back, looking up. High atop the bell tower, the outlines of the two watchmen formed a deeper darkness against the night sky. Sam whistled to get their attention. "All done. Keep off the road!"

"We will," a sentry replied.

"Be sure to warn the replacements, when they come to relieve you."

"When's that gonna be? We been here since before sundown."

"I'll tell Barton."

"See that you do," the watchman said.

"Tell him to get his ass up here, see how he likes it," the other said.

Sam had nothing to say to that. He rode downhill, joining Latigo. They started into town, walking their horses east where the dirt road became Trail Street.

"A good trick, that dynamite," Latigo said, "if the Comanche come this way."

"If they don't, the other approaches to Four Corners are planted, too. We'll get 'em coming or going."

"Is it that you like Hangtown so well or hate the Comanche so much?"

"I like living. If we beat Red Hand here, we live. If not . . ."

Red Hand was wary of mysterious activities his scouts had observed going on around town in the hour before midnight. The Texans were up to something. Groups of two prowled around the edges of Four Corners for reasons unknown. His men were unable to get close enough to determine what exactly it was they were doing.

He would give the Texans something to think about during the long hours of the night watch. He sent in a band of skirmishers to start trouble on the west side of town, shooting it up to draw the whites' attention to that sector. A classic piece of misdirection.

The moon came out from behind a cloud, shafting silver rays. Sam and Latigo continued on Trail Street.

"What now?" Latigo asked.

"We get something to eat and drink, mebbe catch a few hours of shut-eye, and wait for sunup."

They neared the Alamo Bar. *Strange to see the*

Alamo dark—shuttered and locked up, Sam thought. Ordinarily it would just be hitting its stride, riotous and ablaze with light. But it was black and silent as a tomb, as was the rest of Hangtown outside Four Corners, itself dimly lit with few figures showing.

Something burst out of the north sidestreet, streaking overhead. Great wings beat the air as an owl soared up and out of sight. A big one, its flapping wings sounded like a blanket being shaken out.

Startled, Sam's horse upreared, forelegs leaving the ground. He clung to the animal to keep from being thrown. Unseen objects whipped past him in the dark, scorching the air with the speed of their passage.

Arrows!

The thud of a shaft striking flesh meant Latigo was hit.

Shadowy forms shifted in the dimness deeper in the side street.

Sam stopped fighting to hold on and threw himself off the horse, opposite from where the Comanche arrows had come. He hit the ground hard, breaking the fall as best he could as he rolled on his shoulders. It gave him a jolt, stunning him for a moment before he continued rolling to avoid being trampled by his horse as it ran away.

The mule brayed, breaking free and running down Trail Street, too.

Latigo was still in the saddle, hunched forward, with an arrow sticking out of his chest. Grabbing his gun, he fired at the ambushers. Red lines slanted from his gun barrel toward figures huddled in the shadows.

A strangled cry, abruptly choked off, showed that at least one shot had scored.

A bowstring twanged as another arrow was loosed, taking Latigo in the torso. He tilted sideways, firing a shot into the air as he fell off his horse.

A Comanche darted out of the street, tomahawk in hand. Shrieking a war cry, he charged Sam who lay sprawling on his back in the street.

With no time to get the mule's-leg loose, Sam drew the Navy Colt stuck in his belt, firing up at the brave standing above him with war hatchet held high for a skull-splitting downstroke. He pumped several rounds into the center of the Indian. Muzzle flashes from the Colt underlit the brave's face, highlighting stark death-mask agony. The Comanche collapsed.

Rifle fire tore out of the darkness, flying high and harmlessly over Sam. Pushing the dead man away, Sam rolled over. Raising himself on his elbows, he returned fire, tagging a brave who shrieked, spun and fell, the rifle falling from his hands.

The Colt was empty. Sam let it go and drew the mule's-leg. Rising to his knees, he worked the lever, spewing lead into the side street. Muzzle flares pulsed with fiery flashes.

Three braves writhed, shrieking in a death dance as they were cut down.

On his feet, Sam advanced, levering the mule's-leg, cutting down Comanches all the way to Commerce Street.

He watched as the two Comanches who had stayed behind to hold the horses hopped on the backs of their ponies to make their escape. Screened by a row of buildings, they were safe from Sam's bullets.

The deadly little skirmish was over. But Latigo was dead.

TWENTY

The clock tower on the courthouse had been turned into a combination observation post and sniper's nest. It was occupied by two Hangtown marksmen of note, Pete Zorn and Steve Maitland.

Zorn was an old-timer, a burnt-out cinder of a man, gray-haired, grizzled. A veteran of the Mexican-American War and the War Between the States, and countless shooting scrapes with Indians and owlhoots, he was a dead shot with a rifle.

Steve Maitland was a gangly, sixteen-year-old ranch kid with brown hair, a pink beardless face, and the clear cold gray eyes so often found in sharpshooters. He had finished second in the annual Thanksgiving Day turkey shoot the year before—no mean feat in Hangtown with its many top shooters.

Zorn had finished first that day and taken the prize.

The clock tower room was a square space, much

of it taken up by clockwork machinery. Gears, wheels, flywheels, weights, counterweights, and pendulums were corroded with rust and thick with dust and congealed grease.

The walls had louvered side windows with adjustable horizontal wooden slats, allowing for light, vision, and ventilation. They also allowed for many and varied lines of fire covering much of Hangtown below.

The space was supplied with a couple chairs and whatnot to provide Zorn and Maitland with minimal comforts. A kerosene lamp burned smokily, trimmed low to provide illumination with minimal damage to the occupants' night vision. Each shooter had his own rifle plus several extras supplied by the town to minimize time spent in reloading. There was plenty of ammunition, too.

Earlier, they had watched as a number of stealthy two-man teams set out from Four Corners to plant dynamite in the avenues of approach. They'd kept a ready eye out for prowling Comanches, but none had been seen. Not that they weren't there. But if they were, they couldn't be seen from the clock tower.

The first floor of the courthouse had seethed with noise and unrest when so many families had massed in the courtroom. The scene had quieted down with the lateness of the hour, but was still disturbed by anxious men, nervous females, sleepless kids, and squawling babies.

An office in the southeast corner of the second

floor was reserved for the use of Wade Hutto, pursuant to his duties in town council and county administration. Hutto sat behind the desk, comfortably set up in a high-backed, well-cushioned chair. Seated across from him were Banker Willoughby, Alamo Bar owner Chance Stillman, and promoter Rutland Dean. Their chairs were smaller and not quite as comfortable as Hutto's, but they were drinking his liquor and smoking his cigars.

A leather couch, useful for entertaining lady friends or for napping—stood in a corner against the wall. Boone Lassiter lay on his back, hat tilted over his eyes, awake. A lit cigar was clenched between his jaws; he held a tumbler of whiskey on his chest.

Hutto was making the best of a bad situation, but he would gladly have given plenty to be anywhere but where he was, waiting out the night hours before a full-scale Comanche onslaught.

"Good brandy," Banker Willoughby said. "You do yourself right, friend Hutto."

"In this job you need it," Hutto replied. "Especially on a night like this."

Gunfire sounded outside. There were shrieks in the distance. More shots—a death cry.

Boone Lassiter sat up, swinging his booted feet to the floor. Hutto came out from behind his desk and went to the south window. He lifted an edge of the window shade, peering outside. Lassiter went to the desk and blew out the light in the oil lamp.

The room went dark, a line of light showing at the bottom of the door to the hallway.

The others crowded around Hutto at the window. It looked down on Trail Street, including the other three bulwarks of Four Corners. They could see the jail, the feed store, and the Golden Spur.

"What is it, Wade?" Dean asked.

"There's movement down there, but the shooting came from farther up the street," Hutto said. "Can't quite make it out."

Lassiter crossed the hall to the office opposite Hutto's, and entered it. Empty and dark, the room held the southwest corner of the second floor. Standing to the side of a window facing west, he raised the curtain and looked outside.

Hutto and the others came into the room, the last one in leaving the door open.

"Close that door so we don't show against the light," Lassiter growled.

Willoughby shut the door, then joined the others.

The moon came out from behind a cloud, silvering rooftops and shining into the street. Motion swirled on Trail Street. Black forms of horses and men shifted and surged. A gun yammered, striking sparks of light.

A man screamed and fell. More shooting racketed up from the darkness.

The couthouse was astir. Pete Zorn and Steve Maitland went to the west wall of the clock tower, peering out and down through the wooden-slatted windows. They couldn't make out much. The shooting had stopped, and the horsemen had fled, swallowed by darkness.

In the first floor courtroom, men started up out of troubled sleep—those with nerves strong enough to enable them to sleep, or drunk enough to have passed out for a blessed while. Women gasped, girls shrieked, children and babies fussed.

Armed men with sleep-bleared eyes staggered to the west windows for a look, only to be balked by the Golden Spur blocking their view.

Men moved around in the jail, feed store, and gambling house. Defenders made ready, but none ventured outside for fear of stepping into an ambush.

Throughout Four Corners, attention was focused on the dark, west side of town from where the shooting seemed to have come.

Red Hand and twelve followers were hidden in a dark grove of trees a hundred yards east of town. Part of a well-wooded thicket north of Hangtree Trail, it was a tangle of brush, shrubs, and tall weeds.

When the shooting started on the west side of town, Red Hand rode out alone into the open, toward the courthouse. Outfitted in full warlike regalia, he rode a strikingly colored silver horse with a white mane. A bonnet of eagle feathers crowned his head. His face was striped and masked with war paint, his torso was shielded by a chest piece made of buffalo bones, and his arms were painted red from fingertips to elbows. A round buffalo-hide shield was worn on his left arm; his right hand held a flaming spear.

Not the Fire Lance, of course. It was too valuable to be thrown away on a mere ploy, and that's what he was engaged in. A bold stroke to steal the Texans' courage and plant fear in their hearts.

Red Hand wielded a Comanche lance whose spear blade was coated with Medicine Hat's inflammable compound and set ablaze. He crossed the field, charging the courthouse front.

Close to the courthouse steps, he yanked hard on the reins, the bit digging into the soft parts of the animal's mouth. The silver stallion reared, rising on its hind legs.

Red Hand cast the fiery lance, burying it point first in one of the wooden front double doors. It stuck, quivering in a planked panel, its head burning with eerie blue ghost light.

Turning his horse to the right, he galloped away into the darkness. He shrieked a war whoop in parting.

His men in the grove opened fire on the courthouse with repeating rifles, laying down a covering fire for their chief. Once Red Hand was safely clear, they ceased fire, melting back into the woods.

Drawn by this new disturbance, the courthouse folk rushed to the east windows to see what it was all about. Wade Hutto returned to his office, looked outside, and saw the burning spear stuck in the courthouse front door.

"What's it all about?" asked Banker Willoughby.

"A declaration of war, I call it," Hutto said.

"As if any were needed! They've already made their hostile intent clear," Rutland Dean said.

"Comanche medicine, to scare the faint hearts," Boone Lassiter informed them. "Hope nobody falls for it. But they will."

The fiery spear kept on burning. Presently, some hardy souls opened the front door partway, mindful not to show themselves as targets. Somebody splashed the spear with a bucket of water. The fire was oil-based and instead of extinguishing it the water made it burn hotter and brighter.

Next, buckets of sand were thrown on it and blankets were beaten against it and the door until the flames went out. A few door planks were charred, but only on the surface, not too deep.

The door was slammed shut and bolted from the inside.

An hour or so later, the screaming started. It came from somewhere in the grove from which Red Hand had previously ventured. Thick woods and darkness hid whatever was going on there.

Shrill and piercing, the outcry was the sound of a man in mortal agony. Worse, it was only the opening note in what would prove to be an aria of anguish. It was loud and clear throughout the Four Corners.

A small lamp burned in Hutto's office, glowing

dimly. Fresh screams ripped through the stillness of night.

"Gad! What're they doing to that poor devil?" Rutland Dean exclaimed.

"Torture," answered Boone Lassiter.

Chance Stillman went to the east window, looking out. "I don't see nobody. No Injins. Nothing."

"You won't see them until they want you to see them," Lassiter said.

"Who is it, do you think?" Dean wondered.

"Some poor soul unlucky enough to be taken alive, Lord help him," Lassiter said.

"Think it's Coleman or Hapgood?" Stillman asked.

"Let's hope not. They're our only hope of getting word to the cavalry," Willoughby said.

"Don't count on the army," Lassiter said. "We're on our own here."

Hutto's face fell. "There's a good chance that one or both of them might have gotten through . . . isn't there?"

Nobody answered. The shrieking fell off, grew silent. After a moment, Dean said, "Thank God that's over!"

Boone Lassiter snorted. "Hell, they ain't even started yet." He poured himself a fresh drink.

After a while, the screaming began again, steadily rising into ever-higher registers of pain. It lost all human qualities. It was the hopeless wail of a suffering animal in mortal pain and terror.

"What do they do to make a man scream like that?" Willoughby wondered.

"Don't think about it," Hutto said thickly.

Lassiter gulped his drink, setting down an empty glass. "Save a bullet for yourself, if we can't hold 'em today. Save some for your families, too."

The shrieks rose and fell, fading, then starting up again, and again, and again.

"Why don't he just shut up and die?" Stillman said. "Die, damn you, die!"

"Easy," Hutto cautioned.

"Comanches know what they're doing," Lassiter said. "They'll keep him alive for a long time. They're good at that. By working on him, they're working on us, trying to put the fear in us."

"They're doing a pretty good job," Rutland Dean mumbled, grinning weakly.

Wade Hutto rose from his chair. "I better go downstairs and make a show to the folks, take their mind off things. Reassure them. They might need some shoring up."

"I can use some shoring up myself." Dean poured a stiff drink and tossed it down.

TWENTY-ONE

In Francine's room of the Golden Spur, Johnny Cross slipped out of bed, his eyes already accustomed to the dimness. He'd been lying awake in bed for some time. He dressed quietly, then sat on the bed while he donned socks and boots.

Yellow light from the hallway outlined the closed door. Moonbeams shafted through lacy curtained windows, spilling onto the bed. Sheets and blankets were tangled up around Francine.

She lay on her side, legs bent at the knees, one long bare leg showing outside the bed coverings. White-blond hair spilled across the pillows, partly covering her face. Her body was all shining silver and black shadow. *She's beautiful,* Johnny thought.

"Running off so soon?" she murmured.

"Sky's lightening in the east. Things're gonna start happening. I'd best be up and doing." Johnny was restless, couldn't sleep. Eager to get to the showdown. He'd had the loving and was anxious to get to the killing. Usually he did it the other way around. Take care of business first, then have a woman for dessert. That's how he liked it.

But it was fine this way, too. Just fine. He'd satisfied the lust for flesh. Now the need for action was rising in him.

His twin-holstered guns were hung over the top of the brass bedpost. He draped his gun belt over an arm.

Francine moved around in bed, reaching for him. He bent down to kiss her. Her mouth was warm, her breath sweet. After a while, he eased clear of her embrace. Taking his hat from the top of the bureau where he'd left it, he put it on his head and walked to the door.

He turned back to Francine. "See ya."

"Be careful, Johnny. Stay alive. I'll be waiting for you."

He opened the door partway, light slanting into the room, laying an angled yellow rectangle on the floor and bed. Francine turned to him, raising herself up on an elbow. Her long unbound hair spilled across the smooth curve of bare shoulders down to her breasts. Her eyes shone and her lips were parted.

Johnny filled his eyes with her once more, then stepped into the hall, closing the door behind him. It clicked shut. He buckled his gun belt low on his hips, settling holstered guns where the gun butts were within easy reach of his free-hanging hands.

He took off his hat and combed his hair with his

fingers, pushing it back from his forehead and over his ears, out of the way. He put on the hat, tilting it to the angle he liked.

He followed the balcony to the landing and descended the staircase. The long cabinet clock on the ground floor showed the time as a few minutes past four-thirty in the morning.

It was quiet on the main floor. Most of those gathered there, Anglos and Mexican-Americans, were asleep.

Luke sat at a nearby table, slumped in a chair. A sawed-off shotgun lay on its side on the tabletop, the fingers of his left hand resting lightly on the butt of the stock. His hinged wooden leg, straightened out and locked in place, extended in front of him, resting toes-up on the seat of a second chair. His head was propped up by his right arm, the side of his face resting against an open palm. His mouth, partly open, snored softly.

Johnny smiled. He smelled fresh-brewed coffee.

Morrissey stood behind the bar, sleepy eyes heavy-lidded, resting his weight on meaty forearms pressed against the counter. Sam Heller stood by himself at one end of the bar, eating a roast beef sandwich and drinking a cup of coffee.

Johnny went to them. "Coffee smells good. Can you do me a cup?"

"Coming right up," Morrissey said, pushing himself off the counter.

"A shot of whiskey would go nice in that."

"You got it." Morrissey splashed whiskey in a cup,

filling the rest of it with a hot black brew from the coffeepot. He set it down on the bar in front of Johnny.

"Thanks." Swirls of steam rose from the surface of the liquid in the cup. Johnny held it under his nose. It smelled good, the rich, pungent coffee aroma mingling with raw whiskey fumes. It tasted even better.

He picked up the cup and took it down the bar to stand beside Sam Heller. "Latigo?"

"Dead," Sam said.

"Sorry."

"Me, too. He died game."

"Can't ask for more than that."

"I reckon not." Sam finished up his sandwich and drained his cup.

"What's next?" Johnny asked.

"I'll be heading for the church directly. Want to get there and be in place well before sunup," Sam said.

"I'll tag along, if you don't mind."

Sam's eyebrows lifted. "In a hurry to get yourself killed?"

"I'm not one for sitting around. I like to take the fight to the enemy," Johnny said. "'Sides, a Yankee son of a gun like you is a natural-born magnet for trouble. Figure I'll stick to you and get me my share."

"I don't mind. Glad to have you," Sam said.

A Mexican youth in his early teens had volunteered to serve as a runner. Sam charged him to tell

Barton to send an extra horse along with the relief for the sentries in the church tower. The kid went out the front door and ran east along Trail Street to the jail, reaching it without incident.

A quarter-hour later, two riders halted in front of the Golden Spur, one of them trailing two saddled horses behind on a lead line.

"Let's go." Sam and Johnny went out the door, onto the front porch. The moon was low in the west, the star-spangled sky, tending more blue than black. The street was thick with purple-gray shadows. The early morning air was cool and fresh. The east end of Trail Street framed a vertical oblong of empty sky paling at the horizon.

Johnny glanced at the courthouse, wondering how Fay Lockhart was doing. Funny—he hadn't thought about Fay once since he first laid eyes on Francine. He wondered what Fay was like in bed, hoping he'd live long enough to find out.

He carried a repeating rifle. In addition to two guns holstered at his hips, he wore a pair of gun belts slung over his shoulders, the guns holstered butt-out under his arms. Another pair of six-guns were stuck in the top of his waistband at his sides. It was how he armed, pistol-fighter style, when he rode with Quantrill. It was how he armed when he made war.

The high, tight feeling in his chest and the top of his belly was a not unwelcome tension. It contrasted with the relaxed looseness of his shoulders and arms, and his easy, catlike tread.

The two riders waiting outside were Bayle and Lockridge, Dog Star Saloon regulars who often served as posse men for Sheriff Barton. Bayle was a solidly built, brown-bearded six-footer; Lockridge had a thatch of unruly straw-colored hair and a long, bony face.

"Didn't know you was coming along, Johnny," Bayle said, surprised.

"Okay with you?" Johnny asked.

"Hell, yeah."

Johnny and Sam mounted up.

Across the street in front of the feed store stood the barricade built along the store's boardwalk. With wraparound wings on the sides, it would serve as a forward firing platform. The open walkway of the boardwalk between the barricade and the storefront was hemmed in to shoulder height on both sides.

Dark yellow-brown light showed in the squares where the front windows had been. Shortly after occupying the space, the Ramrod riders had broken the glass out of the windows and built a barricade inside the front of the store—tables turned on their sides, barrels, and hundred-pound grain and feed sacks.

Quent Stafford stood looking over the top of the bulwark. "Damn, it's Johnny Cross. Somebody gimme a rifle."

"Here you go, Quent," Marblay said, pitching a rifle underhand at him. Quent caught it in both hands, his meaty paws slapping down on the long gun and pulling it out of the air. He started toward the front of the building.

Dan Oxblood moved to intercept him. "What's your game?"

"I'm gone shoot that sum-bitch Cross," Quent said.

"You ain't got the sense God gave a chicken," Oxblood said, shaking his head.

"Git out the way," said Quent.

Oxblood stood unmoving. "What'll you bet I can shoot your guts out before you get that rifle into play?"

Quent's face paled, then reddened. He started to swing the rifle barrel up.

"Why, you—"

A six-gun filled Oxblood's left hand, leveled at Quent's middle. The hammer clicked, a small sound that was very loud in the large, shedlike space.

Quent froze.

"You lose," Oxblood said.

Quent looked around, eyeing Ramrod riders grouped at the sidelines. He forced a laugh; it sounded sick. "You going up against all of us?"

"Who wants to get burned down to save yore hide? Anyone so minded, step up," Oxblood invited.

Nobody stepped up.

"Looks like it's just you and me," Oxblood said.

Quent let go of the rifle like it burned his hands. It clattered to the floor, but didn't go off. "I ain't no gunfighter."

"You're wearing a gun. Use it."

Quent shook his head. Cold sweat beaded on his lead-colored face.

"I'll give you the same chance Bliss gave Damon." Oxblood dropped his gun into the holster. "Now we're even. What's stopping you?"

Vince Stafford came up from the back of the store where he'd been napping, bullying his way to the fore. His men stepped aside, moving well back out of the line of fire. Clay came up behind his father.

"What is this?" Vince demanded.

"He's goin' against us, Pa!" Quent blurted, his voice thin and squeaky.

Vince frowned fiercely, white tufted eyebrows forming a V-shape, head thrust pugnaciously forward. He kept his hands empty and in plain sight, though. "Thought you was a professional gun, Red. You're working for me."

"Not when your idiot son tries to bushwhack Johnny Cross," Oxblood answered.

"Cross ain't paying you, I am."

"I had a clear shot on Cross, but he stopped me, Pa!"

"Shut up, Quent. What about it, Red?"

"Damned right I stopped him."

"What for? Cross is a dangerous man. Maybe the most dangerous man siding the gambler." Vince said.

"He ain't siding him. He just left the Spur," Oxblood told Vince.

"Now, maybe. But later?"

"Johnny'll kill a lot of Comanches."

"He could kill a lot of our men too. You think of that?"

"I'll worry about it once Red Hand's whupped."

"You're out of line, gunslinger."

"You don't like it, Vince, you know what you can do about it. You're wearing a gun, too."

"Easy, Red," Clay breathed. "Knock it off."

Ignoring him, Oxblood pressed, "How 'bout it, Vince? You and Quent against me, right here, right now. What d'you say?"

Vince sneered. "Shoot me, who's gonna pay you, huh?"

"You're pushing it, Red. Don't push it," Clay said, half threatening, half pleading.

"I ain't so prideful I can't back away," Vince said. "I'm no gunman. I got nothing to prove. I don't want to lose no more sons, neither. I want to live to avenge my boy Bliss. That's what's important to me."

"That your call?" Oxblood asked.

"That's my call. Let it go."

"I won't go against Cross, or that one-legged pard of his. As for the rest of them, they ain't nothing to me, one way or t'other."

"I still want you to brace Teece when the showdown comes with the gambler, if you're of a mind to."

"Want me? You need me." Oxblood laughed softly. "I'm the only one here can take Teece straight-on."

"Prove it," Vince challenged.

"I will when the time comes. When the Comanches are dead or on the run. Not before."

"All right." Vince turned his back, going off by himself into the dim depths of the store.

"Break it up. It's over," Clay told the men. "Get to your posts. Don't let the Comanche catch you napping. Move!"

The Ramrod riders began to disperse. Sidling away, Quent darted bad eyes at Oxblood, muttering, "You cain't hide behind Red Hand all the time."

"Damn you, Quent!" Clay let his breath out slowly and took off his hat, holding it in his hands. Without warning he slashed the brim at Quent's face, whipping it across his eyes.

Quent cried out, raising his hands to his face. Clay kicked him between the legs. Quent doubled over, grabbing his crotch. His eyes bulged, and his face turned fish-belly white. His mouth was a black sucking O.

Clay lowered a shoulder, slamming it into Quent's chest. Quent, knocked off balance, fell. Vince rushed forward, throwing a hand out. "Clay, don't!"

Clay moved in, lifting a booted foot to stomp Quent. Vince clawed at his sidearm. "Clay!"

Clay put his foot on the floor. His voice low, ominous, he said, "You gonna draw on me, Pa?"

"Nobody's drawing on nobody," Oxblood said, resting a hand on his gun butt.

Vince and Clay glared at each other over Quent,

who lay rolling on the floor, holding himself between the legs and moaning.

Vince's hand fell to his side, empty. Clay ran his fingers through his hair, eyes wild in a stiff face. Vince moved away, off to the side.

"One big, happy family," Clay said, then swore. Vince spat on the floor. Quent kept moaning.

"It's a new way to fight Indians," Clay went on. "We scrap like cats and dogs with each other and the redskins are so scared they call off the attack."

A couple of men in the shadows laughed.

"I ain't here to fight Injins," Vince said, giving Clay a dirty look. "I'm here to even up on the killers of my son Bliss—the gambler and his whore."

Nobody laughed.

TWENTY-TWO

Sam Heller, Johnny Cross, Bayle, and Lockridge rode their horses west of town to the church, all unaware of how close Quent Stafford had come to taking a shot at Johnny. Nobody shot at them, neither red men nor white. The two men on duty in the bell tower mounted up and rode back to Four Corners. Nobody shot at them, either.

The windows of the church were boarded up and shuttered closed, making the inside near dark. A couple lamps burned wanly at opposite ends of the central aisle. The newcomers brought their horses into the building, tethering them in the outside aisle between the front wall and the rearmost wooden pews. Plenty of hay had been spread on the floor where the animals were grouped. It was an act of necessity, but even so, Bayle was self-conscious about it.

Sam barred the front doors shut, then moved to

a window, looking east through a gap between nailed-up boards. The others sat in a pew close by.

"It don't seem right," Bayle said dolefully, shaking his head.

"You still going on about the horses? What do you want to do, leave 'em outside so Comanches could steal 'em? That'd leave us in a pretty pickle!" Lockridge said.

"I reckon the Lord won't mind. If Red Hand wins, there ain't gonna be no church. No town either," Johnny pointed out.

Sam turned away from the window. "Gonna be light soon."

"Let's get to it." Johnny hefted a sack filled with bundles of dynamite, slinging it over his shoulder so it hung down his side, leaving his hands free.

Sam slipped his arms into the leather straps of his wooden gun case. It rested flat on his back. The mule's-leg was holstered at his side.

He and Johnny went down the central aisle to the west end of the church and through the door in the wall behind the pulpit. It opened on to the well of the bell tower. A vertical wooden ladder was nailed flat to the tower's west wall, rising to the belfry. Near the top of the fifty-foot shaft was a wooden platform with a square hole in the center. A length of thick hempen rope hung down through the hole, with its fat knotted end dangling a few feet above the floor of the shaft. It was connected to the church bell in the spire atop the tower, allowing it to be rung from the ground floor level.

"After you," Johnny invited, indicating the ladder.

Sam stepped forward. Looking up, his hat almost fell off. He tied the hat strings under his chin and let the hat dangle down the back of his head. He gripped a rung at shoulder height, giving it a good shake. It seemed sturdy enough. He started climbing, testing each rung before trusting his full weight to it.

Up he went. The case on his back brushed against the bellpull, setting it swaying, though not enough to set the bell ringing. The shaft smelled strongly of the wooden planks and beams of which it was made.

The higher he climbed, the less sturdy the wooden ladder seemed, though he told himself that was just an illusion. He was careful not to grip each rung with both hands at the same time. If one of the rungs gave way, he wanted to have a hand on another as backup.

At the top, Sam reached over and pushed the hatch in the platform open. It rose on its hinges and fell back against the floor, making a dull booming noise in the confined space of the tower.

He climbed through the open hatchway to the belfry, stepping onto the floor. Like the tower, the belfry was square. Its walls were waist-high. Above them, it was open to the sky. Four massive corner post beams upheld an obelisk-shaped spire. Four feet of open space stood between the top of the balustrade and the bottom of the spire.

The spire was hollow, its interior shored up by a

skeletal wooden scaffolding of beams and braces. A stout horizontal crossbar supported the church bell. The bell rope was secured to a ring in the clapper.

Sam eased his arms out of the shoulder straps of the gun case and set it down in a corner of the platform. He set his hat squarely on his head.

The air seemed cool after the close confines of the shaft. The sky was a rich purple-blue dusted with paling stars. The horned moon hung way down in the west, as if seeking to hook a peak rising from the jagged skyline of the Breaks.

The eastern horizon glimmered with the glow of predawn. The few lights showing at Four Corners shed a hazy yellow blur against gray-black gloom.

At the bottom of the shaft, Johnny watched Sam climb through the hatch, then started up the ladder. He climbed swiftly, nimbly. Reaching the top, he stuck his head through the hatchway.

Sam sat in a corner with the open gun case flat on his lap, fitting the barrel and stock extensions to the mule's-leg, converting it to a long rifle. It was second nature to him to put the pieces together by touch in the dark.

Johnny climbed up on the platform, shucking off the sack of dynamite and setting it down carefully. He eased the wooden hatch closed. Hands resting atop the balustrade, he took a look around. It was still dark enough to keep him from outlining against the night sky.

Sam finished assembling the long rifle. Closing

the case, he set it down on its side against a wall, out of the way.

Johnny turned to him. "Now we wait."

The wait would not be a long one.

Darkness faded. The predawn sky took on a clear, colorless hue that was not white, not gray, but a mixture of the two.

In Wade Hutto's second-floor office in the courthouse, the air was thick with cigar smoke and whiskey fumes. Rutland Dean stood at a window looking east. He stuck his nose in a space between the nailed-up boards of a barricade, sniffing early morning air.

It smelled fresh, clean in comparison to the stale smokiness of the office. Dean breathed deep, filling his lungs with the air of outside.

White light seeped into the sky, the view gradually brightening. Veils and streamers of mist drifted above the ground. The thicket of trees east of town and north of Hangtree Trail was a black-green wall of foliage. At its base were flickering flashes of motion, flitting shadows that showed so quickly before disappearing that Dean was unsure of what he'd seen . . . if he'd seen anything at all.

The screams from the thicket had ended an hour or so earlier—a blessing, for the unseen sufferer as well as for those forced to listen.

The rim of the eastern sky took on faint shadings of yellow, the first herald of sunrise. A dark blur detached itself from the gloom of trees, crawling west toward town.

Dean stiffened. "I see something."

"What?" Banker Willoughby asked, starting from a fitful half-sleep.

"Don't know. It's coming this way, though."

The others went to the windows, crowding around.

"It's a rider!" Chance Stillman exclaimed.

Boone Lassiter stood at the window, rifle in hand. "One side, men. Gimme some room."

"Don't shoot just yet, Boone," Hutto cautioned. "Something about that rider . . . doesn't look right."

"Don't look like no Injin," Stillman pointed out.

The figure on horseback advanced toward the courthouse at a slow walk, almost a crawl. Moving out from the trees, it crossed the fields at a measured pace. The image blurred as curtains of mist rolled across it, clearing as the mists moved on.

It was quiet in Hutto's office, the sound of the men's heavy breathing clearly audible. A commotion below, shouts and half-stifled exclamations from the first-floor courtroom, indicated the apparition had also attracted attention in that quarter. His brow furrowed, his lips tightly compressed, Lassiter eyed the oncoming rider.

"That's no Injin," Stillman said.

"That's a white man," agreed Rutland Dean.

"It was." Lassiter had good eyesight.

The man on horseback closed on the courthouse. He was lashed to a framework of two vertical wooden sticks with crossbars tied to the back of the saddle. It held him upright.

He was bare from the waist up. Below, he wore brown pants. His feet were bare. A rope tied to his ankles ran under the horse's belly. His head hung down, chin resting on his chest.

The horse wasn't much to speak of. It was old, swaybacked, heavy-footed—crow bait. A disposable animal, one the Comanches could do without. Its legs were hobbled with lengths of rope allowing it to take only slow, plodding steps. The rider tied to the saddle framework swayed and lurched according to the animal's gait, as much as his bonds permitted.

"Who is it?" Hutto whispered. His eyes narrowed as he stared at the rider, trying to figure it out.

"Coleman," Stillman said.

One of the two who had set out after dark to try to reach the cavalry out on the plains west of the Breaks; the other was Hapgood.

"Coleman? Is that Coleman? That's not Coleman," Hutto disagreed.

"It's a big man. Coleman's a big man. Hapgood's a little fellow," Stillman said.

In the dawning light, it could be seen that the field fronting east of the courthouse was studded with a number of irregularly spaced fourteen-inch wooden stakes with red strips of cloth attached to each one.

"He keeps coming straight-on, he'll cross one of

those dynamite pits," Banker Willoughby said. "What happens then?"

"Nothing. The dynamite's safe," Hutto said.

"Unless the horse steps on a blasting cap, maybe," Lassiter reckoned.

"You're a cheerful soul," Hutto grunted. After a short pause, he asked, "You think that could set it off?"

"I don't know. Blasting caps are awful fluky." Lassiter answered.

"They can't be that fluky if our people set them out without any of them blowing themselves up," Hutto said.

The rider neared, closing on a red-staked patch. Banker Willoughby panted, as though trying to catch his breath. Hutto was sweating. In this, he was not alone.

"Something definitely wrong with that jasper," Rutland Dean said.

"He wasn't screaming half the night for fun," Lassiter bluntly pointed out.

"It's Coleman," Stillman said.

The mounted man seemed to have been hung with what looked like strings of gray-white sausages, in thicky ropy loops circling his neck and shoulders, hanging down on his torso, gleaming wetly.

"It *is* Coleman," Hutto muttered.

"What's that hanging around his neck?" Dean asked.

"His guts," Lassiter said.

Stillman gagged. He put out a hand palm-flat

against the wall, bracing himself. He'd gone weak in the knees.

"No," Banker Willoughby croaked. "Oh, no. It can't be."

"They pulled out his guts and hung 'em on him like ribbons!" Stillman cried, his voice crackling with rising hysteria.

Downstairs in the courtroom, somebody started screaming. Hard to tell if it was a man or a woman. Suddenly, the screams were interrupted, cut off as if a hand had clamped down over a shrieking mouth, silencing it.

Scattered shouts, cries, gasps, and wordless exclamations erupted from the horrified spectators on the first floor.

It got worse.

Coleman's head lolled to one side. His eyes opened. His jaw dropped, and he moaned.

"Good Lord, he's alive!" Hutto cried.

"No, he can't be!" Willoughby protested. "Not after that! Must be a trick, the way the horse is moving, something . . ."

A shot sounded, so near that everyone in Hutto's office started, all but the man who had fired it. Boone Lassiter. It was a shot from the rifle in the hands of Boone Lassiter.

Coleman's body jerked, a hole showing over where his heart would be. He slumped against the bonds securing him to the upright framework, sagging.

"He's dead now," Lassiter said.

"Good job," Hutto said heavily. "You did the right thing, the only thing. It was a mercy."

The horse would have broken into a run but for the ropes hobbling it. Its ears stood straight up, its eyes rolled, its nostrils flared, and it frothed at the mouth. Hampered by its bound, hobbling gait, the poor horse angled past the corner, into the mouth of Trail Street.

Sheriff Barton, Deputy Smalls, and the Dog Star bunch manned the defenses around the jail. They watched as three men ran into the street from the courthouse.

"Damn fools! What do they think they're doing?" Keeping under cover of a barricade of hogshead barrels filled with sand and stacked hay bales, Barton cupped a hand to his mouth, shouting to the trio. "Get off the street, you jackasses!"

One of the three, Pastor Fulton of the Hangtree Church, was the town's spiritual leader. A notorious brawler and hell-raiser long ago, he'd seen the Light and repented his ways, becoming a man of the cloth. He carried a Bible in his jacket pocket and wore a gun on his hip. He was a fighting preacher.

Pastor Fulton and the other two citizens hurried up to Coleman on the horse. The man with the rifle stopped dead in his tracks when he got a good look at the thing lashed upright to the saddle framework. His eyes bulged, his mouth hanging open.

"Get back, Pastor!" Barton called, making urgent warding gestures.

Pastor Fulton grabbed the horse by the bridle,

trying not to look at what had been done to Coleman. "We've got to get this obscenity out of sight!"

"Pastor, don't! Clear off!"

Pastor Fulton led the horse west, jogging alongside it. A second man moved with him. The man with the rifle stood in the middle of the street, motionless, except for turning his head to watch as Coleman's horse stumbled into the street between the jail and the feed store.

As the men led the horsebacked atrocity down the side street, away from the horrified eyes of most of the defenders and certainly lost from view to those in the courthouse, a bowstring twanged nearby, followed by a thunking sound.

The man with the rifle staggered backward, an arrow sticking out of his chest. He tripped over his own feet, and lay on his back in the street, thrashing and writhing.

A Comanche stood on the near corner of the front porch of the Alamo Bar, fitting another arrow to his bow.

Pastor Fulton turned, drawing his gun and firing. Bullets crashed into the brave, cutting him down.

Fulton held the horse's bridle in his left hand, a smoking pistol in his right. Turning to the other man with him, he said, "Take the horse, Joe, I'll see to Sanders."

Joe shook his head. "He's done for, Pastor."

Sanders, the man felled by the arrow, lay still, his open eyes unseeing.

Turning away from the dead man, Pastor Fulton

led the horse with its grisly burden toward the Big Corral, Joe following. A gap opened in the Big Corral barricade. The pastor and Joe entered with their grisly burden, sheltered by reinforced walls.

"They made it!" Deputy Smalls exclaimed, breathing a sigh of relief.

Gunfire cracked from the direction of the Cattleman Hotel. "There's more Comanches inside the town!" Barton yelled.

A brave crouched on the second-floor balcony at the front of the hotel, firing a rifle down the street.

"I got him," Smalls said, shouldering his rifle, a single-shot .50-caliber Sharps buffalo gun. He fired, booming thunder.

The thudding sound of the big .50 round tearing into and through the Comanche was audible clear throughout Trail Street. The brave dropped as if he'd been slapped down.

Several rifle barrels bobbed atop the hotel roof. More Comanches.

During the predawn hours, Red Hand had infiltrated a number of skirmishers, riflemen, and archers into Hangtown. They were popping up all over, sniping at the defenders from every which way, sowing chaos, confusion, and death.

Bullets tore into the space in front of the jail where Smalls had been. He'd ducked behind the barricade after squeezing off his shot. Crouching under cover, he reloaded his buffalo gun.

Shooting crackled in and around Four Corners, the volume of firepower steadily increasing.

Chapter Thirty-one

After that, things got real quiet in Swamp Creek, but no one was fooled. Everyone in town knew who shot Amanda Trouville, and why. They all knew I had shot Glan, and nobody mourned him. He'd killed a few right around the district, and maybe lots more somewhere else. He'd been dumped into a three-foot-deep grave in Swamp Creek's cemetery, and was barely shoveled over before everyone got away.

Scruples knew I done it, and I wasn't gonna be his snitch, and I suppose that meant I was marked for a killing, but I didn't much care. I could deal with short-gun men. It was Glan bothered me the most, and now he was under the sod. So I kept a wary eye out for them other thugs, and minded my own business.

I rode out to them woodcutters to see about the paid vacation Carboy was offering, but they wasn't interested, not even with Glan gone. They said they liked the work, being outside and making cordwood, and the mill was buyin' every stick. So I returned all them eagles to Carboy. The summer was stretching into fall, and it looked more and more like Scruples would walk away with the pile of money he wanted, especially now that poor Amanda was no longer around.

Then one day, things got interesting again. A dandy in a black silk stovepipe hat come into town, in a black carriage driven by a monkey in green and blue, and with that dandy was three other fancy-lookin' fellers, in tweeds and walrus mustaches. It was pretty plain that Scruples had himself a buyer for the Swamp Creek District, and the dude was looking the whole place over. And it was clear that them other fellers knew a whole lot about all that stuff. I heard that one was a geologist, another a mining engineer, and the third an accountant. They put up at the town's excuse for a hotel, a dump called the Mountain House, which doubled as a parlor house and had some girls upstairs. Maybe that'd just help the sale along. Anyway, they got settled in there, and pretty soon Scruples showed up in his rig, guarded by some of them toughs he had on his payroll, and then the whole lot drove off for a tour. I kept clear, but sure heard about it from Billy Blew at the Mint, who knew everything there was to know.

"That there gent in the stovepipe, that's Ambrose Marcus, and he's made killings in the California gold-fields, and in the Comstock Lode, and in Butte," Billy told me. "He's lookin' to buy the whole district from Scruples. Those are his experts, along to make sure he doesn't get took."

I'd heard of Marcus a few times. He had a piece of the copper mines up in Butte, and was actually, from what I heard, a good man, paid them hard-rock miners a good wage, and most everyone up there liked him. He was also tough, and went after them that tried to euchre him. He lived in Virginia City, Nevada, but made trips up to

* * *

"This'll put a twist in Red Hand's tail," Hutto said.

He and Lassiter were alone in an office down the hall from Hutto's own. Fronting east, it was in the center of the building under the clock tower, below the face of the dial.

The two men were hunkered down below the windowsill. The glass had been knocked out of the window earlier; its bottom half was boarded up. Lassiter was putting the finishing touches on Black Robe's garment, rigging it for flying. Sam had left it earlier at the courthouse for safekeeping. After the Coleman horror, Hutto came up with an idea for the defenders to get back some of their own against Red Hand.

Lassiter fitted a broomstick inside the shoulders of the robe to open up the garment and spread it out. He tied a short rope to each end of the broomstick, so the rope came out of the ends of the sleeves. He tied a somewhat longer rope to the middle of the short rope where it came out of the robe and secured the other end of the rope to a wall bracket.

Hutto sat with his back to the wall, holding a rifle. Lassiter crouched, testing the knots to make sure they would hold. "That does it, she's ready to go."

"Hold on to your hat, because when Red Hand gets a good look, the fur's going to fly," Hutto said.

Lassiter rose, sticking the top of his head above

the boards nailed over the lower half of the window. The black robe was bunched up in his hands. Holding it over the top of the boards so it was outside, he let it unfurl so that it hung loose and free. The broomstick inside the shoulders spread out the garment so it could be fully and clearly seen for what it was by those outside.

He lowered it by the line attached to the ropes tied to the ends of the broomstick, until it hung five feet below the windowsill.

The black robe hung like a banner out the second floor window, below the clock tower. A ragged black flag, trimmed with buckskin fringe and boldly blazoned with sun, moon, stars, lightning bolts, diagonals, and zigzags, all picked out with yellow, white, and red beadwork.

It stood out in the dawn light shining on the east face of the courthouse.

Lassiter grabbed his hat and rifle. He and Hutto ran for the door, bent almost double. They ducked through the doorway into the hall, peeling off to the sides to put a solid wall between them and the room they had just quit.

The Comanches held their fire while they got a good look at the banner hanging below the clock tower. A banner that until the day before had been the potent medicine shirt of Black Robe, a mighty warrior and one of Red Hand's inner circle.

The display was a way of stealing Black Robe's power, his magic as the Comanches knew it.

Gunfire popped in the woods east of the courthouse. In a few beats, the shooting sounded like a string of firecrackers going off.

Bullets streamed at the courthouse, ventilating wooden barriers, flattening into leaden smears against brick walls. Rounds pelted the building's east face, gouging out cratered bullet holes, beating up a cloud of rock shards, mortar dust, and wood chips.

Hutto had passed the word in advance, alerting those in the courthouse to his stratagem so they could take cover before the Comanches loosed the anticipated barrage.

Riflemen among the defenders were on the alert to look for telltale puffs of gun smoke among the thicket of woods to pinpoint the location of concealed enemy shooters.

The defenders returned fire, crackling reports rising and falling in waves. In the room at the top of the clock tower, sharpshooters Pete Zorn and Steve Maitland fired through slatted side windows.

Muzzle flares sparking through hazy gun smoke in the trees of the east wood gave them targets on which to center their gun sights. They squeezed off round after round, gun barrels heating up, turning red.

A large force of Comanches massed in the thicket was the source of much of the enemy's firepower. But the infiltrators who'd sneaked into town at night were proving to be a more potent and deadly threat.

They'd slipped in on foot, alone or by twos and threes, archers and riflemen, taking up positions around the Four Corners.

They struck from all directions, steadily moving in closer, tightening the noose. They bloodied up the defenders, keeping them off balance and uncertain.

Several storerooms on the west side of the first floor of the courthouse building had been set up as infirmaries to treat the wounded. They began to fill up as the early morning assault opened.

Among others, a gray-haired grandmotherly woman was giving first aid to the injured in one of the infirmary rooms. Some of the wounds were fearsome, the blood flow prodigious. All too soon she ran out of bandages, but not patients. More were being brought in by the minute, children and adults alike.

The caregiver hurried to the room next door to pick up fresh bandages. She went into the hallway. A bullet tore through a pine board covering a window, drilling it and knocking her down. She fell to the floor, blood pooling out from her.

A man ran to her aid, into the path of more bullets tearing through the same window. He fell down dead.

Shot through, the boards over the window broke apart, leaving a large gap. Swift blurred forms of Comanches outside flashed past the gap.

A young cowboy charged the window, a gun in each hand. He slipped in a puddle of blood, booted feet flying out from under him. He took a pratfall, landing hard on his tailbone. One of the guns in his hand went off, narrowly missing a nearby teenage mother with a babe in her arms.

An arrow flew through the hole in the window, whizzing past the cowboy. Getting to his feet, trembling with pain, he clomped to the window on shaky legs.

A Comanche stuck his face in the gap, looking in. The cowboy pointed a gun and fired. The brave's face became a wet scarlet mask for an instant before dropping out of sight.

Vince Stafford's Ramrod riders were astir at the feed store, positioned at the windows and outside at the barricades. Dimaree and Carney were huddled at the northwest corner of the store, behind a makeshift barrier bordering the boardwalk.

Dimaree thrust out his left arm, pointing at the top of the building across the street. "Injins! Climbing the roof of the Golden Spur!"

"Hell, let 'em," Carney said, "that's Damon's lookout."

A quartet of Comanche braves on horseback galloped into view, rounding the corner between the Spur and the Alamo Bar, charging east on Trail Street. Whooping, shrieking, they opened fire on the feed store.

Dimaree, hit in the left shoulder, spun sideways. Bullets whizzed past Carney on both sides. One clipped off an earlobe. Another ripped into Marblay behind him, gut shooting him. He doubled up, grabbing his belly. He tried to scream but lacked the breath.

Carney reeled, off balance. One hand pressed to his torn, bleeding ear, he stumbled around, crashing into Dimaree and knocking him down. Dimaree hit the boards with a thud, a six-gun in the fist of his right hand. His left arm where he'd been hit was numb, useless; he couldn't make it work. Marblay lay beside him, spasming, belly and crotch soaked with dark blood.

A rattle of gunfire ripped out, venting from the blazing pistols of Kev Huddy in the wing of the barricade. Having no dominant hand, he could shoot with equal facility with either hand and alternated shots between the gun in his left and the one in his right, first one, then the other, so fast the reports blended into a roaring torrent of noise. Crouched bent-legged, a toothy go-to-hell grin on his face, he fired into the four Comanches who'd shot his buddies.

Four ponies flashed by, the braves sprawled dead in the street at Huddy's feet. A cloud of gun smoke floated around his middle.

Carney bumped into the bulwark hedging the west end of the boardwalk in front of the store. He held on to the top of the hay bale, propping himself upright and looked up.

Standing opposite him on the other side of the bale was a Comanche with war hatchet upraised.

Grinning fiercely, the brave buried the blade in the top of Carney's skull, splitting it down to the eyeballs. Bits of bone and brain matter spewed, geysering up on a torrent of blood. So deep was the tomahawk buried in Carney's cranium that the brave couldn't get it free.

Carney lurched away, arms and legs thrashing spasmodically as he careened from side to side, bouncing off the barricade and storefront.

Dimaree shot the hatchet-wielder from where he lay on his back on the boardwalk, tagging him high in the chest.

Carney smashed into plank boards nailed over the bottom of a storefront window, tearing them loose, and falling through. He lay half in the store, half out. His shattered head bled into the store, soaking into the top of hundred-pound grain sacks heaped as a barricade. His legs hung outside, squared-off boot toes drumming the boardwalk before giving a final kick.

A running brave angled southwest across the street. Duncan raised his rifle but a section of the barricade blocked the shot. He sidestepped into the street, swinging the rifle barrel in line with the brave's muscular, delta-shaped back and drilled him between the shoulder blades.

A Comanche bowman on the roof of the Golden Spur launched an arrow at Duncan, hitting him in the right breast. Duncan stood in place, weaving slightly.

The bowman sped a second arrow at him. It took

Duncan sideways through the right ear, piercing his skull. Down he went.

Seeing it, Lord cried, "Dirty stinking redskin!" and pointed his rifle up at the archer.

A Comanche at ground level stepped around the corner of the Golden Spur, rifle leveled at Lord. Kev Huddy shot him.

Lord did a double take. A second report from Huddy's gun fell swiftly on the echoes of the first. Lord looked up.

The bowman on the Spur roof was hit, lurching sideways. He ran out of roof, pitching into empty space and impacting the street with a loud booming *whoomp*.

Huddy grinned at Lord over smoking pistols that had just gunned two braves. He'd saved Lord's life twice in two blinks of an eye, but all the same, that toothy grin of Huddy's really burned Lord's ass.

"Thanks," Lord said grudgingly, hating the other.

Knowing it, Huddy laughed.

Up above the street, high on the Golden Spur roof, Swamper and his shotgun got to the roof edge late and only managed to tag the last brave in the line of riders moving south between the Spur and the courthouse. It took a second barrel to blow him out of the saddle.

Swamper broke the piece, shucking out the empty shells and reloading. While he was occupied, several nimble Comanches managed to scale a drainpipe on the west side of the building, mounting the roof.

One, an archer, slew Duncan before being slain by Kev Huddy. That attracted Swamper's attention, causing him to glimpse two other braves ducking for cover. It was a game of hide-and-seek.

He padded toward them, keeping a wide brick chimney topped with several spouts between him and them. Leaning around a corner, he loosed a barrel into a Comanche rifleman.

A second brave dodged around to the other side of the chimney. Swamper stepped out in the open for a clear shot. He fired. The brave jackknifed, pitching off the roof. Swamper did not see, but heard, him hit bottom with a satisfying thud.

A pair of hands came into view along the west edge of the roof. A Comanche chinned himself, heaving up over the edge.

No time for reloading. Swamper rushed to roof's edge, butt stroking the brave's head with the shotgun. It made a wet crunching sound, smearing the other's features, breaking his nose and knocking out teeth. The brave was tough, holding on. Swamper readied to strike again.

The brave defiantly spat a mouthful of bloody teeth up at him.

Swamper struck again. The brave's head snapped back, his hands losing their grip. Backward, outward, and down he went—without cry, curse, or complaint.

Swamper leaned over the edge of the roof for a

looksee. A trio of braves on foot came skulking south down the side street. The shotgun was empty or he would have cut loose on them.

The brave in the lead spotted him, swinging up a rifle toward him. Swamper threw himself back, landing on his ass and elbows, but dodging a bullet. He crawled away from the edge and reloaded.

The braves in the street fired into the Golden Spur's west windows. Bullets ripped through the plank-boarded lower halves of window frames, felling a gray-bearded Mexican and a beardless youth inside.

Flint Ryan went to the grand staircase, rifle in hand, taking the stairs two at a time until he was at the midpoint of the flight. This put him several feet above the tops of the planks nailed across the lower west windows. He half sat, half sprawled across the steps, looking down into the street for a shot. A brave flashed into view rushing a window, and Ryan shot him.

On the roof, Swamper heard suspicious noises coming from the side of the building. He swung his weapon over the edge, pointing it downward. A brave lay flat in the street where Ryan had shot him. A second brave stood beside a window, his back flattened against the wall, edging in for a shot.

Swamper swung the shotgun down at him, but before he could fire he was shot by the third brave in the group, who'd been hanging back from the others, waiting for Swamper to show himself. He drilled Swamper through the forehead, blowing off the top of his skull.

Swamper fell back in a heap on the roof, shotgun falling from his dead hands into the street.

Below, the brave standing beside the window peered through gaps in the nailed-up boards. Plenty of human targets were scattered around inside the gambling hall. He fired inside, cutting down a man who stood on the other side of the floor at the east wall.

Defenders fired back, tearing holes through plank boards, sending splinters flying, but the brave ducked under cover and remained unhit.

Ryan climbed to the top of the stairs, turning left on the landing, moving along the balcony to a window overlooking the street below. The window was unboarded, open.

He peeked out cautiously, looking for the Comanche who'd just shot through the window. Instead, he saw a brave shinnying up a drainpipe, climbing up the side of the building. It was the one who'd shot Swamper, though Ryan had no way of knowing that.

The climber was almost level with Ryan. They saw each other at the same time.

Ryan's rifle was at the ready. He fired into the Comanche at point-blank range, blasting him off his perch.

The climber dropped, narrowly missing a brave standing pressed against the wall with his rifle raised to fire again through the window. Ryan shot him, too.

A lone Comanche came galloping in from the north, riding along the eastern edge of town toward the courthouse. He heaved a ball-like object through the open space of a high window, clear above the plank barricade and into the building. It hit the courtroom floor, rolling for some fair yardage before bumping to a halt against a wooden bench.

Yipping his defiance, the brave wheeled his horse around, racing back to cover.

The object was revealed to be a human head, unscalped, the deliverer having used its longish hair as a handle by which to hold and fling it inside.

Somewhat the worse for wear, it was still recognizable as the severed head of Hapgood, the other rider who'd set out at nightfall to reach the cavalry troop escorting Major Adams's wagon train west of the Breaks.

Whatever else, the cavalry would not be riding to the rescue of Hangtown.

TWENTY-THREE

With violent clashes peppering the Four Corners, Red Hand assembled his men for the main assault.

They came out of the eastern treeline on horse-back, filtering from behind the brush, the woods yielding a seemingly inexhaustible supply of Comanche warriors.

Streamers and banks of morning mist drifted above the earth, giving the initial appearance of the braves a dreamlike aspect, as if they were phantoms materializing from the gloom.

They took on an all-too-solid reality as they came forward—at least a hundred and twenty-five of them . . . or more.

A long line of mounted braves, several ranks deep, stretched out on both sides of Hangtree Trail. They faced the town in a front reaching from Commerce Street north of the courthouse to Hobson's livery stable in the south.

The Comanches sat silently on their ponies, hard, stoic, remorseless.

They carried rifles, carbines, muskets, six-guns, lances, bows and arrows, tomahawks, stone-headed war clubs, and knives. Many wore round buffalo-hide shields over one arm.

They were well armed. Red Hand had seen to that. Anglo and Mexican captives—young women, mostly, but also boy and girl prisoners hardy enough to withstand the harrowing ordeal—had been traded for weapons and ammunition in advance of the Great Raid. They'd been herded overland to secret meeting places deep in the Staked Plains where renegade Comancheros camped, swapping whiskey and guns for human flesh. The captives were ultimately sold into slavery deep in the remote vastness south of the Rio Grande, never to be seen again by friends and family.

Red Hand took his place at the center of the front, brandishing the Fire Lance. The real, authentic Fire Lance, the one he'd taken from an Austro-Hungarian cavalryman who'd come a long way from home to die in service to Maximilian's foredoomed Empire of Mexico.

He used it as a baton, conducting and directing the movements of his men. It was dormant, untorched, for its fiery aspect lost its impact in the light of day.

* * *

In their perch high in the church tower, Sam Heller and Johnny Cross could see some, but not all, of the Comanche battle line where it extended north and south beyond the courthouse. Its center was blocked by the courthouse itself, shielding Red Hand from being targeted by Sam's long rifle with its telescopic sight.

"Looks like Red Hand's getting ready to make his move," Johnny acknowledged.

"He's tricky," Sam stated. "If he's showing himself in the east, it means you better look west. The bunch at Four Corners, Barton, Lassiter, Zorn, and the rest of them are better positioned to deal with him than we are. We're here to guard the back door."

And so they were. East, the ground was open with little cover, affording clear fields of fire to the defenders. West, the approach to Four Corners consisted of the street grid, with much cover provided by blocks of buildings honeycombed with streets, lanes, and alleys.

If Sam had been making the attack, he would have directed his forces to come in singly or in combination from the north, south or west, with minimal concentration of attackers coming from the east. That's why he had set up his sniper's nest in the church tower, giving him good firing lines along the north, south, and west approaches.

By the same logic, the flat west of the church would be a prime staging area to marshal forces for an attack. Charging horsemen could work up a nice head of steam crossing east across open ground.

The knoll on which the church and Boot Hill were sited would screen the attackers from view of those in Four Corners until the charge topped the rise. That's why Sam had planted red-staked blast pits on the flat.

If he'd guessed wrong, and the Comanches did not come from the west, he could still do plenty of damage to them with his scoped rifle from the church tower heights.

So he and Johnny Cross guarded the back door, scanning the landscape for a west-based assault.

Sure enough, Red Hand had divided his forces. A second Comanche band appeared, coming out of the stepped ridges in the north. They crested the nearest ridge, having hidden behind it in a valley.

"I make 'em about seventy-five or so," Johnny said.

This second assault force was quiet, with no screaming defiance, no war whoops. They came downhill, wheeling east to form up in a long line at the far side of the flat.

Prone on the floor, holding his face over the open hatch, Johnny looked down into the dark well of the tower shaft. Putting two fingers to his mouth, he whistled several times, sharp and shrill.

Lockridge entered the bottom of the well, looking up. "They're coming!" Johnny called.

"We see 'em!" Lockridge replied.

"Hold your fire till the first blast."

"Okay—but don't wait too long!"

At the center of the Comanche line leading the sortie was a Titan figure with lines of scalps hanging from the reins of his horse. Ten Scalps. A Bison Eye who'd been with Red Hand since the beginning. A copper-hued Hercules, he was mounted on a big quarter horse, a dappled white and gray charger.

He led his band of seventy-five braves east across the flat toward the rise, their path taking them straight across the field of red-banded stakes. Onward they came, inexorable.

Gesturing with the lance, Red Hand set his warriors into motion. Forward!

The main body of Comanches advanced, coming from a power position, attacking with the rising sun at their backs. The quickening charge unleashed shrieking war whoops and drumming hoofbeats.

The long line swept westward, its swift rush narrowing the distance between them and the defenders.

They rode on, prime targets for sharpshooters Pete Zorn and Steve Maitland in the clock tower, Boone Lassiter on the courthouse second floor, Deputy Smalls and some of the Dog Star marksmen at the jail, and Hobson and a knot of riflemen at the livery stable.

At the last moment, reaching the hinge where the Hangtree Trail ran into town, the Comanche line broke in two at the center. Half the line peeled off to the left, the other half to the right.

A canny campaigner like Red Hand was too smart to charge straight into the guns of the enemy's strongpoint. The twin halves of the line swung around to the sides, setting up a pincer movement to flank the north and south ends of Four Corners. The objective: surround the stronghold and arrow in, swarming it where it was most vulnerable.

His men broke off the full frontal charge well short of the eastern fields where the red-banded stakes lay, circling around to the sides. A lucky break, or the result of foresight and strategy?

The answer remained to be seen.

Red Hand's attack was loud, heard clear across town, to the church knoll and beyond. It cued Ten Scalps to launch his attack.

Digging his heels into his horse's flanks with such force the animal shuddered in pain, Ten Scalps charged forward. His followers did the same. The earth shook under their hoofbeats.

Sam's nerves were taut. The issue would be joined directly, in a matter of seconds. Ten Scalps and his seventy-five braves were fast narrowing the distance between themselves and the knoll.

"Come on, come on. Let them come on."

Ten Scalps was in his glory leading the charge. A bull of a man, a magnificent physical specimen, he held. a rifle in one hand, and motioned his band forward toward the knoll and Hangtown below . . .

charging straight into the field of red-banded stakes.

Sam timed his move with nice delicacy, waiting until the thundering herd was deep in the red-staked field. At the head of the charge, Ten Scalps was almost clear of the flat.

Sam took a stance in the belfry, using the square upright column for cover. Shouldering the rifle, he pointed it downward at the near end of the field. Sighting on the red-staked center of the closest dynamite pit, he squeezed the trigger. A hot round ripped into a bundle of buried dynamite just as Ten Scalps rode over it.

Kaboom! The tremendous explosion erupted like a vest-pocket volcano blowing its top, spewing light, heat, and violent energies. Geysering earth heaved up in a fan-shaped cone of flaming death.

Caught in the middle of the blast, Ten Scalps disintegrated, along with his horse.

Shockwaves ripped through several dozen braves riding nearby, obliterating them and their mounts in an upthrust wall of yellow-red glare. They were hurled skyward in a heap of body parts. Down they came, but not too soon—they'd been blown pretty high up.

The church rocked from the ground floor to the spire. The belfry roost shivered. Having been wrapped in muffling layers of cloth and tied down in place earlier, the church bell did not toll. It quivered with vibrations, sending out a metallic teeth-rattling hum, which Sam felt in his bones.

No sooner had he popped off the nearest blast pit than his rifle swung toward the next. He scoped out another red-tied stake and triggered it, blowing a big hole in the stunned and stricken Comanche charge and shredding men and mounts.

Gore fountained. Dust and chaff showered down from inside the spire above, shaken loose by the shock waves of the blast. Sam hoped the church bell or the spire itself wouldn't crash down on their heads.

He sighted on a red-staked pit toward the left rear of the mass of braves and fired.

Another earthshaking blast rewarded him. Curtains of roiling black smoke rose up, wrapped with writhing red serpents of flame. Dirt, smoke, and debris temporarily obscured part of the scene.

A fresh explosion surprised Sam, detonating in the northwest quadrant of the field of death. It was one he hadn't triggered.

Johnny Cross had, tagging it through the open sights of his rifle. He flashed a tight grin at Sam.

Hangtown had no cannon. Such heavy guns had been confiscated or spiked by Union troops in the unhappy aftermath of the War. Yet the braves' charge was ripped and rended as if shattered by cannon balls. The field was an annex of Hell, scored with blast craters and scorch marks.

Smoking craters vented black-gray pillars of

smoke, creating too much murk and chaos for Sam or Johnny to see the red-tied stakes for a moment. But they could still see plenty of Comanches, outlined shapes streaking through the palls of smoke and fire. A cluster of them changed course, charging the church.

Johnny waved a hand, getting Sam's attention. He held an unlit bundle of dynamite.

Sam nodded.

Pitching it overhand, Johnny heaved the bundle at the oncoming attackers below.

Sam fired, hitting the bundle and detonating it in midair above the attackers. Bodies arrowed outward in all directions from the center of the blast.

Gunfire ripped in the church below as Lockridge and Bayle fired on the foe, knocking them down.

A ragged knot of Comanches rode up the far side of the knoll. Johnny let fly with another bundle of dynamite, a round from Sam's rifle touching it off.

The slope was cleared.

Sam began picking off the remaining braves one by one, shooting them off their horses. Johnny hefted his rifle and did likewise, while Lockridge and Bayle in the church below continued to cut loose.

The charge in the west was broken, its force crushed. Survivors scattered, fleeing the killing field.

Red Hand's man Sun Dog led the Comanches' right wing north, his kinsman Badger taking the left wing south with the all-important task of stealing the horses penned in the Big Corral. The prime stock fenced in behind the barricades was as attractive to them as a bank ripe with gold bullion would have been to outlaws. Irresistible!

His job was to break the ring of the Big Corral and run off the herd. The animals could always be rounded up later. Denied the use of their mounts for a getaway attempt, the townfolk would be pinned in place for conquest. Rape, torture, and slaughter!

The Big Corral was not without its defenses. Hobson, Squint McCray, and a half dozen other top riflemen were posted in the second-story loft of the livery barn. More were on the ground floor.

Shooters were atop the raised firing platform along the east wall of the barricade running between the jail and the stable. More were on top of and in the carpenter's shop and the lumberyard. A squad of riflemen was on the jailhouse roof.

The Big Corral thronged with scores of horses. They were penned in the center of the enclosure, secured by hitching lines and hobbles.

Badger's wing of braves swept south of town, curved west, then swung north to charge the rear of the livery barn and south wall of the Big Corral. The braves massed in a column six mounted warriors wide, ten ranks deep.

With Badger at their head, they came hard and fast, their horses straining at the bit. They were a storm force meant to crash through the barrier at its weakest points, the barricades between buildings.

The charge whipped into open ground south of the pen. It was ground marked with red-banded wooden stakes laid out at regular intervals.

If Badger or any of the charging braves noticed the layout, it was only to reflect for an instant that the White Eyes were always up to some such ritualistic nonsense marking out the lands they'd stolen from others.

The vanguard of the column churned north into the red-staked field. Squint McCray fired first, aiming his rifle through a gun port in the rear wall of the loft and placing a shot into a dynamite pit.

The world blew up and Badger along with it, taking many others at the tip of the Comanche spear.

In the loft, Hobson and other sharpshooters pumped lead into red-staked patches, a sudden succession of shattering blasts scouring the Comanche column and shaking Four Corners.

Having been at the center of the front when it broke in half, Red Hand found himself at the rear of the right wing column as Sun Dog raced north.

His column's left flank raked by gunfire from the courthouse front, he rounded the structure's north end, and bulled west onto Commerce Street. Sun Dog's group swarmed the area when suddenly the street itself exploded, detonated by the snipers in the clock tower shooting into red-staked patches of earth positioned throughout the thoroughfare.

Solid ground turned into a torrent of hellfire, blasting Sun Dog and his band. Shockwaves pulped the braves, pulverizing them into white-hot jelly. Men and mounts went up like dead leaves tossed onto a bonfire, heat waves searing flesh off the bone, turning bodies into charred wreckage.

Red Hand and those at the tail end of the column were stunned by the sudden fury. They were dazzled by flashes of white light bursting on every side. The light turned red-yellow-orange, throwing up clouds of debris and inverted pyramids of black smoke.

Between the blasts, high-pitched cackling—laughter—rung out from the clock tower. Pete Zorn was having fun. "Lookit them feathers fly! Better'n a turkey shoot!"

Ever alert, Red Hand swiftly reined in his silver horse, curbing it violently. For most of the column ahead of him it was too late to turn back.

By the time the last dynamite pit had been detonated, the main attack was blunted and broken. The explosive hellfire was the equalizer, the secret weapon that evened up the odds.

A number of braves filtered into Trail Street. Seeking the quickest way out of town, they looked west, finding not open space and empty sky, but rather a curtain of gray-brown clouds rising to the heavens—mute testimony to the killing field beyond the knoll. The church and the Hanging Tree on Boot Hill showed as vague, indistinct outlines wavering in the smoke.

With much of Hangtown a chaos of fire, smoke, and carnage, the citizens unleashed their counterattack. Rifle squads fired fusillades through swirling smoke, dealing mass death to the stunned Comanche survivors of the dynamiting. Pistols were pressed into service for close-in work.

With Red Hand's horde decimated, discouraged and disoriented, the townfolk were able to complete the rout, cleaning up isolated pockets of resistance.

Even the most fanatic Bison Eye stalwarts—those few who remained—lost heart. The truth was plain to see: the raid was a failure.

Red Hand was unlucky. No more devastating indictment could be leveled against a war chief than to be unlucky. To have bad luck was to be in disfavor with the gods. That was all it took . . . it was more than enough.

The coalition of mighty warriors had agreed by mutual consent to enlist under Red Hand's sway when he looked like a winner. That was done . . . and so was his leadership. The Great Raid was over.

The Great Flight began. Braves pointed their horses' heads at open spaces and raced toward them, eager to put as much distance as possible between themselves and the avenging guns of Hangtown.

TWENTY-FOUR

Red Hand's luck had not totally deserted him. He'd managed to stay in the saddle through to the last blast.

This was no battle. It was a massacre. And not the one he'd planned. Those of his warriors who'd survived the explosions were being cut down by gunfire. No fool, Red Hand knew that Death ruled in Hangtown, death for his war party and his dreams of conquest.

The Great Raid was dead. What remained of his war party had become a mob of fugitives. And he, Red Hand, was one of them.

His silver horse was near out of its head. Its bulging eyes rolled, its mouth foamed. Red Hand could not restrain it. All he could do was hang on tight and fight to keep from being thrown as the animal galloped blindly into Hangtown. He felt he was riding into the whirlwind.

Yet his gods were still with him. Miraculously the

horse somehow avoided falling into bombed-out craters, where it would have risked throwing its rider and breaking a leg.

The silver horse broke through the gap between the jail and the courthouse, plunging west. The Four Corners was a blazing buzz saw of violence as vengeful defenders shot bomb-dazed braves.

Red Hand's senses were numb. He was seeing double. He shook his head to clear it and his eyes focused as a gap in the drifting smoke revealed the length of Trail Street stretching ahead. Other braves streaked west along it, fleeing town.

The silver horse ran that way. Red Hand leaned forward, letting the animal have its head. The sooner he was quits with Hangtown, the better!

A long, hard ride lay before him if he hoped to reach Comancheria. The defeated must slink home with their tails tucked between their legs.

But a man must live to fight another day. Other chances would present themselves, opportunities for advancement and redemption. New great deeds would wipe away stinging defeat, winning fresh acclaim.

First one must live. Then all else would follow, sure as the turning of the earth.

So Red Hand told himself, taking heart.

The front doors of the church crashed open and Johnny Cross came riding out.

Like the others manning the church, he'd kept

his horse inside to avoid betraying their presence to Comanches. Johnny had done all he could to help wipe out Ten Scalps' attack force on the killing field. Those whom the dynamite had spared had fallen to the deadly accuracy of the riflemen in the church. Straggling survivors fled toward the far horizons, away from Hangtown.

That was not enough scrap for Johnny. He was just getting warmed up. Killing at a distance was all very well and good, but he preferred to work up close and personal, where he could look in the faces of those he slew. There was still plenty of mopping up to be done in town, where the Comanches' main force was being routed.

Johnny Cross was loaded for bear and his fighting blood was hot.

If there was one thing he hated above all else, it was being crowded. Since coming to town with Luke on Saturday—*was it only yesterday?*—he'd been crowded by gunmen, lawmen, and Indians. He'd had a bellyful of Red Hand and his war party and of being pinned in the Golden Spur, unable to come and go as he pleased.

The Spur was a gilded cage, spiced by the delights of lissome, lustful Francine, free-flowing whiskey, and the fellowship of a few boon companions. Despite that, cage it still was, and Johnny Cross was born to run wild and free.

He'd had a bellyful of Staffords and their Ramrod bunch, too, but they'd won a temporary stay of execution due to the Comanche-based emergency, when all Hangtown had to put aside private quarrels to unite against a common foe. The period of grace would last only so long as the current crisis.

Johnny trusted none of the Ramrod bunch, save maybe Dan Oxblood, and the redheaded gunman was no real Stafford hand. At that, he wouldn't be turning his back on Red, either.

All that aside, his mission was to clean up Comanches.

The bombardment in the killing field had been hellacious, each earth-shattering blast making his heart beat faster. He'd envied Sam for the magnitude of the death-dealing abilities rendered him by a scoped rifle and a field full of dynamite. It almost, but not quite, took some of the sting off him being a Yankee.

Oh well, a person can't help where he comes from, Johnny supposed. *Not everybody is lucky enough to be born a Texan. Hard luck for them!*

Sam Heller could no more help being a Yankee than the Comanches could help being what they were. They were born marauders and it suited them just fine. That was what they knew and they wanted no other way of life.

Which didn't mean Johnny wasn't going to kill every last warrior he caught on the business end of his guns. Of which he had many—two on his hips, two under his arms, and two stuck in the top of his pants.

He spurred his horse so it jumped from the wide platform of the top step to the ground without touching any steps in between. Wind brought the smell of fire smoke and cordite to him. He rode downhill, east on Trail Street, and right into the heart of the action. Smoke, screams, shots, pounding hoofbeats, and the smell of gunpowder. It was totally wild!

Twin .44s were in his hands and the reins gripped between his teeth as a passel of Comanches came racing toward him. Johnny opened up, guns blazing, leaving them sprawled in the dirt and their riderless horses coursing by.

Holstering the gun in his left hand, he gripped the reins one-handed, slowing the horse. He had fallen into the rhythm of battle without thinking; a habit of mind that came as naturally to him as breathing. It helped make him a natural-born pistol fighter.

Farther east along the street Comanches were giving a couple fellows a hard time. Johnny urged the horse forward.

Three mounted braves had two citizens trapped on the boardwalk fronting the Alamo Bar. The townsmen had their backs to the wall

Johnny rode up to the braves and cut loose, throwing lead. No sportsmanship, no fair play, that wasn't what it was all about.

Leaving three riderless ponies and two grateful citizens in his wake, he moved on in search of the next encounter. A cloud of smoke blew up, stinging his eyes, choking him.

The smoke thinned, revealing a handful of

mounted braves coming at him. He fired, the pistol in his right hand emptying after two shots. But each shot hit its man.

Letting his empty gun fall, Johnny reached across his chest under his arms, right hand reaching left, left hand reaching right, each hand snaking a .44 out of the shoulder holsters.

No longer a leader but a follower, Red Hand regained control of his horse and raced to join the group of braves riding fast out of town.

Through the murk of smoke, the lone figure of a mounted man emerged—a Texan. Opening fire, the rider shot the two lead braves out of their saddles before his gun clicked on empty.

The others rushed him. Quick as thought, guns filled the Texan's hands and he came at them shooting.

A Comanche warrior raised a rifle for a kill shot. Before he could bring it into play, slugs hammered into his chest, nailing him.

The clash was so quick, so sudden, the contending parties so close to each other, any advantage rifle-bearing braves might have had was nullified as they shot it out with Johnny Cross at point-blank range.

Fire lanced from Johnny's gun muzzles, pistols milling out a wall of lead. Bullets whipped past, one creasing his left arm. Deadly .44s roaring, he swept braves from the scene, gunning them down with lightning speed

Red Hand gaped in astonishment as those before him fell torn and mauled under hammering six-guns.

A Comanche crowded within arm's reach of Johnny, his face filling Johnny's field of vision. A gun blast erased that face, wiping its features into an unholy mess that dropped out of sight with its bearer.

A war club wielded by another swiped viciously at Johnny's head—a near miss, the breeze of its passing fanning his face.

Johnny didn't miss. Space opened up around him as the foe fell away, and then suddenly he was face to face with Red Hand. Not that he knew him from Adam. All he knew was that he was being rushed by a particularly fierce-faced Comanche with a spear.

Red Hand still had his lance, the unlit Fire Lance. Somehow he'd managed to hold on to it during the rout. His right hand gripped the lance at mid-shaft, pointing it at a tilted angle at Johnny.

One of Johnny's guns was empty; he leveled the other on Red Hand, squeezing the trigger.

Click. That gun was empty, too.

Red Hand's grimace widened into a grin of triumph. The gods were indeed with him. His luck had not yet run out!

Red Hand thrust at Johnny, the spear blade seeking the other's heart.

An empty pistol was still a weapon. Johnny threw it at Red Hand's face. Red Hand ducked his head to avoid it.

Johnny turned his horse, kicking its flanks and slamming it into Red Hand's mount. The animals crashed together with jolting impact.

Getting under and around the lunging lance, Johnny came up on Red Hand's left side. He kicked free of the stirrups and climbed out of the saddle. Hands reaching, clawing for Red Hand, he jumped him.

The thud of flesh striking flesh sounded as Johnny tangled with Red Hand. The two pitched over the right-hand side of the Comanche's horse, spilling into the dirt, kicking up dust.

Red Hand absorbed most of the impact of the fall. He let go of the lance, no longer an asset, but a liability.

Horse hooves hammered the ground near their heads. They grappled, throwing punches. Grunting and panting, they worked fists, elbows, and knees.

Red Hand was strong and slippery. Johnny couldn't get a good grip on him, but he got the Comanche under him.

Red Hand drew his knife. Johnny grabbed Red Hand's forearm, tough as a tree limb and harder to hold than a rattlesnake. The blade quivered, seeking Johnny's throat, chest, and heart.

A reversal put Red Hand on top, Johnny on the bottom, gripping the wrist of the other's knife hand. He brought his knees up to his chest and pushed out, flipping Red Hand up and over. His hold on the wrist of the Comanche's knife hand was broken.

Red Hand went with the throw, tucking his head down, taking the impact on his shoulder. Going into a roll, he got his feet under him and jumped up, whirling to face his opponent. Shifting his grip on the knife for an underhand thrust, he lunged at Johnny.

Scrambling to meet the Indian's rush, Johnny reached for a gun stuck in his waistband, drawing and firing several times. The reports came so quick they sounded like one continuous blast.

He shot Red Hand point-blank in the middle, firing from so close the other's flesh was tattooed by gunpowder burns.

Doubled up, the Comanche kept on coming even as he was folding. Johnny sidestepped to get out of his way, and Red Hand fell facedown into the dirt.

Johnny crouched low, gun in hand, looking around for the next foe. The slaughter had peaked and was moving into a lull. Most of the surviving Comanches had already fled town.

Three stragglers raced up. Johnny shot the lead rider off his horse. He swung his pistol toward the next man, but before he could pull the trigger a burst of gunfire sounded from behind him, blowing the rest of the stragglers out of their saddles. Their horses rushed past.

Johnny glanced over his shoulder to see where the shooting came from. Through drifting gun smoke he saw Sam Heller on horseback, the mule's-leg in his hand. The Winchester Model 1866 was once more cut down for close action.

"Trust a Yankee to show up when the dirty work's over," Johnny croaked.

"Trust a Texan to bag the bragging rights," barked Sam.

Johnny didn't catch his drift. "Say again?"

"Don't you know who you were tussling with?" Sam asked.

"Nope, 'cepting he was an ornery cuss even for a Comanche, and that's saying some."

"Take a better look."

Johnny went to the body. It lay facedown. Working a boot toe under the corpse's shoulder, he flipped it over on its back. The face meant nothing to him, but he saw that the dead man's arms were painted from fingertips to elbows with scarlet signs and symbols.

"Red Hand."

"The big chief." Sam nodded.

"Huh. Ain't that a caution?"

"Yup."

"So that's the one who kicked up all this fuss," Johnny said. "Well, he's stone dead now."

"And he never looked better in his life."

TWENTY-FIVE

You've got to hand it to Hangtown. No sooner does it get shut of one round of killings, than it gets set for another," Sam muttered.

"I'm getting set," Johnny retorted. "My name's penciled in on this dance card."

They stood near the Alamo Bar, off to one side, facing Four Corners, where the next big gunfight was shaping up.

Johnny was checking his hardware. One fully loaded gun was stuck in the top of his pants over his left hip. He transferred it to the empty holster on his right hip.

Sam stood puffing away on a corncob pipe, liking the way the taste of the rough-cut tobacco caught in his throat. He held the pipe with the bowl cradled in his left hand. His right hand hung down easily by his side, brushing against the butt of the holstered mule's-leg.

Their horses were tied to a hitching post. Red

Hand was stretched facedown across the back of Johnny's horse.

"One loaded gun," Johnny muttered. "Feels like I'm comin' to the party half dressed!"

Sam drew the Navy Colt worn holstered under his left arm and proffered it to Johnny. "Try mine."

Johnny took it. "Thanks." Instinctively he checked the .36 revolver, making sure it was loaded.

Sam smiled, not offended by Johnny's caution. Only a damned fool took a gun that wasn't his without inspecting it first.

"Red Hand's carcass should be worth something. Keep an eye on it for me, will you?" Johnny asked.

"Sure."

"See ya." Johnny started across the street.

"'Luck,'" Sam said, giving the other a two-fingered salute.

The Comanche raiders had fled. The victorious townfolk were not minded to take up pursuit. Most were simply glad to be alive. Others had yet to slake their thirst for blood. Chief among those was Vince Stafford.

Now that the battle of Red Hand was done, Vince was moving fast to strike hard against the man he regarded as his main antagonist. Damon Bolt.

The sun was up. It was already hot. A light breeze from the west blew much of the smoke and dust out of town. The air was still hazy, and stank of cordite, blood, and death.

Four Corners bore all the marks of the war zone it was. A number of small fires burned where flaming debris had fallen on rooftops, porches, or boardwalks, sending up long, thin fingers of gray-black smoke. The street grid was pocked with the craters of exploded dynamite caches and strewn with the dead bodies of horses and men.

Wooden walls were riddled with bullet holes. An intact pane of window glass was not to be found for blocks. Glass shards littered the streets, reflecting sunlight like a diamond mosaic.

From all sides came a mixed chorus of the shrieks and groans of the wounded and the dying. A disemboweled horse lay on its side shrieking, legs churning empty air.

Vigilant and bloody-minded citizens roamed among fallen Comanches, delivering the coup de grâce to those still alive or any who looked doubtful.

A shot sounded and the wounded horse stopped shrieking. Frown lines in Sam Heller's face smoothed out. The horse's outcries had been getting on his nerves. He was glad someone had put it out of its misery.

Men were sure pure hell on horses. They were hell on each other, too, but at least they had a choice. The horses didn't. *Maybe the men didn't have a choice, either, but that was the way of it,* Sam told himself.

* * *

The Ramrod bunch, what was left of them, was mustering in front of the feed store to take their fight to the Golden Spur. They gathered around Vince Stafford as if by some law of gravitation, all the lesser satellites falling under his heavy sway.

Of the top guns, Dan Oxblood, Kev Huddy, and Clay Stafford were intact and unwounded. Ted Claiborne had been hit several times. None of the wounds was mortal, but he was out of action. Among the next rank, Duncan, Kaw, and Lord were unhurt or had received minor flesh wounds. Five other lesser, mid-range Ramrod gun hands were in shape for the showdown. Vince Stafford was unharmed, as was Quent.

Vince took stock of the situation and found it good. Most of the citizenry was still staying off the streets. Sheriff Barton and his men were busy at the Big Corral, shoring it up to prevent any horses from escaping.

Vince gripped a rifle, holding it horizontally across the tops of bowed, spindly thighs. An oversized horse pistol was strapped to his hip.

"I come out of that scrap all right, by God! I got my two strong sons to side me and more'n half my men alive," he crowed. His face scrunched up, squinting across the street at the Golden Spur.

Clay and Quent Stafford fell in alongside Vince, flanking him, Clay on his left and Quent on his right.

Clay's face was tiger striped with blood streaks

from where a glass shard had opened a cut on his forehead. A blue bandanna was knotted around his forehead. It was stained a purple-wine color, but the makeshift bandage had stemmed the flow of blood from the wound. His hair was disarranged. It stood out in yellow-white spikes, some stained red. His face was taut, haggard, his eyes watchful. A smoking six-gun was held at his side.

Quent loomed large, a brutish hulk dwarfing his wizened father and tall, lanky younger brother. The battle had left not a mark on him. His little piggy eyes were bright and glowing. His wide mouth twisted into a leering grin.

"Where's the gunfighter?" Vince asked.

"Right here," Dan Oxblood said, stepping forward into the front rank. He took off his hat, running his fingers through sweat-damp, brick-colored hair. His face was soot smeared from the smoke. Green eyes glinted. No tremor disturbed those quick gunfighter hands.

Vince began to rally his troops. "Get set, men. We gone clean up on the Golden Spur crowd."

"Now, Boss?" somebody asked.

"There'll never be a better time," Vince said. "The townsmen have had a bellyful of killing. Them that's still alive ain't gonna risk their precious skins to save the gambler's hash. We finish it here and now."

"What about all them Mexes forted up in the Spur?" asked another.

"If any of 'em buck us, kill 'em," Vince snapped.

"They won't fight. What's Damon to them?" Clay said.

Quent spat. "Might as well clean up on them, too. They's already too many of the dirty greasers around."

"Their money's as good as anybody else's, and we got beef to sell them—"

"Hell, brother, them beaners ain't got a pot to piss in. To hell with 'em."

"Shooting at them's the best way to make them throw in with Damon," Clay argued. "Why go picking fights when you don't have to?"

"'Cause that's what I like to do," Quent said stubbornly.

"Clay's right. Don't go burnin' down nobody less'n they throw in agin' us," Vince said, laying down the law in his best because-I-said-so tone of finality.

Quent changed the subject. "And the girl, Pa? Damon's whore? What about her"

"I'll tend to her later."

"You still bulldogging that, Pa?" Clay said, not bothering to hide his disgust.

"You know me, son. Once I set my mind to a thing, it's done. That's the way it is and that's how it's always going to be, as long as I'm in charge of this outfit. And that's gonna be a long, long time."

"Let me do it, Pa. I'll fix her," Quent said, licking his lips. A little spittle drooled down the corner of his chin.

"Keep your mitts off her, boy. An overgrowed

galoot like you don't know your own strength. You git your paws on her pretty neck, you're liable to snap it like a twig."

"I might—after . . ." Quent's little round eyes were hot, dreamy.

"That's too quick," Vince said, his voice strident. "She's gotta live as a warning and a reminder of what happens to those who trifle with a Stafford. She worked woe on poor Bliss and I'm gonna do the same to her and she ain't never gonna forget it. And this town ain't never gonna forget it, either."

A couple dead Comanches and townsmen lay sprawled on the street in front of the gambling hall. The façade of the building was shot up. Shadows that could have been figures flitted behind boarded-up front windows.

"Looks quiet," a Ramrod rider said.

"I pray the gambler still lives," Vince said fervently. "Don't do me out of the pleasure of killing him myself!"

"Don't trouble yourself, Pa. Damon's not dead," Clay said, sour-faced.

"How do you know?" the old man demanded.

"Because there he is." Clay gestured north toward the street between the Golden Spur and the courthouse.

Damon Bolt rounded the corner of the Spur, stepping into view, Creed Teece beside him. They halted, facing the Staffords and company, hands hanging low over holstered guns.

Vince bristled like a mountain cat getting its back arched for a fight.

A courthouse door opened. Out came Ace High Olcutt, poker faced, his complexion looking a little grayish. Moving alongside Damon, he stood with him and Creed Teece. Olcutt turned hard eyes on the Stafford crowd. He swept back his coattail, out of the way of the gun holstered on his hip. His hand hovered over the gun butt.

Damon smiled. "Decided to get in the game after all, eh, Ace High?"

"You know me, I'm a gambling man. I got to be where the action is."

"Glad to have you. I made a bet with myself on you, and it looks like I won."

Keeping his eyes on the Stafford party, Creed Teece said, "I take back what I said about you being a yellow belly, Ace High."

"Thanks," Olcutt said sarcastically.

Flint Ryan and Charley Bronco came out the front doors of the Golden Spur and took up a stance on the front porch. Ryan held a rifle. His long, thin horse face looked tired. His eyes were heavy lidded. Suddenly he showed a bucktoothed grin.

Charley Bronco was hatless, long dark hair hanging down to his shoulders. His face was sweaty, almost feverish. His slitted eyes glittered. He was a little unsteady on his feet, swaying slightly. His fringed buckskin shirt was stained with dark blood on his left side where he'd been hit. He'd been tagged high in the left arm, too. The arm hung down straight along his side. His right hand hovered over the gun on his right hip.

Barkeep Morrissey appeared at the window to the right of the front door, wielding a double-barreled shotgun.

Luke Pettigrew showed in the window at the left, thrusting a double-bored shotgun muzzle through the space between a couple boards nailed across the window frame.

Johnny Cross eased into view, anchoring the southeast front corner of the building, a .44 on his right hip and the Navy Colt worn butt-out in the top of his pants on his left hip.

"Hey, hoss," Luke called to him.

Johnny grinned. "So you made it for the showdown, huh?"

"Wouldn't miss it," Luke said. "Hell, I can't miss—not with this here scattergun."

"The way you shoot, I ain't so sure."

"Spread out, men," Clay Stafford said tightly. The Ramrod gunmen stepped to the sides to confront the Golden Spur bunch across the street. "You know what to do, Red."

Dan Oxblood's left hand hung loosely at his side, over his six-gun in its black leather holster decorated with silver stars and sunbursts. His tone was mild and conversational as if he were passing the time of day. "I got Creed covered."

"You do, huh?" Creed Teece called, his voice as flat and even as his level-eyed gaze.

"That's right."

"Tell me another one."

"Gambler! This's Stafford, Vince Stafford!" the old man shouted.

"I hear you," Damon Bolt said mildly.

"I'm calling you out!"

"Here I am."

The hot morning air quivered with tension, hate, and the promise of more violence. Nerves were stretched thin. The contending parties were frozen for a timeless instant, like an electrical storm in the gap between a lightning strike and a thunderclap.

Sam looked at Sheriff Barton standing midway between Trail Street and the Big Corral. Deputy Smalls stood beside him, his head close to Barton's ear, obviously speaking to him.

Barton frowned, eyes narrowed. Smalls pointed toward the Ramrodders. Barton's frown deepened.

It occurred to Sam that it might be a good time to have a word with the sheriff. He untied his horse and Johnny's from the hitching rail. Taking hold of both sets of reins, he walked the horses across the street toward the Big Corral.

Sam had a plan, or at least a strategem. He pitched it to Barton. Barton was game. But—

"We've got to act fast, there ain't much time," Sam said.

Deputy Smalls rushed to the Big Corral to round up some sidemen. They came back in quick time, fifteen men or more, mostly Dog Star hardcases and a handful of small ranchers. They all hated Vince Stafford's guts. Barton gave them their orders.

Sam handed off the horses to Hobson's boy for safekeeping, but not before reaching into his saddlebag. He had a few bundles of dynamite remaining. He took out a spare stick.

He and Barton went ahead of the others, approaching Trail Street. Sam shouldered the mule's-leg. Barton held the stick of dynamite.

"No need to light the fuse," Sam said.

"I hope you know what you're doing," the sheriff said doubtfully.

"I hope you know how to throw."

"Don't worry about me, Yank."

"Throw it high."

"I will."

"Don't wait too long, the boys're getting ready to pop. NOW!"

Barton threw the stick of dynamite underhand, tossing it high into the air above the middle of Trail Street.

Sam shot it at the height of its arc, tagging it on the wing and detonating it. He and Barton ducked back behind the corner of the feed store to avoid the blast. It shook things up pretty good. Smoke, fire, and a deafening blast knocked men down, shaking buildings and scattering debris.

The gunplay stopped before it could get started. Nobody in the fighting factions knew what the hell was going on.

Drawing his gun, Barton motioned for his men to move up. Their guns were drawn, too. As the smoke cleared on Trail Street. Ramrodders and Golden Spur faction members began picking themselves up off the ground where they'd been knocked down. No one was seriously hurt but they'd all taken a hell of a bruising from the concussion. They were stunned, shaken, and unsure.

Before they could recover their wits enough to get back in and fight, Barton and his men had poured into the street, guns drawn, and leveled. They had the drop on them—on both sides.

"Stand down!" Barton shouted, standing at the head of the militiamen armed with rifles, shotguns, and six-guns. Most were leveled on the Ramrod riders, but some covered Damon's faction across the street.

Sam kept to the rear, off to one side. The situation was volatile enough without injecting his Yankee self into the picture. He'd done his bit; now it was the sheriff's play.

Kev Huddy was one of the first to stagger upright. His front was all dirty and he had a nosebleed. He trembled with a skinful of adrenaline, his eyes bulging, and his neck cording. "You loco? What'd you do that for?"

"To get your attention," Barton stated.

Huddy swore.

"I'll overlook that, considering," Barton said flatly.

"You crazy peckerwood!"

"That's one too many. Mind your manners." Barton wagged his gun in Huddy's direction.

Big Quent Stafford was one of the few to have remained on his feet despite the blast. "I'll kill you." His hand closed on the gun butt, tensing to pull it from the holster.

Barton held his pistol at arm's length, pointed at Quent's head. Despite the ringing in everyone's ears from the blast, the sound of the hammer clicking into place was loud indeed. "Pull that gun and I surely will blow out what little brains you got, Quent."

Quent froze. "Don't shoot, Sheriff!"

"Move that hand away and make sure it stays empty."

Quent eased his hand off the gun butt, his thick fingers uncurling. He raised his hands shoulder-high, holding them there. Barton moved in, shucking Quent's gun out of the holster and tossing it into the street.

"What do you think you're doing, Sheriff?" Clay asked.

"Calling a cease-fire. There's been enough killing today. Boot Hill's running out of space to bury the dead."

Flint Ryan was in disbelief. "You threw dynamite at us to get our *attention?*"

"Worked, didn't it?" Barton said, smug.

"What if you missed? We'd 've all got blowed up!"

Johnny Cross spotted Sam lurking on the sidelines. "Never mind, Flint. They got an hombre over there who don't never miss."

"Careful how you wave that rifle around, Ryan. It's be a damned shame for you to get yourself shot this late in the game," Barton said. "We've got the drop on all you boys—on both sides—so don't anyone do anything stupid."

Vince Stafford stood hunched up in a knot of outrage, fuming. "I told you we was gone tangle, lawman."

"We're tangling now. You want it so bad? Quit running your mouth and make your move, Vince."

"You gonna give me a chance on a fair draw?"

"No. I told you, I'm calling a cease-fire. I'll bury the first man to go for a gun."

"You got the whip hand now, but it ain't gonna end here."

"Yes, it does." Barton's tone held a convincing note of grim fatality, enough to make Vince Stafford take a few steps back, hands held palms upright.

Vince cried, "No. Don't!—"

Clay quickly interrupted. "You're a sheriff. You can't kill him in cold blood."

"What'll you bet?" Barton asked. "I've got a proposition. If this is a private war, let's keep it that way. Limited to the interested parties. No sense any of the rest of you getting shot up for no good reason. You're so all-fired set on gunning down Damon, Vince—fight him yourself. I'm talking about a fair fight between the two of you."

"Sounds good," Dan Oxblood opined.

Vince's face purpled. "You're working for me, damn you!"

"I quit."

"Good for you, Red," Johnny Cross called across the street.

"What do you say, Damon?" Barton asked.

"I'm agreeable."

Vince scoffed. "Fair fight, you call it. He's a gunman! I'm just an honest rancher. I make my living selling cattle. What's fair about that?"

Sam stepped forward. "There's a way to even it up so it's a test of nerve rather than who's the fastest gun."

Heads turned his way, many with unfriendly eyes. Vince glared, worked up into quite a state. "Nobody asked you to throw your two cents in, Billy Yank!"

"His idea about the dynamite pits didn't work out too badly. Hear him out," Johnny Cross said.

"Fight an old-time duel, like the gentry used to do in New Orleans," Sam suggested. "You ought to know about that, Damon."

"I may have heard," Damon allowed.

"Each man has a drawn gun. Stand back-to-back, walk five paces, turn and shoot. That's all there is to it. Who's faster on the draw won't matter," said Sam.

"Sounds fair to me," Oxblood agreed.

"Sure—it ain't your neck," said Vince.

"Got a better idea? No? Anyone?" Barton asked. "Because one way or another this thing is gonna be settled for good. I don't aim to have it hanging fire over me or the town. It ends here—now. . . .

"What do you say, Damon?"

"I have no objection."

"Vince?"

"Goddamn you!"

"That a yes or a no, Vince?"

Vince was so mad he chewed his lower lip, a clot of froth bubbling in the corner of his mouth.

"Vince?" Barton prompted.

The man was silent. The silence went on for a long time.

"He won't fight. He's yellah," somebody yelled.

Clay cleared his throat. He looked anguished. "Pa, for the honor of the family, the Ramrod brand . . ."

"Is it a go, Vince?" asked Barton one more time.

"All right, I'll do it. Damn your eyes! Nobody can say Vince Stafford ever backed off a fight."

"Good."

"A duel of honor," Damon said mockingly.

Barton held up a hand palm outward. "First, though, we got to disarm both sides, in case there's any soreheads. Take off your gun belts, boys, and you won't get hurt."

He motioned the militiamen forward. "You men move in and collect 'em."

Somebody said, "The gambler's men will slaughter us."

"No they won't, because we're taking their guns, too," Barton said cheerfully. "This ain't a matter of choice. Anybody reaches 'll get a bellyful of lead. That goes for you with the scatterguns in the windows. Am I joshing? No!"

"I trust you, Sheriff," Clay said, unbuckling his gun belt.

"You're a damned fool, brother," Quent sneered.

"You didn't seem so eager to throw down on Barton when you had the chance."

Smalls led the militiamen doing the collecting. Some went among the Ramrodders, others circulated among the Spur faction, taking rifles and gun belts with holstered guns. Others of the militia held guns leveled on both sides.

"I don't give up my guns to nobody," Creed Teece said, when his turn came.

"You heard the man, Creed. Stand down," Damon said.

Teece hesitated.

"What're you afraid of? I gave up my guns," Dan Oxblood called across the street.

"Hell, if you can do, I can," Teece said, unbuckling his gun belt and handing it to one of the collectors.

"I'll give my guns up to Mister Yankee." Johnny Cross gave Sam his .44 and the Navy Colt. "What'd you do with Red Hand?"

"He's in the Big Corral for safekeeping," Sam said.

"Good. I got me a feeling that rascal's hide's gonna be worth big money."

"I wouldn't be surprised."

The hardware made quite a pile. Two piles actually—one for the Ramrod guns, the other for the Spur's.

"You'll all get your guns back—afterward," Barton promised.

Damon Bolt and Vince Stafford stood back-to-back in the square formed by the intersection of Trail Street and a cross street. Each stood holding a six-gun at his side, pointing down. Damon's jacket was off. He wore a maroon vest and long-sleeved shirt. He was half a head taller than Vince.

Damon faced the north of the cross street, Vince faced south. It was blocked out that way so neither party had the disadvantage of facing into the morning sun.

Barton stood to one side, gun held level at his hip, pointed in the general direction of both men. "It's simple enough. I'll call out the count. You step off and keep the pace. At the count of *five,* turn and fire. Keep shooting till it's done. Any questions?"

Silence.

"Anybody's got any kick, speak now or forever hold your peace. Damon?"

"Ready."

"Vince?"

"Get on with it."

A crowd of spectators had gathered. Luke Pettigrew sat on a chair on the front porch of the Golden Spur, Morrissey standing beside him. The batwing double doors of the Spur swung open.

Out came Mrs. Frye, her long, ankle-length skirts swishing. Her face was taut and pale, her lips tightly pressed into a line. She and Damon crossed glances.

The Stafford brothers stood off to one side, Clay behind and to one side of Quent. Clay nudged Quent in the small of the back with something hard and metallic. "Hsst! Take it!" Clay whispered.

Quent started.

"Easy—don't give away the game. Reach behind you," Clay said.

Quent put his hands behind his back. Clay surreptitiously pressed a gun into the other's palm, a short-barreled .32 revolver.

"A pocket pistol they forgot to look for. I've got one, too," Clay said, low voiced.

Quent grunted. His oversized hand closed over the gun, hiding it. It disappeared inside his big fist.

"Not now, though. Wait," Clay said. "Follow my play, in case Pa don't make it."

"I know what to do."

"I thought you would," Clay said, smiling.

The sheriff gave a last word to the duelists. "Start walking when I start counting. At the count of *five,* turn and shoot. Anybody turns before *five,* I'll shoot him dead, savvy?"

"And if he misses, I won't," Squint McCray said from the sidelines.

Barton took a few steps back, away from the duelists. "Ready, gents?"

They were. Barton stood with his gun held hip high, elbow at his side, calling, "One!"

Damon and Vince stepped off, guns held pointed downward at their sides.

"Two."

"Three . . . Four . . . *Five!*"

Vince spun around, whippet-quick. Bringing the gun up, he jerked the trigger, banging away.

At the same time, Damon turned in one easy, fluid motion, leveling the pistol. A slug tore through the muscle at the top of his left shoulder. He fired once, shooting Vince Stafford in the chest.

Vince wavered, shuddering. He planted himself in a wide stance, stiff-legged, like a man trying to keep his balance on the deck of a storm-tossed ship at sea.

Damon squeezed out several more shots, cutting Vince's heart to pieces. Vince fell, measuring his length in the dirt of the street. His right foot kicked several times, the way a dog's might when it dreams of running. He stopped kicking. He was dead.

An inarticulate cry of rage and pain came choking from Quent. Clay rasped, "Now!"

Quent was already in motion, raising the gun in his hand. The pocket pistol looked like a toy in his big fist. He pointed it at Damon.

Clay slammed into Quent, pushing him to one

side, into the open. Quent howled, outraged by the betrayal. His shots went wild, missing Damon.

Damon didn't miss. Quent was huge, a monster of raw animal vitality; he could take a lot of body shots and keep on coming. Damon went for the headshot, planting a slug above Quent's eyebrows.

Quent's head snapped backward, as if kicked by a mule. A round black dot, coin-sized, flashed into being in the middle of his low forehead.

His massive form followed the violent snapback of his head, toppling. A jet of blood so dark as to appear black spurted from the wound, fountaining out, tracing a curving arc as it followed him down to the ground. He landed with a thump, head lolling to one side.

Damon stepped forward, gun raised, ready to continue the fray to a finish with the last of the Staffords.

Clay was having none of it. He wasn't reaching, had never made a move toward his gun. He stood with his hands held way out away from his sides. Empty hands.

"You want some, too?" Damon asked.

"Not me," Clay said, breathing hard. "I've got no gun."

"Get one. I'll wait."

Clay shook his head. "No. It's over."

"Expect me to believe that?" Damon scoffed.

"Believe it."

"Man, I just killed your father and brother!"

"That makes me boss of the Ramrod. Thanks."

Clay smiled then, slow and sardonic, a smile to give one pause.

"You sound none too grief stricken at that," Damon conceded.

"You beat Pa in a fair duel. Quent threw down on you. I'm not kicking," Clay said. "I'm not armed, either. Shoot me and it's murder, cold-blooded murder, and you'll be dangling from a rope on the Hanging Tree. Ain't that right, Sheriff?"

Barton, more than a bit taken aback by the turn of events, said at last, "Uh, yeah. That's right."

Damon said warningly, "If this is a trick, Clay . . ."

"No trick. Like the man said, there's been enough killing today."

Damon lowered the gun to his side. "Damned if I can figure you out."

Clay turned, facing his riders. "None of us Staffords are big on explaining ourselves but I'll give you all this much, once. Pa was—well, you know what he was like. The whole town could be sacked and burned by Comanches if that's what it took for him to get his revenge. I didn't see it that way, but there was no telling him different while he was alive.

"He's dead now and I'm in charge and what I say goes. You take orders from me. Any of you don't like it, draw your time and get out. You want to make war on the Spur, be my guest. But you'll be doing it on your own, with no help from me. No help and no pay! I reckon you savvy that.

"This town's going to need a lot of rebuilding. Let's bury our dead and get on with it."

Clay turned back to Damon. "I'm quits with it if you are. As far as I'm concerned, we're square. You go about your business and I'll do the same."

"A smart man knows when to fold his cards and cut his losses," Damon said thoughtfully.

"We're square?"

"If that's what you want."

"That's what I want."

"You'll pardon me if we don't shake hands. Peace or no peace, I prefer to keep my gun hand ready," Damon said dryly.

"Do as you please," Clay said.

"I generally do."

"I don't expect us to be chums, but at least we can stay out of each other's hair." Clay nodded toward Damon's arm. "Better see to yourself. You're leaking."

Damon's white shirtsleeve was bloody from left shoulder to elbow. Red droplets fell to the street. "I'll live."

"Then you can count it a good day, gambler," Clay said, turning away. He almost bumped into Dan Oxblood.

"All dressed up and no place to go," Oxblood said, grinning wryly.

"You'll be paid for the work done, Red."

"Thank you kindly, Clay."

"If you want to try out Creed, though, it's on your dollar."

"Some other time, mebbe. See you," Oxblood said, fading into the background, making himself absent.

Francine Hayes came out of the Golden Spur, going down the stairs and into the street. Breezing past Damon without a glance, she went to Clay, who rushed forward to meet her with open arms. Her eyes shone and her face glowed.

Clay swept her up, embracing her slim yet nicely rounded form. They went into a clinch, Clay crushing his mouth against hers, Francine kissing him back passionately. When they came up for air, Francine said, "Thank God you're alive, Clay!"

"It was you I was worried about, darling."

Mrs. Frye stood beside Damon. He looked surprised; she was level-eyed, her mouth quirked in a cynical, knowing twist. Arm in arm, Clay and Francine went to them.

"Something you want to tell us, Francine?" Mrs. Frye said, her tone lightly mocking.

Clay spoke. "It happened when Pa sent me as a go-between to buy off Francine to leave Bliss alone. Turned out I had things upside down. She didn't have her hooks into him, it was he who wouldn't leave her alone. That's when I learned what a fine girl Francine is. I couldn't help it, I fell in love with her. I only hope she feels the same about me."

"You know I do, Clay. I love you!" Francine said.

"I mean to make her my wife, if she'll have me," said Clay, with a show of sincerity.

Francine squealed with delight. "Of course I will, darling!"

"I hope that meets with the approval of you two," Clay said guardedly.

Damon Bolt and Mrs. Frye exchanged glances.

"Miss Hayes is a free agent, as are all the ladies in the employ of the Golden Spur. As long as your intentions are honorable, sir, you have my blessing," Damon said.

"I want to marry this woman," Clay declared. Francine squealed some more.

"I'll send for Pastor Fulton," Mrs. Frye said, adding, "before you change your mind."

"No worry about that, ma'am!" Clay said quickly. Francine kept a tight hold on his arm anyway.

"Now come along, Damon. I'll patch up that arm while you've still got some blood in you," Mrs. Frye said.

She and Damon went into the Golden Spur. A runner was sent out to fetch the pastor. Francine stuck close to Clay, showing every sign of staying glued to him until she was safely wed as Mrs. Clay Stafford.

Standing nearby were Sam Heller and Johnny Cross. Johnny said, "Now don't that beat all? Women! Who can understand them?"

"Not me," Sam said. "I reckon Clay found something he liked filling his hand with better than a gun."

Johnny made a sound of disgust.

They left the center of the street and went to the Big Corral. A knot of onlookers clustered around Red Hand's corpse, gawking.

"Is that him? The big chief?" somebody asked.

"Sure," another said, "you can tell by the war paint. That's him all right!"

A third sneered, "Huh! He don't look so big now!"

Johnny had heard enough. "You should've seen him coming at you, charging with that lance. He looked big enough then."

TWENTY-SIX

The Comanches fled north, most of them. A cavalry force from Fort Pardee eventually set off in pursuit, accomplishing little.

Two days later, Sam Heller took Latigo's body to Rancho Grande. He wanted to bring back Lydia Fisher, and, no less important, get Dusty, his horse. Pastor Fulton had found a home for Lydia with one of the families in his church.

Johnny Cross went with Sam. "I liked Latigo. He had sand."

Johnny had borrowed a wagon to take the body back. Nobody would lend a wagon to the Yankee. Latigo was laid out in a handsome coffin of dark, shining wood fashioned by master artisan and carver Joe Delagoa. The box was secured to the wagon bed.

Riding north out of Hangtown, they crossed green prairie under blue skies. The ranch's white adobe walls shone in the sun. Closer, the ramparts showed signs of battle. Ironbound, old oaken gates showed scorch marks where unsuccessful attempts had been made to burn them down.

The portals opened for the wagon to enter. Sam pulled up inside the courtyard. He and Johnny climbed down from the wagon.

They were greeted by the foreman, the segundo, big, bluff, swaggering Hector Vasquez. "Hey, gringo! I knew you would come through all of this. You must have had an easy time of it in town while we men were doing the real fighting here, no?"

"No," Sam said.

"And you, the young hawk, the young falcon with the quick gun! Still fast as ever?"

"Faster," Johnny said.

"No need to prove it. For once even Vasquez has had his share of fighting. And . . . Latigo?"

Sam indicated the back of the wagon with a tilt of his head. Vasquez looked inside, saw the coffin.

"I thought as much, when I did not see him riding with you, yet I hoped he was but wounded," Vasquez said.

"He was a brave man. He killed many enemies," Sam said.

"He was an hombre," the segundo agreed, sighing.

"Was it bad here?" Johnny asked.

"The Comanche *bravos* lost their taste for fight after a few cannon balls," Vasquez said, smiling at a memory of epic destruction.

Two figures came out of the front entrance of the hacienda, crossing the tiled plaza. Lydia Fisher hurried into the courtyard, Lorena Castillo following at a more measured pace.

"Hey, Sam! I knew you was just too plumb ornery to kill!"

"That's what I figured about you. Lydia, I want you to meet a friend of mine, Johnny Cross. Johnny, this is Lydia Fisher, one of the bravest gals I've ever known . . . and she can shoot, too!"

"Glad to know you, miss," Johnny said, taking off his hat and sweeping it before him in a kind of courtly bow.

Lydia blushed, suddenly shy and withdrawn, demure. "Uh . . . howdy, mister," she said, small voiced.

"Call me Johnny." His big, friendly grin made her face light up.

They grow up fast, Sam thought. His eyes were on Lorena, making her way toward them. Her hair was a magnificent mane, her eyes were bold, and her red lips were curved at the corners.

Sam politely touched the tip of his hat. "*Buenas dias, señora.*"

"*Buenas dias, hombre,*" she said, smiling radiantly. "A good day, no?"

"Yes, a good day."

TWENTY-SEVEN

They hanged Red Hand. No matter that he was dead, dead as they come. They hanged him anyway, as a kind of object lesson, stringing him up on a limb of the Hanging Tree.

Noose around the neck, he hung with moc-casined feet head-high above the ground, swaying slightly, pendulum-like, according to the whim of the winds. The taut hempen rope creaked under his weight.

A three-man guard was posted to watch the body at night, for the Comanches were ever-bold, un-likely to be chastened by their recent stinging defeat.

The crows first pecked out Red Hand's eyes. The crows were always first on the scene after a hanging and the eyes were always the first to go. Later, bigger birds arrived. Buzzards, battening on to the corpse, tearing it apart bit by bit, bite by bite. It wasn't pretty. After a few days under the hot Texas sun, the aroma got pretty ripe.

Four days and three nights had passed since the riotously happy folk of Hangtown had hoisted the corpse. The night guards kept their distance, sitting around under a mesquite tree, smoking and passing around a bottle of redeye. A blurred horned moon floated in and out of high, thin, hazy clouds.

"He's gone to rot and ruin. Ought to take him down and bury him. It ain't Christian," a guard said.

"Neither was he," said another.

"What're they gonna do, leave him up till he's nothing but bones?"

"I reckon."

The guards were being watched by hidden lurkers, nearby, but unseen. Arrows came whizzing out of the darkness, striking the guards, slaying them. They fell in a heap, bodies bristled with feathered shafts.

A small band of Comanches rode up Boot Hill, leading a riderless horse. A brave cut the hempen rope, dropping Red Hand's corpse into the arms of the others reaching up for him. Wrapping the body in a blanket, they threw it across the back of the horse, binding it in place.

The dead guards were plundered of weapons and personal belongings, their hair lifted by scalping knives. Their horses were taken away on a lead rope.

The braves fled north, taking Red Hand home. The remains would be buried in a secret place where the Texans would not find it.

* * *

In a camp hidden in the heart of Comancheria, two aging warriors sat around a low fire late at night.

"It is well," Wahtonka claimed. "It was not fitting for the Texans to delight in the birds picking clean the bones of Red Hand."

"He had a vision of great slaughter," Laughing Bear remarked.

"The slaughter was of our braves, not the whites. The vision was false. It led Red Hand to his own doom."

"Waugh! It is so."

The fire burned very low. In its wan red glow, the faces of Wahtonka and Laughing Bear were like a pair of old ceremonial masks.

Laughing Bear threw some kindling on the fire. It flared up, burning hotter and brighter. All too soon it played out, the darkness drawing in, darker than before.